TARNISHED

JULIA CROUCH

headline

First published in Great Britain in 2013 by
HEADLINE PUBLISHING GROUP

First published in paperback in 2013 by
HEADLINE PUBLISHING GROUP

1

Cataloguing in Publication Data is available from the British Library

B format ISBN 978 0 7553 7805 0

Typeset in Sabon by Avon DataSet Ltd, Bidford-on-Avon, Warwickshire

Printed and bound in Great Britain by Clays Ltd, St Ives plc

Headline's policy is to use papers that are natural, renewable and
recyclable products and made from wood grown in sustainable forests.
The logging and manufacturing processes are expected to conform
to the environmental regulations of the country of origin.

HEADLINE PUBLISHING GROUP
An Hachette UK Company
338 Euston Road
London NW1 3BH

www.headline.co.uk
www.hachette.co.uk

After a drama degree at Bristol University, Julia Crouch spent ten years devising, directing and writing for the theatre. During this time she had twelve plays produced and co-founded Bristol's Public Parts Theatre Company. She lives in Brighton with her husband, the actor and playwright Tim Crouch, and their three children.

Also by Julia Crouch and available from Headline

Cuckoo
Every Vow You Break

To my family (no relation)

Especially my Nana, who got the love just right.

Acknowledgements

Thank you:

To all the librarians and booksellers of the UK.

To Rosemary for introducing me to Tankerton (and a lot else); to Laura Escott for advice from the mortuary; to Aitor Basauri and @EddieYeah for Spanish translation (much of it lost in the edit – sorry about that); to Lin Dillon for her generosity; to Orlagh Stevens for her insights.

To my agent Simon Trewin at WME and my editor Leah Woodburn for just the best notes ever; to my indefatigable publicist Sam Eades, Emily Kitchin, and everyone else at Headline for providing the best possible home for my books.

To my homeys: Brighton Beach Hut Writers (beachhutwriters. co.uk), and Queen's Park Lowbrow Book group; to my family: Tim (generous first reader), Nel (for her eagle eye and enthusiasm), Owen and Joey, and to my parents, Jane and Roy Collins and in-laws, Pamela and Colin Crouch.

1992: Beachcomber

IT WAS JUST ABOUT DAWN, BUT THE MOON STILL HUNG, enormous, above the sea. The lowest spring tide of the year was due in an hour, and Colin Cairns had been looking forward to it like a child waiting for Christmas.

He crunched down the shingle, over the extraordinary collection of cuttlefish bones the tide had brought in at its highest point the night before. It always made him wonder where they came from when they were thrown up like that: was there a mass cuttlefish murder event, an orgy of tentacles entwining round necks? Did cuttlefish even have necks? He stopped and made a note in the little pad he carried with him, carefully writing the question in capital letters.

A wind blew in from the east, whipping loose tangles of kelp and net over the sand-and-mudflats like tumbleweeds in a Western. Glad both of his cagoule and the balaclava his mum had knitted for him, he pressed on, lugging his equipment down the slope towards the mud, which, today being a Proxigean Spring Tide, stretched on almost as far as he could see. Only a tiny hint of movement on the horizon suggested that there might be any water at all out there. All that mud! All that sea-bottom to explore! As he reached the end of the shingle his joy overflowed into an awkward little dance and he skipped round the straggles of seaweed and worm casts towards The Street.

There was no better place for detecting than The Street. Even on a normal day, the ancient strand of clay and shingle took you right out, so far that you felt like you were that old King Canute, or Jesus even, walking on the water. Today it was so far that Colin reckoned he could walk out to the horizon as far as the Maunsell sea forts, whose history and facts he knew by heart.

But that wasn't what he was there for this morning. He pulled his big headphones up over his balaclava'd ears, switched on his battery pack and started on his long walk outwards, sweeping his detector from side to side as he went.

From his study of tidal flow in the area, Colin had come to the conclusion that, if you wanted a good find, The Street was the place to go. Created by two currents converging, it had a tendency to catch interesting things. So far, in his hours of splashing around its edges with his detector, Colin's most valuable discoveries included several coins he thought to be Roman, a gold ring that probably wasn't all that old, something circular and rusted that he liked to think was a Saxon neck adornment, and part of some sort of helmet. He had a private museum in his bedroom where he displayed his prizes, each labelled with the date of discovery, his own name as the discoverer, and his estimate of the provenance of the item. He spent a good deal of time in the library, looking things up.

His odder finds included a payphone coin box (sadly emptied), a set of dentures and the remains of a corset with metal stays. He had also found the skeleton of what he reckoned was a dolphin, as well as a leathery, beached angler-fish. Once he had come across the corpses of fifteen giant ray fish – dismembered heads, long, whippy spines, chomped fins.

Someone must have been having a feast, was what he had thought.

He took photographs with the Kodak Instamatic he kept in his rucksack. He always photographed what he found out here. It was important to keep a record.

Absorbed in his task, listening intently for a change in the crackle, buzz and beep of his detector, his eyes going blurry with the effort of keeping sharp, Colin didn't at first notice the sea fog rolling in on the wind. He had travelled out for what he reckoned was about three-quarters of a mile and things were going well. He had already stopped three times, digging up five ancient nails that he imagined might have come from a medieval boat, three pound coins in a waterlogged leather purse and a beer can of a type he didn't already have in his collection. He had also nearly stepped in, then photographed, a wobbling jellyfish that must have been over two feet across.

Then he realised that he could no longer clearly see the ground at his feet. He stopped and cleaned his glasses, but that wasn't it. For an alarming second he thought he had got his timing wrong and the tide, which he had thought was going out, had in fact turned. If that was the case, he wouldn't get back in time to cross the shore-end dip that filled in early, and he would be stranded: cut off by the incoming tide, like the sign on the promenade warned.

But then he looked around and realised that the twinkling lights of home were now hidden, and his destination – the tip of The Street as it emerged from the still-outgoing tide – was also not to be seen.

He lifted his headphones from his ears and listened.

3

While the fog cloaked almost everything from view, it seemed to have brought the sound of the sea closer, as if it were lapping at his feet rather than the murk.

It was off-putting – eerie, even.

Colin thought perhaps he should return to the shore and the flask of tea he had hidden behind a beach hut.

But the pull of The Street – the fact that he would, very soon, be stepping on ground which, because of the lowness of the tide, people touched perhaps only once every couple of years – was too strong to resist. So instead, to get his bearings, he walked sideways, to the very edge, just to confirm that the sea was indeed still going out.

He stood and waited for five minutes as he watched the water recede from the wet mud and gravel, travelling out beyond an old metal post stuck in the ground. He wondered as he waited how old it might be. Perhaps it had been used by the Saxons to tie their boats to when they used The Street as a landing point before the harbour was built. Satisfied that the tide was still outgoing, he put his headphones on again and resumed his journey, keeping the water just to his right.

Apart from another metal post, he didn't find anything in the next five hundred or so yards. Visibility improved: the fog was slightly thinner out here. He stopped and cleaned his glasses again, pulling his T-shirt out from underneath all his layers to polish them. As he slid the frames back up onto his face, he caught sight of something interesting, a lumpish shape at the water's edge, about ten feet away.

Thinking perhaps it was a ball, possibly kicked over-enthusiastically by a sailor enjoying a little R and R on a warship somewhere out there, Colin wandered over to take a look. He turned the thing over with his wellington boot, and, not quite believing what he saw, he laid his detector on the drier ground to his left and squatted to take a closer look.

A tiny crab scuttled in one of the black holes that once would have been eyes looking back up at him. What remained of her face told him that she had probably been quite pretty, and she had lovely blond hair. Long. It made him sad to see her there, and he knew he should do something about her.

He took a photograph. Then, taking his rucksack off and laying it next to his detector, he drew out one of the carrier bags he kept for what he called wet specimens. Ever so carefully, using the bag as a sort of glove so that he didn't have to touch her, he eased her inside it. She just about fitted. She was surprisingly heavy, though, for just a head. He put her into the rucksack and eased it on to his back. Finally he picked up his detector and had a look about to see if there was any more of her to be found.

But he couldn't see a thing. The currents went all over the place this far out. The rest of her could end up anywhere, Sheppey, Walton or perhaps even Dutch Holland, which is how he thought of it to differentiate it from Holland-on-Sea, Essex. He took one last wistful look out to where he had been heading. He supposed he wasn't going to go out there now, not with the weight he was carrying on his back.

The poor girl.

He had better take her back and give her to the police so that perhaps they could work out who she was.

Her mother, if she had one, would be worried about her.

Then

BREATHE.

OK then.

I'm trying to see her face.

But all I can remember is the weight of her arm round me, and the scent of her: almondy orange, thick. And the feel of her nightie, which is pale blue, cotton, with frills on the front.

I've got my eyes shut and we're in her bed and she has a cup of tea, which, with her free hand, the one that isn't on me, she reaches and drinks from. And, although I can't hear the words, I can feel the rumble of her voice as my ears are pressed up against her ribcage.

If I had a clear photograph, I could see her face.

But I don't have a clear photograph. There were hardly any photos of anyone, which, not knowing any different, I never really questioned. Not until recently. The only one I've got is of me, where I'm sitting on her lap, all chubby knees and corn-rowed hair, leaning against her slim elegance.

And in it, her face is a blur.

I try to look forwards, but always I'm pulled back to the blank space before I was ten, and the void that has filled me since then.

I wonder if it's because I can't see my mother's face that I feel like this.

One

WHEN PEG TURNED UP FOR HER WEEKLY VISIT AND WAS GREETED with a scream, she knew things had reached the point of no return.

'Who the fuck are you?' Doll said over the blare of the TV.

It was the first time Peg had ever heard her grandmother swear.

'It's me, Nan, Meggy.'

The sticky fly tape behind Doll twisted in the fruited thermals of the lounge. Despite the fact that it was now winter, it was full and no longer doing its job. Peg noted that it needed to be changed.

'Never seen you before in me life.'

Doll frowned and patted her immaculately set grey curls – the mobile hairdresser always came the day before Peg.

Then, tilting up her head with a birdlike movement, she squinted at the large, crinkle-haired girl in her lounge. 'Stand in the light so's I can see you.'

Peg moved further into the greasy sunlight filtering through the net curtains and allowed her face to be taken by her grandmother's cold, lumpy fingers. As the old lady leaned forward she brought with her a tang of urine that flared Peg's nostrils.

'Oh yes. Now you mention it, there *is* something familiar about you. You're Raymond's girl Margaret, ain't you?'

'That's me, Nan,' Peg said, pressing her lips together, trying to appear neutral. 'Shall I make us a nice cup of tea, then?'

'Nice cup of tea.' Doll nodded and folded her hands back into her lap, on top of the blanket Peg had crocheted with her one wet Easter holiday many years ago.

Peg went out to the tiny kitchen and hunted for the teapot, teabags and milk. Doll had taken to putting things away in peculiar places. Only last week, the milk had been in the washing machine and the teapot – full of treacly tea and with the chicken-shaped cosy on it – in the fridge. Today wasn't such a challenge; by rooting in the saucepan cupboard, she found everything she needed.

While the kettle boiled, Peg began her regular clean of the kitchen, the work coloured this week by a realisation that the situation was becoming untenable. But it was so difficult. It was all down to her to sort out, but what could she do to help Doll while at the same time respecting the old lady's fierce independence? She had tried to get help in, had gone through all the means-testing that showed Doll was entitled to home care. But every time a home help, carer or shopper came to the bungalow, Doll sent them packing.

'They're all idiots. That or savages,' she explained to Peg, who knew exactly what sort of shorthand her grandmother was using. The mobile hairdresser – the only help allowed past Doll's threshold – was an unswervingly cheerful woman in her mid-fifties. She was also English and, underneath her spray tan, lily-white.

Even with her weekly mini-cleans, Peg could see that the battle against the chaos of stuff in the small bungalow had been all but lost. A teenager in the war, a young mother in the rationing years, Doll had never knowingly thrown out anything potentially useful in her life, and after eighty-nine years that added up to a hell of a lot of stuff, none of it as clean as it could be, most of it smeared with a thick layer of dust.

So the kitchen drawers were crammed with objects that were unlikely ever to come in handy, but which had been saved just in case. There were packets of sugar from every café Doll had visited in her life; beer mats swiped, she had told Peg, from the days when she and Frank used to go for a weekly drink in the local pub; a handful of British Rail spoon, sugar and milk-powder sets she made him take from the train on his daily commute to Wapping after they first moved down; various lengths of string rolled into balls like wool, and boxes and boxes of plasters, out-of-date antiseptic wipes, scalpel blades and yellowed latex medical appliances. There was a drawer almost entirely full of rubber bands, some so ancient as to be returning to the original sap. Another sharply compost-scented drawer was stuffed solid with the thin, filmy plastic bags you put supermarket fruit and veg into.

The grimy cupboards above the drawers held the leavings of generations of cheap, cracked and partial dinner sets, unidentifiable electrical appliances with dangerous-looking twisted and frayed cloth-covered cables and enough vases to furnish a small florist's shop. Off-puttingly jammed in among the dinner plates were stainless steel kidney dishes, a grimy bedpan and lengths of stained rubber tubing.

Four years earlier, shortly after coming home from boarding school after her A levels, Peg had – amid much consternation from Doll and Aunty Jean – moved out of the bungalow, away from Tankerton and up to London to start the job she still held at the library. On her weekly visits she had watched with alarm as the tide of clutter and neglect almost immediately began to roll in. It was as if Doll, who had been impeccably – even obsessively – clean and tidy when she was growing up, had been holding it all back until she was gone. It hadn't helped that, with the almost inhuman strength of a determined old woman, she had pulled what looked like hundreds of boxes and bags of ancient stuff into the lounge from the garden shed. It had been as if she were somehow taking stock, finding a way of rooting her increasingly free-floating sense of self.

Two years after she had moved out, after months of guiltily wondering if she should intervene, Peg had spent a whole weekend trying to organise things. She thought if she managed to clear just one cupboard or shelf in each room for the small number of items Doll actually used, then it would be possible to keep the other stuff under control. But it had been a far more difficult job than she had anticipated. Doll had perched on the kitchen stool, watching her every move with as steady an eye as she could muster, making sure that nothing Peg moved was thrown away. Then she had followed her around the house, saying 'I might be able to use that' each time Peg, questionable object in hand, glanced at the recycling box she was optimistically pulling behind her.

She wondered if, when the time came, she could get the phrase put on Doll's gravestone.

'And why are you nosing through my stuff anyway?' she once asked, to which Peg had no answer that didn't sound insulting.

In the end, Peg threw her hands up and decided she would just stage tiny, imperceptible and secret interventions whenever she visited. So, while the situation had steadily worsened, at least it had done so more slowly than had she not lifted a finger.

She tipped a beetle thing out of the teapot, gave it a rinse and popped in five teabags – Doll liked it 'so strong you can stand a spoon in it'. Then she put it on the tray she had already set with cups, saucers and sugar, the blue Princess Diana milk jug and a plate of Bourbons only just past their sell-by date.

But, as seemed increasingly to be the way, when she got back to the lounge Doll was fast asleep in front of the roaring gas fire, snoring slightly, jaws open, a string of spittle threading between the top and bottom sets of her loose dentures.

Peg batted away the couple of flies that threatened to invade her mouth.

On the TV, Lorraine Kelly and friends were chatting at such a volume that the hundreds of dusty glasses in the cocktail cabinet tinkled along with them. Peg put the tray on the sideboard, prised the remote from Doll's grip and turned off the TV. She poured herself a cup of tea, picked up a Bourbon biscuit, pulled her red notebook and pen out of her bag and settled down on the settee in front of the whistling gas fire. Her brain whirring, she leaned back and gazed at the creeping damp patch on the ceiling. But she had other things to worry about than the state of the roof, which she knew nobody had the funds to repair anyway.

She turned to her red book.

List: what to do about Nan? she wrote, and underlined it twice.

She stared at the blank page, but nothing came, no great insights or solutions.

So she closed her eyes, slowed her breathing and practised the mind-clearing technique she had been learning. She tensed and relaxed each of her muscles and started to count down from a hundred, imagining she was climbing down steps, down to a room with stars on the walls . . .

'Meggy!' Peg felt a hand on her knee. 'So nice of you to come, Meggy!' Far from coming up with any great revelations, she had simply fallen asleep in the humming, airless heat of the double-glazed bungalow.

'Hello, Nan.' Peg smiled and looked at the lined face twinkling down at her. She took her grandmother's cold hand, feeling the wedding ring that had been on that finger for sixty-six years. It had always been loose, but now it was only saved from slipping off by a lumpy, arthritic knuckle. The engagement ring, a decent-sized diamond that Frank had bought second-hand with his saved wartime earnings, was long lost. Washed away with the potato peelings, Doll always said.

'You'd better sit back down, Nan,' Peg said, getting up and helping her to her chair. Then she went over to the teapot and lifted the cosy. 'It's still warm. Want a cup?'

'Probably strong enough for me now,' Doll said, and they both laughed.

The intercom buzzed sharply, cutting across the thick air and making them jump even though they had heard it countless times before.

'Mummy?' Jean's voice crackled from the little white box on top of the low bookcase. 'Mummy? Is Meggy there?'

Putting the teapot down, Peg picked her way across the room to the box and pressed the red button on the top.

'Hello, Aunty Jean.'

'Oh, thank goodness you're there. I was getting ever so worried.'

'I've been here for a bit, Aunty Jean. It's only eleven.'

'Is it only eleven, then?'

Peg glanced over at the wrought-iron clock on the mantelpiece. 'Yes. I'll be over at about four-ish, as usual.'

'Oh.'

The tone of her voice stirred in Peg the familiar feeling that she was doing something wrong. 'I'll see if I can't come over a little bit earlier, then,' she said.

'All right, darling. Thank you, darling.'

The intercom crackled as Jean cut the connection.

'You know,' Doll said as Peg finally poured the tea, 'I don't know where Keithy's got to. Do you?'

Peg turned, cup in hand, and looked at her. 'Keithy? Who's Keithy, Nan?'

'My Keithy. I miss him, you know.'

Peg put the tea on the occasional table by Doll's chair, cleared six copies of the *Daily Mail* from the grimy pouffe and sat down next to her. She took her hand and laced their fingers together.

'Your Keithy, Nan?'

'You know.'

'No?'

'You know, Keithy, my boy. My poor baby.'

'Your boy's Raymond, Gran. My dad, remember. Raymond.'

'Oh yes. Raymond's a lovely boy. Ever so clever.'

Peg felt a lump in her throat.

'My Raymond's done ever so well. In spite of *her*.'

Peg closed her eyes. She could hardly bear it when Doll started on her mother.

'She broke his heart, you know,' Doll said.

'She died, Nan,' Peg said. She needed to soften her tone. 'And Raymond's not here any more, remember?'

'I miss him so much.' Doll looked up at Peg and closed her heavy eyelids, which were so papery Peg thought she could see the irises through them.

There was very little Peg could say to this. What do you say to a confused old lady who hasn't seen her only son for sixteen years?

They sat for a few minutes, holding hands, the hiss of the gas fire underlining the silence in the room. Outside, a car rolled past, bumping over the tarmac seams in the patched-up concrete road.

Then Peg noticed that Doll had started to snatch at her breath in staccato rasps. Her tiny, concave chest shuddered under the food stains on her brown acrylic jumper.

'Nan?' Peg bent towards her grandmother, a flush of panic sheening her face. 'Nan? Are you all right?'

Doll didn't respond. Peg put her hands on her shoulders and gently tried to rouse her, but she seemed to be lost somewhere inside herself.

'Are you all right, Nan?' Peg grabbed for the old lady's wrists and found the pulse point. It was fast, but steady.

She looked into her face again and, with relief, saw a fat, wet tear work its way out of the drooping corner of her grandmother's eye.

The old lady wasn't dying.

She was crying.

Then

I'M WHAT, SEVEN?

More or less.

Every night I stayed at the bungalow, until I was twelve or thirteen, Nan cuddled me up in my bed and told me a story. She never read from a book. She preferred the stories in her head, she'd say. Each night the story would be different.

She never repeated herself. Not once.

Not that I remember, anyway.

But that's not saying very much.

'Story!' I go.

'Tuck in then, Mrs Fubs,' Nan says, pulling my eiderdown over me. 'And hodge up.'

I shuffle myself right up against the wall and Nan stretches her little legs out beside me. Even though I'm still very young, my feet are already further down towards the bed-end than hers.

'They stopped watering me when I could reach the postbox,' was what she always said.

When I was younger than I was here I really believed her, thinking what cruelty that was.

'Well then,' she says, putting her arm round me. I catch her smell of lavender handcream and roast beef. 'What's it to be?'

'A story about a broken-hearted king!' I say, snuggling right down into the wiry firmness of her brown, freckly arm.

'Another one?' she says, and I nod my head up and down, up and down.

'All right then,' she says.

I settle down and let my eyes go hazy. There's a seagull stamping around on the flat roof above my head. He's been up there for a couple of weeks now; every night before I go to sleep, I hear him. He's up to no good, Aunty Jean says, and if she weren't handicapped, she'd be up a ladder with a broom to shoo him away. But I like him. I pretend he's my pet.

'The story of the Very Sad King,' Nan announces.

'The Very Sad King!' I go.

'Here we go then,' she says. 'Once upon a time, in a land far, far away, there was a king and he was a very happy king.'

'Why was he happy?' I ask, fiddling now with the bangle that's wedged up on her arm above the knobble of her elbow. Put there, she says, by her owner, when she was a slave-girl. And then she ran away and got free and it was stuck.

'He was rich beyond compare. And he had a lovely, lovely, lovely wife. A dark beauty she was. He'd found her in a foreign land even further away than his own country, and had fallen in love with her and brought her back to be his queen.'

'What did she look like?'

'She had brown skin—'

'Like mine?' I interrupt, holding up my arm. Which, to be honest, isn't all that brown these days. Not with the sunblock Nan puts on me all the time.

'Even browner. And her hair was long and curly, like yours, but darker: dark, dark brown, almost black. And she was tall and slim with a tiny waist. And the king loved her with all his kind and goodly soul. The only sad part was that they couldn't have a baby, which was the one thing they wanted that they didn't have.

'Now, it so happened that there lived in the kingdom a wise old woman. Hearing about the heartbreak of the king and queen, the wise woman went to them and cast a spell, and one fine day the king couldn't believe his luck when his queen gave birth to the most perfect tiny baby girl.'

'What was she called?'

'She was called Meg.'

'Like me!'

'Just like you! And little Meg grew and made the king and queen the happiest people in the world. She looked so like her mummy that sometimes, except for the difference in size, it would have been hard to tell them apart. But then, sadly, the queen got very, very poorly and died.'

'Sad.'

'Sad indeed. And the king was so broken-hearted that he got on his horse and rode away, far away, and was never seen again.'

'But what about the little girl?'

'He left a note for the wise woman. And this is what the note said.' Nan puts the king's voice on, which is very posh, not like how she talks at all. '"Dear wise old woman. Although I love my little daughter to bits, I cannot bear to look upon her because she reminds me so much of my beloved late queen.

You are a good, wise woman. Please take her and bring her up as well as you can, as if she was your own."'

'So the wise woman got the little girl.'

'She did. And that's the end.' Nan leans in and kisses me on the nose.

'But what happened? Was the little girl happy?'

Nan thinks for a bit. 'She was mostly happy,' she says. 'Perhaps even happier than she would have been with her mummy and daddy.'

'And that's the end?'

'That's the end.'

'But that's not a proper ending.'

'That's because it's a real story. And real stories sometimes don't have those neat pat endings like they do in those books you read.'

I think about this for a while. I suppose she's right. But I still feel a bit cheated.

'Can I read now?' I ask.

'Well . . .' Nan says.

I have to read, because I want to get the story out of my head. 'Please,' I go.

'All right then, twenty minutes and no more.'

She creeps out and shuts my door and I hear her making her way down the steep steps from my attic to the rest of the bungalow.

I sit there with *What Katy Did* in front of me, but my eyes aren't taking in the words. All I can think about is Nan's story and how the little girl sounds like me. I've got the dead mummy and the broken-hearted daddy, who rode away, and I suppose Nan is a bit like the wise old woman.

Later, Nan comes up and checks on me and gives me my sniffy blanket so I can sleep well.

Was I happier than I would have been with my own parents?

Who's to say.

I don't remember them. I don't even have an image for either of them.

All I have are these vague moments from my childhood.

Breathe, Peg.

Two

'SHE WAS CRYING ABOUT RAYMOND,' PEG SAID.

'Oh,' Jean said. She was trying to reach for something with her grabber stick, but couldn't quite work up the momentum to raise herself to sitting. 'Oh bugger it. Pass me my cigs, will you, Meggy? There's a darling.'

Peg reached down for the Marlboros, which had worked their way across the candlewick bedspread and fallen onto the lino. 'I'd really like to find him, so they can see each other again before it's too late.'

'Not much chance of that. Thank you, lovey.' Jean propped her oxygen mask on the top of her head, pulled a cigarette from the pack and put it between the Rimmel-red lips she referred to as her 'trademark look'. Peg picked up the lighter and held the flame to the tip for her. Jean's fingers were so swollen, so distended by her own flesh that she had problems with motor tasks. And it didn't stop with her hands – she had been stuck in bed now for over ten years.

She inhaled deeply, then let the smoke trickle slowly from her nostrils. From his position parked on her belly, her ageing cat Lexy batted lazily at the plume with his paw. That cat was a nuisance: he regularly sprayed Jean's room. But, away from the focal points where he marked out his territory, his pungent cat musk had nothing on the fug of Jean's cigarettes and the rankness that crept from the deep folds of her body. Having grown up with it, Peg was used to it. But the almost visible odour still always hit her like an olfactory boxing glove when she entered Jean's extension – even after the warm-up of having spent some time in Doll's side of the building.

'What do you mean, not much chance of that?' Peg said. She had always wondered if Jean knew more about Raymond than she let on.

'There's no way of finding him. That's what I mean,' Jean said, looking at Peg through the corners of eyes which, despite their customary slick of frosted blue shadow, could only be described as piggy. 'Get me my Guinness, will you, Meggy?'

It had always been like this. Jean met any mention of her missing brother with a blank wall.

What she didn't know, though, was how right she was about there not being much chance of finding him.

What she didn't know was that Peg had been making quite an effort to find Raymond and had so far turned up a nothing as big and as fat as her aunt. For all she knew he was dead. But something inside her said he was still around and, if he was, she was determined that she would find him for Doll. It must be awful to be an abandoned mother.

What she felt as an abandoned daughter was also worth noting, but, she reminded herself, far less urgent at the moment.

She went through the wide doorway into the kitchen to fetch Jean's afternoon pint of Guinness. Frank had built this extension for his daughter almost entirely on his own when they moved down from London. While the rooms were no bigger than those in the adjoining bungalow, he had built the doorways and passageways wider than standard, to accommodate Jean's bulk back in the days when she was mobile. It mattered little, now she was bed-bound, that she had probably outgrown even the generous dimensions of his handiwork.

Popping in on Jean was the most challenging part of Peg's visits. After she and Doll had shared their ritual fish and chip lunch – she only had chips herself, but Doll had never seemed to notice – she would settle her grandmother down in front of *Countdown* with a slice of her favourite Jamaica Ginger Cake while she went 'next door'.

Part of Frank's design was that, for her independence, Jean would have her own back door. So visiting her involved going out of the back of the bungalow, down a slope, turning back on yourself to go up another, then into Jean's door, which was right next to Doll's. There was also an internal door in the partition wall between the bungalow and the extension, but it only opened from Jean's side – another feature Doll said Frank had designed to 'give the girl some dignity'.

He sounded like he had been a kind man. Peg wished she could remember him, but all she had to go on were family stories and a photograph Doll kept on the mantelpiece of their wartime wedding. Other than that, her grandfather was as lost to her as her mother: a hazy figure.

On top of the worry of what to do with Doll, Peg's other problem was that when she tried to think of anything that happened before she was ten or so, she found nothing. She could almost feel it in her skull: a big, empty hole. Time that she must have lived through, but where either nothing had taken root, or from which everything had been erased.

But the leavings of this forgotten past were all around her.

Evidence of her grandfather's kindness, for example, coming up against the harsher realities of the present.

Because, despite Frank's best-laid plans, there was very little dignity left for Jean now. And that was where Peg found the challenge in visiting her. Doll's decline was brutal, but far easier for Peg to deal with – it was the kind of thing you might expect from an eighty-nine-year-old. Up until about a year ago, not only had she been able to cope with her own needs, but she had also single-handedly looked after her disabled daughter. This had been a matter of great pride and importance for her.

So, with certain qualifications, Doll had seen a good innings.

But Jean. It had been a tough life for her all round. There she was, twenty years younger than her mother, yet thanks to her forty stones of rebellious flesh, horribly, horribly stuck.

She had been handed the very shortest of life's straws; even the thought of her beached there at the back of the bungalow brought Peg out in a rash of guilt and despair. Although she barely admitted it to herself, it was partly because of this that she had moved away from the bungalow so soon after she had finished school.

As she slowly poured the Guinness down the side of the glass so that it didn't froth up too much, Peg noticed that Julie – for whom Wednesday was a well-earned night off – had left out a cold supper for Jean under a shell of cling film. Julie was Jean's care worker, contracted by the council to come in three times a day. This arrangement had been put in place after Doll slipped on the outside slope while delivering her daughter's daily full English breakfast. Luckily, Mrs Cairns the next-door neighbour was in curtain-twitching mode at the time, so Doll was carted off to A&E for a check-up and Peg was called in and given the usual Mrs Cairns head-waggling tirade about how on earth could she leave her poor aunt and grandmother with no help after all they'd done for her.

It wasn't like she'd asked them to look after her, Peg thought, as the memory of the shame she had felt at that moment flushed her cheeks.

But that was when Peg had finally won the battle to get Doll some help with Jean, and the first of a succession of carers was brought in.

They didn't last long. It was hard work, shifting all that unwilling flesh around a bed, and Jean, quite understandably, didn't take to being cared for by strangers.

But Julie, the fifth carer to come along, had been with Jean for eight months now. She had been new to the job, so hadn't known any different, hadn't known that other clients could be grateful and meek. She was also the most patient person Peg had ever met.

She poured herself a small Guinness – Jean liked company when she had a drink – and carried the two glasses through to the bedroom, where she adjusted the electric bed-head to make it easier for her aunt to put the glass to her mouth.

'Thank you, darling,' Jean said, as the whirring contraption shifted her immobile bulk up to a sitting position. 'What's the girl left out for my tea?'

She always referred to Julie – who was at least forty – as 'the girl'. Not once in Peg's experience had she called her by her real name.

'It looks like ham salad,' Peg said, helping Jean to light another cigarette.

'Oh no,' Jean said, poking out her lower lip. She didn't really consider salad to be proper food. 'Did you have fish and chips again with Mummy?'

'As soon as it's less icy, we'll come over and eat with you again,' Peg said. 'But Nan can't go out in this.'

'Is it still icy, is it?' Jean said. Her drink had given her a tan moustache. Peg pulled a tissue out of the box on the bedside table and wiped it off, taking care not to disturb her lipstick. 'Pass us the ashtray, there's a dear.'

The pelican-shaped ashtray was well within Jean's reach, since she had only just put out her last cigarette, but Peg moved it closer without comment.

'Nan mentioned something about a Keithy,' Peg said, when Jean had everything she needed.

'*Did* she now?' Jean said, raising her eyebrows, which she kept immaculately plucked in high arches above those elaborately made-up eyes. She drew her face back into the flesh of her neck, giving herself a couple of extra chins. 'Well, that's a turn-up for the books.'

'I thought she was getting Dad's name wrong or something.'

'No.' Jean took another slug of her Guinness. 'No, she wasn't doing that.'

'So who's Keithy then?'

Jean looked at Peg and sighed. Eventually, she appeared to make a decision. 'I'll tell you. Just for Mummy's sake. So if she brings it up again you'll know to steer her clear. Because we'll NEVER EVER talk about it again after this, Meggy. Not in front of Mummy.'

'Never talk about what?'

'Keith – Keithy, as Mummy always called him – was our brother.'

Peg frowned. 'Whose brother?'

'Mine and *his*. You know, your dad's. Not for long, though. It was a dreadful accident. He was only a baby. Not even two.

He fell off the edge of the docks into the river, hit his head on a stone and was swept away.'

Peg gasped. 'I never knew . . .'

'A really and truly dreadful accident.' Jean clocked Peg's reaction and nodded to herself. 'Pass us that tissue, will you, darling? Well, that's the story we told everyone. I saw it happen, though . . .'

'What does that mean?'

Jean dabbed at her eyes and took a deep breath, as if she were about to say something more. Then she checked herself and, at last, she spoke.

'Your father saw it too. He was there.'

'How horrible for you both,' Peg said, compassion almost blanketing an initial flash of annoyance that no one had thought to tell her about this piece of family history before. Was it any wonder she couldn't remember anything when chunks of the past had been withheld from her like that? 'How horrible for everyone.'

'There's some things it's impossible to forget,' Jean said, leaning back on the pillows and rubbing her forehead. 'I know I'll always remember it. All my days. The little baby toddling on the edge of the dock. His face as he lost his footing. And the sound as his head hit the rock. Crack.'

Jean watched as Peg shuddered.

'I've asked myself if I could have done or said anything to stop it happening,' she went on. 'But I was too far away. I never could have got there in time to stop him.'

'You're not to blame, Aunty Jean. You were only a little girl yourself.'

'I was eight. I know what I saw. But it nearly killed poor Mummy. She wasn't there. She was busy somewhere else. She'd left him in our charge. So she blamed herself. She said it to me, at his poor little funeral. "I'm never looking away from my children again," she said.'

'So it must be *really* horrible for her not to have seen Raymond for so long,' Peg said.

'I suppose,' Jean said, brushing crumbs from her bedspread. 'But do you know what and all?' She narrowed her eyes at Peg. 'That was when Mummy stopped eating. She used to be a fuller-figured woman, big, a bit like me. But after Keithy died, she started starving herself.'

'I can't imagine Nan big,' Peg said. 'I always thought she's skinny because that's how she is. I never knew.'

'Well, dear,' Jean said, wedging the balled-up tissue between her flesh and her sleeve. 'You can't know everything, can you?'

Indeed, Peg thought. So it seemed.

She served the salad supper and, despite Jean's protests about being forced to eat rabbit food, the entire plateful disappeared in a few bites. With it went the best part of a large loaf of the doughy white bread that formed a major part of her diet, half a bottle of salad cream and almost an entire tub of Utterly Butterly.

'I'm worried about Mummy,' Jean said, wiping her mouth with a Wet One. She put another cigarette to her lips and looked up at Peg, a depth of seriousness in her eyes.

'You and me both, Aunty Jean.'

'It's just, if she's talking about Keith, then, well . . .' Jean drew on her Marlboro again and blew the smoke out up at the ceiling, adding another tiny tint of yellow to the nicotine stain blooming on the Artex.

'She didn't know who I was when I turned up,' Peg said.

'Oh dear.'

'We need to start thinking what we're going to do with her, Aunty Jean. She won't have any help, but she can't go on like this.'

'No. I know. It's a dreadful problem, I know.'

Peg braced herself and finally gave voice to the thought that had been gnawing at her since she witnessed Doll's earlier confusion. 'It's just I don't know how much longer she's going to be able to stay in the bungalow.'

Jean shot Peg a horrified look. 'You're not talking about putting Mummy in a *home*, are you, Meggy? You can't do that, though. It would kill her to move away, away from all her things. Away from me. Do you want to *kill* her?'

'Of course I don't,' Peg said, twisting her fingers into knots so tightly that they hurt.

'I won't have it, you hear me? I won't have it.' Jean stubbed her cigarette out in the mouth of the pelican-shaped ashtray. She screwed the Wet One up into a ball and jabbed it at her eyes, which started to bulge as a coughing fit took her over. The spasms racketed through her, making her fleshy body quiver. Tears blobbed in her eyes and spilled onto her blotchy cheeks.

Peg rushed to the kitchen to fill one of Jean's special sipping cups with water. She held it in front of her aunt, who gulped it down between desperate wheezes for breath. Then she took the oxygen mask from where it was still perched on the top of Jean's head and pressed it to her face.

'Thank you, dear,' Jean gasped. With quivering fingers she pressed the mask tight against herself, fell back against the pillows, closed her eyes and breathed in as deeply as she could to activate the oxygen.

Peg hovered anxiously over her while the moments passed. Then, without warning, Jean shot out a hand and squeezed

Peg's arm so tightly in her hot fat palm that she nearly yelped.

'And if you throw Mummy in a home, Meggy,' she said, lifting the mask away to speak. 'Then what about me? What's to become of me?'

Peg knew this was the big issue. Thinking about it made her head ache; she had no answer for it. But she couldn't let Jean know that. She took a deep breath and looked her aunt straight in the eye. 'Don't worry, Aunty Jean,' she said. 'I'm never going to do that to either of you.'

She made sure both Jean and Doll were comfortable for the night. Then, her brain like scrambled egg, her eyes tight like two little raisins stuck on the front of her face, she steeled herself for the chilly walk to Whitstable Station, which she decided tonight would be the longer, beachfront route. She wanted to be whipped clean by the salt-sharp wind.

She had just fastened the front gate when she turned and nearly bumped into Mrs Cairns.

'Heel, Scotty,' Mrs Cairns said to her greying Jack Russell which, as usual, greeted Peg with bared fangs. 'How are they doing, Margaret?' she asked, her blob of a face a picture of solemn concern.

'Oh, they're fine, Mrs Cairns,' Peg said, hitching her rucksack on her back and fixing a smile onto her face. 'All jogging along nicely.'

Allowances had to be made for Mrs Cairns. Her only child – a 'hulking great slow boy', as Jean put it – had hanged himself in a police cell about twenty years ago, and, according to both Doll and Jean, she had not been right since then.

'Your grandmother didn't look all that smart yesterday. She was out the front here in her dressing gown at eleven o'clock in the morning calling for her late husband.'

'Really?' Peg said, her heart sinking down somewhere near her Doc Martens.

'It's a crying shame that she's on her own here, without any help.'

'I know, Mrs Cairns, but Nan won't have anyone else in the house. And at least there's Julie now, for Aunty Jean.'

'And about time too.' Mrs Cairns folded her arms across her battleship bosom and settled her chin into her neck.

'I'm working on it, though, Mrs Cairns. I'll get in touch with the council tomorrow. I promise.'

Mrs Cairns made a little harrumphing sound.

'If you'll excuse me,' Peg said, trying to stay brave, trying to hold back the tears of helplessness fizzing in the corners of her eyes, 'I've got a train to catch . . .'

'Yes. I suppose you've got a life to get back to up in London,' Mrs Cairns said, unfolding her arms and swinging a bag full of scooped poop from her hooked forefinger.

'I've got work tomorrow, if that's what you mean.'

'Well, don't let me keep you.'

Peg set off, but before she had got more than a couple of steps, Mrs Cairns spoke again.

'Oh, just before you go, what are your plans for that garden, Margaret? It was a jungle out there in the summer, and it really needs a good tidy.'

This was one of Mrs Cairns's favourite themes.

'Poor Mr Thwaites made it ever so lovely,' she told Peg for the millionth time. 'And even after he passed away so suddenly, Mrs Thwaites looked after it, kept it neat and presentable. But after you left, she let it drop, you know. And it's in a right old state now. And all those weeds have seeds, you know. And they blow over my way.'

Peg nodded, itching to get away. It wasn't as if she hadn't

tried to tidy things up. But her time was limited and, never having had a garden of her own, she had no idea where to start. Two years ago she had succeeded, during one enthusiastic bout of weeding, in pulling up a whole load of ground-cover geraniums.

'What Frank put in for our golden wedding,' Doll had informed her. 'Just before he passed away.' Oblivious to the effect she was having on Peg – who had ended up going home and crying until she was sick – she went on to say how the purple flowers coming up every spring had lifted her heart and reminded her of him.

'Well what do you say, Margaret?' Mrs Cairns said.

'I'll see what I can do, Mrs Cairns.'

After the geranium debacle she bought some new plants to put in, carrying them on the train in a soggy cardboard box that leached muddy water through to her jeans. But she planted them just before a late and devastating frost, and they all died.

'I'd be very grateful,' Mrs Cairns said. 'I don't like to nag, but it's a bit depressing to look at. It can't do poor Mrs Thwaites much good either.'

'No,' Peg said.

Mrs Cairns turned towards her gate, and Peg was finally dismissed. With time now at a premium if she was going to catch the one train she could use with her cheap advance ticket, she set off on the quicker, more dreary walk to the station, past the crumbling chalets of Tankerton, whose streets stood as yet unchanged by the tide of gentrification washing in from Whitstable.

As she reached the corner of the street, she heard a vehicle pull out in the road behind her. She needed to cross, so she glanced back. It was a white van. There were so many white vans on the roads and they all looked the same. But she had an eerie feeling that she had seen this one not only here in Tankerton, but also several times in the past couple of weeks as she made her way to or from the library. As the van passed, she caught a glimpse of the profile of the driver in the inadequate yellow streetlight.

And, although she couldn't place him, she thought he looked oddly familiar.

Three

PEG ENDURED A TENSE JOURNEY BACK TO LONDON IN AN overheated train carriage with the bouquet of the bungalow lingering in her nostrils and – she knew it – on her clothes.

Her only fellow traveller was a trashed boy who slouched in his seat, earphones blaring, and eyed her with menace.

If she had been Loz, she would have asked him what he thought he was looking at and told him to turn his fucking shit music down. But she was Peg, so she suffered in silence and tried once more to count her breaths, to take herself away and zone him out, using the same technique she had tried before failing and falling asleep in the bungalow.

She had found the method in a book on age regression and self-hypnosis borrowed from the self-help section of her library. The aim was to use the breathing and counting to put yourself in a state of what the book called 'inner flow'. Then, by visualising yourself floating along a personal timeline, and seizing on glimpsed sensory details – your bedroom wallpaper, for example, or the smell of a favourite meal – you could access long-repressed memories.

Yeah, right, she had thought when she first flicked through the book.

The fact of her missing memory hadn't particularly troubled Peg until recently, when it had begun to dawn on her that, apart from her year-long relationship with Loz, she had very little going for herself. With no ambition and few friends she wasn't too clear who or what she was. Something seemed to be blocking her up. It felt to her as if there were a wall between her and most other people, Doll, Jean and Loz apart.

It had been Loz, in fact – whose mother Naomi was a psychotherapist and who was therefore very conversant both with herself and the power of the mind to heal itself – who had made her realise this.

'You need to do something about it Peggo,' she had said one evening when, coming home from the restaurant after an early shift, she found her slumped in front of really crap TV. 'Before it gets too late and you're completely fucked.'

It was also Loz who suggested that the reason Peg felt so blurred round the edges – for that was as close as she could get to describing how she felt – had something to do with what Loz had decided to call her 'weird childhood', and how she couldn't remember anything about it.

She had offered Naomi's services, but Peg had felt it was too close to home. It would feel . . . incestuous. Instead, ever her grandmother's self-improving girl, she checked out the self-help book from the library.

Following its suggestion, she had gone out and bought a digital voice recorder with five hundred and thirty hours of recording time. A bit of a Luddite, she had taken a full day to become conversant with the workings of the thing, but now she carried it with her everywhere, ready for the moment when she might engage with her 'inner flow'. She had also bought a new red notebook and a slightly expensive pen, for more conventional recording of what her thoughts revealed and, if she were honest with herself, she much preferred this quieter, more contemplative method. After all, she had been brought up by her grandmother to record everything in notebooks – or, as Doll called them, 'Commonplace Books'.

But the voice recorder had cost thirty quid, and, even if she didn't use it all that much, she had – partly out of the hate of waste she had also learned from Doll – elevated it to a sort of totemic level. If she wasn't going to use it, at least it might provide a sort of prop to spur her on. So she kept it constantly in her pocket, more to stroke than to use.

Her breathing took on the rhythm of the train, then grew slower and deeper. Almost magically, the boy's horrible music became little more than a background hum: hardly troubling at all.

She felt the recorder's comforting weight in her pocket. From a position of scepticism about the process, she had now moved on to holding out great hope. She even had an idea it might be starting to work. Not that she felt any more defined, but her childhood – which had been a foreign land to her – had started, albeit tentatively, to reveal itself.

She took out her red notebook and started to write.

Then

'I WAS A NURSE IN THE WAR.'

This is another of Nan's stories.

I'm about eight, I suppose, and again she's tucked up beside me in my bed.

'I was a nurse in the war,' she says, her voice rumbling in my ear. I'm resting my head on her chest, and her arm is round me. It's so comforting, this feeling. Anything could happen, but I'm safe against my nan, here in my little attic bedroom with its stars on the walls which are also ceiling.

'I was a nurse in the war. I was younger than I should have been when I signed up for the training. I loved it, Meggy. They saw how excellent I was as a nurse, so very soon they put me into surgical, and I was in theatre throughout all the bombings, helping with all the poor boys back from the front and the people burned in the Blitz. We mended people whose whole bodies were covered in burns, put smashed jaws back together, cut off blood-poisoned legs.'

'Yerk,' I go.

'You see this?'

She pulls a hair from her head and holds it up in front of me.

'My hair is very fine, see. And it was long back then, too – I had it pinned up most of the time under my hat. It was perfect for stitching up the delicate work on the nerves and such. They sterilised it first, of course. Keep the germs off.'

'Would mine work for stitches?' I ask Nan, pulling out one of my own hairs and holding it up against her straight one.

'Yours is much thicker than mine, see, and a bit curly.' She holds them up together and I see that she's right.

'Oh,' I say, disappointed.

'But never mind,' Nan says. 'They could have used yours for the outside skin, where they needed really strong thread to stop it bursting open.'

I wind my hair tightly round my finger. She's right. It's really strong. So strong it makes the tip go white.

'Did you get to be a doctor in the end?' I ask Nan, thinking that's how it goes: you work your way up through nursing then you become a doctor.

'No, dear. Girls weren't doctors back then. Not girls like me, anyway. You had to be posh. But I'd have *loved* to have been a doctor. I could have been. I worked hard at it, you know.

'At the end of each day I'd sit up at the desk in the nurse's dorm and write down in my Commonplace what I'd seen being done, with diagrams and that. It's like I always say to you, Meggy. If you want to remember something, write it down. By the end of the war, if the surgeon had dropped down dead in the middle of an operation, I'd have been able to step in and finish it off!'

'So why aren't you a nurse any more, then?' I ask.

'Oh, I'm much too old now to be anything,' Nan says. 'And of course we girls didn't work back in those days after we got married.'

'That's not fair,' I say.

'But we had to look after our husbands and children,' Nan says. 'And quite right too. It's better than nowadays, when everyone feels the need to go out and work all the time and dump the poor children with strangers.'

'But your nursing comes in handy with Aunty Jean, doesn't it?' I say.

'Oh yes. It comes in very handy,' Nan says. 'I'm lucky I've got her, and she's lucky she's got me.'

'And I'm lucky I've got both of you,' I say, squeezing her tight.

Four

MUCH LATER, PEG STOOD UNDER THE RESTAURANT AWNING AT
Seed – the first vegan fine-dining restaurant in the West End –
stamping her cold feet on the hard pavement, waiting for Loz's
shift to end.

She needed to talk.

From behind the cover of a baytree in a chained planter, she
watched Gemma the Kiwi waitress as she wearily toured
the dining room, blowing out candles and putting chairs upside
down on tables ready for the cleaner in the morning. Gemma
was pretty, like a little imp, but tonight she looked exhausted.
Even though it was only a November Wednesday, the party
season had already begun to kick in. Seed's owner Cara was
working the staff into the ground, and every night Loz staggered
home with news of mutinous rumbles in the kitchen.

Peg chided herself: she should have just gone home and not
bothered turning up at the restaurant. Poor Loz would be
knackered. All she would be wanting after a night in the kitchen
would be to cycle home quickly and quietly, then to shower

and slip into bed. Why on earth should she want to be loaded up with Peg's family baggage?

She was just thinking about quietly turning away to get the bus home when Loz appeared, coming out of the back store-cupboard and into the open-plan kitchen, looking as fresh as if she had just jumped out of bed on a good morning. She stopped and had a brief word with Gemma, who seemed to be apologising for something. Loz playfully tapped her knuckles on the weary waitress's arm, then kissed her lightly on the cheek.

Peg was astounded by the flash of jealousy that grasped at her belly, rising and sticking in her throat. For a second she wanted to storm in and knock that Gemma flat to the ground. But she was being ridiculous. Loz was like that. She was a toucher, a kisser.

Rummaging in her bag for her bike-lock keys, Loz slid back the latch on the restaurant door and stepped out into the street, ready to cross the road to the cycle rack. But then she looked up and saw Peg standing there, right in front of her.

Without a beat, delight flooded her face. She reached up, took Peg's face in her hands and kissed her full on the lips.

'Peggo! How lovely! How are you? Fancy a drink? How's poor Dolly?'

I am an idiot to doubt her, Peg thought, as Loz fetched her bike and they set off for the dingy little late-night drinking club.

A fucking idiot.

'You're such a *good* girl,' Loz yelled as she placed two pints on the table in front of Peg. 'You're so *responsible*.'

'There's no one else.'

'There's social services.'

'What?' It was hard to hear what she was saying over the loud music thumping from the dance floor.

'There's social services,' Loz said, sliding into the seat and putting her mouth up close to Peg's ear.

'She'd never have it. Charity, she calls it. And look: Julie's great, but she's always in a rush. Four other clients besides Jean and she has to get all of them up, all of them fed, all of them changed. It's not a system for human beings.'

'What other choice is there, though?'

'I don't know,' Peg said, yawning and rubbing her fingers through her hair. 'I could move back in with them?'

Loz snorted. Then she saw the look on Peg's face.

'You're not serious?'

The club was the attic floor of a tall building down a greasy alley off Old Compton Street. It didn't advertise itself – there wasn't even a sign on the wall outside, just a discreet entry phone buzzer into which you whispered the current password. It was noisy, drab and dark, the floor was permanently sticky and, winter or summer, the whole place sweltered. But it stayed open till four and charged pub prices so didn't really have to try all that hard. It was always busy, crammed with actors and restaurant staff letting off steam after a night's work.

'Yes. No. I don't know,' Peg said.

Loz bit her lip and looked away. Then she turned back to Peg and levelled her fierce green eyes at her.

'Listen, Peg. You've had a rough time of it, a grim little childhood.'

'It wasn't *that* grim.'

'How do you know? You've got great blank bits.'

'I forgot.' Peg smiled at her own weak joke.

'Anything could have happened. And usually if you can't remember something . . .'

'I know. "You're repressing something."'

'My momma knows, you know.'

43

'But—'

'No buts. I know it.' Loz winked and wagged a stern finger at her. 'Anything come to light yet, with the old "look into my eyes" thing?'

'Not a lot yet. Only that I can't remember my mother, which I knew anyway. And some stuff about Nan, but that's hardly relevant.'

'You've got to dig deep,' Loz said. 'Time will help, and other platitudes.' She took a swig of her pint then laced her fingers with Peg's. 'But don't move back in with them, Peggo. Don't be such a wet blanket. They're adults. One's old and one's disabled, but your responsibility stops with sorting them out with the best care you can find for them. You can't do anything more than that. You have to live *your* life. It's your turn now.'

'But council care's not good enough, and they can't afford anything else. They're as skint as we are.'

'But *someone* isn't skint,' Loz said, sitting back and crossing her arms.

'What do you mean?'

Loz muttered something that Peg couldn't hear.

'What?' Peg said.

'God, you're so dense sometimes. I need a fag. Coming outside?'

They put their coats back on and went out on to the club's roof terrace, high above the Soho streets, where they stood shivering while Loz rolled and lit a cigarette.

'You know who I mean,' Loz said at last, exhaling.

Peg matched the effect with the steam coming out of her own warm mouth into the cold night. Growing up in a bungalow full of stale cigarette fumes and dodgy lungs had rendered the idea of smoking herself utterly unappealing.

44

'Look,' she said. 'I've got no idea where my father is and he doesn't want anything to do with us anyway.'

'How do you know that?' Loz said. 'HOW DO YOU KNOW THAT?'

'He could be dead for all I know.'

'And he could be alive and wondering about you.'

Peg shook her head, drew her hands tight round herself and looked away. The noise from inside the bar – Beyoncé's 'Crazy in Love', almost entirely drowned by party-level shouting and laughter – made her feel like her head was going to explode. Loz leaned back on the parapet and looked at her, piling on the pressure with her extraordinary eyes.

'And anyway, who's to say he's got money?' Peg said at last.

'He paid for that fancy-pants school of yours.'

'That's not definite.' Peg tried to avoid Loz's gaze.

'You know he did.'

Peg shrugged.

'See what I mean about being such a good little Meggy? Doll tells you *once* that asking who was paying was prying and your brain shuts down and you don't ask *ever again*. For fuck's sake! Look: I love you so much, Peg, but sometimes you drive me mad. You just always assume that everything's going to be too difficult, so you never even try. You never even *try* to make things better.'

'But things *are* so difficult,' Peg said, fighting to stay in control, feeling the tears pricking at her eyes. The metallic tang of the cold London night seeped into her bones, making her feel so alone, despite Loz being right beside her. 'And I *have* tried. I've looked for him. I've searched the Internet for him, but he's nowhere. And if I did find him, then what? He's hardly going to be delighted, me tracking him down. If he knows where Nan

45

is – which he does – then he knows where *I* am. If he hasn't found me, then he doesn't want to find me.'

'Jesus.' Loz flung her cigarette over the wall and Peg hoped it wasn't going to land on someone's head in the street below. '*He's* the one in the wrong, not you. Don't you think it's time he took some responsibility – for his mother at least, if not for you? He deserted you. I'm ninety-five per cent certain he's at the root of why you feel so lost. He *deserves* to pay.'

'It's not like that,' Peg said, hugging herself and gazing at the silent, sodium-lit street below, her eyes fogged with freezing tears.

Loz put both hands on Peg's shoulders and pulled her round to face her. 'If you go back to Tankerton, to your little room under the roof in the tiny bungalow, you'll have let him off the hook, won't you? It'll be the end of you and the end of us. You'll be like some sad old spinster, looking after sick elderly relatives, "never once thinking of meself". Well, listen, Peg. If you're going to get anywhere at all in your little don't-worry-about-me life, you're going to have to start putting yourself first. You need to find your father and look after Peg.' She jabbed a finger at Peg's chest. 'Harsh but true.'

'But—'

'But what?' Loz stood, and clicked her fingers repeatedly, waiting for it.

'But I don't know who that is.'

'What do you mean?'

'I don't know who "Peg" is.' And, despite all her best intentions of holding back, she burst into tears.

'Fuck's sake, girl, c'mere,' Loz said at last. She reached up, took her in her strong, wiry arms and let her cry there, holding her face against her nicotine-scented sleeve, until there were no tears left.

As she usually did when heading home with Peg, Loz left her bike tucked indoors, locked to the bottom of the stairs that led up to the club, with the arrangement that she would pick it up the following night.

As the chilly night-bus rattled through the deserted, diesel-scented South London streets, Peg told Loz the Keith story.

'And they never mentioned him before?' Loz said, astounded, her mouth open.

'Not once,' Peg said, looking at a pink bra that had somehow found its way on to the top of a bus shelter and wondering if it had been thrown from the ground or a passing bus, and whether the owner of the bra had been upset or in on the joke. 'Well not that I remember, of course, given the gaps. I don't suppose it's the kind of thing you talk about all that much.' She cradled the voice recorder in her pocket. It hadn't occurred to her until now that she might have been told and had forgotten.

'If that was my family it would be a story repeated so often it would have grown legs and wings and taken off. There'd be some sort of shrine in a prominent room, with photographs and candles and shit.'

'And that's why we're so different,' Peg said.

'I'd be angry not to be told.'

'But it's not really my business, is it?'

'Fuck's sake.'

The bus went on its way, bare tree branches rattling on its windows. Peg and Loz sat, hands twisted together, bleached by the fluorescent lighting of the upper deck. The coconut-oil smell of the immaculately groomed man sitting a couple of rows in front of them coloured the bus with an improbably exotic tang.

It *was* none of Peg's business, though. Thinking about the

silence around Keith's awful death made Peg feel indescribably sorry for her tiny, grief-shrunken Nan, and this in turn made her feel bigger and more blurry than she had ever felt before.

'You're right, Loz,' she said.

'I'm liking the sound of this.' Loz squeezed her hand and put her head on her shoulder. 'What am I right about this time?'

'I'm going to give finding my dad another shot. He *does* owe us. I'm not going to ask him for money, though. I just want them to get back together.'

'Of course.'

'It would mean the world for Nan if she saw him again before – before she . . .'

'Shhh,' Loz said, as another wave of tears took hold of Peg. 'Shhh now.'

Five

'KEEP STILL.'

'It tickles.'

Loz ran the clippers one more time over Peg's head, then stood back to admire her work.

'You've got a lovely head,' she said, fetching a hand mirror from the bedroom. 'So smooth. And your scalp's the same colour as your hair so you look just like honey.'

'Jesus,' Peg said, examining her reflection in the cold morning light filtering through their living-room window. This hair-styling session had been Loz's way of attempting to cheer Peg up after the upsets of the night before. But Peg wasn't too clear how much better she actually felt on viewing the result.

'You'll get used to it. It's lovely.'

'Marianne will have a fit.' Peg's team leader at the library affected a flowing, earth-mother style – the complete opposite to Peg's new, number-one-all-over look. She was also wondering what on earth Jean and Doll would make of it.

'Fuck Marianne. She doesn't own your head. I do.' Loz bent and ran her lips over the smooth velvet on Peg's scalp. 'It

49

sharpens you up, Peggo. Like how you should be more like inside. Here, hold on. I've got just the thing to complete the effect.'

Loz dashed into the bedroom where she bashed about opening and closing drawers, searching for the effect-completer, whatever it was.

As she waited, Peg looked around the flat and marvelled at the changes Loz had already wrought.

When Peg's old flatmate – fellow-librarian Petra – lived here, it was a purely functional space that they used for sleeping and eating. When Petra moved away to live with her boyfriend in Brixton, Peg suggested to Loz that, as they spent nearly every night together anyway, it would make sense if she took Petra's place on the rent book. She would have put it more romantically had she the equipment to do so; Loz was, after all, the love of her life, her first proper serious relationship. But practical forms of expression came more easily to her.

Loz had accepted like a shot, and Peg couldn't quite believe her luck.

And now, already, after just four weeks, Loz had turned the bare little flat into a home. She had scattered old kilims and new cushions and hung paintings and art photographs that she had 'nicked' from her parents' house up in Camden. She had filled the empty old fireplace with pillar candles and placed an essential oil burner on the mantelpiece.

Peg's hundreds of novels – of the kind that might constitute the entire reading for a degree in English Literature at one of the older universities – had been joined on the growing shelves by Loz's equally vast collection of real-life crime books. She liked nothing better after a night sweating at the pass than to relax with a story full of brutal descriptions of dismembered corpses or ghastly doing-away-withs. Her addiction to this sort of book was the one big inconsistency in her otherwise politically exemplary life.

'It's good to measure my goodness against how bad other people can be,' she had once tried to explain to Peg. 'And the fact that it's all actually happened makes me feel I'm learning about the real world, not just reading what some writer makes up.'

Loz didn't need the filter of literature to answer her existential questions. In this she was the complete opposite of Peg, who had liked nothing better than to lose herself in a fictional world. At least, this had been the case until Loz had shown her the seductions of real life.

'Naomi and Richard hate my sort of books of course,' Loz had said of her parents. 'They think they're awfully lowbrow. But it's not all that far from Freud, if you think about it, and God knows Naomi's read *him* enough times.'

But Loz's biggest impact on the flat had been on the kitchen area. Before she arrived it had been so basically equipped that it would have been a real challenge to do anything other than microwave a ready meal. It now had the air of a semi-professional enterprise, with a block of razor-sharp knives, all sorts of chopping boards, and top-notch saucepans and woks. Previously empty shelves were now crammed with enough oils, herbs, spices and vinegars to stock a small specialist shop.

'Kitchenware. It's my only extravagance,' she explained to an awestruck Peg as she breezed through the kitchen, emptying drawers and cupboards of their blunt, chipped and broken contents, scrubbing them clean, then restocking them with her state-of-the art kit.

Cooking was Loz's passion. She was ambitious and would tell Peg bedtime stories of the restaurant she was going to run once she had saved enough, and how Peg would run the front of house and they'd live in a little flat above the shop.

Peg wasn't so sure how much of an asset she'd be to Loz's restaurant. She didn't think she was really a front-of-house type, what with the wall that stood between her and everyone else.

It seemed harmless to humour her girlfriend's dreams, though.

'Here we are!' Loz said, finally returning to the living room with two enormous silver earrings. 'I got them when I was in India. Put them on.'

Peg did as she was told.

'You look perfect!' Loz said, clapping her hands together. 'Look!' She held the mirror up.

Peg watched herself in the glass, with her sharp-smooth head and the dangling jewellery. Her eyes looked bigger. She almost looked like she knew what she was doing.

She hardly recognised herself.

Peg wasn't due in at work until after lunch, so, after Loz had set off for Seed, she thought she'd have another go at tracing her father.

She switched on the ancient jelly-coloured iMac she and Loz had found in a skip and which to their amazement worked when they plugged it in. It was the first home computer either of them had ever had: Loz's parents hadn't allowed them in the house, because Naomi said they encouraged insularity and undermined family interaction, and of course there had been no way that Doll and Jean could have either afforded or wanted such a thing.

Peg had inherited the family lack of interest in technology. At school, she was the kind of girl who escaped social purdah by curling up on her bed with a real book rather than the sort who hid in the impressively equipped IT suite. Under duress, she used computers at work, but she didn't really know what to do with one at home or why, indeed, everyone else seemed to find it necessary to own one. In the same way as she favoured her pen and notebook over the voice recorder, she preferred looking things up in real books and sending proper letters.

The old computer finally completed its elaborate and long-winded firing-up process and Peg scanned the available networks for PARTYBOYZ, the sporadically available and appropriately named unsecured wi-fi belonging to Sandy, the nocturnal boy downstairs. She was in luck, so turned immediately to the Facebook account Gemma from Seed had helped her to set up. Or, as Loz had put it, the Raymond Bait.

'If you can't find him, perhaps you could reel him in,' she said.

The account was in the full name she detested: Margaret Thwaites. It carried no information but her date and place of birth. The profile picture was a smiling, gap-toothed school picture taken when she was about ten which she had borrowed from its place on Doll's bookshelves and which Gemma had scanned for her.

Peg was entirely sceptical – and her argument about her father already knowing how to find her if he wanted to still held true – but, with few other options, she thought she might as well just go along with it.

The downside was that, over the two weeks since she set the account up, she had acquired lots of friendship requests with messages from old schoolmates – she couldn't really call them friends – asking how she was doing and telling her at length how brilliantly their lives were going in their entitled, graduate world – the world from which Peg had excluded herself.

Despite the vocal disappointment of her teachers and her straight-A A level results, Peg hadn't taken the expected path of going to university. Instead she set off in search of the low-paid, low-stress jobs she felt she was more suited to.

These Facebook messages unsettled her. She thought she had done with those girls: despite a lack of specific early memories, she knew from a lingering rotten taste in her mouth that her schooldays had been harshly unhappy, and it was doing her no good at all to see these faces and hear these names again. This led her to wonder if perhaps Loz was right – if perhaps her lack of memory was some sort of defence mechanism masking a hideous lurking truth too horrible for her conscious mind to deal with.

She shook the thought from her mind. She was over-glamorising her situation. She just had a poor memory, that was all.

The PARTYBOYZ network, infuriatingly slow at the best of times, took ages to load her page; she sat looking at a blank screen for what seemed like an hour. Then the blue header bar appeared and she saw, wearily, that she had four new friend requests. More girls she wished gone from her life.

But of course there was nothing from Raymond.

She had exhausted Google, too. His name returned quite a few results, and she had written to the Raymonds whose addresses were listed and who seemed to be about the right age. She received a few replies in the SAE she had enclosed in each letter, but, while they showed sympathy for her situation, none was her father. She supposed she should go and turn up on the doorsteps of those who hadn't got back to her. But, with some as far away as Durham, Aberdeen and even California, the expense of doing so was beyond her, especially with such a slim chance of success.

It was hopeless. It was a big world and she was never going to find her father.

As she shut the whirring, clicking computer down, the old familiar feeling crept up on her.

She was useless.

Six

'I DO MISS HIM, YOU KNOW, MEGGY. OH, DEVILS. THIS IS ALL skew-whiff.'

Two weeks had passed, Peg had got no nearer to arriving at an answer to the problem of what to do with her grandmother and her aunt, and the decline in Doll's thought processes seemed to be accelerating.

They were sitting together in the bungalow lounge and Doll was looking down critically at the mess of items on the hospital-style wheeled table suspended over her chair. She had bought it many years ago for Jean, but it hadn't really fitted over her, even back then. Now it wouldn't have a chance. Never one to entertain waste, Doll had taken the table for herself, using it to store the essentials of her daily routine: tissues, the TV remote, three pairs of smeared glasses, a prayer book, a tin of sticky humbugs, a magnifying glass. She also kept her pencil case to hand, and two elastic-band-bound bundles of jotters full of diagrams and notes – her Commonplace Books.

She had always kept these notebooks, maintaining that they helped her keep her 'bearings'. Peg had been taught the habit too, although it had tapered off for her some time in her teenage years, and she had lost or thrown away her early efforts. Her new red notebook was, in some way, an attempt at a revival, she supposed.

As with everything else, Doll had of course held on to all hers. Filled with personal observations, recipes, knitting patterns and little drawings that reminded her, for example, how to wire a plug, or how to bone out a chicken, they were sort of illustrated diaries. Until recently, she had kept them tucked away. 'Private and personal', she called them, and Peg understood that to look in them would be as bad as spying on her naked. But with her fading focus, Doll had taken to leaving her current pages open and visible, and Peg had unavoidably seen that they now were filled with indecipherable, shaky spider handwriting and random doodlings. If these were her bearings, then here was evidence of how rapidly she was slipping away from them.

'Who is it you miss, Nan?' Peg asked. Remembering Jean's warnings, Peg hoped she wasn't about to bring Keithy up again.

'This goes *here*, not *there*.' Doll tutted at the objects in front of her and shifted them around. 'Have you seen my thingamabob?'

'Which one?'

'This.' Doll reached for her lipstick, which had its own place next to a tiny gilt hand mirror. 'Raymond. I miss Raymond of course.' She took the top off the lipstick and, using the mirror, drew a line as shaky as her handwriting round her mouth. 'He's been gone for days, hasn't he?'

'Years I should say,' Peg said.

Bloody years.

'Oh, what did you do to your hair, dear?' Doll said, reaching up and touching Peg's scalp. It was the fifth or sixth time she had asked the same question, and Peg gave her the same answer as she had on the previous occasions.

'It helps me think more clearly, Nan.'

'Does it, dear? Perhaps I should have a go at that hairdo myself.'

They both laughed.

'Do you know what I fancy?' Doll said, twinkling her eyes up from behind her glasses. 'A drop of sherry. With a cherry in. Cherry in me sherry.'

Peg went to the cocktail cabinet and swung down its horizontal door. The shiny interior, with its peppery smell and neatly arranged bottles and glasses, was as familiar as an old friend. She poured two small glasses of treacle-sweet sherry from the decanter, topped them with cherries speared on wooden cocktail sticks, and carried them over to Doll.

'What's this?' Doll said.

'Sherry with a cherry. Like you ordered, madam,' Peg said, bowing slightly as if she were a waiter.

'Did I? Well I never. A cherry on a sherry! Well we can't put them down on the surface. It's ever so precious,' Doll said, stroking the tiny bit of free space on her wheeled table. 'You'll have to get a mat for the glasses. From the cocktail cabinet.'

Happy to humour her – she was in no rush and quite enjoyed Doll's capriciousness when it dealt with stuff rather than memories – Peg went back to the cabinet and rummaged in its two drawers.

'Nothing here, Nan,' Peg said.

'They're there. You've just got to look. Try the little wotsit behind the potato wine.'

Among all her confusion, Doll still retained some extraordinarily sharp laser beams of particularity. Peg lifted aside the bottle of potato wine Doll had made over ten years earlier and, just as she had said, there was a wotsit – or, rather, a cardboard box – full of identical drinks mats emblazoned with the word 'Flamingos' and a cartoon of a bright pink snooty-looking long-legged bird.

'I never knew that was there,' Peg said. But she recognised the flamingo mats; they were like a cocktail stick of clarity piercing into the fog of her childhood. 'We used to have these out at Christmas,' she said, setting two down on Doll's table.

'That's not the right place,' Doll said, repositioning one of them. 'That's better. Yes, well of course, we've still got loads left. We used to have the serviettes too, but I don't know what happened to them. He brought them back for me. Never look a gift horse.'

'Who brought them back?' Peg said, pausing briefly, sherry glasses in hand.

'Pass me that drink, come on. I'm gasping, dear.'

'Sorry.' Peg handed the glass to Doll, who downed it in one.

'Lovely,' she said, wiping her lips with the back of her hand.

'Who brought the mats back?' Peg went on, picking up the one meant for her own glass and examining it.

'My Raymond brought them back, of course. From his club. You know. The one down London Bridge. You know.'

'Club?'

'You know, Jeanie.' Doll tapped the side of her nose, then picked up a mat and showed Peg the reverse, where an old 01 London telephone number swooped above the legend TOP BIRDS FOR TOP GENTS. 'Flamingos.'

'He had a club?' Peg said.

'You know, just off Tooley Street. Remember? It's been a while since we was there, though.'

Peg's heart raced. She had scoured the real- and cyber-world for her father, and all the time her first real concrete clue to

59

where he might be had been sitting in her grandmother's cocktail cabinet, behind her grandmother's potato wine.

'Do you think you could find it on a map?' she said, quickly fetching Frank's old 1960s *A to Z* from the glass-fronted bookcase. She found the page with London Bridge on it and held it open for Doll, who put on her readers – placing her normal glasses just so on her table – and peered at it.

'There, look. It's marked anyway. That green cross,' she said, stabbing a knobbly finger at a biro mark on the page.

'No way,' Peg said, smiling.

At last, things were beginning to look up.

With sherries drunk, glasses washed up and put away, and Jean visited, Peg finally left the bungalow. She studiously ignored Mrs Cairns, who came out of her front door as she passed, her nagging gears clearly engaged and ready for action.

The unfamiliar sensation of a springy step carried her all the way to the station, fuelled by the knowledge that she had a Flamingos drinks mat and the old *A to Z* in her rucksack.

She had a lead to her father. At last she had a lead. And she knew where she was off to in the morning . . .

As she stepped out into the road, a white van cruised past. All she could see of the driver in the dark was that he was bald, big and black. But those three features stirred something inside her and she paused for a minute, trying to work out what on earth it could be.

Seven

THE SHABBY, CUT-OUT FLAMINGO CAST A SUPERCILIOUS EYE down on her. The door he straddled with his long legs was locked and unresponsive to her knocks. He seemed to be mocking her for the naive hope which had propelled her to this grimy alley off Tooley Street.

Perhaps she should've come the night before, straight from Tankerton. Nightclub: the clue was in the name. But it had been late, she had wanted to get back to see Loz, and, with her DMs, hairdo and lack of ID, she wouldn't have got past the doorman anyway.

Besides which, this place looked as if it was not only closed, but closed down.

She sat heavily on the dog-end-littered steps and put her head in her hands. Having made the mistake of allowing herself a shred of hope, she had really thought she was on to something. The cold of the concrete bit into her, and she shivered with uselessness.

'Are you all right, love?'

Peg looked up and saw a middle-aged woman peering down

at her, puffing on a cigarette. Swamped by a big puffa coat, she was too skinny and had a front tooth missing. But above their sunken dark circles, and beyond a taint of sadness, her eyes were warm and brown. Motherly, Peg thought.

Like my mother's eyes?

'I'm fine, thanks,' Peg said, embarrassed at being caught out at a low ebb. She rubbed her cold, blue fingers together, regretting that she hadn't brought gloves with her. 'Thanks.'

'Well you'll have to move, girl, because I got to get in there.' The woman ground her cigarette into the pavement and gestured at the doorway with a bunch of keys she had pulled out of her canvas shopper.

Peg jumped up, propelled partly by a small leap of hope. 'Are you something to do with Flamingos?'

The woman stood back and looked Peg up and down. 'Yes. But I can tell you here and now, if you looking for a job, don't bother. You're not the Flamingos type. Not by a long shot.'

'Oh no,' Peg said, touching her shorn head and smiling. 'I'm not looking for a job, thanks.'

'What you want then?' the woman said, one hand on the door. 'I gotta get in there and get it clean for tonight.'

The woman was nearly as tall as Peg, and behind her air of damage there was a remnant of something more commanding about her – something that made Peg feel she could trust her. Besides which, she was the only thing standing between her and a wasted journey.

'I think my dad works here. Or used to.'

The woman looked at her through the corners of her eyes. 'So?'

'I haven't seen him since I was little and now my nan's really ill and I want him to see her before—' Peg didn't know why she was telling all this to a complete stranger, but the relief of doing

62

so brought the tears to her eyes. 'I'm sorry,' she said, trying to force them back and failing. She hugged herself and stamped on the icy pavement.

The woman sucked her teeth and glanced up and down the alley.

'Look, it's freezing out here. Come on in and I'll make us both a cuppa and you can tell me all about it. And you can give me a hand with the bar shutters. They're a bastard to do on your own.'

She led her in and along a black-painted corridor.

'My name's Carleen,' she said as she switched on lights to reveal a ticket booth.

'I'm Peg.'

'Nice.'

They went down a narrow flight of stairs and Carleen snapped on several rows of fluorescent lights to reveal a vast black room set with tables and chairs all pointing towards a podium with a pole and a backdrop of greasy slash curtain. Dusty red velvet alcoves lined the room, and a shuttered-up bar ran along the wall to their right.

'Shit heap innit,' Carleen said, surveying the dingy basement, which, although the tables and bar were mostly clear of empty bottles and glasses, had the air of the morning after a party. The sharp smell of old wine and the dun stink of damp walls enhanced the effect.

'Like me these days, looks a lot better in dimmer light.' Carleen cackled, then wound her way through the tables, picking up a stray champagne bucket as she went. 'Bar staff should've cleared that away,' she tutted.

'Come backstage,' she said, unlocking a black door flush with the wall. 'Far cosier. Jeeze, these girls are such a mess.' They were in a sort of dressing-room-cum-green-room with a wall of mirrors above a long table littered with black or sparkling underwear, make-up and hair-styling equipment. 'Mind you, I wasn't too tidy myself back in the day.'

'You used to be a dancer?' Peg said.

'I was the best.' Carleen flashed a gap-toothed smile. 'Don't look so surprised.'

'I wasn't, I—'

'But there comes a time you got to give it up.' She flicked the switch in a kettle on the side of the dressing table and dumped teabags into a couple of mugs. 'So this dad of yours. Was he like a barman or something?'

Peg shook her head. 'I think he was the boss.'

Carleen rolled her eyes. 'They *all* think they're the boss, honey. What's his name?'

'Raymond. Raymond Thwaites.'

Carleen whistled softly.

'You know him?' Another stirring of hope made Peg catch her breath.

'Well of course, I know him. He's the gaffer. Always has been. Knew him quite well back in the day, if you catch me.'

Peg put her hands to her mouth. 'Where is he? Is he coming in today?'

'Let me get this straight,' Carleen said, eyeing Peg. 'How long is it since you saw him?'

'Why?'

'I just want to know.'

'I haven't seen him since my mum died. When I was six.'

'Not at all?'

'Nope. And my nan and gramps brought me up. But I need to contact him because—'

'Yeah. I know. Your nan's sick.'

'Yes.'

64

'And you got no idea where he went?'

'No.'

'Jesus.' Carleen sighed heavily and poured boiling water into the mugs. 'You got a fuck of a lot of catching up to do, girl.'

Peg frowned. 'What does that mean?'

'Not really for me to say, though, is it. You'll have to ask him when you see him.'

'But can you tell me where he is?'

Carleen handed a mug to Peg and levelled her gaze at her. 'You look a bit like your mum,' she said.

'You knew my mum too?' Peg said, her heart leaping.

Carleen nodded. 'A bit.'

'What was she like?'

'Kind. Nice. Good-looking. Great dancer. The best. After me, of course.'

'Dancer?' Peg thought of the pole on the stage in the club room next door.

'Yeah, she worked here,' Carleen said, and Peg tried not to think of the slim brown arms that used to hold her instead wrapping themselves round that pole for hungry male eyes. 'That's how she met him. She took him off me, if you must know.'

'I'm sorry.'

'What you apologising for, girl?' Carleen laughed, her tired eyes misted with memory. 'I was so jealous. But you know, you get over it. She was such a sweet thing, you couldn't hate her for long. When he married her, though, we all thought she was so lucky. Can you believe it?'

'What do you mean?'

'Nah, it's just . . .' Carleen shook her head, as if trying to dislodge something from her mind. 'Well, she got ill, didn't she.'

Peg nodded. They both stood there, leaning against the dressing table and peering into their steaming mugs.

'So do you want to know where your dad is or not?' Carleen said at last, breaking their impromptu moment of silence.

'I need to find him.'

'He's in Spain.'

'What?'

'He's what you call arm's-length. I don't think he can come back here anyhow.'

'Why not?'

'Reasons. You need to ask him that.'

'Do you know his address?'

Carleen shook her head.

'Well I've got him narrowed down to one country in the whole world, I suppose.' Peg peered gloomily into her mug. 'It's better than nothing.'

'Don't be so downhearted, girl. I don't *know* his address, but I know how to *find* it. Follow me.'

Carleen unlocked a door at the back of the changing room and led Peg into a small office.

'The Flamingos nerve centre,' Carleen said. 'Best not to know all the deals going on in here. But they still need it cleaned, and Charlie the manager's mostly an idiot. Or must think I'm one.' She jiggled a mouse on the desk and the computer screen sprang to life. 'See? He leaves it on and he's still signed in. Useful for me if I want to do a bit of surfing, but still an idiotic thing to do. Especially when —' she clicked a couple of times through to the email software — 'there's stuff of a highly confidential nature. Like Raymond's address. I know about it because the idiot couldn't work out how to buy plane tickets online, so I had to help him. And he never clears anything out, not a thing.'

She stood back and let Peg read the email, which dated back four years and concerned the hiring of a club dancer called Brandi for an event at a house called Casa Paloma Blanca, including a full itinerary and directions from Malaga airport.

'That's his house. It was for his wedding.'

'He's married?'

Carleen nodded. 'He wanted the best dancer from each of his clubs.'

'Really?'

'Yeah, I know. For a wedding. Tacky, innit. Brandi said the kid was there too, watching like.'

'Kid?'

'Raymond's kid.'

Peg was stunned. Having clung on to Doll's stories of the heartbroken king, she hadn't imagined that he'd have a new wife, let alone another child.

'Oh honey,' Carleen sighed. 'You're going to be doing a lot of finding out if you contact him. You sure you're doing the right thing?'

Peg nodded.

'I mean sometimes it's best to let things lie, you know?'

'What does that mean?'

Carleen ignored Peg's question. 'Look. I got to get on. And you need to help me with them shutters.' She printed off the email and handed it to Peg. 'Don't whatever you do let him know it was me gave you the address.'

Peg nodded. 'Thank you.'

'I got enough trouble without you landing me in it with him.'

'I won't say a word.'

'I hope it turns out all right,' Carleen said. 'I hope he gets back in touch with your nan, and everything's OK.'

'I'm sure it will be,' Peg said. 'This is completely the right thing to do!'

Carleen fixed her with her dark brown eyes.

Peg wasn't sure – it was almost imperceptible – but she thought she saw her shake her head.

Then

I'M SIX YEARS OLD HERE. VERY YOUNG INDEED. THIS IS GOOD progress.

We're whizzing along the front, bombing down the slopey paths towards the sea, charging down, down, down to the promenade below. The wind whips my hair and tears stream down my cheeks, brought on by the cold air and the fact that I'm laughing like a wild thing, wedged up between Aunty Jean and the steering column of her trolley.

'Faster, Aunty Jean! Faster!'

She ramps up the throttle so the trolley makes a high-pitched, juddering sound, and we bump and jump and fly over those lumps in the tarmac that look like giant, armour-plated moles tried to push their way up.

'Hold on, Meggy,' Aunty Jean says, and she makes a perfect, high-speed turn at the bottom of the slope. The trolley's side wheels lift up and thump down and we're hurtling along, the sea on our right, to Whitstable.

* * *

This was the first day of my regular holiday visit. It's the Easter holidays before the summer I went to live full-time with Nan and Aunty Jean, but of course I didn't know it at this point.

I had no idea what was coming for me.

Old bags and silly bitches tut as we pass them. I know they're old bags and silly bitches because that's what Aunty Jean calls them. She says they don't like the handicapped having fun, and she's out to prove them wrong.

When we get to our café, I go in and get the boy and, as usual, he makes out like it's a big problem to open the double doors to let Aunty Jean and her trolley in. The first time we went there he said it couldn't be done and she argued with him and said that he had to because it's against the law to discriminate against the handicapped.

'We'll have our usual, darling,' she says to me, handing me a tenner. I go up to the counter to get our fish and chips.

She has large with lots of vinegar and I have normal with no vinegar, but she always helps me out because I can never finish my chips and I don't like the skin part of the batter. Aunty Jean does. She says it's the best bit. I also get her a can of lager and me a can of shandy, which has real beer in it, she says. It makes me feel a little bit squiffy.

'So, how's Mummy doing, darling?' Aunty Jean asks me as I bring the food over to our table. We're right in front, in the window, because it's the only place you can fit the trolley in. The tide is out, far, far out, and there are old twits milling around the sandbanks with their metal detectors. The smell of mud, a bit like river mixed with stink bombs, is everywhere.

'She's all right,' I say. 'I think.'

'She looked a bit peaky when she dropped you off. A bit thin.'

'Perhaps she's been on a diet,' I say.

'Doesn't suit her. Fellas prefer a bit of meat on a woman,' Aunty Jean says, slapping the ketchup bottle so that a big dollop of red lands on her chips. 'Look at that.' She points at a lady walking past with big bosoms wobbling under a tight white T-shirt. 'Lovely.'

I agree even though she just looks chilly to me. It's a day when you should be wearing an anorak. 'I do prefer Mummy when she's more cuddly.'

I dip my chip into Aunty Jean's ketchup.

'Oy, get your own!' She reaches over and tickles me with her oily, salty fingers.

Later, we trundle along the front to the far end of Whitstable, me walking alongside the trolley and Aunty Jean leaning back, steering with one hand and smoking a ciggy with the other so that she looks like the bad guy in a Western. We reach the point where we can't go any further because the flood defences are up – big bits of wood they slot into the gaps in the sea wall when there's storms or big high tides. Sometimes, Aunty Jean brings her crutches and we struggle up and over the steps and go to this old wooden pub on the beach, where they let me buy the drinks at the bar like a grown-up because Aunty Jean has to sit down. I always get a lemonade for me and a port for her and we sit outside at the old tables and chat about this and that. My favourite things Aunty Jean tells me are about when she and Daddy were little, and the naughty things they did.

But Aunty Jean hasn't brought her crutches with her today, and, in any case, the weather's looking a bit iffy to sit outside the pub. You can see the clouds getting together over the sea and I spit on my finger and hold it up to the wind. A storm's coming. I'm quite pleased because I'm pretty pooped. I only stopped school yesterday and Mummy got me up really early to drive me down here because she's got somewhere she's got to be in London today.

'That's a nasty bruise she's got,' Aunty Jean says, as we reach the harbour and draw up in front of an ice-cream van.

'Where?' I say, looking round. I'm only half listening because I can't make up my mind between a Screwball, a Nobbly Bobbly or a Double Ninety-Nine. I'm thinking I'll go for the Double Ninety-Nine because, even though it's probably more than I can manage – Aunty Jean says my eyes are bigger than my tummy when it comes to ice cream – it *is* the first day at Tankerton.

'Your Mummy, silly. On her face.' Aunty Jean points to her own forehead. 'You'd think it wouldn't show on her skin, but it's all purple, isn't it?'

There's one thing about Nan and Aunty Jean that's boring: if they get a chance, they'll get in something about Mummy's skin. I'm glad mine is more like Daddy's. 'You'd hardly know,' Aunty Jean always says when she rubs in my sunblock, 'if you remember to stay out of the sun.'

'Oh that,' I say, meaning the bruise. 'She walked into a door, she said.'

'They all say that.' Aunty Jean hands me a tenner out of her purse. 'I'll have a treble Ninety-Nine today, darling. Celebrate your arrival. Get yourself whatever you want.'

'Two treble Ninety-Nines, please,' I say, standing on tiptoe so I can see into the van. The ice-cream man looks a bit dirty to me, so I watch him carefully. He touches the flakes and I have to pretend I don't see it so that I can eat them. I decide, though, that I'll leave the bottom bit of the cone, because his hand has been on there for ages.

'Looks like your daddy duffed her up,' Jean says as I carry our ice creams to a seat where she can park alongside me and we can watch the seagulls peck at the bits in the fisherman's nets.

I look up at her, shocked. Daddy doesn't hit anyone, not even me when I've tried his patience beyond all limits. But Aunty Jean is laughing. It's a joke. I feel this massive relief.

'Raymond hasn't got it in him to hurt a fly, you silly!' Aunty Jean slurps the top off her ice cream, just before it tumbles down onto her hand. Then she leans over and whispers in my ear so that I can feel the cold on her breath. 'It's the treatment, isn't it?'

'Treatment?' I say, looking round at her.

'For the cancer,' she says, pulling one of the flakes out of her cone and sucking the big blob of ice cream off it.

'Cancer?' I say.

'I thought as much.' Aunty Jean sighs and looks sadly at me. 'They haven't told you, have they? That's no way to treat a child, keeping it in the dark.' She draws another deep breath and takes my hand in hers. 'Your mummy's having radiotherapy, darling. For the lymphoma.'

I don't know these words. I frown and look at the horizon, which is a silver line between a grey sea and a grey sky. The clouds have rolled right in now, all the way from Essex, I suppose. Essex is what's on the other side, beyond the sea forts that look like little trees out in the middle of the water. I looked it up in Gramps's atlas. A spot of rain hits my nose and my ice cream suddenly seems too cold to eat.

Back at the bungalow, we're in Nan and Gramps's front room and the gas fire is lit and it's *EastEnders* and they're all watching it and drinking Nan's elderberry wine. They sometimes let me have a tiny glass, but not tonight, because Nan says it's a strong batch.

I'm on a cushion on the floor, in my favourite place near the fire and the sliding-glass bookcase, which I open up. Inside are all Nan's medical books. I pull out the big one called *Diseases and Symptoms*, open it up on my knee and look up lymphoma. Then I have to drag out the big *Collins Dictionary* to find out what lymph nodes are and what a prognosis is.

And then I am filled with dread.

Eight

PARTYBOYZ WAS READY AND WILLING, SO PEG ZOOMED IN ON Raymond's address in Google maps.

'Massive,' Loz whistled from her position peering over Peg's shoulder. 'Out in the middle of nowhere. And look at the size of that pool. Daddy's loaded.'

'I hope his new family's OK with me showing up.'

'Jesus Christ, Peg.'

'I wonder what he's going to say, me turning up out of the blue.'

'It'd better be "sorry",' Loz said, moving over to the fridge and pulling out a cling-film-covered bowl. 'Fucking off and leaving you just when you needed him most.'

'He was broken-hearted when Mum died.'

Loz whacked the bowl down on the work surface. 'And you weren't?'

Peg closed her eyes and rested her forehead in her hands. 'Please, Loz. Don't.'

'You've got to put yourself first sometimes and—'

'Please? I just need to get him to make whatever it is up with Nan before it's too late. That's all. I don't want to complicate it all with the other stuff. Not now.'

'I know.' Loz crossed back to Peg, put her arms round her and kissed her on the top of her head. 'I'm sorry. Sorry.'

'I just want to be practical about this.'

'Of course. It's just I don't know how you *can't* get involved with all the other stuff as well.'

'We're just different people, aren't we?'

'You can say that again.' Loz kissed her a second time. 'Now, I've got to dash. Mouths to feed.'

'What's in the bowl?' Peg said.

Loz fetched the bowl, whipped off the cling film and showed it to Peg.

'Well now. The tofu's nicely marinading, and I've chopped all the veg for you – so you just whack it in the wok. Do the onions, ginger and garlic first for a few minutes, and stir-fry. Then you throw on Loz's teriyaki marvel sauce from here,' she pulled a jam jar full of a dark purple sticky substance out of the fridge, shook it twice and replaced it. 'And bish bosh, Jean's your aunty, supper for Saint Margaret.'

'I don't deserve you,' Peg said, looking up at her.

'You bloody well do, you know.' Loz bent to kiss her on the nose, then pulled on her jacket, grabbed her backpack and stuffed her sequinned Union Jack purse inside it. 'Raymond won't know what hits him when we turn up on his doorstep, expecting him to step up to the mark, Prodigal Son style.'

'We?' Peg said, alarmed.

'Well, I'm not letting you go out there on your own. You're going to need some support.'

'No, no, no,' Peg said, getting up and taking Loz's hands in her own. 'I have to do this on my own.'

'What?' There was a long silence as Loz bored her green eyes into Peg. '*What?*'

'I need to keep it as simple as possible.'

'You mean you don't want him to see you turn up with me,' Loz said, pulling her hands away. An angry flush spread across her cheeks. 'You don't want Daddy to see you've got a girlfriend.'

'Of course it's not that.'

'It is, you know. You're such a coward sometimes, Peg. You're just so . . .' Exasperated, Loz shook herself away from Peg. 'Look. Let him see you for what you are. It's not that bad, you know, Peg. It's really not so bad.'

'I need to see him on my own.'

'This is why I've not met Doll and Jean yet, isn't it?'

'That's rubbish.' But Peg knew Loz had a very good point.

'Because you're scared to let them know. You're buying into some homophobia you're imagining for them.'

'I'm not!' She wasn't. She didn't need to imagine homophobia. It was rife in the Tankerton bungalow – on Jean's side, at least. Peg had witnessed it in full flow many times, as disgust vented at a TV soap storyline or some tabloid article.

It was all right for Loz, with her right-on Camden parents who loved the fact their fourth daughter was a lesbian, and who had been especially over the moon when they met Peg.

'Extra kudos for the skin tone,' Loz had remarked *sotto voce* as Naomi and Richard had danced round her, failing to restrain themselves from asking about her parentage – which, of course, she could do very little to fill them in on, particularly on the more interesting brown side. The only thing Peg knew about her mother was that she had been brought up in care. Jean had told her this once, adding that all she knew was that she had been the unwanted daughter of an 'Irish good-time girl' and a 'Coon jazz musician'. Peg knew where Ireland was. She had looked up Coon in Frank's atlas, but failed to find it.

The racism in the bungalow wasn't imagined, either.

'It's why you don't ever hold hands with me,' Loz said. 'You're scared of people seeing and judging.'

'That's not true!'

Apart from one month with a girl called Ed, short for Edwina – with whom the only thing she really had in common was being named for a Conservative politician – Peg had not had a proper relationship with anyone before Loz. While she loved the quieter intimacies and sharing that being together offered, she had difficulties with publicly declaring any sort of partnership. For example, whenever they held hands – always instigated by Loz, of course – she felt stiff and awkward. Loz usually picked up on this discomfort. Since letting things lie wasn't her style, a discussion usually followed which, depending on her mood, took a form somewhere between gentle questioning and the full-on haranguing of the type she was currently dealing out.

Peg closed her eyes. Loz's constant challenging of her was a good thing, she supposed. It forced her to swim her life, rather than just float it, which is what she had been doing before they met. In fact, how they got together said it all about the two of them.

Halfway between relieved and devastated about Ed – who two weeks earlier had pounced on someone else while they were at a party together – Peg had been at one of her boss Marianne's library team-building meals. It was being held all the way in town at Seed because Marianne was friendly with Cara the owner, and a generous discount had been promised. As Peg tucked into her quinoa-lime salad, she noticed a beautiful young chef working in the open-plan kitchen. She couldn't keep her eyes off this tiny, tattooed firework of a woman as she darted from grill to pass to orders board, keeping tabs on what everyone was doing.

Peg told herself she could dream on. This was someone completely out of her league. Yet, to her surprise and delight, the morning after, that very same beautiful young chef approached her at the library desk with a pile of real crime books.

'What a coincidence,' Peg had said as they spent her lunch break in Starbucks, her stomach churning with a sort of excitement she had never felt before.

Loz later confessed – when Peg had acted on her suggestion and bunked off sick for the afternoon to take her back to her bed – that it had been no coincidence at all. The night before, she had felt the gentle presence of the striking, tall woman at the table full of nerds so strongly that she could barely concentrate on her work. Thanks to Marianne's connection with her own boss, tracking her down had been simple.

But even though, a year later, she and Loz now shared a life and a flat, Peg had not managed to broach the subject of their relationship with the other two important women in her life, Doll and Jean. She had DNA in common with them, and had grown up under their care, but she was so different to them that she might as well have come from another planet. It was something her father – because, despite her protestations to Loz, of course she knew it was he who had paid for her school fees – had bought for her. By sending her away to private school, he had made her something very different to the person she might have been. Sometimes she thought that in doing so he had created some kind of Frankenstein's monster out of her. But mostly she acknowledged that something had been set free in her that otherwise would have remained hidden. Like, for example, the way she was comfortable with the fact that she was drawn to girls. Boys had just never really occurred to her.

Looking at it objectively, she had to be grateful to him for that, at least.

'Open your eyes, Peg.' Loz's hands were again encircling her own. 'I'm sorry.'

Peg looked at her, then, smiling, she fished in her pocket for her voice recorder. 'Can I have that for the record?'

Smiling, Loz leaned toward the mouthpiece. 'I'm sorry, Peg.'

'Good!' Peg said. 'I'm going to keep that forever and listen to it whenever you piss me off.'

'I *am* sorry, Peg. But sometimes I just feel like you edge me out. You know?'

'Look. I'm sorry too,' Peg said. 'But I've got to do this on my own.'

'But what if you get really upset? What if you need me there?'

'I'll phone.'

'Promise?'

'I promise.'

Nine

THE TAXI DROPPED PEG OFF BY A MASSIVE PAIR OF GATES SET IN a tall wall that stretched as far as she could see each side. She watched as the car drove away, bumping over the dirt track and blooming dust clouds in its wake. Its driver had been singularly uncommunicative, only grunting when Peg showed him the address, and holding out his hand at the end for his fare.

Her knees were still a little wobbly from the journey she had just endured, first on a motorway so petrifyingly fast and crammed with traffic that she had found herself gripping the back of the seat in front of her until her knuckles turned white, then on a switchback road climbing up out of the town and into a landscape of sheer drops down to irrigated fields, greenhouses, palm trees and cacti.

At least the fear that she might die any second had taken her mind off what lay at the end of the journey. But now she was standing in front of her father's house, she had to put up quite a fight to stop herself running away.

She was on her own.

She couldn't even call Loz for moral support. When her plane landed she had, as promised, composed a sweet little 'arrived safely, thinking of you' message for her. But she had never taken her basic, no-frills phone abroad before, and it told her it had no reception.

Heart pounding, she tried the gates, but they were locked. There was an entry phone in the gatepost, with a camera on a pole about six feet above her head.

She pushed the call button and waited, holding her face up, trying to draw strength from the sun. Nothing came back at her but the rustle of leaves in the still-warm breeze, broken occasionally by the odd buzz of a late cicada.

She was just about to press the button again when there was a crackle and a woman's voice issued from the speaker grille underneath.

'Hello? Can I help you?' An exaggeration around the 'o's showed up a failed attempt to mask the Estuarine mud of her accent. Jean used the same voice when she was on the telephone.

Peg leaned in so that her mouth was right against the mesh. 'Is this where Raymond Thwaites lives?'

'Who is it wants to know?'

Peg took a deep breath and plunged in.

'It's Peg. Margaret. Raymond Thwaites's daughter.'

'Oh,' the woman said, drawing it out into several syllables. Then she fell silent.

'Hello?' Peg said.

There was no response.

'Hello?'

Eventually, just as Peg had started to scan the wall for climbing possibilities, the entryphone croaked back into action.

'Look up so's I can see you,' a new, male voice said.

Unsmilingly, Peg looked up at the camera.

'Jesus Christ,' the man said. 'It *is* you.' There was a rustle and crackle at his end, as if he were putting his hand over the microphone. 'It's her all right.' Then he sighed. 'Well, you'd better come in then, Margaret.'

A buzzer sounded and the gate swung open. Peg picked up her rucksack and walked through, along a smooth driveway leading through some sort of orchard. On the other side of the trees, a vast, emerald lawn gave way to an enormous, spanking-new villa, sparkling white and pink in the afternoon sunshine, soaring columns surrounding a double-width front door. The scale and brightness dazzled her and made her feel as if, with every step she took, she was walking on a tightrope that was bending further and further towards the ground.

As she got closer to the house, the air filled with the sound of dogs barking, chains rattling and clanging metal.

Peg froze.

'*Cállate, Atilla y Bronson!*' a gruff voice shouted from somewhere behind the house and instantly the noise faded into a couple of whimpers.

Composing herself once more, Peg crossed a terrace of salmon-coloured crazy paving that looked like a melted strawberry milkshake. From somewhere over the back of the house, she could faintly hear the sort of music you might get in a hotel lobby. The driveway was surrounded by huge shrubs bearing highly scented, waxy pink flowers. Their sweet smell, which reminded Peg of candyfloss, didn't quite mask the sour aroma of sewage which percolated thickly through the air.

The front door swung open to reveal a lot of gold worn by an overweight grey-haired man in a pink-and-white striped shirt and straining white chinos. A cigar protruded from the corner of his mouth.

If this was Raymond, he didn't look a bit as she had imagined

– not the faintly glamorous picture built from Doll's glowing account, nor the fine catch poor Carleen lost to her mother.

He was fatter, older, smaller and on an altogether more human scale.

He was, in short, a disappointment.

Although she still had to fight the urge to flee, with him standing so unimpressively in front of her, her task looked a little bit more doable: she thought she could see the type of man he was.

'So. Margaret. Well then,' he said, looking her up and down – but not, she noticed, in the eye. 'My, haven't you grown, gel.' His voice – at once highly pitched and gruff, in accent every bit as South London as his mother and sister – gave nothing away. But the weakish lines of his face couldn't disguise the shock he was clearly feeling.

'Hello, Dad,' Peg said, surprising herself. She had decided she was going to call him Raymond, but the other word just slipped out. She put down her rucksack, stepped forward and held out her hand, but he took the cigar out of his mouth, opened his arms wide, then enfolded her in a tight but awkward hug. As he held his face against her chest – he was shorter than her by about four or five inches – she thought she heard him sigh.

He smelled of coal-tar soap, tobacco and alcohol.

After a thankfully short while, where she had to work hard not to stiffen under his embrace, he stood back and looked at her.

'You're tall,' he said.

'Yep.'

'Six foot?'

'Six one.'

'Fuck me. Mind you,' he waved his cigar in the air, 'your

84

mother was tall, too. But not that tall. Leave your bag. I'll get the girl to take it in for you. Well then. You've caught us on the hop a bit. Come on through and meet Caroline and Paulie.'

Caroline and Paulie. Must be the new wife and son. Her stepmother and half-brother, Peg supposed. Her head was bursting with all the new information she was having to process. She wondered again if she couldn't just go home and forget all about this.

As she followed him through the marble hallway, Peg caught her reflection in one of the many immaculately polished mirrors lining the walls. She felt like a Greggs bun in Harrods food hall, a Primark T-shirt on a Versace catwalk, a mis-shelved library book.

Raymond opened a pair of double doors and led Peg into a vast living room. Two squashy white leather sofas the size of lorries sat in front of a monolithic stone fireplace and the whole of the back wall was glass, looking out onto a terraced swimming pool as big as the old baths Peg tried to visit three times a week back at home.

She thought of the grim little bungalow in Tankerton and the injustice of it all made her nostrils flare. It was obscene how this man had deserted his own mother and sister.

The pool steamed in the November air. In its middle, frolicking on a Li-Lo, was a small blond boy with an alarmingly deep suntan. On a brown wicker seating unit curving round a matching circular glass-topped table, an equally mahogany-coloured woman sat underneath a glowing patio heater. She was smoking a cigarette and looked a little on edge.

Raymond slid open the glass window and the woman and boy looked round. The low-level music Peg had heard from the driveway was in fact Rod Stewart, crooning through speakers on the terrace.

The woman stood quickly, stubbed out her cigarette, took off her vast tortoiseshell-and-gold sunglasses and extended her hand. 'You must be Margaret. I'm Caroline. Hello, my darling.' It was the same voice Peg had heard at the gate: the type of girlish tone that sits uneasily on a middle-aged woman.

'Hi,' Peg said, noticing the rock of diamond on the third finger of the left hand wielding the sunglasses.

'And this is Paulie,' Raymond said, lifting a towelling robe from the back of the seating unit and taking it to the pool where he held it out for the boy, who swung himself up and onto the side. 'Come and meet Margaret, Paulie.'

'Pleased to meet you,' the boy said, nodding his head rather formally, but keeping his distance.

'He's a special fella,' Raymond said, his eyes shining, his voice catching slightly. 'One in a million.'

There was a brief silence while Raymond rubbed the towel over the little boy. Peg shifted from foot to foot, fighting hard to stop her first-ever sibling emotion from being jealousy.

'How was your journey?' Caroline said, making small talk as if she had been expecting Peg, as if all this had been planned. She rang a little hand bell on the table in front of her. Almost instantly, a short, dark woman appeared, apparently from underneath the terrace.

'Manuela. Can you bring us up some Cava, please?' Caroline said, slowly and clearly.

'And a beer for me, Manuela, cheers,' Raymond said.

'And some olives and crisps,' Caroline added.

'And a Coke for me,' Paulie said.

Manuela nodded silently and disappeared back under the terrace.

'You run in and get some proper clothes on, Paulie,' Raymond said.

'But—'

'No buts. You'll catch your death in those wet trunks.'

Reluctantly, Paulie ran inside the house. Raymond turned to Peg.

'I don't want him to know who you are just yet. He needs a bit of preparation. You OK with that?'

Peg nodded. It wasn't Paulie's fault, she supposed, that her father had so completely failed her. Although, however much generosity she was trying to feel towards the little boy, she couldn't help a small part of her wanting him to suffer just a little bit. Just as a learning process.

'We haven't told him about you, you see,' Caroline said. 'Or anything about the past.'

Raymond shot her a sharp look.

'Well we haven't. But I'm so glad to meet you at last, Margaret,' she went on. 'Raymond's told me so much about you.'

Peg wondered what on earth he had to say about her, not having made contact for sixteen years. She was having to bite her tongue so much she was afraid of chewing it right off. She was really glad Loz hadn't come. It would have been impossible for her to keep her lip buttoned, and that would have completely sabotaged the mission.

No, she had to keep quiet and choose her moment.

'Why don't you sit down, dear?' Caroline patted the seat next to her. Raymond sat opposite them. He still hadn't looked Peg in the eye. She supposed that this was down to a deserved sense of shame at confronting the daughter he had abandoned, so she took heart from this.

'This is nice, isn't it?' Caroline said, to break the awkward silence between them all.

'How did you find us?' Raymond said at the same time.

'Through the club,' Peg said. 'Flamingos.'

'Really? That surprises me. They're not supposed to give out my address. Who did you speak to?'

Peg thought of the sadness in Carleen's eyes. 'I didn't catch their name.'

Raymond relit his cigar. 'Well I suppose it had to happen sooner or later. I was thinking of getting in touch myself. You beat me to it.'

That's easy to say, Peg thought.

'He was, darling,' Caroline said, turning to Peg as if she could read her mind. 'He was always wondering how you were doing.'

'Whatever, Caroline,' Raymond said. 'Hey. Interesting haircut you've got there,' he said, sitting back and letting out a stream of cigar smoke.

'Oh, you know. It was such a nightmare to look after,' Peg said, running her hand over the velvet of her scalp, astounded at the bollocks she was spouting. 'Nice house,' she said, to change the subject. The pool terrace was a very sheltered spot. In the full beat of the sun and the patio heater, she could feel the sweat beading on her upper lip.

'We moved in last year,' Caroline said. 'We had it built specially. To our own design.'

'We used an architect, though,' Raymond said. 'We done it proper.'

'Ooh, it cost the earth, it did. But it's worth it. It's my dream home,' Caroline said. 'And Paulie loves it too, don't you, lovey?'

Raymond looked at Peg and tapped the side of his nose as a nodding Paulie returned and sat next to him.

'Well, we done it for him, really,' Raymond said. 'It's a great house for him to grow up in, and I'm just there.' He pointed to a smoked-glass extension reaching from the back of the house to form an L shape round the pool. 'That's my offices.'

'Lovely,' Peg said.

'He likes to be a hands-on dad,' Caroline said.

A sudden breeze brought with it the sewage smell Peg had detected when she got out of the car.

'Pooh,' Paulie said, wrinkling his freckled little nose.

'You need to call that guy about the cesspit, Kitten.' Raymond pointed a finger at Caroline.

'I've left him a message.'

'Well, call him again, Caroline. That stink's disgusting. Here, come in under the heater a bit, Paulie. You still look a bit chilly.' Raymond turned to Peg. 'He's a proper water baby. I'm training him up for the Olympics. Do you like swimming, Margaret?'

Peg shrugged. She swam, but it was more out of duty than passion.

'You should give it a go, girl. Good exercise. Keeps the weight down.'

'Raymond!' Caroline said, putting her diamond-laden hand up to her plumped-up lips and giggling.

Raymond shrugged and puffed on his cigar. Peg fought to keep the smile on her face. She was not going to allow any of this to get to her.

Manuela reappeared and they all watched as she set out drinks and nibbles from a silver tray.

'And Manuela, we've got one extra for supper tonight,' Caroline said. 'You are staying for supper, aren't you? And please stay the night, too.'

'She might have other plans, Caroline,' Raymond said.

'I'd love to stay, if that's all right,' Peg said.

'So make up the mauve room, Manuela please,' Caroline said.

'So what do you do, then?' Raymond said, after Manuela had gone.

'I work in a library.'

'You're a librarian?'

'Well, a library assistant. You need a lot of qualifications to be a librarian,' Peg said.

'I thought you might've got qualifications. I thought you might've gone to uni,' Raymond said. 'After all that money spent on your posh school. Paulie's going to uni, aren't you lad?'

Paulie nodded and smiled, revealing a mouth full of gaps stopped by teeth that his young face had not yet grown into.

'He's a bright boy,' Raymond said. 'There's a lovely private English school down in the town and he's top of all his classes.'

Raymond reached for his Heineken, which he poured into the pewter tankard Manuela had set before him. 'Got a fella?' he asked.

'Um, no, not at the moment,' Peg said.

'Never mind. Early days, eh? You're, what, twenty-odd?'

'I'm twenty-two.'

'You knew that, Goosey!' Caroline said, laughing again and tapping Raymond on the arm with the back of her hand. 'Of course he knows how old you are, darling,' she said from behind her sunglasses. Despite obvious surgical attentions – her mouth and eyebrows had an uncanny upward turn to them – Caroline's face was criss-crossed with lines from spending far longer in the sun than she should have with such fair colouring.

Peg thought how her own skin would have blossomed under this sky, given the chance.

'Oh well, Margaret. Better get a move on with the blokes then,' Raymond said. 'Don't want to be left on the shelf!'

'Oh, stop going on, you,' Caroline said. 'Crisp, Margaret?'

After the bottle of Cava was finished – mostly by Caroline, who drank all of it except the one glass taken by Peg – Manuela was summoned again to show Peg to her mauve room so that she could, as Caroline put it, 'Have a wash and brush-up before we meet down in the lounge for pre-dinner drinkies.'

As Manuela led her indoors, Peg wondered if she was a disappointment. Then she checked herself. Despite everything, she seemed to want Raymond's approval. But, as Loz had pointed out, it was for *him* to make things up to *her*. She had to remember that. And, to be honest, her main reaction to meeting her father was so far just that: disappointment. He was unimpressive. She didn't think she liked him very much.

She was surprised at how good this made her feel. Loz had been absolutely right, of course: engaging her anger, putting her sense of injustice into gear felt perversely empowering.

Despite Peg's best efforts to stop her, the tiny, wiry Manuela carried her rucksack up two flights of sweeping marble stairs to a large room. She put the bag on a suitcase rack and mutely showed her the en suite bathroom and the balcony, where the view of the pool and swathes of golf-course-quality lawn was set off by a backdrop of bruise-coloured mountains. Festooned with draped purple fabrics and furry cushions, the frill-encrusted bed was big enough to set up home in. The open windows ushered the cesspit stink into the room, but an air freshener plugged into the wall put up a valiant chemical battle against it.

Peg sat on the bed and ate one of the home-baked granola bars from the beautifully wrapped package Loz had presented her with at the departures gate – she had, of course, insisted on accompanying her to the airport. The recipe was the best, Loz had said, the dog's bollocks, and each bite soothed her and reminded her of home, of love.

Enjoying the expensive toiletries – no doubt a Caroline touch – she took a shower. Then she wrapped herself in one of the thick towels and rummaged in her rucksack to see if she could find anything suitable to wear for dinner in a house like this.

Again Loz popped up somewhere in her brain, telling her to wear what she wanted: *he* should be working to please *her*, not the other way round.

There wasn't much evidence of that yet: he seemed to be as unreachable now as he had been when she couldn't find him, which didn't bode well for getting him back together with Doll. That, and the fact that so far he had not mentioned or asked after his mother once.

She wondered what it was that had driven him so fully away. She had more or less got over the poisonous suspicion that it might have been something *she* had done – she had only been six, after all. But if not that, then what?

But it wasn't the time to think about that. She had one evening to accomplish her task, so she needed to prepare. Instead of clothes, she pulled her red notebook and pencil out of her rucksack. Then, still wrapped up in the towel, she sat on the balcony, wrote herself a speech, and did her best to commit it to memory.

Somewhere over the other side of the house she heard a car draw up, which set the dogs off again.

The sun slipped down behind the mountain and, feeling the chill of the evening, she decided to get dressed.

Being a pared-down packer, she hadn't given herself a lot of choice. In the end, she decided on a stripy smock. It was too short to wear on its own away from the beach she had somewhat deludedly thought she might be spending some time on. So she pulled her jeans back on and accessorised the outfit with Loz's dangly earrings and a bit of kohl.

'Almost a normal,' she said to herself as she checked the result in the mirror. 'Might just about do.'

Then

'I CAN'T REMEMBER HOW TO HOLD THE WOOL, THOUGH,' I SAY.

I'm trying to crochet a square for the blanket me and Nan are making for Aunty Jean, but the wool keeps tangling and the stitches don't loop properly. It's looking like a right old mess and I'm not getting anywhere.

Me and Nan and Gramps are in the lounge. The telly's on and Gramps is smoking a cig.

He smoked Players. They smelled completely different to Aunty Jean's Marlboros.

Less spicy.

He's still alive here, so I'm about nine years old, I suppose.

'Twice round your little finger, then weave it through the middle and ring and hook it up over the index,' Nan says, as her own fingers flash away with hook and yarn. She's already half done her own square and I've not even started.

'I JUST CAN'T DO IT!' I say, and I fling the stupid hook on the floor.

'Temper,' Gramps says. 'Temper, Meggy.'

'Shhh,' Nan says, though I'm not sure if it's at me or Gramps.

She gets out of her rocking chair and comes over to sit next to me on the settee.

'Here you are,' she says, producing a toffee from her pinny pocket as if by magic.

I pop it in my mouth and start chewing. As if by magic, it calms me down.

'Now then,' Nan goes. 'We can get this right. If you can't remember how to do something, what do you do, Meggy?'

'Write it down,' I say, with a bit of dribbling difficulty. The toffee is really chewy.

'Exactly. Write it down. Or you'll never get anywhere. It's all down to you, remember, to make the most of yourself. So where's your Commonplace Book?'

I go and fetch it from my bedside table, where I left it last night, after writing up my day.

Back in the lounge, Nan dictates her wool-holding instructions and I copy them down.

Then, posing for me so that I can get the drawing right, she makes me do a diagram because, as she says, 'sometimes you need more than words'.

That's easy for her to say, but my diagrams are useless. I'm not as good as her at drawing.

Gramps always says she could have been an artist, but she says she would rather have been a doctor and he says, 'Stop it now, Dolly.'

I've looked for the books I made when I was a child. But they seem to have disappeared. They must have got thrown out at some point.

If I still had them, then all of this remembering would be much easier.

And I'd know for sure that what I was recalling was true, because it would all be there – every day of my early life, recorded in my own childish handwriting.

Nan was wrong about one thing, though.

Writing it down didn't help me remember anything.

Ten

'WELL, YOU LOOK NICE,' CAROLINE SAID RATHER TOO BRIGHTLY as Peg joined them in the vast living room.

Raymond sat by the fire, warming his hands, and Paulie sprawled on one of the sofas, headphones on, engrossed in something on an iPad. He didn't even look up.

'G&T?' Caroline handed a large glass to Peg. 'I had Manuela bring them up half an hour ago, but the ice is still fine.'

'Sorry I took so long,' Peg said.

'No, no, no. You had to get yourself settled in. Rome wasn't built in a day.' Caroline let out a long, tinkling laugh. 'We've told Paulie who you are.' She reached across and tapped the boy on the knee. He looked up and slipped off his headphones. 'Say what you said, Paulie, when we said Margaret was your half-sister.'

'She's too old to be my sister.'

Both Raymond and Caroline seemed to find this hilarious. Pleased at their response, Paulie put his headphones back on and plugged himself back into his game. Peg was glad to see she had made such an impression on him.

'How did you like that school I sent you to, then?' Raymond said as Peg sat down on the sofa opposite him. He was smoking a cigar again, filling the room with blue plumes.

'It was fine,' Peg said.

'*Liar,*' the Loz-voice hissed in her ear.

'Cost me enough. I'm surprised they didn't get you into uni, though,' Raymond said. 'They've got a very good record. It's why I chose them.'

'I was the only one in my year not to go,' Peg said.

Raymond lowered his chin, bit his lower lip and nodded, as if he were taking some time to digest this.

'So why not, then?'

'I didn't see the point.'

'I'd have paid whatever it cost.'

'It wasn't the money. I just didn't feel up for it. I didn't really see what it would give me that I couldn't find out in the real world.'

'But you done all right in your exams, though, ain't you?'

'Yes.' She wasn't going to tell him that she got straight As. She wasn't going to give him that satisfaction.

'That's something, at least. And you speak nice, too, which'll be a help.'

'*You got your money's worth, then,*' Loz thundered in Peg's head, daring her to say it out loud.

'And I suppose,' Raymond went on, 'if you want to go when you're a bit older, well there's nothing stopping you.'

'Nothing to stop me at all.'

'And of course, if you need help of the money kind, I'm here.'

'I'll be fine, thanks,' Peg said.

'You make it sound as if you've got no money worries.'

'I haven't.'

Raymond snorted.

After a silence just long enough to feel uncomfortable, a gong sounded from somewhere within the house.

'Ah!' Caroline said brightly, jumping up and stumbling slightly. 'Dinner at last!'

And they all trooped through to the dining room.

Peg had forgotten to mention that she was a vegetarian, so there was little she could eat from the meal of steak and gravy-smothered chips. As she picked at a portion of the accompanying salad, Raymond mused about how vegetarianism was unnatural because man was designed to hunt and eat flesh. A more concerned line of argument came from Caroline on how dietary advice was all about protein these days.

'If you want to lose a stone or two, just cut out the bread and pasta,' she said helpfully to Peg.

'So what do *you* do?' Peg asked Raymond, in an attempt to divert the beam of attention away from herself.

'Same what I started back home,' Raymond said, sawing into his steak, which, as he put it, was so rare it was almost mooing.

'Nightclubs?'

'Yep,' Raymond said, chewing. 'And bars.'

'He owns a chain of establishments all along the Costas,' Caroline said.

'Thatcher's, I call 'em,' he said, reaching for a toothpick. 'After Maggie. After you in a way.' He laughed, a deep booze-and-tobacco-stained chuckle, then dug into his gums and extracted a lump of chewed meat, which he sucked off the end of the toothpick. 'Bit gristly this steak, Kitten.'

'I'll have a word with Manuela,' Caroline said.

'Nan would love to know about all that,' Peg said.

It was as if her words were a large stone she had dropped in the middle of the dining table.

'All you've achieved,' she went on into the silence. 'She'd be ever so proud.'

'Not in front of the boy, Margaret,' Raymond said, inclining his head towards his precious son.

'Who's Nan?' Paulie asked.

'Our dad's mum,' Peg said.

'Enough,' Raymond said, his voice low. 'He doesn't need to know.'

'But why not?' Peg went on, determined not to be put off now she was clearing the way for her speech. 'They were ever so kind to me – Nan and Jean and Gramps, I mean.'

The air in the room seemed to tighten. Caroline let out one of her stupid, silvery laughs.

Raymond silently attacked the bloody steak again, sawing off a chunk and tearing it from his fork with his teeth.

'Are you sure you've got enough to eat there, Margaret love?' Caroline asked Peg. 'Shall I ask them to make you an omelette or something?'

Perhaps it was due to the plastic surgery, but she didn't seem to be able to stop smiling. It made her look like she had air for brains.

'I'm fine, thank you,' Peg said, then, as if she had Loz's hands at either side of her face, forcing her not to let things lie, she turned once more to face Raymond. 'I had a very happy childhood, in fact.'

No thanks to you, Loz thundered in her head.

Raymond looked at his plate, chewing furiously.

Peg closed her eyes so that she could go on. The words she had practised on the mauve-room balcony came out, like a telesales script.

'I found you again because Nan isn't very well and I know that not seeing you makes her very sad. You need to come over and see her and Aunty Jean – who isn't too great herself – and make whatever it is up between you all.'

She could hear Raymond breathing, heavily, but she forced herself to go on.

'Before it's too late. You need to see her. And Paulie needs to see his grandmother. You have to think of him.'

This last part wasn't part of her script, but she truly believed it to be the case, and thought perhaps it might carry some weight with Raymond in his role as Paulie's Doting Father.

Raymond let out a gasp. This was good, she thought. She was hitting home.

'Raymond love, are you all right?' Caroline said, quite urgently.

'Take the boy away!' Raymond said in a strangled voice.

'If you don't do it now,' Peg forged on, her eyes still closed, fighting her way to the end of her speech, 'it's going to be too late and it will be very sad for them and for you and for Paulie.'

Her father made a wheezing, retching sound.

'You might regret it for your whole life.'

'RAYMOND!' Caroline cried.

Her speech over, Peg opened her eyes. Paulie was being hurried out by Manuela, as her father reached forwards in his seat, choking, his eyes bulging from their sockets, the veins standing out on his forehead.

For a fleeting second, Peg marvelled at the effect her words had worked on Raymond. But then she realised what was going on. Well taught by Doll, she jumped up, hoisted him from his seat – surprisingly easy, because he was lighter than he looked – and swiftly administered the Heimlich manoeuvre. A stringy chunk of half-chewed steak and gristle shot out of his mouth and onto the white tablecloth in front of him.

'Glass of water, Caroline,' she said, sitting him back down again. Gasping for breath, Raymond allowed her to feed it to him, the tears still streaming down his face. It reminded her of looking after Jean.

Peg and Caroline – who had been fluttering round her husband like a startled chick – watched from a respectful distance as he attempted to regain his composure.

'Thank you for that, Margaret,' he said at last. He breathed slowly, in and out, then closed his eyes. 'Thank you.'

Peg picked up a paper napkin and, with Caroline protesting that 'The girl will do that,' she scooped up the meat that Raymond had spat on the table and placed the crumpled ball on his dirty plate.

'Sit down girls,' Raymond rasped, and the two women did as they were told. When they were settled, he turned and, for the first time since she had arrived, looked squarely at Peg.

'All right. I'll just tell you this, Margaret. Just once and then we're not going to mention it ever again. You've not got one snowball's chance in hell of getting me back there,' he said, emphasising each single word. 'I want nothing to do with that place. That lazy, fat, bad bitch of a sister of mine is history to me.'

'But what about Nan, though?'

Raymond's lips fell into a scowl and he flared his nostrils.

'I can't have anything to do with either of them. It's all in the past. This is my life now. And Paulie – and Caroline – will never, ever, meet them. Never. You hear?'

Peg gasped at the fire behind Raymond's words. It was like he was spitting another lump of gristle out of his throat.

'You hear me?' he went on, his eyes cast down now to the floor, his voice trembling. 'So don't waste your breath.'

'But—'

'That's all I'm saying about it,' Raymond said. He took up his knife and fork and sawed into the remaining chunk of flesh on his plate. 'You hear me?'

'Are you sure I can't tempt you with some more salad?' Caroline asked, smiling her smile as if nothing had happened.

Eleven

AFTER A STRAINED DESSERT OF CHOCOLATE MOUSSE, RAYMOND said he had a few phone calls to attend to. Peg was led by Caroline back into the living room, where she took a seat on one of the squashy sofas and contemplated just how badly her mission had failed. She felt like just getting up and walking out, but she couldn't find the energy to do so.

'Raymond's very hands-on with the business,' Caroline said as she settled down next to Peg in front of the living-room fire. A younger woman in a black blouse and skirt – a nanny, perhaps – appeared at the door with Paulie so he could kiss his mother goodnight.

'The doctor said he should take it more easier,' Caroline said as the little boy was led away, a red smudge of lipstick on his cheek. 'But there's no stopping him.'

'Doctor?' Peg said.

'He had a triple bypass a year or so back. I thought he was having another heart attack back there!' Caroline giggled.

Nan should have known about that, Peg thought as she

stared into the flames, watching them curl round the olivewood logs like witches' fingers.

'You don't talk much, do you?' Caroline said, pouring herself a second brandy and tucking her legs up underneath her. 'Just like him.' She stretched her arm along the back of the sofa and laid a claw-nailed hand on Peg's shoulder. 'Like I said, he's wanted to get in touch with you for ages. "Go on, then," I said to him whenever he mentioned it, but it was "never the right time", or "she won't want to know".'

Peg wondered if this was the truth, or if Caroline was just telling her what she thought she wanted to hear – keeping her sweet because she knew how furious she must be feeling.

Caroline smiled to herself and looked out at the pool, which glowed in the chilly night with pink underwater lights. '"Silly old Goosey," I said to him. I call him Goosey sometimes. "Of course she'll want to know. You're her dad. Of course she'll want to hear from you." And wasn't I right? Here you are. Just like that!' She snapped her fingers.

Peg looked at the woman she supposed she should refer to as her stepmother and wondered if they even came from the same species.

'You mustn't judge him too harshly,' Caroline said.

Why the hell not? Peg felt her inner Loz urging her to say.

'His mother and sister said it was best for you, darling.' Caroline stroked Peg's shoulder, her pearly pink nails rasping on the material of her smock. Peg fought the urge to bat her hand away. 'When he got out, you were so settled and happy. You said so yourself at dinner – you were happy, you said.'

'Got out?' Peg said, turning to face her, so that she could no longer reach her shoulder.

'Of the nick,' Caroline said. Then, seeing Peg's reaction, her face fell, as if the stitches holding it in its happy position had been scissored. 'Oh shit,' she said. 'You don't bloody know, do you?'

Peg shook her head slowly. She wished she hadn't had that third glass of wine at dinner. She wasn't used to drinking and her head now felt like it was going to explode. She was really worried that she might end up splattering her brains all over the white sofa.

Caroline's phone pierced the silence in the room with a tinny rendition of the opening line of 'La Cucaracha'. Relieved at the distraction, she looked at the screen, at the same time trying to rearrange her face into a more pleasant aspect.

'It's Raymond,' she said, jumping to her feet with a gasp of relief. 'He wants a word. Would you just excuse me for a mo, darling?'

'Tell me, though,' Peg said.

Caroline paused, glass in hand.

'Tell you what, lovey?'

'Why was he in prison?'

'Oh, well, um, that's not for me to say, my darling.' Caroline went over to Peg and patted her hand. 'Best leave it to him to explain, eh?' With that she was out of the door as if she had the hounds of hell at her heels.

What was it with all these women – first Carleen and now Caroline – leaving everything for the shut-jawed and inarticulate Raymond to explain?

Peg leaned her head back on the sofa headrest and closed her eyes. She wanted to talk to Loz so badly. But even if she knew how to get her phone working, she wouldn't have been able to contact her, because she'd be at work and phones weren't allowed in the kitchens of Seed. It was a rule that Loz had brought in herself, so she would be the last to break it.

Peg counted her breaths and tried to clear her overloaded

mind. A long time passed. Sleep must have got the better of her, because when she looked up and saw Caroline standing in the doorway, the once-roaring fire had all but burned out and died.

'Could you pop into his study for a bit, please darling?' Caroline said, indicating with her head some indefinite place beyond the hallway. Despite the effortful cheeriness of her voice, her lipstick was blurred and her mascara was ground round her eyes and swept across her face like random watercolour brushstrokes. Her hand shook as she gripped the edge of the door.

'Are you all right?' Peg said.

'Me? Course I am, dear.'

Peg got up and picked her way across the vast room to follow Caroline across the echoing hallway to a closed door in the back wall of the house. These, Peg supposed, were Raymond's 'offices'.

There was a doorbell in the wall, the kind you get in buildings that have been divided up into flats. Identical in fact to the doorbell in the flat Peg shared with Loz. Steadying herself against the door, Caroline pressed the buzzer.

'Yes?' Raymond's voice rasped like a Dalek's through the device.

'I've got Margaret here,' Caroline said, as if she were a secretary with a client arriving for a meeting.

'Show her in,' Raymond said. The door clicked open.

'Should I come in as well?' Caroline said into the speaker, in a tone that suggested that she really, really didn't want to.

'Nah, you go to bed now, Kitten,' Raymond said.

'In you go,' Caroline said, ushering Peg through the door, her relief again palpable. 'It's the second on the right.'

The door swung shut behind Peg and she found herself in the reception to a suite of offices. She crossed the black marble floor to the door Caroline had indicated and tried the handle. It was locked. She rattled it a couple of times, but nothing happened. Then she knocked.

'Open,' she heard from within, and the door swung away from her.

'Good eh?' Raymond said from behind a vast desk in front of an arched wall of glass. 'Voice-controlled door. Only recognises me.'

'Yeah,' Peg said, hovering by the door, which had closed behind her with a gentle hiss.

The room was sparsely furnished in black leather, chrome and glass, its air layered with cigar smoke and Raymond's coal-tar-soap scent.

'Well, take a seat, girl,' he said in that strange, high-pitched croak of his.

He swung his chair to face her.

Peg edged forwards to the smaller, lower swivel chair in front of the desk.

'Good girl,' he said. 'Now then, I hear from my lovely wife that she let the cat out of the bag, so to speak.'

Peg nodded. She hardly felt able to look at him.

'I think it's time we had a little chat,' he went on. 'I expect you've got some questions.'

Peg nodded again. 'I—'

'Well, girl. I want you to know this,' he said, sitting back and folding his hands on his belly. 'I'm not proud of what I done in the past. Not proud at all. I'm glad you had a happy childhood, as you say. But it's a new life now for me. I've got all this.' He gestured at the pink pool, at the sweeping view of the house all lit up in the sliding glass wall to his left. 'I've got Caroline and I've got Paulie. I'm very happy now, Margaret. After difficult times, I've reached a point in my life when I can say I'm at peace.'

'I'm very glad for you,' Peg said, trying to keep any hint of sarcasm out of her voice, trying to still the voice inside – her own now, and nothing to do with Loz – screaming 'WHAT ABOUT ME?'

'And you see,' he went on, as if she hadn't spoken, 'I've got this nice little boat now and I don't want it rocked.'

'I'm so sorry,' she said, too aware of the angry tremble in her voice.

'Now there's no need to take that tone, Margaret. It's interesting to see how you've turned out. What they've done with you.'

'And?' she said, holding his look.

He let his eyes drift to the view of the pool again. She was certain she was a disappointment to him. He would have liked her straight in every sense: married, nicely groomed, with a degree and some sort of business acumen. She had failed him on every count.

And part of her was glad.

'Well then, *Daddy*?' She stood up and held out her arms. 'How have I done in your complete and utter absence, then?' she said, her voice catching on an edge of something gritty.

'Oh, sit down and keep your hair on, Margaret,' he said, raising one eyebrow at her but keeping the rest of his body very still.

'Peg. My name is Peg now.'

He laughed until the tears ran down his face. For a second, she thought he might be having another heart attack. For a second she thought: *good*.

Then he stopped laughing.

'Peg? What kind of name is that, Margaret? A peg is a *thing*, not a *name*. Anyway, what you don't know is, ever since you left that bungalow, I've been looking out for you.'

'What do you mean?'

'I've got these people, just to keep a little check, let me know what you're up to.'

'What?' Peg sat down, her mouth open.

'I'm worried about you. Now you're grown-up I want you to get a chance at your own life.'

'What do you mean?' Peg could hear that her own voice was now raised.

'It's complicated. Look: I had no choice but to leave you with them, and—'

'What were you in prison for?'

Raymond stopped in his tracks. For the first time – apart from when he had been choking – she thought she could see behind his defences. Then, in a beat, he checked himself, stood up and moved round so that he was next to her, peering down into her face.

'This is how it is, right?' he said, quietly. 'I don't talk about the past. I don't even *think* about it. I apply the same rules to your aunt and your grandmother too. And your mother, rest her soul, come to that. And no amount of questions or requests from you are going to get me to change my mind. *And* you are certainly *not* going to get me going back to that place.'

He straightened up and examined his preternaturally neat fingernails, then he looked back at her, his voice level. 'So you can save your energy by not going on at me. Understood?' He turned his back on her and returned to his chair, as if that were the end of it.

'But—' Peg jumped to her feet again and hit her chair so that it spun like the magazine of a gun. 'What about *me*? What about how *I* feel?'

He sat entirely still and looked at her, absorbing her outburst so that the energy of it fell to nothing and her hands dropped to her sides. Then he spoke. 'You don't know the half of it. And we're going to keep it that way. All right? And that is how we are going to deal with this issue of "*how you feel*".' He used his fingers to describe the inverted commas.

'But—'

'If you can't play it by my rules, then you can't play at all. Understand?'

'It isn't a game, Raymond!'

He shot her a warning glance.

'It's real life,' Peg went on. 'And it's about your own mother, and your own sister, and your own daughter, and if you can't take that on, well then, sorry, but that's that. We have nothing more to say to each other.'

Astounded at herself – no, *pleased* with herself – Peg turned and crossed the room to go.

But there was no door handle, no way of letting herself out. She looked back at him. 'Open the door, please,' she said, with as much dignity as she could muster.

'But I haven't finished,' he said from the far side of the room.

'You've said all I need to hear. Now open this door, please.'

'After you've heard this, girly.' Raymond spread his arms wide, gripping the edges of his desk. 'And I want you to think seriously about what I'm going to say, because it could do you a lot of good. I want to make you an offer. As you can see, I've not done too badly in life. I left when you was what, five?'

'I was six.'

'Six, then. Look. I know you're angry at the moment. I can understand that. I don't blame you.'

'That's very big of you.' Peg felt her mouth pursing with anger.

He waved his hand, brushing her comment aside. But he

chose not to see that in doing so he had only fanned the flame of her fury.

'I want to make it up to you,' he went on. 'If you can leave the past behind, let it lie, then we can move forward. You live in a shitty rented flat above a Paki in the arse end of South London.'

'You know where I live?'

He smiled and ignored her. 'Well I'd like to get you a little place closer into town. Something more comfortable, where you don't have to worry about the bills. Pay for you to go to uni, so you don't have to do this library job.' He said the last two words as if they might have been 'dog turd'. 'And an allowance so you can, I don't know, get yourself some nice clothes, a proper haircut. That kind of shit. Keep away from that bungalow.'

'Why this, so suddenly?'

'Call it making amends.'

'You think you can buy me?' Peg dug her fingers into the flesh of her thighs in an attempt to short-circuit the outrage coursing through her body.

'Oh Jesus, don't tell me she's one of those don't-care-about-money types,' Raymond appealed to an imaginary audience. 'One of those let's-camp-and-show-the-bankers-what-baddies-we-think-they-are hippies? Jesus Christ. My own flesh and blood.'

'Keep your money. "Dad".'

'Don't be an idiot, girl. Don't bite off your nose to spite your face. Tell you what: why don't you sleep on it, eh?'

'Please will you open the door?'

'Take this first.' He held out a business card and waited until Peg crossed the room to take it from his hand. It was thick, glossy and purple, with his name, phone number and email address reversed out in a slanting, looped font, and his club logo – the word 'Thatcher's' displayed in letters created from naked female silhouettes.

'Good girl. Now even if you don't see sense while you're here, you can still get in touch with me when you finally come round. OPEN!' He barked this last word so suddenly that Peg jumped, nearly dropping the card.

The door swung out with barely a whisper. Raymond took his cigar from where it had been resting on the ashtray, put his feet up on his desk and watched as Peg left his office with as much dignity as she could muster.

Once out of his sight, she fled, nearly colliding with Manuela as she crossed the hallway from the living room to the kitchen with brandy, glasses and ashtrays stacked on a tray.

'*Perdona, Señorita*,' Manuela said.

Mumbling an apology, Peg went upstairs to her fancy bedroom and threw herself on the king-size bed, where she sobbed until her face felt like a full and soggy sponge.

Much later, unable to sleep, she sat on her balcony staring at the stupidly lit pool. The lights in Raymond's offices were all out, so he was probably sleeping soundly in some over-draped cushioned bed, happy he had said his piece.

Something was buzzing in her mind and she couldn't forget about it.

He knew where she lived. He knew where she worked.

He must have been keeping *very* close tabs on her.

She thought about the white vans that had been popping up everywhere she went. She hadn't been imagining things. She had been followed: trailed like an animal.

That chilling thought alone made her want to run away from the house and away from Raymond.

There was nothing here for her anyway. She had been a fool even to consider that she might get anywhere with him.

Her decision made, she went back into the room, stuffed her few belongings back into her rucksack and hitched it up on to her back. Then, as quietly as she could, she headed down the stairs and slipped out of the front door, hearing it lock shut behind her.

She set out down the porch steps and cut across the lawn. She had half-covered the distance to the first gate, which led to the orchard, when the whole lawn lit up as if it were a stage and she the only actor on it.

Stuck like a rabbit in headlights, unable to move, she looked back to the house in terror as she heard mechanical whirring, barking and clanking coming from the side of the house.

Almost instantly, two Rottweilers, teeth bared, muscles glistening under their glossy, floodlit coats, steamed out from behind the bushes. In an instant, Peg weighed up her chances of outrunning them and realised, panic gripping at her chest, that they were virtually nil.

As the dogs pelted across the lawn towards her, their eyes glowing with red, she cast around wildly for a stick, or a stone, or some sort of weapon. Lights had started to go on in the upstairs rooms of the house.

Then, out of nowhere, the words came to her. The words she had heard shouted in the driveway the day before. She stood her ground and looked firmly at the beasts.

'Cállate, Atilla y Bronson! Cállate, Atilla y Bronson!'

The dogs stopped as if they had run into a wall. Then, obediently, they sat. If Peg hadn't been in such a state, she might have laughed at their evident confusion. She reached into her bag for the last of Loz's granola bars and threw them on the ground as far away as possible from where she was standing.

'Here, boys, *Atilla y Bronson.*'

The dogs loped over towards her and bent their heads to the grass to lap up the granola bars.

'The dog's bollocks,' Peg said, smiling with relief as she slipped into the trees at the far edge of the lawn. 'Thank you, Loz.' She reached cover just in time to avoid being seen by Raymond, as he appeared at the front door in his dressing gown, a gun in his hand.

'Atilla, Bronson, what the fuck you playing at?' he said. 'What you got there, you bloody softies?'

His gun still at the ready, he walked over to join the animals. 'Was it more bloody rabbits setting it all off again, boys? We'll have to have a word with Kitten to get it sorted.'

With one hand on the biggest dog's head, he scanned the bushes. Peg stayed completely still until, satisfied there was no intruder, he had taken the dogs back to their quarters to the side of the house. Then she pelted to the first gate – almost jumping right over it – and darted through the orchard towards the big front wall. Twice she fell and twice she picked herself up, scared that Raymond might decide to take a second look for what had disturbed the dogs.

When she reached the wall, panting and shaking, she realised it was far too high to climb. Desperately, she hauled over a nearby wheelie bin, climbed wobblingly up on it and lobbed her rucksack over to the other side. Then she hurriedly picked her way over the barbed wire and broken glass on top of the wall. Her pulse racing, she finally let herself down on to the silent road on the other side.

Pulling her rucksack back onto her shoulders, she set off down the mountain towards the stretch of moonlit sea, in the direction of the orange glow in the sky she hoped was Malaga.

It was nearly dawn when she arrived at the airport. She

rather guiltily spun a story at the airline desk about her grandmother being ill, and managed to change to the early-morning flight for just a small administration fee.

It was only when she was visiting the lavatory in the departures lounge that she realised she had a nasty gash in her knee. She sat on the toilet and got out the small first-aid kit she always carried with her and cleaned and plastered the wound. She would have put a couple of stitches in, but she had left her suturing kit at home, because needles weren't allowed on planes.

Night-worker Loz was still fast asleep when Peg got home, oblivious to everything that had happened since they had said goodbye at the airport. Peg slipped into the sheets beside her, snuggled up to her lovely, welcoming, warm back and fell into a deep, obliterating sleep.

Twelve

PEG SLEPT TILL ABOUT MIDDAY, WHEN THE SMELL OF COFFEE pulled her from under the duvet. Dragging on the old, rose-patterned dressing gown she had worn as a child and which somehow still fitted her, she stumbled into the living room, where she wrapped her arms round Loz, who was whizzing up pancake batter.

'What is it?' Loz said, switching off the food processor and turning to take Peg's face in her hands. 'Why are you back so soon?'

She led Peg to the sofa, where she teased out every detail of what had happened the day before, stroking and kissing her tears away. Then she fetched her a cup of coffee and continued making the breakfast feast.

'What a bastard,' she said as she slipped a ladleful of pancake batter into the frying pan. 'And prison. I can't believe no one told you. What were Doll and Jean thinking?'

'I don't know,' Peg said. She was miserable and hungry, but glad to be back home.

'We'll go over there and get it out of him.' Loz flipped the pancakes over. 'The whole story. It's outrageous that he expects you not to want to know what happened. This is about you, not him.'

'I don't think he sees it that way. And there's no way I'm going back there.' The thought of standing behind Loz as she thumped on Raymond's colonnaded front door made Peg feel sick. 'And it's like he had this portcullis that slammed shut as soon as I started talking about the past or Nan or Aunty Jean . . .'

She frowned and twisted her fingers together. 'And he's just full of hate. The way he talked about poor Aunty Jean.'

'But "poor Aunty Jean" kept you in the dark all these years.'

'I suppose she thought she was protecting me. And the way I'm feeling now, she probably had a point.'

'For God's sake,' Loz said, retrieving the soda bread from the toaster. Soda bread! Peg had never heard of such a thing before she met Loz. She held on to the thought as a consolation.

'I should've stayed and had it out with him. I'm such a coward.'

'No you're not. He deserved to have you walk out on him.'

'And when Caroline came in and got me, she looked so, well, scared.'

'Bastard,' Loz said again, plating up the breakfast.

'And, oh my God, I didn't tell you: he's been having me followed. He knows where I live and everything.'

Loz paused open-mouthed, a pancake flopping over the edge of her spatula. 'What?'

'I know. Really creepy.'

'But why?'

'See if he got his money's worth from that awful school?' Peg shuddered.

'I wonder if he knows about me?' Loz said.

'I should imagine he does. I wish I'd never gone.'

'You did the right thing.'

'He seems to have just wiped the past out completely.'

'Except why's he following you about? It's got to be because he's feeling guilty. He told you he wanted to make it up to you?'

'Yes, but . . .'

'Bingo. Guilty.'

'But I don't want his stinking money.'

'Here, come to the table and get this down you,' Loz said. 'Grilled field mushrooms, fried eggs – sunny side down, guaranteed snot-free – pancakes, maple syrup, baked beans and soda bread toast with unsalted Breton butter.' She put the plate down in front of Peg, who had, like a good child, taken her place at the table.

'Thanks. I so wanted you there, though,' Peg said, almost fully meaning it.

'See? What did I say?' Loz said, picking up her mug and sitting opposite Peg. She reached over and gave her hand a squeeze. 'I should've gone with you.'

'Bloody lovely mushies,' Peg said, tucking in.

'Field-foraged by this old lady who brings them in from Surrey. Nicked them from work.'

'Loz!'

'Not that they'd notice. Not that I don't deserve a perk or two.'

'So what am I going to do now then, Loz?'

Peg's phone buzzed at her side. Cautiously – she hadn't told Raymond her number, but she wouldn't have put it past him to have some people find it out – she looked at the screen.

'Is it him?' Loz said, seeming to read her mind.

'No. It's just Marianne.' Peg put on her Marianne voice – all passive-aggressively soft – and read out the text: '"We're five down because of the flu. I know you're supposed to have the weekend off but can you come in tomorrow?" Bollocks. That's the last thing I feel like doing.'

'You can say no.'

'I know. But . . .'

'Yeah yeah, but you won't. Do you want ketchup?'

'Brown sauce, please.'

'Ew.' Loz pulled a face, but fetched the bottle anyway. 'I think you need to find out what Daddy did,' she said, sitting down again. 'To get put away.'

'What if it was something really terrible?'

'You won't rest until you know, though, will you? Then, once we've got the size of him that way, we'll know how to approach him.'

'I'm not sure I want anything more to do with him now, let alone once I find out he's a – I don't know, some sort of murderer or kiddy fiddler or something.'

'Look: he's got money. Doll and Jean need money. He wants to "make it up to you",' Loz said, putting on a gruff, East-End-gangster voice which, apart from being an octave too low, actually sounded a bit like Raymond. 'If he won't help out willingly, he can help out without knowing it, and you can divert some funds their way. Then everyone's happy and you get on with your life. You play him to benefit them.'

'Sounds like it could get complicated . . .'

'Look: put your fork down a second, will you?'

Peg did as she was told. Loz reached for her hand and curled her small, almost translucent fingers with their cooking-scar badges of honour round Peg's own, softer hands. 'Look, Peggo. I love you. I want to live here with you. We have a great future ahead of us: I'm going to start my restaurant and make a load of money and we'll have a lovely life. I don't want you moving back to your box room in Tankerton to look after two ailing old ladies. I want you to be happy. Us to be happy. Listen to me. I'm dealing out wisdom here. He fucked you over. He deserves everything he gets. It's a serious thought: get the money off him.'

Peg wished she could see everything so clearly. But Loz had never met any of the people involved so didn't really appreciate the complexities. She knew it was more than time to take her down to Tankerton to meet Doll and Jean, to show her the part of her life that no one else knew about. It was something she had been avoiding, an issue that Loz had, with uncharacteristic tact, allowed her to determine for herself. She closed her eyes and imagined introducing everyone. It certainly wouldn't be like going up to Camden to meet Naomi and Richard.

'I couldn't do anything like that, though. I couldn't take his money through lies.'

'It wouldn't be for you, though. Would it? And he's clearly no angel. I shouldn't imagine the way he got hold of the money bears much looking at. You'd be doing the world a favour taking it to benefit two old women, turning something filthy to good.'

Peg shook her head and, despite herself, smiled. Loz could construct an impressive argument. 'I don't know. I need to know what he did first.'

'You could ask Jean perhaps, or Doll?'

'No!'

'Why not?'

'It wouldn't be right. They've obviously got their reasons for not telling me.'

'Oh, Peg . . .'

'It's true. I'm supposed to be making their lives easier, not upsetting them. I've got to find out some other way.'

'But how,' Loz said, leaning back and stroking her chin. 'If only there were some way one could look up things that happened in the past . . . perhaps using a computer . . . on a worldwide web sort of thing . . .'

'As you know, I've searched for him on the Internet for years and nothing's ever come up about prison.'

'But you're not exactly the world's most expert geek, are you?'

Peg shrugged.

'Think though,' Loz went on, her eyes lighting up. 'Your mum died when you were six, and you didn't see your dad after that.'

'Yep.'

'So, we're looking at something that happened mid to late nineties. Where did you and your mum and Raymond live back then? Guildford was it?'

'Just outside. Farnham.'

'And I suppose there's a local newspaper for round there?'

'I suppose . . .'

'Boom.' Loz pointed at Peg, her eyebrows raised, waiting for her to catch up.

Of course. When she had been looking for Raymond, she had been searching more recent records. She needed to look backwards, in more specialised archives, from before the time when everything automatically went online. As someone who supposedly knew a thing or two about libraries, she should have seen that without having it pointed out to her by a technophobic chef.

They both leaped over to the old iMac and Peg turned it on. But sadly, after waiting for it to perform its whirring and clicking start-up routine, PARTYBOYZ was nowhere to be found.

'Come on, Sandy, switch it off and switch it on again,' Loz said.

'He's probably too busy "entertaining",' Peg said.

'Hey, just think: if you could bring yourself to take Raymond's money, we could get ourselves an Internet connection . . .'

'Stop it,' Peg said, smiling. Loz had a way of fixing her mood, however low she was feeling.

'Oh the luxury of just going online, just like that,' Loz clicked her fingers.

'That doesn't sound like you.'

'I maintain my Luddite position solely on economic grounds,' Loz said. 'Bung me a couple of grand and I'll turn into the queen of geek.'

'Hmmm . . .' Peg said, scrolling fruitlessly for another unsecured wireless network. 'Oh fuck it. I'll go into work tomorrow and do it there.'

She picked up her phone and texted Marianne to say she was willing to provide sick cover. It would be better all round to use the work computers – they had access to all sorts of normally paid-for resources, including loads of local newspaper archives.

Then she turned to Loz. 'OK. Let's try to forget about it and have a day off today.'

'I'm all for that,' Loz said. 'Come this way, then, madam.' And she led her to the sofa where the gas fire was burning warm enough to get rid of Peg's rose-patterned dressing gown, and Loz held her and kissed her and felt her and stroked her and licked and bit and opened her up, and Peg gave as good as she got, or better.

And for a few short hours, she forgot all about Raymond, Spain and the awful, awful Caroline.

Then

BREATHE.

Oh.

Oh.

This is when I was six. It's the summer half-term after Aunty Jean told me about my mother's illness.

I'm lying in my bed, tucked in under the roof, reading *Alice in Wonderland* and cuddling my sniffy blanket, which is still a bit scented from the night before. I smell bacon and sausages frying and suddenly I hear Nan's voice. She's talking to Gramps in the kitchen.

I'm bursting with excitement, because I'm staying here for the whole week. I've never done that before, not for the whole of a holiday – I always go home first. But this is a special treat to have the whole time by the seaside, and the weather's lovely. Lovely!

I'm hoping Nan's got us a beach hut for the week.

Wayne the driver brought me back from school last night in

The Car, but it was only Gramps here, because Nan and Aunty Jean hadn't got back from a trip they were on.

This is from when Aunty Jean could still get about and Nan could still drive – I remember now that they had a special car to fit the trolley in. Not that they went away much. This is the only time I remember them ever doing so.

For now, at least.

Anyway, it was nice to see Gramps, and I remember we had fish and chips from the Chinky, as he called it.

But it was always Nan I loved the most. So when I heard her voice downstairs, I was really pleased she was back.

As I get out of bed, I hear Radio Two on in the kitchen, and the Carpenters are playing. I know it's the Carpenters because they're Aunty Jean's favourites. They're singing the one called 'Goodbye to Love'.

I like that one. I can almost sing it all the way through, and I imagine I'm all thin and wafty like Karen is on the video Aunty Jean's got, *The Life of the Carpenters*. 'It's sad she died,' Aunty Jean says when we watch it, all cuddled up on her big old bed that smells of cigs and Guinness. 'But she was too good for this world. That voice. She was an angel.' Sometimes I have to get the tissues, because she cries a little bit.

Nan and Gramps's voices are too quiet to hear properly down there in the kitchen. It's serious, because the sounds are all low and rumbly with none of Nan's usual higher, laughy bits.

As I slip my feet into my fluffy slippers, I look at my clock that looks like a sunflower. It's still quite early, only seven thirty, but Gramps will have been up for ages.

Nan says he'll always be up with the larks, because every

day from when he was fourteen to when he was sixty-five, he had to get up early for his work printing the newspaper. He'll never learn to lie in and take it easy like everyone else, she says. If it's nice, he goes to the garden, but if it's not nice, he goes into his shed, where he makes things – like my Wendy house, which is in the back garden – and mends stuff. Mr Fixit we call him. If there's something broken around the house, it will disappear for a couple of days and then it'll be back in place, all perfect again.

I can see him now!

A big, gentle man.

Clever, but he didn't say much.

And I don't know why, but when I think of him, I feel sorry for him.

I pull on my enormous rosy dressing gown. My room is so small up here I can just about reach out and touch both the walls now, so I always do that before I go downstairs, just for good luck. Touch the stars on the wallpaper.

I pull back my sheets and eiderdown – that's what they make us do at school, and I suppose it's become a bit of a habit – and, clasping *Alice in Wonderland* to my chest, I quietly climb one-handed down the ladder to the ground floor. Then I pad across the carpet to the kitchen door, where I stand still and listen, holding back the moment I'm aching for: the moment when I burst in and throw my arms round Nan.

'It's a blessing, really,' I hear her say.

'Don't say that, Dolly,' Gramps goes.

'My poor boy,' she says, and I hear her sigh hard, like she's pushing all the air out of her whole body. 'She was breaking his heart.'

I peer through the door, which is open just a little bit. Gramps is perched on the stool by the breakfast bar – we call it that, even though it's just a bit of kitchen top he cut to fit on top of the big chest freezer. He's got one knee bent and his bad leg is stretched out so that Nan has to walk round it to get to the sink. She's mostly at the cooker though, working away at the frying pan. I can only see the back of her, but her elbows jiggle as she slides the sausages about, flipping the hanky she keeps tucked into her bangle from side to side.

'He never should have married her,' she says. 'Look at this mess she's got him into.'

'Don't,' Gramps says, looking at his big hands with their moon-shaped nails. 'It's not as if it's her fault.'

'What's he going to do now, though, eh? How's he going to look after the poor girl?' Nan says, turning to look at Gramps. As she does so, she catches sight of me in the doorway, rushes to me and buries me into her front with a big hug.

'Who's my favourite girl?' she says, holding me so tight I feel like I'm going to squeeze out of my mouth.

'Where were you, Nan?' I say, my voice muffled by the folds of her pale-blue pinny.

'I was just off visiting, lovely,' Nan says, letting me go and putting her hands on my shoulders. She's only a bit taller than me and it's so funny, because I'm only six!

'What were you talking about?'

'When?'

'Just now?'

'Oh, just a silly story,' Nan says, brushing her hands together and moving away back to the stove. 'I'm making the best breakfast for you today dear,' she says. 'Bacon and sausages and all the trimmings. You're just in time to have it fresh.'

'Yum,' I say. I am starving hungry. I always am when I come

here from school. It's the sea air, Nan says. Makes me hungry – and sleepy too.

'Sit down over there, dearie,' Nan says, pointing to the other stool, opposite Gramps.

I sit on the stool and swing my feet backwards and forwards on the side of the freezer. I open my book at the place where I was reading with the plan of getting stuck back in while Nan gets on with plating up our breakfasts.

'No swinging and banging, Meggy. And no reading at the table, please,' she says. Remembering yet again how much these things I do annoy her, I stop. She puts two big plates of food in front of me and Gramps. Two sausages, three bits of bacon, fried potatoes, baked beans, fried bread and yuck, though I pretend it's yum, a fried egg.

'Where's Aunty Jean's?' I ask.

Usually Gran makes up another plate for Aunty Jean and takes it next door for her to have in bed. It takes a while for Aunty Jean to get up in the morning. Everything takes her double time because she's so big and she's handicapped.

'She's not here, darling,' Nan says. 'She's stayed out visiting.'

We say our grace and tuck in. Gramps looks over at me. He looks like he's about to say something, but Nan coughs and he stops.

'Cheer up, Gramps!' I say, because he looks sad. 'It might never happen!'

It's what he says to me when I'm down in the dumps. I bite the end of a sausage that I'm holding up on a fork, like a meat lollypop.

'Manners, Madam Miss,' Nan says, but not very crossly. 'I just came back early, because I wanted to see you.' She leans back against the sink and smiles at me. She never sits down when me and Gramps eat our breakfast. There aren't enough stools for one thing, and she says she likes to watch us enjoy our food. 'I do worry about Jeanie though,' she says to Gramps. 'She's not used to being without me to help.'

'You don't need to worry, Dolly,' Gramps says. 'She's perfectly able to look after herself for a bit.'

Nan folds her arms and shakes her head, bunching her shoulders up by her ears so that her pointy chin disappears into the bones of her chest.

'And I'm sure Raymond will help her out if she's got any difficulties,' Gramps says, popping a fried tomato into his mouth with his fingers.

'Frank!' Nan says. 'Fingers!'

'Is Aunty Jean with Mummy and Daddy, then?' I ask.

'Yes, dearie. She's visiting,' Nan says.

'Oh,' I say, and I get this tight feeling in my chest, and out of nowhere I wish that I could go home and see my mummy and daddy and be there with Aunty Jean. It's great at Nan and Gramps's but I'd like to go home to my own bedroom. It's big and comfy there and I've got my own special bathroom. And sometimes . . .

. . . Oh God, sometimes, on nights when my father was out – which was very often – my mother would slip into bed beside me and hold me in her arms and stroke my nose and sing to me until I fell fast asleep.

I still can't see her face, though.

If only I could see her face . . .

I've got a pink net thingy over my bed at home, and I've got kittens on my wallpaper. With pink and blue ribbons.

I feel sorry for the kittens, because by the summer holidays, they'll have been all on their own for the whole term.

I'm quiet while I finish up every bit on my plate, even my egg, even though it's a bit snotty. I wipe it up with my bread and try not to look as I pop it into my mouth. Nan likes me to eat up every last bit; if I don't she asks lots of questions about what was wrong with it, and am I feeling all right. Nan thinks if you don't eat your food up then there's something wrong with you.

Then I ask the question that's been building up in my mind. 'Why's Aunty Jean visiting Mummy and Daddy?'

Nan claps her hands together. 'Who'd like a nice cup of tea then?' she asks.

'Ooh, me please, Dolly.' Gramps rubs his tummy and puts his hand up in the air.

'Me too!' I cry, doing the same.

Nan picks up my and Gramps's plates then turns to the teapot, which has been brewing for a long time under the chicken-shaped cosy I chose for her Christmas present last year. She pours out three cups of her lovely, thick, orangey tea. She adds our sugars – three for Gramps, four for me, and a Hermesetas for herself. Then, instead of putting them down in front of us, she switches off the radio, cutting off some lady singing 'Killing Me Softly With His Song', which isn't half as good as the Fugees one, which is loads better to dance to. In the quiet bit that follows, Nan turns to face us.

'I think we'll have it in the lounge today. What do you think, Gramps?'

Gramps purses his lips together tightly, frowns and nods. 'Definitely,' he says.

This is a real treat because Nan got a new suite at Easter and I'm not allowed usually to have any food or drink in the lounge.

Nan puts the cups and saucers on a tray and carries them

through. Gramps can't carry tea. He's too bumpy because of his gippy leg.

'Get the occasional tables out, Meggy,' Nan says and I run on ahead and slide the shiny teak tables out of their nest, putting one each in front of Nan's and Gramps's chairs, and one in front of the settee for me. Nan puts a cup on each table, on top of a mat, and we all sit down.

'This is nice,' I say, feeling quite grown-up. I sit and try not to scratch at the new settee. Its brown nylon looped cover makes me all jangly, but something in me forces me to run my nails over it, which makes the shivers run up my back and my tongue squirm.

Nan and Gramps look at each other.

'What?' I go, smiling at them and pushing my tongue through the gap in my front teeth, trying to keep it still. 'What is it?'

'Meggy, we've got a bit of sad news for you,' Nan says quickly, and I see Gramps shoot a look at her.

'Gently, Dolly,' he says.

I sip my tea. 'Is it Mrs Cairns?' I say. Mrs Cairns next door had a nasty fall when I was here in the Easter holidays and the ambulance came. I lifted up the nets so that Aunty Jean and I could see as they carried her out on a stretcher. Mrs Cairns looked like whatever it was was hurting a lot. We really enjoyed watching and wondering what might have happened. Aunty Jean said if she passed away it would serve her right because she was an interfering old bag. But when Nan came through with our cake she told us off for being Nosy Parkers and closed the nets, although not before she had a good look herself and shook her head, saying that the ambulance men were lifting her all wrong and they'd feel it in their backs if they carried on like that.

I know Mrs Cairns was quite poorly with a broken hip, and I haven't seen her since I arrived, so I think perhaps she *might* have passed away.

'No, it's not Mrs Cairns, dear,' Gramps says.

'Good,' I say, and I really mean it. No one really deserves to pass away.

'It's your mummy, dear,' Nan says.

I put my cup back down on its saucer, sloshing a bit of tea over the edge. I think back to *Diseases and Symptoms* and what the *prognosis* was for a patient with *lymphoma*.

'Is it Hodgkin's or non-Hodgkin's?' I ask Gramps. He knows everything because of his job. Reading his newspaper word by word every day to check for printing mistakes taught him, he says, 'as much as any la-di-da university could'.

'It was non-Hodgkin's, Meggy,' he says, and I catch the word 'was'. He doesn't use a lot of words, Gramps, but he is very particular about those he does.

'Well, I don't know about that,' Nan says, trying to smile, but closing her eyes.

I'm tucked right into myself, clasping *Alice in Wonderland* close to my tummy. I try to fold myself round it. I wish I could fall down that hole and drink that medicine and shrink right away.

'Mummy's dead, isn't she?' I say, looking up at them both. I want to cry, but I can't. I can't really believe it.

They both nod. Nan still has her eyes shut.

Even though I have only very vague memories of my mother, they are all warm. They are all about being protected, about being safe, about being loved. So I suppose this news must have been very hard indeed to take in at this point. I don't think I even believed it.

It was like I was dreaming it and I just needed to wake up . . .

I didn't know what to do or say. I just felt cold and small. It was all so serious.

I'm scared I'm going to start giggling.

'She's a clever little girl, Doll,' Gramps says. He takes Nan's thin little hand in his big paw and they both sit there and look at me. 'She picks up more than you'd know.'

I wish.

Thirteen

'EXCUSE ME,' THE MAN IN THE GREY OVERCOAT ASKED, LEANING over Peg as she sat at one of the library computers. 'Could you find this book for me, please?'

He handed her a crumpled piece of notepaper on which he had written in pedantic capitals, *SEXUAL DEVIANCE IN PACIFIC PEOPLES*.

Peg looked up at him and forced a customer-service smile. He was a regular visitor. Almost daily he sent someone off looking for something risqué or borderline obscene. They tolerated him because he was harmless and clearly lonely. The sour smell he carried with him was the hardest thing to bear, really.

'I'm terribly sorry, Clive,' she said. 'I'm on my lunch break. Do you want to ask Marianne?'

He never asked Marianne. She frightened the life out of him.

Annoyed at her genealogy session being interrupted by the chatter of other people, the elderly woman at the next computer made a harrumphing sound and buried her chin further into her buttoned-up cardigan.

'It's all right. I can wait,' Clive said, gently pushing the paper onto the table beside her. 'I'll be over by the magazines.' He shuffled off, leaving his distinctive odorous wake, and Peg returned to her investigations, still feeling slightly tucked-in and small, the memory of receiving the news of her mother's death newly wedged into her consciousness. Part of her wanted just to curl up, to hold it close and forget about everything else for the day. But her curiosity spurred her on. It was, after all, part of the same process.

She had not managed to find Raymond Thwaites on any of the specialised search engines she had tried – not on court records for London or Guildford, nor on company records, nor in any of the national newspapers. While she could view PDFs of the local papers for Farnham and Guildford, they weren't indexed for search engines before 1998, so she had resigned herself to a long trawl through screen images of every edition.

She decided to search the *Farnham Herald*, on the basis that, to the best of her knowledge, her father had certainly been around up until then and it was the paper nearest to where they had lived. She thought she recognised the masthead: had she seen it at her parents' house when she was young? She worked through, starting at the date of her mother's death, the day before she sat in her grandparents' lounge and had the news dealt out to her: the second of June 1997.

When she reached the seventh of June edition, she gasped. The picture on the cover struck into her like a chord at the beginning of a familiar song. A slender, beautiful, coffee-skinned woman in a pale linen shirt waister stood laughing at the camera, her long, slim, brown arms raised, her hand defending a wide-brimmed hat from the wind that was blowing her skirt around her knees.

Something inside Peg said 'wedding', and she was hit with a

memory of feeling lumpy and tired in a white broderie anglaise dress, with people bending over her and muttering disapprovingly that she was 'white with the bride', and her mother – her mother, for here she was, in front of her at last – saying that she wasn't to take the slightest bit of notice of what other people said, that she looked beautiful.

It was the first fully focused photograph of her she had ever seen. She zoomed in and for a few minutes she just gazed, taking in the lines and planes of that face. She brought her finger up to the screen and touched the tip of the nose – a reflex gesture, one she barely knew she was making – and, once again, the almond-orange smell of her mother was with her.

She allowed herself a couple of moments. There were lines in that face she recognised – partly from seeing them reflected back at her by the mirror, but partly from knowing she had once seen them on that woman every day. She waited for more memories, but nothing happened. Perhaps she couldn't get there without the breathing exercises.

But she didn't have time for that.

Remembering her purpose, she zoomed back out and that was when she saw the headline:

FARNHAM MAN ARRESTED IN TRAGIC WIFE MERCY KILLING.

Peg gasped again – so loudly this time that the woman next to her hissed another sharp 'Shh!'

Her heart pounding, Peg craned forward to read the article.

Farnham man Franklin Thwaites, 47, was arrested at his £1m luxury home yesterday afternoon after admitting causing the death of his wife, Suzanne Donoghue, 37.

Miss Donoghue had been suffering from cancer, and her doctors had given her six months to live.

'You were due back ten minutes ago.' Marianne's face appeared above Peg's computer monitor, her eyes angled at the big white clock on the wall.

His sister, Jeanette Thwaites, 51, who was visiting at the time, said: 'I overheard Suzanne begging him to end it all for her, and he was crying, saying he couldn't do it.'

'What?' Peg said, tearing her eyes from the screen, feeling as if her skin had been stripped from her body.

'Lunch break's over,' Marianne said, shaking her head so that the many strings of glass and stone beads round her neck clattered dangerously. 'I need to release Paula.'

Peg drew her fingers up her face and over her scalp. 'Sorry,' she said.

'Just get on now, please, Peg. The returns trolley is over-flowing.' Marianne bustled over to the desk, her Indian print dress billowing behind her, a galleon in full sail.

Feeling sick, Peg sent the article to print and logged off. She folded the printout and slipped it in her back pocket. Then, barely able to walk, she headed for the returns trolley and her afternoon's work.

'Excuse me.' Clive flew across the library floor, like a missile homing in on her. 'Could you look up that volume for me please, now, miss.'

Stomach churning, she pushed her trolley into the secret cul-de-sac of the C section of fiction, the one spot where she knew she was unlikely to be found by Marianne. Squatting behind the trolley, she pulled the article out of her back pocket and, hoping she had made some mistake, she reread the whole thing.

But there was no mistake. Raymond's real name was Franklin, after his father, no doubt. That was why he had been so impossible to find.

He had killed her mother.

Her father had been imprisoned because he had killed her mother.

She wished she couldn't believe it, but the tragedy was that she wouldn't put it past that weak control-freak she had met in Spain.

She realised she was breathing too quickly, that she was nearly hyperventilating.

She pulled her phone out of her pocket and called Loz.

'Fucking shite,' Loz said when Peg told her what she had found out.

'It says it was a mercy killing,' Peg said. 'It says that Mum's doctor said she would have died anyway, and sooner rather than later. But it was still murder, and that's what he was arrested for.'

'Jesus.'

'I'll bring the article home tonight,' Peg said, craning round the bookcase to see Marianne crossing the library, heading in her direction. 'Gotta go.'

'Is everything all right, Peg?' Marianne said as she hove into view.

'Yes,' Peg said, hastily pocketing her phone and trying to look busy. It was practically a sacking offence to be caught with a phone – like Loz, Marianne had this very strict rule about staff keeping them in their lockers while working.

'Hurry up then. We've got a backlog to shame the Royal Mail.'

Peg made herself look busy until Marianne returned to her desk. Then, when the coast was clear, she looked back at the article one more time.

When her father disappeared after her mother's death, Peg had swallowed wholesale the vague and coded story handed to her by Doll about being such the spit of her mother that, in his broken-hearted state, he couldn't bear to see her. She had accepted this line so fully as a child that she hadn't felt the need for any further explanation. It had even, in some way, made her feel special.

But here in front of her was the real reason.

Her father had murdered her mother.

Because, in Peg's eyes, mercy killing didn't really wash.

In Peg's eyes, he had robbed her mother of her life. And how could someone do that to someone they were supposed to love?

Peg screwed her face up and pulled on her ear lobes until they hurt. She wanted to run out of the library, all the way to Tankerton, force her way into the bungalow, grab Doll by the neck and demand why she hadn't told her the truth.

Had she been trying to protect her?

That's what she would have thought, perhaps even a couple of days earlier.

But for the first time ever, the art of understanding – at once her blessing and her curse – deserted her. To be left to discover this, on her own, was an outrage.

As she sat there, huddled into the bookshelves, the indignation running through her like a hot needle and thread, her phone rang, bursting its rally of birdsong call-tone out into the library.

She hurriedly pulled it out of her pocket and switched it to silent, planning on stuffing it back unanswered. She didn't feel like talking to anyone else. But then she saw the caller was

Julie, Jean's carer, so she answered. Julie didn't call unless there was an emergency.

'Hello?' she whispered, closing her eyes.

'Meggy?' Julie's voice sounded harried, and Peg could hear a strange keening in the background.

'Yes, Julie. What is it?'

'Oh Meggy, you'd better get down here quick. Doll's had a bit of a turn.'

Fourteen

IT TOOK AN AGE FOR PEG TO GET TO THE HOSPITAL, WHICH WAS in Margate. The train crawled unbelievably slowly along the Thames Estuary. A man called Toby in the seats across the aisle from her declared to his Bugaboo-Hunter family that it would be quicker to *walk* to Whitstable. He got on his phone and loudly told someone called Davina that they were going to be late for the restaurant. When the train guard nasally informed them over the tannoy that, due to a points failure, there would be a bus replacement service between Chatham and Sittingbourne, Toby's reaction verged on the murderous.

Sweating with her own stress, Peg felt like telling him to shut up, that at least he wasn't trying to get to a collapsed grandmother. At least he hadn't just found out his father had killed his mother.

To calm herself, she tried to call Loz, but there was no reply – she would be at work now. So she sent a text, explaining what had happened to Doll.

On the replacement bus, she pulled the *Farnham Herald* article out of her pocket, unfolded it, smoothed out the creases and tried to read more meaning into the words in front of her, but there was nothing else to discover. However, there was the picture of her mother to gaze at. In all of this, that at least was something to be grateful for.

The newspaper seemed to be on her father's side, portraying him as the heartbroken husband of a very sick woman. But this image of him as grief-stricken had been challenged too many times in the past couple of days for her to buy it: she didn't know that she could talk to him again. Loz's plan of screwing him for his money had seemed morally difficult to start with, but now it struck her as impossible. She slipped the article into her red notebook for safekeeping, then spent the rest of the journey trying to think it through, how it might work, but every time she came back to the point that she wanted nothing more to do with him. And she felt foolish for having been taken in by all the lies told to her all her life.

Why should she compromise herself by going to him for money and redistributing it between the two women who had kept all this from her?

She hated the fact that she was being made to feel so bitter, so angry.

When she arrived at the hospital, after a journey that had taken over four hours, it was nearly five o'clock. The A&E department rustled with incongruously jaunty Christmas decorations, even though it was only the beginning of December.

'I found her on the slope outside of your aunty's when I came by to do her lunch,' Julie said, struggling with the arm of her coat, which must have turned inside out when she pulled it off in the heat of the hospital. 'She'd been fetching through a snack for her. She was cold – freezing – and she'd slipped on the ice and barked her knee, but she was also very confused and dithery. I took her in and sat her down with a cup of tea and she was all "Where's my Jeanie?" this, and "We've got to get my Raymond" that, and she kept going on about some Keith? Like she was gathering everyone together for supper or something. I called the ambulance.'

They both looked at Doll, who lay motionless and tiny underneath a green waffle blanket on a wheeled bed. Her arms lay on the covers, a drip jutting from her wrist. The plastic disc of a monitor clung to her chest, held in place by clear tape that smocked her thin skin. A machine by the side of her beeped, registering mysterious numbers on windows on its front.

She looked worryingly peaceful.

'She got a bit agitated in the ambulance so they gave her a shot of something to calm her down,' Julie said, reading Peg's concern.

'What do they say it is?' Peg asked Julie, lifting off her rucksack and placing it on the floor by Doll's bed.

'They think it was a mini-stroke, they've done a scan and there's no sign of any damage, but they can't rule it out, they say. The main thing is she's malnourished, they say, and dehydrated. And she might have some sort of infection down there. They're waiting to find her a bed.'

'They're keeping her in?'

'They want to keep an eye on her for a day or two. She was pretty confused.' Julie glanced up at the red digital clock above a notice containing a stern warning against abusing NHS staff. 'Look love, I've got to go. I got a neighbour to mind the kids but they'll be needing their tea.'

'Of course,' Peg said. 'Thank you so much.' She leaned forward and gave Julie an awkward hug, not made any easier by the fact that she towered over her by more than a foot.

'I got cover in for your aunty,' Julie said, breaking away, clearly not used to such close encounters with clients when cleaning or feeding weren't involved. 'So you don't need to worry about her tonight.'

Peg's thoughts went out to Jean, lying alone in her big bed, being ministered to by a stranger. It was the first time she would ever have spent a night in the house without Doll.

'Did you come here in the ambulance?' Peg asked. It was a ten-mile journey back to Tankerton.

'I'll get a cab back. There's a Freephone in the foyer.'

'Here.' Peg pulled her wallet out of her parka pocket. 'Take this.' She fished out a twenty-pound note and handed it to Julie.

'Thanks love, but you keep it. I can probably claim it on expenses if I make enough of a noise.'

'If you're sure . . .'

The twenty was the only money Peg had with her, and the unplanned, full-cost train fare out had set her meagre weekly budget completely off-kilter. But she felt she ought to offer, at least. Julie probably only earned a tiny bit more than her, and had two children to support. Peg was also aware that, with an education that was – objectively viewed – privileged, she could have had the world as her oyster. That she earned a subsistence wage shuffling books around shelves in a South London library long-listed for closure was a matter of choice – even though it didn't feel all that much like it.

'You keep it, Meggy,' Julie said, closing Peg's hand over the note and pushing it away.

The kindness made the tears prickle in Peg's eyes.

Julie kissed Doll on her cheek. 'Take care, Doll, love. We'll have you back home in no time.'

'Hope so,' Peg said.

Julie smiled on one side of her face and shook her head

slightly. As a parting gesture, it didn't much fill Peg with confidence.

Peg pulled off her parka and sat next to Doll, who skittered her wizened hand over the bedclothes as if she were gathering lint from a child's coat, or playing some wayward invisible piano. She took the hand, held it still and examined her face. The old lady's skin hung loosely on her cheeks and jaw, revealing the shape of her skull.

'Why didn't you tell me about Dad, Nan?' she whispered. 'Who were you trying to protect? Me? Or Raymond?'

Without warning, Doll's eyes shot open. Her hand darted from the waffle blanket to grip Peg's wrist, digging her nails into the base of her palm, the metatarsals and tendons rigid like chicken bones.

The beeps of the machine picked up pace.

'Raymond?' Doll said in a voice so papery that Peg had to lean forward to hear what she was saying. 'Where's my Ray?'

'He's not here, Nan.'

'He's not here,' Doll repeated to Peg, sharing a confidence. 'He's in Spain.'

Peg blinked. Doll had known all along where her son was. Of course she had known. How much grief and effort would Peg have avoided if she had just asked Doll outright, and Doll had simply answered?

Not that she could imagine either happening.

And of course the grief and effort of finding her father was nothing in comparison to what she was enduring having done so.

'It's such a pity,' Doll went on. 'I wanted to show him the baby. He was so looking forward to it.' She let go of Peg's arm and peered about her. 'Where is he?' she said. 'Where's my baby?'

'There's no baby, Nan. You're in here because you had a funny turn.'

'I had the collywobbles.'

'You had the collywobbles.'

For a second, Doll seemed to be content with this explanation. But she started casting her eyes around again – slowly at first, then faster as her agitation grew, her hand working double-time on its mystery task on the blanket. Her darting fingers suddenly grabbed a fistful of her bedding and ripped the whole lot free from its tightly packed hospital corners, fully exposing herself where her NHS back-fastening gown had ridden up. Surprisingly pale and smooth skin made her thin, knob-kneed legs look like they belonged to a little girl, rather than an old woman. Peg was glad to see that someone had managed to put a pad of sorts on her and some kind of surgical webbing knickers to save both the sheet she was lying on and her modesty.

'Where's my Keithy?' Doll cried, struggling to get off the bed. She rounded her eyes furiously on Peg. 'Where's my baby, nurse? What did you do to him?' The rapid beeping of her machine had now turned into an alarm call.

'You haven't had a baby, Nan. You had a bit of a turn.'

'Keithy!' Doll swung her legs off the bed and attempted to stand, wires tangling with her gown, her drip threatening to topple.

'Nan, no. You've got to stay still,' Peg said, trying uselessly to restrain her. She was scared to use any sort of force on her in case she snapped her delicate bones. Assistance arrived in the wholesome apple-dumpling shape of a young nurse who hurried into the cubicle, bearing a cardboard dish with a plastic syringe full of a sickly looking orange liquid.

'My baby,' Doll went on, looking wildly around her.

'There there, Mrs Thwaites,' the nurse said. She expertly applied just the right amount of gentle force to swing the old lady round so she was once again lying down. Then she picked the blanket from the floor and tucked it back over her, effectively hemming her in. Swiftly, she stuck the plastic syringe in her mouth and dispensed the orange liquid. Doll swallowed and the nurse put a plump hand on her cheek as she calmed down. In a few short moments she was stilled; her eyes closed again, her breathing and the beeping returning to normal.

'She's got a bit of a UTI,' the nurse said, speaking to Peg over the top of Doll's head.

'UTI?'

'Urinary tract infection. We've just got the labs back. Makes them a bit disoriented. It'll take a while for the antibiotics to kick in.'

Peg nodded. 'She thinks she's had a baby. She can't find him.'

'Does she? Oh, poor lady,' the nurse said. 'Did she lose a baby ever?'

'Her youngest died in an accident.'

'Oh, that'll be it then. They never get over it.' The nurse stroked Doll's brow as she gave one last shudder of distress. 'I've seen it loads of times. Of course, it was a lot more common back then to lose a child. But it still hurts, doesn't it?'

'What's going to happen next?' Peg said.

'Doctor's seen her and we're just waiting for a bed for her upstairs,' the nurse said, standing up and clicking cot rails into place at both sides of Doll's bed. 'He'd like to keep an eye on her for a couple of days, get that infection cracked, feed her up a bit. She hasn't been eating properly and she was badly dehydrated when she came in.'

'Poor Nan. I try to make sure she eats . . .'

'It's difficult to keep tabs when you don't live with them, though, isn't it?'

'She won't take any help,' Peg said, gripping the bed rail. 'I've tried so many times.'

'I think the time might have come where she's going to need a bit of support.'

'She won't like it.'

'Tell you what, I'll see if I can find the hospital social worker to come and have a chat with you, perhaps point you in the right direction.'

'Thanks.'

A furious beeping set off from another part of the ward.

'I'd best be off, then,' the nurse said, smoothing down her skirt and tucking a stray hair behind her ear. 'We're a bit short-staffed at the moment. Everyone's got that lurgy thing that's going round.'

She scurried out, leaving Peg alone with the quieted Doll. Again she took her hand and stroked it, watching her wheezy sleep.

She searched the lines on the old lady's face. Could she read loss there? To lose a baby. To have your other children watch helpless as he fell off a dock edge into the murky river, cracking his head, being swept away to his death. How terrible. And how awful that, again, no one had talked about it, not ever. She wondered if Raymond remembered it at all, and what witnessing something like that could do to a person as they grew up. Was that an allowance she had to make for him?

Poor Dolly. Both her sons, lost to her. Was it any wonder she made up stories to make it all sound better?

Was it any wonder she had never told Peg the truth?

Fifteen

'HELLO THERE!'

A youngish woman with two dangling plaits put her head through the cubicle curtain, reminding Peg of some comedian in a repeat Christmas special she had watched many years ago with Doll, Frank and Jean.

'So, you must be Mrs Thwaites's niece,' the woman said, sliding into the cubicle clutching a bundle of folders to her chest. Her tone was elaborately solicitous, as if she had already decided that Peg was someone to feel sorry for.

'I'm her granddaughter actually.' Peg stood up and shook the woman's hand.

'Mandy Dawkins, duty social worker.' The woman looked as exhausted as Peg felt. 'Please, call me Mandy. You've just caught me. I'm due off in ten minutes.' She pulled a chair from the other side of Doll's bed. 'I understand you wanted to have a little chat about Mrs Thwaites here.' Her eyes drifted over to Doll, and she reached out and patted the waffle blanket somewhere near the old lady's thigh.

'The nurse said you might be able to help with some ideas

for when she's ready to come out.'

'As I said, I've only got about ten minutes, but I'll give you these.' She pulled out a pile of leaflets from one of her folders and handed them to her. 'If Mrs Thwaites is beginning to have difficulty managing by herself, I want you to know that council policy is to provide support so that people can remain in their own homes as long as is practicable. If that's what they want.'

'Oh, that's definitely what she wants,' Peg said. 'She'd want to be back at home close to Aunty Jean.'

'Aunty Jean?' Mandy's eyebrows shot up into her high, short fringe. 'Would that be Jean Thwaites?'

'Yes. Aunty Jean's already got a care worker, Julie Maltby.'

'Before I started here I was in the Domiciliary Care department. Miss Thwaites was very well known to us.'

'She is pretty distinctive.'

'So this is the mother. Well, I can see that Mrs Thwaites here would want to be close to her daughter after all those years caring for her single-handed.'

Peg bristled slightly. Was she in for another Mrs Cairns-type telling-off?

'She's quite a lady, your grandmother. How she managed to keep it all under the radar . . .' Mandy said, looking at Doll with new respect.

'How do you mean?'

'It was astounding how she managed to look after your aunt as long as she did without any help whatsoever. Quite a feat.'

'I tried to get her to get some help. It took years before she admitted that she couldn't do it any more.'

'Quite a lady.'

They both sighed. It was heartbreaking to see Doll lying there, passive, while decisions were made on her behalf that she would never agree to had she known what they were.

'But it's time though,' Peg said at last. 'It's her turn to be looked after.'

'So.' Mandy flicked through the leaflets. 'These explain the services we offer, from domiciliary care, through meals delivery, and various aids and adaptations for the home. This is the Mrs Dorothy Thwaites who, in the past, refused a walking frame?'

Peg nodded.

'The lack of which is probably why she's ended up in here. And she'll be a perfect candidate for our new TeleCare alarm system, so if she takes another tumble, she'll be able to summon help. I expect you're quite familiar with most of this because I believe it was you who instigated the care programme for your aunt?'

Peg nodded again. She felt weary just remembering the altercations she had had with Doll, who had railed that she didn't want any 'busybody social services do-gooders prying into my life'.

It would, Peg hoped, be easier this time. Doll wasn't exactly in any position to argue.

'What's the next step?'

'I'll arrange for you to have a visit at Mrs Thwaites's home. It needs to be done as soon as possible, before she leaves hospital.'

'But they said she'd only be in here for a couple of days.'

'To look at her, I'd be very surprised if that were the case,' Mandy said. 'In any case, it goes against the council's duty of care to let a client go home before we've put the appropriate measures in place.'

'What will the home visit be about?'

'We'll be assessing Mrs Thwaites's house for any health and safety concerns, such as tripping hazards and fire risks.'

Peg sighed. The whole bungalow was a tripping-hazard fire risk.

'It's also council policy to conduct a deep clean of a client's home at the beginning of a contract, so that an adequate state of hygiene can be maintained. It's quite usual for clients, when they reach the point of needing help, to have slipped into a challenging state domestically.'

'But she has everything just how she likes it,' Peg said, spreading her hands out in front of her. 'She hates people interfering with her stuff.'

'We have to think of our employees as well as our clients, I'm afraid,' Mandy said, looking at her watch, brisk now. She stood up and handed Peg a form. 'Now, if you could just fill in your contact details here and here,' she pointed to the form. 'Then someone will be in touch in a day or two about arranging the home visit.'

Peg did as she was told and Mandy bustled out, leaving her to fret alone. So not only was Doll going to have her autonomy stripped from her, but all her belongings would be gone through by strangers in the name of hygiene and health and safety. Peg was contemptuously familiar with all this: the heavy hand of the council bureaucrat was never far away at her own work, telling her how many books she could lift, and where she was allowed to walk with a hot cup of tea in her hand.

It was as if, by collapsing on Jean's steps, Doll had set a juggernaut in motion to cart her own identity and self-determination away. It made Peg think of Solzhenitsyn, or Kafka. It was the stuff of horror.

The only way Peg could see round it, the only way she could help Doll retain some dignity, would be to do the clearing and cleaning part herself. To set herself up in the bungalow for however long it took to sort the place out.

But what would Loz say?

Loz.

If only she could call her. But she'd still be in the middle of it all at the restaurant.

So she sat there, by her grandmother, waiting.

Doll looked so innocent, lying in that bed like a baby. It was impossible to think that she had anything but the best motives for not telling the truth about Raymond.

Peg knew her grandmother loved her fiercely. Because of that love, she could truthfully say to Loz that what she could so far recall of her childhood wasn't so bad – even the death of her mother had been dealt to her in a careful and loving way. It was because of that love that Doll had shielded her from the truth. It had been a form of protection. But it had also been as if she had held a blanket over her, unwittingly smothering whoever she really was with white lies. Blurring her. Rendering her – how did Loz put it? – without edges.

And what else hadn't she been told?

Doll sighed and quivered. She looked so desperately alone there, hemmed under the waffle blanket. Her decline had begun, and Peg wondered if she was now ever going to have a chance of a proper conversation with her. She closed her eyes and tried to clear her mind to allow a chink of light into the fog. It took a while, but slowly something began to dawn.

If Raymond's imprisonment – and specifically the reason for it – was the lock he had put on the past, then, if she told him she had found out, wouldn't they be in a better position to move forward? Then perhaps Loz's plan to take his money for Doll *would* work. It would even give her a subversive thrill of satisfaction. And anyway, didn't she owe it to her grandmother – because of the love she had shown her all her life – to at least try?

She pulled her red notebook and pen from her rucksack and wrote:

1: Tell Raymond that I know about Mum's death.

Sixteen

BY THE TIME A BED HAD BEEN FOUND FOR DOLL, IT WAS GONE three in the morning.

Loz had called when she got out of work and Peg told her she planned to go to the bungalow after the hospital. Thankfully, Loz had been nothing but understanding.

Peg took the first morning train. When she arrived at Whitstable, it was still dark. A brisk, icy wind whistled the reek of low-tide mud all the way inland to the station, the cold air whipping at her eyes, making them water so that the station lights appeared at once blurry and sharp. She had plenty of time before Jean woke up, so she pulled her rucksack on and set off straight down the hill on her favourite, seafront route to the bungalow, taking care not to slip on the patches of black ice on the pavement.

Unlike Loz, who always seemed a little jumpy at night, Peg completely lacked any street smarts. It never occurred to her to look around her or worry about walking anywhere alone in the dark. If anything, lack of light made her feel safer. Even from close up, and especially in her parka, her height and build was such that she could easily be mistaken for a sizeable man. Sizeable scary man, even.

However, when she passed a white van on the hill down towards the sea, her antennae prickled. And when it pulled out after she had walked twenty or so metres beyond it, she stopped, turned angrily and stared at where she imagined the driver must be.

'Piss off, Raymond,' she yelled.

As the van passed her, the skinny white driver was caught in the glow of a street light. He looked alarmed.

Then Peg saw the ladder on top of the van and the sign-writing on the side. He was only a builder going to some early-morning job.

Chiding herself for being so jumpy, she pulled her parka hood close to protect her frozen cheeks and slipped down between the shadowy tennis courts and over the concrete steps of the sea wall. The tide was far out, nearly on the turn, and the moon hovered in the clear, cold sky, spilling silver light on the distant, shifting water.

She loved this walk; it was a perfect antidote to the sleepless hospital night she had just endured. She followed the concrete path along the edge of the beach, past the wooden cottages that opened right onto the shingle. Some were still as dilapidated as they were in her childhood, but many of them had been fixed up and painted Farrow and Ball colours, with Derek Jarman-esque stone and driftwood gardens.

She remembered now the Whitstable of her childhood, when it had still been a slightly down-at-heel Kentish seaside town of dingy B&Bs and day-tripping Londoners.

It was on this very path that Jean had told Peg of her mother's illness. The realisation brought the taste of the ice cream and chocolate to her mouth as vividly as if she were holding the triple Ninety-Nine in her hand.

She stopped for a minute and squeezed her eyes tight shut, pinching at her frown with her mittened fingers. Had she ever been here with her father? Could she see Raymond on this beach? Or Suzanne, her mother?

She had no recollection whatsoever about either of them being there. But even so, she could feel her mother very close by. Perhaps it was finally seeing her face in the newspaper photograph that did it, but Suzanne's presence right then was strong enough to send a shiver down Peg's back.

She skirted the harbour, where she stopped and, half hidden behind a closed oyster stall, watched fishermen, long returned from the night's work, cleaning their mud-stranded boats and loading their catch onto lorries. She would have liked that straightforward sort of life: go out there, catch your fish, come back and clean up. Even the dangerous bits – the possibility of being swamped by a colossal wave, or of having your ankle lassoed by an anchor chain and being dragged beneath the keel – seemed to be real, tangible problems, compared to the ever-increasing mess that her own life seemed to be churning out for her.

Too cold to stand still any longer, she moved on down the road to rejoin the coastal path. She passed the Continental Hotel which stood silently, held by the first fingers of dawn, the only inside light coming from somewhere behind the dining room where, she imagined, some lonely chef would be setting up for the breakfast rush hour. This brought Loz to her mind, and she sent her love to where she imagined her to be – warm, tucked up and fast asleep on her own side of the bed at home.

The Street, the long strand of shingle that juts out from the shore at low tide, was almost entirely visible. Beyond was the offshore wind farm, just discernible in the pale light, its blades turning like ghosts waving to the living on the shore.

Normally Peg resisted the urge she always had to strike out along The Street when it was laid bare like this – her reason for being here was usually to spend the time with Doll and Jean. But Jean would be asleep for at least another hour, then Julie would take a further hour to wash, dress and feed her. So, with time to kill, she dropped down off the concrete path, across the shingle and on to the mud and gravel. At sea level, the expanse of exposed seabed before her seemed so vast it appeared to tilt.

She headed out along the spit of land. The breath-counting, 'inner flow' work and note-taking were beginning to have an effect: the act of drawing her parka hood round her face called up a vivid memory of tightening her anorak in the same way when Jean had brought her down here one blustery evening many years before.

Unable to take the trolley onto the sand, her aunt had sat and watched over her as she ran out to sea towards the end. Two interfering old bags stopped her and asked where her mummy was.

'Mummy's dead,' she had said. 'But Aunty Jean's watching me on her trolley.' And she pointed to the path, where her aunt cut a large blob of a figure, easily detectable even from half a mile away.

'You taking the mick?' one of the old bags said, to which Peg had shaken her head and pointed again at Jean, who raised a hand to wave.

'Poor mite,' the other bag had said.

How right the interfering old bag had been. Peg saw it now. She had, indeed, been a poor mite.

She hunkered down into her parka as the wind whistled in her ears and sinuses, freezing her brain. Gulls dropped shellfish all around her, swooping then picking them up, then smashing them down again. Some just missed her head.

'Dangerous game,' Peg said out loud to the birds.

She crunched out to the very far point and looked at the mudbank beyond the tip, unreachable now because the tide had started its obliterating journey back to shore. The lowest tides were called Proxigean Spring Tides and they only happened once every eighteen months or so, when the moon was really close to the earth. She had looked it up in Frank's *Pears Cyclopaedia* once when she had managed to get out to the other side of the mudbank. But there was no chance of that this morning.

As she stood and stared out at the empty waterscape, the plan she had started to form in the hospital flowed into focus. The situation was as clear and stripped-back as the line of sea meeting sky in front of her:

Doll needed help.

She deserved the best.

That meant money.

Exhilarated by the simplicity of this, she stood where she was until the incoming tide lapped at the soles of her DMs. Then she turned, and with purposeful step began the long walk back to land. The briefly exposed sea floor, unable to dry in the cold air, glistened frostily in the pink light of the sun as it crept above the horizon.

On her way back, she breathed in the muddy, ozone-heavy air and exhaled it in warm clouds. The sky was clear. If it hadn't been for the biting cold, the twinkling lights of Tankerton in the distance could have been the Spanish coast, viewed from a plane.

Back on the beach, she turned to watch the waves slide in, each one covering a little more of the ground, closing it up for its next showing twelve hours later. Then she moved on, following the litter-strewn tarmac path up the grassy Tankerton Slopes. From the number of vodka bottles and cigarette ends, some sort of party had been going on. Avoiding a used condom splatted in the middle of the path, she wondered what had happened to the place she associated, rightly or wrongly, but very, very strongly, with childhood and innocence. It seemed to have lost its sense of a place of safety.

But perhaps that was just because she knew that, for the first time ever, Doll wasn't there, waiting for her in the bungalow.

Or perhaps it was what she had found out – and what she was starting to remember . . .

Or perhaps this was just growing up.

Seventeen

IT WAS HALF-PAST SEVEN WHEN PEG ARRIVED AT THE BUNGALOW. Julie's little Metro was parked in the driveway. Towards the back of the house, Jean's bedroom light blazed behind closed curtains. Doll's side was in blackness, with no sign of life. In the past few years she had become scared of the dark and had taken to keeping the hall lights on. But Julie must have switched them off.

Bracing herself for the olfactory onslaught, Peg let herself in through Doll's front door. Viewing the place in the light of that social worker Mandy Dawkins's comments made her realise just how much work had to be done. Apart from a grubby few inches of carpet leading from chair to settee to kitchen to bedroom, very little floor space remained that wasn't taken up with piles of stuff – carrier bags full of odd, unwashed pop socks, yellowing stacks of old copies of the *Daily Mail*, saved foil wrappers from decades of Christmas boxes of Quality Street, bags stuffed with Commonplace Books that Doll had hauled in from the shed.

Picking her way through the kitchen to the back door, she

found the remains of Doll's lunch from the day before: a thin ham sandwich with just one tiny bite out of it and an un-drunk glass of milk. She had left it on the side, called – perhaps by Jean's intercom buzzer or possibly just maternal whim – to pop next door with a snack for her daughter.

Peg tipped the leftovers into the bin and emptied and washed the glass and plate, stacking them on the crowded draining board.

Time to start as she meant to go on.

She took the key to Jean's from its hook by the back door – Julie must have replaced it the night before, or perhaps Doll had forgotten to take it with her – and carefully negotiated the scene-of-the-crime slope down and up again to Jean's back door. It was horribly icy. Doll should never have been outside, and she, Peg, should have at least made sure the paths and slopes were gritted. What sort of dutiful granddaughter was she?

One that had been lied to, perhaps.

Batting that unhelpful thought away, she unlocked Jean's back door.

'Congratulations'.

Cliff Richard sang so loudly in Jean's bedroom that the floorboards rumbled with the sound. Her aunt liked music in the mornings, especially Cliff.

'He keeps my pecker up, dear,' she said once to Peg. 'And I know they say he's one of them, but he isn't. He nearly married Sue Barker, you know. And he was in love with Olivia Newton-John.'

Peg could hear poor Jean complaining loudly as Julie tried to wash and move her. One of the many dangers for someone of Jean's size was bedsores and chafing in the folds of her flesh, which, if left unattended, could become infected. Peg knew all this from helping Doll.

'It's just like it was in the war,' Doll used to say, as she made Peg take notes on flushing open sores.

'Ouch,' Jean cried from the bedroom.

Cliff sang on about wanting the world to know he was as happy as can be.

'Hello!' Peg called, hovering behind Jean's closed door. 'It's me, Meggy.'

'Just a minute!' Jean gasped, then she gave out a long, low moan.

'I'll wait here,' Peg said, squatting down in the hallway. 'Call me when you're done.'

She leaned back against the wall and closed her eyes. The stale smell of cigarettes saturated every surface in Jean's extension, even overflowing onto the edges of Doll's side. The resulting airlessness, the cloying, top-of-thermostat central heating and the wheezing and panting of Jean's anti-bedsore air-bed – like the sound of some ancient iron lung – almost lulled Peg to sleep after her night of hospital wakefulness. But her new clarity about what she needed to do kept her sharp enough to hold her eyes open.

'All done!' Julie said brightly as she burst out of Jean's bedroom, a bulging plastic bag marked Clinical Waste under her arm. She was rubbing a white cream into her hands, which Peg noticed were sore and chapped. 'How's poor Mrs Thwaites?'

'Comfortable as she can be. They got her a bed eventually.'

'Good!' Julie said loudly. Then, rolling her eyes back towards the bedroom she added, under her breath, 'We're not in our best mood this morning.'

'Thanks for the warning.'

Julie went through into the kitchenette and Peg clasped her

hands together and closed her eyes briefly to steel herself for Jean.

'I can't believe it,' Jean said, loudly blowing her nose on yet another tissue. 'Poor Mummy.'

Cliff had been replaced by the *Jeremy Kyle Show* on the TV. Two women were screaming bleeped-out insults at each other and grabbing each other's hair.

'She's fine, Aunty Jean. I can't tell you how comfy she looked. And it might even be a good thing in the long run. It'll force her to understand that she can't go on all alone any more.'

'But she's got you, though, Meggy.'

'I'm not enough. Not any more.'

Jean reached for her cigarettes and lit up. As she inhaled and exhaled, Lexy the cat jumped up onto the bed and burrowed his bloated, fluffy body underneath the folds of one of her breasts.

'She's a right bitch that one,' Jean said, nodding at the TV, which showed a snarling close-up of one of the women. 'She had a baby by her sister's husband and she never told her it was his. Pass us the ashtray, there's a dear.'

'I'm going to stay for a few days, sort things out a bit in the bungalow before Nan comes back,' Peg said, handing Jean the pelican-shaped ashtray that, even so early in the day, overflowed with lipstick-stained cigarette butts.

Jean looked at her through bloodshot eyes. 'She won't like that, Meggy. You going through all her things.'

'Don't worry; I'm just going to clean and tidy up a bit. It's got to be done.'

Jean shrugged and looked away, her eyes glazing, fixed on the TV, where, restrained by two burly bouncers, the two women were trying to get at a skinny tattooed man, who was shouting something unintelligible and pointing furiously at the studio audience. He didn't appear to have any front teeth.

'It's got to be done, Aunty Jean,' Peg said again, trying to draw her aunt's gaze with her own eyes. 'The social worker said.'

'Heartless bastards,' Jean said.

'Mandy Dawkins. Said she knew you.'

'That bitch.' Jean's eyes narrowed. 'I'm not surprised. Made my life a living hell when I had those first girls come here. Told me I wasn't a good patient. Me! If anyone knows how to be a patient it's me. Told Mummy off for looking after me, too. I ask you. A mother's got the right to care for her own daughter, surely?' Jean scrunched her face up and sighed. 'I only wish I could pay Mummy back in her hour of need, but look at me. I'm no use to anyone. Can't you come and look after her, Meggy? After all the sacrifices she made for you?'

Peg shook her head, trying to brush off this attempt at emotional blackmail. 'I've got to work, Aunty Jean. Nan needs proper carers, coming here. It's how it's got to be. In the short term at least.'

'What do you mean, in the short term?' Jean looked up sharply. 'You're not going to put her in a home? You promised.'

'Of course not,' Peg said, hurriedly. 'No. There are other possibilities.'

'What other possibilities?'

'Well, I could get the place done up for her and we'll have full-time carers come and live here for you both.'

'But the council won't pay for that, surely? It'll cost the earth. We haven't got that sort of money. Anyway, Mummy won't have it. She hates all that sort of charity.'

'It won't be charity. There'll be no council involved.' Peg took a deep breath. It was time to lay her beautiful, newly

164

formed plan on the table and get Jean on board. 'I'm going to get my dad to help us out.'

'What do you mean?' Jean said, grinding out her cigarette.

'He's got money. Lots of money.'

'How do you know?'

Peg took a breath. 'I went and visited him in Spain.'

Jean blanched and put her hand up to her chest. For one second, Peg wondered if she was doing the right thing by telling her, but she had to plough on.

Like one of those films of a slowly developing foetus, Jean's face took on a look of horror as Peg told her an edited version of her trip to Spain. She left out, for example, the fact that Raymond had called his sister a lazy, fat, bad bitch.

'You went all the way to Spain and we didn't know?' Jean said, at last. 'That doesn't sound like you, Meggy, hiding things from us.'

Peg chose to brush this aside. 'Also,' she said, the sense of release grasping at her belly like excitement, 'I know about him being in prison, Aunty Jean. And I've found out why he went there.'

'Oh no,' Jean said, bringing her nicotine-yellowed hand up in front of her eyes. 'Oh no.' Her whole vast body seemed to deflate, as if someone had stuck a pin in it.

'Why didn't you or Nan tell me?' Peg said quietly. She looked away and focused on the collection of model pelicans sitting on Jean's dressing table.

A commotion from the TV drew her attention. One of the women had launched herself at the man, pushing him to the ground where they grappled, four bouncers trying unsuccessfully to pull them apart. The audience bayed, loudly.

'Can we turn that off, please?' Peg said, reaching for the remote on the pillow on the other side of Jean, who still held her hand over her eyes. She pointed it at the TV and they were plunged into a silence punctuated only by the wheeze of the air-bed.

Peg breathed in and out quietly and tried again.

'Why didn't you tell me?'

Jean sighed heavily and the whole bed rumbled. 'Why didn't you tell *us* you was going to Spain? Because you didn't want to upset us. Same thing our end. We thought it best you didn't know. It was a dreadful thing he did.'

'Was it so bad? Whatever you or I think, he was doing what he believed to be best. What Mum wanted. If it happened today, he'd probably not even have got a sentence.'

'You can think what you like, Meggy.' Jean shook her head and reached for a big pack of Monster Munch from her bedside table. She pulled out a handful and crammed them into her mouth, crunching them quickly. A few orange crumbs spilled onto her brightly coloured giant smock, one of a set of ten that Doll had sewn for her a couple of years back when off-the-peg became impossible for her, even from specialist mail order outlets.

'What does that mean?' Peg said.

'Nothing.' Jean took another mouthful and offered Peg the bag.

'No thank you. What do you mean, I can think what I like?'

'I don't want to talk about it,' Jean said. 'But—'

'But what?'

'Well, if you have to know, you shouldn't believe everything that brother of mine tells you. Your mum didn't want to die.'

Now it was Peg's turn to look horrified. 'What do you mean? It said in the article . . . *You* said to the paper . . .' She pulled her notebook from her bag and held the article out in front of Jean. '"His sister, Jeanette Thwaites, 51, who was

166

visiting at the time, said: 'I overheard Suzanne begging him to end it all for her, and he was crying, saying he couldn't do it.'"'

'I hate that name,' Jean said.

'What?' Peg said, putting the printout down on the bed.

'Jeanette. So prissy.'

'But you said here, to the paper, and to the police, that Mum wanted to die. And now you've just told me the complete opposite.'

'What was I to do?' Jean said. 'He did it. There's no undoing that. And then he'd have got life for murder if I'd told the truth. And what would that've done to Mummy?'

'Why did he do it then? Why did he kill Mum if she wanted to live?'

'It was inconvenient for him to have a sick wife. Draining. Poor soul. She was in dreadful agony.' Like Doll, Jean always inserted a 't' sound into the middle of the word dreadful, which, added here to the trembling emotion of her voice, more than made her point.

Peg looked at her and wondered if this was really the truth. 'Perhaps she had asked him, though. When you weren't around?'

'I knew everything that went on between them two,' Jean said. 'He shared everything with me and Mummy. Mummy was so upset about it all that when it all came out what he done, she came to pick me up and on the way home she crashed the car and I ended up in hospital. Don't you remember the car crash?'

Peg shook her head.

'That really surprises me, Meggy. It was dreadful. But then I suppose you was only six.'

Peg watched Jean crunch on the Monster Munch. Then, unable to contain herself any longer, she finally came to the question she realised she needed properly answered. 'Why did he never come back here though, Aunty Jean? After he got out? Why didn't he come and get me?'

Jean folded her hands across her vast bosom, shook her head and smiled at her. 'No idea, Meggy. You'll have to ask him about that, now you're such good friends.'

Peg felt herself blush. She couldn't help it. It always happened; she hated this barometer of her internal state being so visible to everyone.

'Look, darling,' Jean said, her voice a little softer. 'You've got to stop asking these questions. You were settled with me and Mummy, weren't you? And happy? It was probably for the best that he never came back. Why can't you just leave it at that and stop stirring up the mud.'

'The mud?'

Jean held up her hand. 'Oh yes. Mud.'

'What do you mean?'

Jean took Peg's hand and squeezed it in hers, locking her eyes on her. After a long pause, she finally spoke.

'Oh Meggy,' she said. 'I thought you'd never have to hear this.'

'Hear what?' Peg's chair was low against Jean's bed with its specialist mattress and reinforced base. The position she was now in, looking up at her aunt, reminded her of being at a school assembly, being forced to kneel and pray.

'Your dad is not a nice man, Meggy. Not a nice man at all. He's very troubled. By what happened when we was little. By what he did.'

'What? What happened?'

'Keith.'

'What about Keith?'

'The baby. He didn't fall into the dock.' Jean's voice fell to a whisper. 'He was pushed. By your dad.'

'What?' Peg drew her hand away from Jean's soft, hot clasp.

'It was dreadful,' Jean went on.

'But Dad was only a little boy then. He couldn't have done it on purpose.'

'He was old enough to know what he was doing. I was *there*, Meggy. I saw the look on his face. He *hated* Keith. Hated the fact he, Raymond, wasn't Mummy's baby any more. He put his hands out in front of him and ran forwards, his eyebrows down, and he looked like a little devil, like a beetle, running straight at our baby brother and pushing.' Jean breathed in deeply and heaved her chest. 'Pass us a tissue, darling, will you?'

She dabbed at her eyes and blew her nose, then continued, her voice wavering and hoarse. 'Keithy was only two. A little sweet thing he was, running around by the docks near our house back in London. We was supposed to be looking after him for Mummy. But Raymond saw his chance and . . . Boof!' Jean scowled and thrust her hands out with remarkable force.

'You told me he fell, though,' Peg said.

'That's what everyone thinks. That's what I told them. Even Mummy. It would've KILLED her to know the truth. She must never know, Meggy. Never, you hear me?' Jean licked her fingers and wiped them round the inside of the Monster Munch bag, picking up the last salty, orange crumbs. 'Even now it will kill her. That was the first time I saved your father's neck, but it certainly wasn't the last. He was always in trouble, always doing bad things.' She crumpled up the empty packet and handed it to Peg. 'Could you pop that in the bin, please, dear?'

'But he was so young. He couldn't have known what he was doing.'

'He did. I saw it. He knew *exactly* what he was doing.' All Jean's earlier depression about her mother's collapse seemed to have deserted her. She was truly warming to her theme. 'Do you really want to know why we never told you about your dad, Meggy?'

Peg nodded silently.

'He's *evil*, girl. That's what he is. And the sooner you forget about him the better.'

Peg clasped her hands together, pressing them into her chest, and looked down at her lap.

'You were better off not knowing, weren't you? Oh, Meggy. You see?'

Jean grabbed her hand again and held it with such force that Peg felt her bones creak.

'If you need to know it, here it is. Your dad was a wild one. Mummy and Daddy couldn't control him. He was awful to the both of them, a terrible son and a worser brother. He did unimaginable things. Really. Things you don't want to think about. He'd have been no good at all as a father.

'There you are. Now you know.

'If we'd told you back when you was a nipper, how would that have made things for you? It would have been dreadful. How do you tell a little girl her daddy killed her mummy? Eh? Or that he killed his own baby brother?'

Peg shook her head, numb.

'Now, you say he's got money. Listen to your old Aunty Jean, darling.'

She pulled at Peg's hand so that she was forced to lift her head and look her in the eye.

'We can do without his money. We don't want nothing else to do with him. Not never. Be the good little Meggy I know and love, and do as I say. Forget all about him. And whatever he's told you about anything, anything at all, take it with a pinch of salt. He's worthless.'

She smiled at Peg, something like triumph tinting her look. Then, her energy spent, she laid her head back against the pillows.

A few minutes later, she raised weaker eyes to look at Peg. 'Now then. How about a nice cup of tea, dear? You look as worn out as I feel. You should go and get forty winks. I don't know, you youngsters think you can keep going all night without a moment's sleep. You'll make yourself ill, Meggy.'

Peg's phone rang. She pulled it out of her pocket and saw it was Loz. She couldn't answer in front of Jean, not the way she was feeling, so she flicked it off.

'That's not your father, is it?' Jean said, narrowing her eyes at Peg.

'No. It's just my friend. Loz. She can wait.'

'Loz?' Jean frowned. 'What kind of name is that?'

'It's short for Lorraine.'

Jean frowned at Peg, letting her eyes linger just long enough to show that her mind was working on something new. 'Close friend is she?'

'Yes,' Peg said, her blasted beacon cheeks firing up again. She put the phone back in her pocket and went through to the kitchenette to make the tea.

As soon as she could escape, Peg shut Jean's back door behind her and closed her eyes, grateful to be outside in the icy morning.

She tried to return Loz's call, but there was no answer: she was probably back in work. So she texted her to say that she was going to be staying for a couple of days to sort things out and that if she fancied and if she could get a day off, she could come out and help her.

It was an olive branch of sorts: a hint to Loz that, by deciding to stay, she wasn't putting in place the first part of a move back to Tankerton that would exclude her or alter their lives in any permanent way.

Then she phoned Marianne, who begrudgingly agreed to allow her to take the entire following week off, due to the exceptional circumstances. Her irritation was a little bewildering – she was forever on at Peg to use up her annual leave because she wasn't going to have her taking the entire three weeks in a chunk at the end of the financial year. But Peg knew that Marianne wasn't one to say yes to anything without some sort of fight.

She took one last breath of fresh air, then went inside and made another cup of tea among the chaos of Doll's kitchen. Perhaps the week ahead of physical labour sorting out the bungalow would distract her from what Jean had told her about her father, and help her to reassess her plan.

She wasn't so sure she was going to be Jean's good little Meggy and not contact her father again. If what her aunt had said was true, he was even fairer game for any kind of treachery, and if Peg could channel some funds to Doll, then wasn't that still the right thing to do? Even more than before, he owed his mother everything.

She opened her red notebook and looked at the photograph of her mother. Then she unfolded the article and, once again, read it through.

TRAGIC WIFE MERCY KILLING

Something didn't feel quite right about Jean's story. Peg didn't think she liked Raymond, but she wasn't sure he measured up to quite the monster his sister would have her believe. She had learned her lesson about taking what she was told at face value.

She had a very strong sense that she didn't yet have the full picture.

But, with a sleepless night behind her, she was so tired she couldn't think straight. She slipped the article back into her notebook, which she tucked under her arm. Then, in a movement so often repeated it had ingrained itself into her bones, she opened the ceiling trapdoor to let down the sliding wooden ladder to the attic.

Balancing her cup of tea in one hand and steadying herself with the other, she climbed up to her musty old bedroom with its damp patches and mould spots where the dormer met the roof. Jumping quickly under the clammy sheets – the heating and insulation up there were minimal – she closed her eyes and started to count her breaths.

Then

I SHOULD HAVE REMEMBERED, OF COURSE: IT WAS A NASTY crash and Aunty Jean hurt her leg quite badly. It was never the same again for her after that.

Perhaps it has been eclipsed in my mind because it was the same week my mother died.

The very same week.

Perhaps that's a good enough excuse.

'Come on dear.'

Gramps has me by the hand and we're walking along a really long corridor in the hospital. I'm not all that keen on being there, but he says I've got to come along and cheer Nan and Aunty Jean up after the horrible car crash. I've got to be bright and happy, he says.

Luckily Nan was all right though, because the driver's side wasn't involved. But she's really upset.

'She blames herself, ducky,' Gramps said to me.

Gramps says I shouldn't be sad about Mummy dying because it's a blessing seeing as she was so poorly.

I've tried not to be sad but I'm not very good at it.

My main concern back then – and this I find incredible – was not to be a burden to my grandfather.

Remember: *my mother had just died.*

Quiet.

Breathe.

Even though she wasn't hurt, Nan's been staying in the hospital, sleeping on a little camp bed beside Aunty Jean. It's not really allowed, but Gramps says if Nan wants something she doesn't let people say no.

She says Aunty Jean needs her.

So it's just been me and Gramps at the bungalow. I try not to get in his way, but it's a bit boring just being with him. He's always in the shed, mending things or making things.

I've got a Caramac in my pocket. Gramps has bought it for me because he says I'm a good girl. I hope I'll have time to eat it before we get to see Aunty Jean.

But I don't, because Gramps steers me round a corner and we're in Aunty Jean's ward. She's in a private room. Daddy's paying for it because it was on account of Aunty Jean looking after him that Nan was driving her back and they had the crash.

I haven't seen Daddy at all since Easter, and I really miss him. But Gramps says he's too upset to see anyone at the moment.

As we walk towards the nurse's desk, Nan hurries out of one of the side-rooms, almost bumping right into us.

'Oh,' she says, putting her hand to her chest. 'Thank goodness you're here, Frank.'

'What's the matter, Dolly?' Gramps says. 'What is it, girl?'

'It's this place,' Nan says. 'They have no idea how to do things proper. It's filthy and I tell them it's filthy and they just look at me like I'm mad. And they're so rough with her; it's horrible to watch. And they're nearly all foreign too. Don't speak a word of English. It's not like it was in my day. And the doctors don't know a thing about her special needs. It's a very different thing, looking after a bigger person.'

She's standing ever so upright, her arms folded, her shoulders up near her ears, her mouth working.

'Hello, Nan!' I say, as happily as I can manage.

'Oh, hello, dearie,' Nan says, smiling at me. 'I'm sorry I'm a bit upsy-daisy, but I don't think we can stand to be in this place one more day.'

'What are you going to do, Dolly?' Gramps says.

Gramps was always asking Nan that. He never seemed to be able to make up his own mind on anything.

Was it because he was a weak man?

Or was it because Nan was a strong woman?

And do I remember that he wasn't all that well? That he had these pills he had to take to stop him – and I don't know why this phrase comes so quickly to me – 'having a turn'?

Poor Gramps.

'What are you going to do, Dolly?' Gramps asks again, because Nan is clearly deciding something.

'I'm bringing her home, Frank,' she says at last. 'I'm discharging her.'

'Do you think that's wise, dear?' Gramps asks.

'I wouldn't be doing it if I didn't, would I?'

'Of course not, dear.'

'She's all I've got left, Frank.'

Nan's face does a funny little wobble, and Gramps puts his arms round her and says, 'There, there, dearie,' and, 'You've got Meggy now, too.' Nan puts her hand out and I hold it for a while, not quite sure what's going on, but glad I can help her feel a bit better.

I go in to see Aunty Jean while Nan and Gramps go and sort out getting her out of this place. She's got her leg in plaster and a thing round her neck.

'Whiplash,' she says. 'It's ever so painful, Meggy.'

'Will you be able to walk again?' I say.

'Mummy says this is the final straw for my poor old legs,' Aunty Jean says. 'There'll not be much walking for me any more.'

'You're very lucky you've got the extension and she's so good at looking after you,' I say, again trying to talk brightly.

'I am, Meggy,' Aunty Jean says. 'With Mummy, I'm the luckiest Aunty Jean in the world. Here, pass me my cigs, will you.'

I get her Marlboros from her bedside table. It's a new pack, so I slide the cellophane off, a job I love doing because it always feels so neat and so lovely.

Then I help her to light up.

A minute later, a nurse bustles in with a clipboard, with Nan and Gramps hot on her heels.

'Mrs Thwaites. How many times have I got to tell you that smoking is not permitted in the wards?' She snatches Aunty Jean's cig clean out of her hands, which is so shocking I gasp.

'Which is another reason I want her out of here,' Nan says. 'It's dreadful they don't allow you to have the few simple pleasures you've got left. Sign the self-discharge paper, Jeanie, and we'll get you back home where we can look after you properly.'

The nurse holds out the clipboard, her mouth a thin line. Jean signs it with a great flourish, like she's King John signing the Magna Carta – which I've just been learning about at school – and the nurse leaves.

'We'll be home in time for supper, darling. I've got you a lovely ambulance,' Nan says. 'On the private as well. Raymond can pay for that and all.'

'That's the way, Dolly,' Gramps says.

'He can't take it with him,' Jean says.

'Jeanette!' Nan says, sharply, her face more serious than I've ever seen it. She's really telling Aunty Jean off with that face.

Aunty Jean blinks.

'Who can't take what where?' I ask, pulling the Caramac out of my pocket and unwrapping it.

'Ooh, Caramac,' Aunty Jean goes. 'Can I have a bit?'

'Go on Meggy,' Nan says. 'Your poor aunty.'

I hand it over and Aunty Jean breaks a piece off, which she hands back to me.

She eats the entire rest of it herself.

Eighteen

PEG WOKE IN HER OLD TINY EAVES ROOM AND LOOKED AT THE stars on the wallpaper twinkling down at her from the sloping walls. The cracked spines of her Enid Blytons were standing in wait like faithful friends in her crammed bookcase. She rolled onto her back and took in her collection of Spanish dolls, which stared dustily at her from the top of her wardrobe. Every school holiday there would be a new one, in a different-coloured flamenco dress, added, Peg had believed, by Doll.

But: *Spanish* dolls?

Now she wondered.

She swung her feet out of bed and landed her toes on the familiar texture of her old Spice Girls rug. The sunflower-shaped bedside clock said it was six o'clock. Disoriented, she reached for her phone and saw that it was in fact only eleven in the morning. She had managed to sleep for less than two hours. Loz had texted, though.

Lov 2 cum n hlp.

She had written in the text language Peg always found so hard to stomach.

Wl wrk somit ot. Don't do 2 mch. Lov u xxx

Peg crawled back under the covers – the insulation in the roof was so bad that in this sort of weather there was ice on the inside of the dormer window. She tried to call Loz back, but there was no reply, so instead she called the hospital.

Mrs Thwaites was stable, they said. She was awake now, and, although she was a little confused, seemed to be in better spirits than the day before. Peg checked on visiting times, then, wrapping herself in her parka, she got out of bed and braved the cold bedroom. Out of habit, she touched both the walls at the same time. These days she hardly had to reach out to do so.

Dressing in yesterday's jeans and some fresh underwear and an old T-shirt she found in her chest of drawers, she climbed down to the ground floor and looked around her at what she had to do.

Not being a fan of throwing things away, Doll had amassed hundreds of free council bin bags. Peg pulled out a handful and, trying to ignore her grandmother's voice muttering in her head about the plans she had for each bit of useless rubbish, she made a start on the lounge, sorting and bagging the obvious waste. She hauled the bags out into the garden, where she made two piles – one for recyclables and the other for landfill. Anything that struck her as ambiguous she placed in a big pile round the settee to be dealt with later, once she had cleared some space.

Her inner librarian was out in full force.

Into the bin bags went three carriers full of stray pop socks and stockings, six opened then abandoned packs of soggy Bourbon biscuits and five disgusting carrier bags full of used tissues – what had Doll been thinking? That she'd use them again?

Another bag went straight to the back garden full of hole-riddled woollens, which had been sitting, unheeded, in a mending pile for a decade or more.

Peg paused for a second when she recognised a long-outgrown pink and lime jumper that she had caught on something – barbed wire, perhaps – over ten years earlier. She wondered if she could save it because, although she couldn't recall the details, she remembered feeling really bad about ripping it; sick, even. Perhaps it was because she had witnessed Doll sitting in front of the telly knitting it for her, wincing through the pain in her arthritic fingers.

She hesitated about throwing it away, but as she lifted it from the pile, she realised it was crusted with moth larvae. There was no ambiguity. It had to go.

By lunchtime, she had a considerable pile of boxes and bags waiting for re-examination by the settee. But, more satisfyingly, the two mounds of bin bags in the back garden were at least twice that size. It was most rewarding, on each return to the lounge, to see a new, dusty square of swirly brown carpet emerge from under all the junk.

Peg's phone rang. She saw with the leap in her stomach that she still got just at the sight of her name that, at last, she was going to have her chance to talk to Loz. She sat on the settee to give her full attention, trying – as she now knew she also did as a child – not to scratch it.

'Hello, you,' Loz said. Peg could hear her inhaling on a roll-up, the hum of an extractor fan muffling heavy traffic and laughter behind her. It was the soundscape of the alleyway at the side of Seed, where they stored the bins and where the kitchen staff took their fag breaks.

'I didn't know you were on lunch today.'

'I've moved my shifts around so I can take tomorrow, Wednesday and Thursday off and come down to help you out. What time's the last train tonight?'

'Are you sure that's OK?' Peg said, feeling slightly alarmed. She hadn't planned on Loz spending the night in the bungalow. It felt wrong, somehow.

'No problem at all. Cara owes me one anyway. I worked an illegal seventy hours last week.'

'I've only got a tiny single bed here.'

'Cosy!'

'It's pretty grim, too. Pretty mucky.'

'You've told me. It'll be good to be part of making it nicer for her.' Loz sounded amused. Like she knew Peg had a problem with her staying.

'It'll be hard work, though.'

'Am I afraid of that? Oh look, Peg. Shut the fuck up. I'm coming down to help you and that's that.'

'Sorry. I'm being stupid, aren't I?'

'Yes, you are,' Loz said. 'A stupid cow.'

'But don't get the last train. Come tomorrow. Have a lie-in first.' Peg wanted to buy time so that she could get the worst of the jobs done before Loz arrived.

'We'll see what I feel like – hold on a sec.' Loz put her hand over the receiver and said something muffled to someone. 'Peggo, gotta go, babe,' she said, returning to her. 'There's an unprecedented run on my beetroot-horseradish starter. Love you.'

'Love you,' Peg said, smiling at Loz's name as it faded from the phone screen. She had, once again, had all her irrational qualms and hesitations impressively and comprehensively flattened.

It was an education.

She scratched the settee fabric and winced.

The pile of boxes and bags to be examined seemed to be her next job.

Her first cursory glances had revealed that, apart from the bags stuffed with Doll's Commonplace Books – which, of course, she wasn't going to start nosing through – some contained loose leaflets, others papers, letters and postcards. There were boxes of books, an old Bible and some baby clothes. Peg was curious about the contents, but given her recent discoveries about her family, wary of what she might uncover.

She took a deep breath, pulled a box towards her and flipped open its lid. It was full of old bank statements in faded ring binders. Pulling them out, she realised some went back as far as the 1970s. There was very little activity on the earlier statements: Frank's monthly pay from Times Newspapers – or, in later years, his pension – was the only entry on the credit side, and there was only one withdrawal every week. Doll always dealt in cash – Peg remembered a big fat red purse she kept it in – she said that way she could keep a track.

After checking that every single one of the ring binders dated back to the previous century, Peg bagged them up ready to be hauled out to her recycling pile. She knew somewhere in the back of her mind that you only needed to keep a financial record for the past seven years. Tucked into the front of the box was a bundle of more recent, unopened bank statements, as well as four empty bank-issued ring binders, one each for the four years since Peg left home. After a moment's pause where she considered

Doll's privacy, Peg started to open the bank statements, stacking them into a date-sorted pile with the most recent at the top.

As the statements piled up, they painted a worrying picture. Despite her regular pension – which, as the widow of a lifetime unionised newspaper print worker wasn't too bad at all – Doll had worked up a significant overdraft. Regular tiny cash withdrawals added up to a small mismatch between what she had coming in and what went out. Over time and with interest this had grown to a debt of over five thousand pounds.

Doll was in a financial mess.

If a sign were needed that Peg had to go to her father for money, then here it was.

But it wasn't going to be simple. Jean had told her not to do it, so there would be trouble from her if she did. And then how would she, Peg – the woman Loz had once said made the Dalai Lama look like a roguish old schemer – ever manage to deceive her father so massively? And even if she did, how far would she be able to string him along, perhaps even pretending to buy a flat and siphoning the funds off to Doll, before he took control? She couldn't imagine the man she had met in Spain letting her buy property with his money without having a very firm hand in the process.

Puzzling on this, she pulled over an old Gordon's Gin box heaped with photographs. Someone – Doll, perhaps, but it was difficult to tell – had written FOR HEYWORTH on it in thick black capital letters.

She was itching to see what was inside, because, as far as she knew, the only other photos in the house were the three in silver frames on the bookcase: the school portrait of herself which she had borrowed for the Facebook page, Doll and Frank's wartime wedding picture – being a printer and a nurse, they had both been in exempted trades – and one of a very young Jean looking voluptuous in a tight mini-dress, with a cropped-off Doll looking admiringly, adoringly even, up at her.

Peg wondered if she might find more of her mother in this box.

The first photograph she pulled out was of Jean sitting, cigarette in hand, in a gift-wrapped motorised wheelchair. It had a giant red ribbon tied round it and a bunch of tulips in the basket. Doll stood beside her and both women were beaming and exultant. It was good to see them looking so happy. On the back, Doll had written:

1 Nov 96. Jeanie gets her trolley.

Peg knew the trolley was now under a blue tarpaulin in the garden shed. It hadn't been used for nearly a decade, since Jean took to her bed for good. A few months earlier, Peg had suggested to Doll that it would make her life easier if she were to learn to use it.

Doll had dismissed the idea out of hand. 'I'm not handicapped,' she had said, as if Peg had insulted her.

The next photograph was also of Jean, but taken size-wise somewhere in between the miniskirt and the trolley pictures. Here she was, again, smiling and happy. Standing next to her was a man in a black lounge suit. One of his arms rested on her shoulders and with his other he held out her hand, showing the camera the sparkling ring on her engagement finger. He looked as if he might be handsome, but it was hard to tell, because his face had been scribbled over in green biro.

Jean? With a fiancé?

It clearly hadn't ended well.

Peg put the picture to one side to show her aunt. Despite the fact that it was mostly turning out difficult to swallow, she was developing an appetite for the truth.

Underneath that picture, Peg found two identical prints of an older black-and-white professional portrait with the Bermondsey photographer's name and address embossed in gold on the back of each deckled cardboard frame. In the formally posed studio portrait, a woman – shortish, plumpish and in a fifties patterned sundress, sat between a young girl in a nautical-themed, full-skirted dress and a younger boy with short back and sides who scowled up at the camera. On the woman's lap was a fat baby in a pale dress.

Although she had a pretty clear idea who the people in the portrait were, Peg slipped the top photograph out of its frame and looked on the back, where, as she had hoped, Doll had noted in the neat, slanting and looped handwriting of her former, pre-senile self:

2 April 1953, Jeanie, Doll, Keith and Franklin Raymond.

Peg turned the photo face up and peered at the uncle she never knew. His eyes stared shiny and blank back at her, like pennies.

Would his family have ended up like this had he not died?

She looked at Raymond in the picture and tried to read something into the way he stood next to the brother who – if Jean were to be believed – he would kill twelve months or so after this photo was taken. But there was nothing to see. It all looked perfectly innocent, just a picture of three kids and their mum.

She propped one photograph on top of the bookcase and the other on top of the fiancé picture, to take through to Jean. Then she carried on rummaging.

At first glance, she thought the next picture she pulled out was a smaller version of the school portrait of herself that Doll kept framed on the bookshelf. On closer inspection she realised that, blue blazer and striped tie aside, the girl looked nothing like her – her curly hair was in fact red, and she had freckled pale skin, sharp, Anglo-Saxon features and a mouth full of cemented-in braces.

Why would there be a photograph of some schoolgirl stranger in this box?

At least, Peg thought she was a stranger. But something about that face, that hair, unsettled her, made something shift in her stomach.

Perhaps it was just the uniform and all the misery it signified. Possibly the school had accidentally sent this portrait home instead of her own, and Doll hadn't got round to returning it?

She slipped the photograph inside her notebook, to think about later.

Perhaps it would come to her who it was.

Near the bottom of the box, she came across an old Kodak wallet with *For Raymond xxx* written on it in a hand she didn't recognise. In it was a series of colour photographs of a small, pretty, blonde woman, dressed in the way only small, pretty, blonde women seem to manage. In one she was in a bar, blowing a kiss at the photographer. In another she stood in front of the Flamingos doorway – although with its neon and fresh paint it looked a world away from the shabby place Peg had visited. In another, Raymond – much younger than the man she had met in Spain, but still recognisable – stood next to the blonde as she perched on the bonnet of a shiny white Jag.

The tiny woman made him look enormous, far bigger than the Raymond Peg had stooped to greet, and there was something proprietorial about the way he stood beside her, his big arm on her dainty young shoulders.

What were *these* photos doing here? Did her father have yet another family that she didn't know about? Was this a half-sister that Doll and Jean had seen fit to keep from her, 'for fear of hurting'? Peg bent closer to look. Even though her knowledge of what constituted a paternal pose was limited, she could see that Raymond was striking something quite different in this picture.

This was a classic rich-man and younger-woman pairing: sexual and possessive.

There was nothing to date any of the images, but from the woman's hair and clothes they didn't look like they were from as far back as the seventies, and one of the few facts she knew about her parents was that they were married in 1979.

So, as well as being a child murderer and wife-killer, was Raymond an adulterer too?

And why did this not surprise her?

She put a couple of the pictures of the blonde with the other photographs she had pulled out.

She wanted some answers.

As she stood up slowly, shaking her leg, which was tingling with pins and needles from having sat still for so long, the tinny sound of Jean's buzzer made her jump nearly clean out of her dusty skin.

'Meggy? Meggy? Are you there?' Jean wailed. 'I need you! It's urgent. OH!'

Nineteen

PEG LEAPED FOR THE BACK DOOR, GRABBED JEAN'S KEY AND dashed round to the extension. When she reached the bedroom she found Jean trying to heave herself up out of bed.

'Oh, there you are,' Jean said, falling back against the pillows, her voice weak from effort, sweat beading on her upper lip. 'Thank goodness. I didn't know if you was still there . . .'

'What's the matter?' Peg said.

'Oh, Meggy. I've run out of ciggies and the girl didn't leave me no more.'

'I thought you were in real trouble, Aunty Jean. I thought something awful had happened.'

'Sorry, I'm sure.'

Peg went through to Jean's kitchenette and looked in the cigarette drawer, where Julie stockpiled the Marlboros. By Peg's reckoning, Jean got through three packs a day at least, which might have made some sort of contribution to the hole in Doll's bank account. She slipped out a new pack and removed the cellophane – an act that still brought her pleasure, despite her irritation at her aunt.

'Could you pour me a little Guinness, please darling, too? And perhaps fetch us some crisps?' Jean called from the bedroom.

Peg poured the Guinness, put a tray together and took it back through to the bedroom.

'The girl says you're piling up bin bags out there,' Jean said, after she had settled herself down with crisps, stout and a cigarette.

'It's just pure rubbish, Aunty Jean. No one could want any of it. Some of it's just got to go; you couldn't move in there. And it's filthy.'

'It can't be that bad, surely?'

'You wouldn't believe how bad it's got, Aunty Jean.'

Jean wouldn't know, of course. Since she had got too big to wrench herself into the trolley, Jean hadn't been anywhere but her bed.

'Poor Mummy.' Jean picked at the duvet, using exactly the same gesture as Doll had in the hospital, although where her mother's shrunken fingers were sharp and worried, Jean's were lost and grabbing, like a baby pounding at the breast.

'I'm only clearing out the rubbish and cleaning things up. You really couldn't walk about in there without tripping over something. If we want her back—'

'Which we do.'

'Which we most certainly do—'

'She'd rather die than go in a home.'

'I know that, Aunty Jean, and I'm doing everything I can to keep her here.'

'Oh, I know you are, Meggy. You're a good girl. I know that. It's just she likes her stuff around her, and it would kill her to lose it all.'

'I know.'

'And she's a very private lady. She'd hate you nosing through all her stuff.' Jean looked up at Peg with one eyebrow arched. 'All her Commonplaces and stuff.'

'You said. Look, I'm not nosing. I'm just glancing to see what's what. And of course, I'd never look at her Commonplaces.'

'They're like her diaries.'

'I know that. Look, so far it's just old papers and photographs anyway. No incriminating evidence yet.'

Jean looked up sharply. 'What do you mean, incriminating?'

'It was just a joke.'

Jean picked up a hand mirror from her table and looked at herself, patting her hair down.

'I found some photos, actually,' Peg said. 'You might find them interesting. I think there's one of Keith.'

Jean continued to peer at her reflection, smoothing the line of her lipstick with her finger.

'And there's a couple of you looking pretty glam.'

'Oh,' Jean said, now checking her nostrils.

'Tell you what. I'll bring some through. See if you can tell me any more about them.'

'I'm a bit tired, though,' Jean said, laying her mirror down on the bed.

'It won't take long, Aunty Jean. I've got to go and visit Nan in a bit.'

'If you like, then, dear.'

When Peg let herself back into Jean's extension with the photographs, she was struck by a smell so strong that it overpowered even the stale cigarette stink. A keening, moaning sound came from Jean's bedroom.

'Aunty Jean, are you all right?'

'Ooh. Oh dear,' Jean said, squirming in her bed. 'I think I've had a bit of an accident. I've made a mess, Meggy.'

Reaching the bedroom, Peg looked at her immobile aunt beached on the bed and sighed. She had helped Doll often enough, in the days before Julie, so she knew what had to be done. From Jean's supplies cupboard she pulled out wipes, a clean pad, a waste bag and a disposable mat to save soiling the bed.

The council had installed a system involving straps, a hoist and the inflatable mattress, which meant that it was possible even for little Julie to change Jean single-handed. When the woman from the medical aids company came round to draw up the specifications, she had actually thought that Peg was joking when she told her that the even tinier Doll had managed to care for Jean with no lifting equipment whatsoever.

With a little direction from Jean about which hooks went into which eyelets, which Velcro strap did up where, Peg managed to roll her over onto one side, so that she could get at her back.

'Don't take too long,' Jean said, panting through the flesh of her face. 'It's hard for me to breathe like this.'

Peg laid the mat underneath her and removed her pad.

'Have you got a bit of an upset tummy then?' she said, breathing through her mouth as she started to clean her up.

'I had a curry last night,' Jean said. 'The new girl didn't give me enough, so I had to have a curry.'

'How did you manage that?'

'Mummy had a word with the Taj Mahal. In case of an emergency. They've got a key and they can deliver straight to my bed.' Even from her squashed position, Jean said this as if it were the most marvellous thing in the world.

Doll had stressed how important it was to 'get everything down there completely clean', otherwise Jean would end up with impetigo, a urinary infection, or worse. So Peg took great care, making sure every deep crease and dimpled fold was spotless.

'Don't forget the talc,' Jean said. She was in a great deal of discomfort, gasping for breath through gritted teeth.

Obediently, Peg sprinkled medicated talcum powder over the area she had cleaned. Since she had last cared for her, Jean must have put on a good few stone – she was bigger than ever, which was odd, because Julie was supposed to keep her on a healthy diet. Peg wondered how liberally Jean interpreted 'an emergency'; perhaps feeling a bit peckish was reason enough for her to call in a curry.

When the waste was sealed in the special scented disposal bags, Peg allowed herself to breathe through her nose. She strapped on Jean's new pad, tugged a fresh pair of netting retaining pants over the top and rearranged Jean's smock to cover her modesty.

'Let me down now,' Jean said. 'Let me down, Meggy!'

Peg parted the straps and deflated the mattress, and Jean gradually subsided onto her back.

'Thank you, Meggy.' Jean smiled up at her as sweetly as if she had just received a bunch of flowers.

After spraying the room with Oust, Peg carried the bagged-up waste to the wheelie bin in the back garden, silently praying that some cruel twist of genetics wouldn't see her end up like her aunt.

She would truly rather be dead.

She wondered if that was how her mother had felt about her own illness. Whether she *had* in fact begged with Raymond to help her out.

In Jean's kitchenette, Peg washed her hands thoroughly and gave them a quick blast of the sanitiser from one of the bottles Doll kept posted in every room – beacons of hygiene standing as constant reminders of how well-run her dusty and neglected home had once been.

'Cleaner,' she used to tell Peg proudly, 'than an hospital.'

Back in the bedroom, she found Jean smoking a cigarette, eating a biscuit and fiddling with the remote. *Cash in the Attic* was on at full volume.

'It's my programme,' Jean protested as Peg went to turn down the volume. 'Hadn't you better go and see Mummy now?'

'I've got a bit of time,' Peg said. 'The train's not for an hour or so. I thought we could look at these.' She reached for the photographs on the dressing table, where she had left them while she changed Jean.

'But it's my programme,' Jean said.

'I'll record it for you,' Peg said. She took hold of the remote and pressed the red button. Then she switched off the TV.

Jean sighed heavily and let her head flop back onto the pillows.

'Please, Aunty Jean. It won't take long. Look.' Peg thrust the top photograph into Jean's hand.

'Pass me my glasses,' Jean said.

She peered at the picture, as if having difficulty focusing on it.

'Here.' Peg switched on the bedside light and angled it so there was no chance of her aunt saying she couldn't see.

Jean held it up, her lips working as if around some imaginary food.

'Yes,' she said at last. 'That's Keith.' She rubbed her fat fingers over the photograph, as if trying to wipe a smear from it. 'Me and Raymond and Keith. Before, obviously.'

Peg handed her the next picture.

'And that's me and Tony. At our engagement.'

'Tony?'

'Oh, it was a long time before you was born.' Jean sighed and peered again at the photograph. 'It was before I got my weight, too, look.'

'You both look very dashing,' Peg said. 'He looks very handsome under that green biro.'

'He was,' Jean said, grimly. 'A handsome devil.'

'You didn't marry him though, did you?'

'He turned out a bad 'un.' Jean clamped her lips together. 'Vanished completely. Just as well, really. It turned out on top of buggering off, he was a crook and he played around with the dolly birds.'

'Crook?'

'Your father employed him. And that Tony thanked him by embezzling.'

'I'm sorry.'

'No need. It wasn't your fault.' Jean let out a great sigh and turned, smiling brightly to Peg. 'What are them other ones, then?' She laid the picture of her fiancé on the bedspread and pointed at the remaining photographs in Peg's hand.

'I was wondering who this girl is. And that's Dad, isn't it?' She handed over the photographs of the blonde.

Jean looked at them, and as her eyes focused on the images she became stiller, more concentrated. 'You found these next door?' She looked up sharply.

Peg nodded. 'In one of the boxes Nan kept by her chair.'

'They shouldn't've been in there,' Jean said. Then, before Peg could really register what was happening, she started to rip the photographs up. 'This is a girl that should not be remembered,' she said as she tore. 'She were trouble then and she'd be trouble now, if she wasn't in the past. And him and all.'

She picked up the photo of Tony and started tearing it, too. Then the family portrait of Doll, Raymond, Jean and Keith.

Peg stood there speechless as Jean continued, shredding the photos until they were tiny pieces of confetti, her cheeks wobbling, the flesh on her arms swinging as she worked. Then, finally, when she was finished, she brushed the pieces away from the bed as if they were radioactive, as if they could in some way harm her. When at last the bed was clear, she looked up at Peg.

'Are there any more in there?'

'There are loads of photographs.'

'I mean of them. Of that . . . that floozy and him,' Jean said, almost spitting the words out. There was something dark in her look; something that could have been anger, but which also had the colour of fear in it.

'A few. I think so, yes.'

'Get rid of them. Burn them.'

'But what about Nan? What if she wants to keep them?'

'Listen,' Jean said, grabbing Peg's arm and pulling her close. 'Mummy doesn't even know who that little whore is. She's never heard of her, all right? She means nothing to her and she never, ever will. Understand?'

'Yes. But if she didn't know her, why did she keep the photos?'

'You ask too many questions, Meggy. I want you to stop it now. It's no good for any of us.'

As if she had been unplugged, Jean fell back onto her pillows. She closed her eyes and sighed so heavily that, for a second she confounded the automatic bellows that worked so hard to keep her air-bed inflated.

'Hadn't you better go and catch that train, Meggy?' she said at last, without opening her eyes.

Then

'IT'S NO COINCIDENCE THAT YOU JUST TAKE ONE LETTER AWAY from brother to get bother,' Aunty Jean tells me as I do her toenails for her.

I'm doing what Nan has taught me, following the instructions I've written down in my Commonplace Book. I'm almost as good as a professional chiropodist, which means foot doctor.

'Dr Meggy come to save your soles!' I say to Aunty Jean's feet whenever I start my sessions.

I'm about nine here.

Aunty Jean only walks a little now – from her bed to her toilet or to her trolley, which is parked at the top of the slope outside her back door. But Nan says even that little time plays havoc with her poor feet, the weight she is now. They're completely flat underneath, completely puffed up on top, and all splayed out with hard skin and little white bobbly bits which Nan says

197

is thrush, which I think is quite funny, like a bird growing out of her toes.

Then I look up thrush and I see it's down to sweaty feet that don't see the air enough. So I tell Aunty Jean this, and every time I'm in there I make sure those feet are out of their covers, having an air.

'You're as good as Mummy,' Aunty Jean says.

'I'm training her up well, aren't I?' Nan goes as she bustles by with a pile of clean sheets for the airing cupboard.

I lift Aunty Jean's feet out of the warm water bath I've been soaking them in.

'I wouldn't mind a brother, though,' I say as I start to file away at her softened calluses.

'No, you're better off on your own, Meggy,' Aunty Jean says. 'So you don't have to share with anyone else. The things I had to give up because I had brothers.'

'Brothers?' I say, laughing. 'You only had the one brother, silly.'

'Yes. Silly me. Brother, I meant.'

She just blustered over her slip and I swallowed it whole.

Hook line and sinker.

If I hadn't been such a gullible child, I'd be having an easier time now.

Stop.

I've got to stop blaming myself.

Breathe.

'What did you have to give up?' I say, wiping the flakes of dead skin away from her feet then patting them dry.

'Where do I start? I always had to share everything, from Mummy's cuddles to sweets, to felt tips. I even had to share my pet rabbit.'

'No!' I go, using an orange stick to scrape away her cuticles.

'Yes. I won him in a raffle with my own ticket, but Mummy said I had to share him with Raymond. "You must share, Jeanie", she said.'

'That's not fair,' I go.

'He didn't do his fair share of the work, though, and the poor, poor rabbit died in the end.'

'No!'

'Yes. And it was all his fault, because he didn't shut the cage door properly after he'd been cuddling it and a fox got it and ate it all up except for the little powder-puff tail.'

'That's horrid.'

'I loved that rabbit like it was my baby,' Aunty Jean says. 'Keith, I called it.'

SHE CALLED HER RABBIT KEITH!

I'm about to say what a funny name that is for a rabbit, but I look up at her and I see her eyes are tiny staring slits, like she was that fox getting ready to pounce.

'But I suppose Daddy was only a silly little boy back then,' I say instead.

'He was old enough to know better.' And just for one second, Aunty Jean turns her angry stare on me. But then she goes back all soft again and looks at her toes. 'You're doing a lovely job there, Meggy. Light me a cig, will you?'

I do as she asks and she sits there puffing away while I rub the special oil round her cuticles and set to with the clippers.

'Gently now,' she says. Once I cut a bit too low and she screamed the bungalow down. I'm ever so careful now.

Aunty Jean rests her cig on the pelican ashtray and helps herself to a chocolate digestive from the pack by her bed.

'Want one?' she says, only half holding the pack out to me.

'I'm all right, thanks,' I say.

Thrushy feet don't really make me very hungry for chocolate biscuits.

'And of course brothers are always the favourites,' Jean goes on. 'We girls don't get a look in if there's a boy. If there's a fight, and you go to your mummy and say that he started it, she'll never believe you.'

I rub the anti-fungal cream into her feet, taking care to get it right down between the toes. Then I wipe my hands with a tissue and fetch the five bottles of nail varnish from the dressing table.

'What colour is it today, madam?' I hope one day she'll choose all five and I can paint each toe a different colour, but she hasn't yet.

'Red, I think,' she says.

I put the toe dividers on – her toes are so puffy they overlap. Then I lean over her feet, holding my breath so that I don't smudge. Nan's shown me this, too. Three firm lines up the nail, the first in the middle and the other two either side of it. Not too much varnish on the brush.

I really am like a foot doctor doing this.

'Ten-bob note goes missing from Mummy's purse and you tell her you saw him take it, but he says he didn't, and guess who gets believed, eh? Not the sister, that's for sure.'

'Poor you,' I go.

'He eats all the biscuits, and who gets the blame? Old

muggins here. No, Meggy, you're lucky you don't have to share anything or anyone with anyone else.'

I nod as I screw the nail varnish lid back on.

But I'm thinking that if I had anything or anyone to share and if there was someone I had to share her or it with, I wouldn't be unlucky.

I'd be glad.

I'd be really glad.

And now of course I wonder if there ever was a rabbit called Keith.

Twenty

'HOW IS MRS THWAITES?'

'Mrs Thwaites . . . ?'

The nurse's hostility was only slightly undermined by the seasonal tinsel headband she wore like some sort of ersatz halo.

'Mrs Thwaites. She was admitted last night.'

'Oh.' The nurse jiggled her mouse and peered at something on her computer. 'Yes, she's not doing too badly. A little confused, but she's eaten well and she's been, so it's all good signs. Oh.' She looked up at Peg for the first time and saw the bunch of lilies she had bought in the hospital shop. 'You can't bring them in here.'

'But . . .'

'It's an infection risk. Hospital policy.'

'So why do they sell them in the shop?'

'You'll have to ask them that. We have to take care on the wards. I'll keep them in the nurses' room until you go.'

'I've brought her wash bag and some overnight things,' Peg said.

'Good. Now if you'll excuse me. You'll find Mrs Thwaites

in bay F.' The nurse took the flowers from Peg and swept them away into a room with a laminated 'Private' sign on it.

Peg blinked and shook her head as if trying to clear her ears of water. Then she found her way to Doll, who was fast asleep, looking even tinier than before, lying with her mouth open and her hand still pick-picking at the blanket.

Peg took her hand and held it lightly. A sweet smell rose from her grandmother's body, like mouldy bread or very old biscuits in a tin. Poor old Dolly, she thought. How awful to have given all your love to your family and for it to come to this – a long-dead husband, a son who won't talk to you and a bed-bound daughter, completely dependent on others for her well-being.

But then, if a person lived to be as old as this, wasn't a certain souring inevitable? Didn't things always, ultimately, end badly? There's almost always disease and disability at the end of a long life, and no family was ever simple.

Peg checked herself, shocked. When did she start thinking this way?

When everything had started to get complicated.

It was as if Doll had been the seal on a Pandora's box of secrets, which, as she unravelled, flew out like moths hungry for fabric to gnaw into and lay their eggs.

As if she could read her granddaughter's thoughts, Doll sighed heavily and opened her eyes. 'Hello, Meggy dear,' she said, as if she were in her lounge and Peg had just been out in the kitchen.

'Hello, Nan,' Peg said, leaning forward and kissing her on the cheek.

'I'm ever so hungry, dear. Is it lunchtime yet?'

'You've had your lunch, Nan. Shall I see if I can find you a cup of tea and a bit of cake?'

'You're a good girl,' Doll said, and Peg went off to the WRVS shop at the ward entrance, where an apple-cheeked woman of indeterminate middle age presided over a tempting array of home-made cakes and biscuits. She selected a nice slice of fruitcake for Doll and a slab of chocolate sponge for herself, then took them back to the ward.

Doll polished her cake off before she even touched her tea.

'Nothing wrong with your appetite, then, Nan.'

'I want to go home,' Doll said. 'It's horrible in here. She—' She lowered her voice and pointed to a red-faced woman in the bed opposite sitting with her hands folded in front of her and gazing out of the window. 'She swears all the time. It's sending me demented, Meggy. Makes my ears bleed. And her next door –' Doll nodded to the closed curtain to her left – 'farts all the time. It's parp, parp –' she blew a raspberry – 'twenty-four hours a day. I don't think I've slept more than a wink all night long, Meggy.'

'You'll be out of here before you know it, Nan.'

'They don't run this place properly either. It's filthy – look at that.' She pointed to a ball of dust and hair resting where two grimy skirting boards met in the corner of the cubicle. 'I'd have got the chop if I'd let it get like that. The matron's not in charge and they all seem to just do their own thing.' She leaned forward and whispered: 'And not one of them speaks proper English.'

'I'm sure they do, Nan.'

'And they've got to clear up. The mess is dreadful – there's blood all over the floor. Look at it. Can you get the mop, Jeanie?'

'It's Meggy, Nan.'

'Meggy?' Doll peered at Peg and nodded. 'Where's Jeanie, then?'

'She's back at the bungalow.'

'Is she now? Silly girl. Doesn't she know she's needed here? But Meggy, what I don't get is how those rooms there,' Doll said, pointing to two doors off the main corridor at the end of her branch of the ward, 'are empty and I've got to be in this bed here. Why can't I go in them?'

'I suppose they're private rooms, Nan.'

'Oh.' Doll looked glum. 'Private, are they?'

''Fraid so.'

'Can't Raymond pay?'

'Eh?'

'He's the reason we're in here, isn't he?'

'Not this time, Nan.'

'Really?'

'You just had a bit of collywobbles.'

'Oh. I thought . . .' Doll's hand strayed over her hair, as if trying to find somewhere to land.

'I'll ask about the private rooms, if you like. Just to make sure.'

'Don't make a fuss on my account though, will you, Meggy?'

'Of course not.'

'I don't want a fuss made.'

'No.'

Peg settled Doll down with a *People's Friend* magazine and packet of chocolate digestives she had bought at the same time as the flowers. Then she kissed her and, with a promise to come back the next day, started to put her parka on.

'I wish Jeanie could pop in and see me,' Doll said. 'She never comes and visits.'

'It's a bit difficult for her, Nan. Remember?'

'Is she still running round after that bastard Tony?'

Peg blinked. How strange that Doll should mention him just

hours after she had uncovered his photograph. 'It's not Tony, Nan.'

'He's a right little fucker,' Doll spat.

Peg had to stop herself from gasping at not only the language but also the venom in her grandmother's voice. The woman opposite – the one Doll said swore a lot – shot over a disapproving glance.

'Aunty Jean's a bit stuck in her bed,' Peg said, steering her away from the subject of Tony.

'Oh yes,' Doll said, shaking herself as if she were coming to after a dream. 'She's an invalid, my daughter. Did you know that?'

On her way out, Peg had a word with a different nurse about the side rooms.

'They're sixty-five pounds a night and we can't guarantee that we won't need them for acute cases, but they're free at the moment.'

'I'll take one,' Peg said, suddenly reckless. 'For my nan.'

She signed the necessary forms, but slipped away before Doll was moved, leaving instructions that she wasn't to be told the details of who was paying and how much.

On the rackety, delayed train back to Whitstable, she thought about money. She had five hundred pounds available on an emergency credit card, taken out when she moved out of the bungalow as a financial safety net. And what was this if not an emergency? But sixty-five only went into five hundred what, eight times?

Eight nights.

By taking on the private room, she had made her statement of intent.

She had finally made her decision.

Twenty-One

Dear Dad,

Sitting at Doll's dining table, which she had pulled out into the newly cleared lounge floor space, Peg stared at the words. Writing them had set a coldness into her pen hand that even the hissing gas fire couldn't touch. She took a bite of the pizza she had picked up on the walk back from the railway station – without Loz's good influence, she was reverting to bachelor-girl form.

She crossed out the words and replaced them with:

Dear Raymond,

That felt better. Less involved. First she had to pretend to eat a slice of humble pie.

I'm sorry about my behaviour when I visited you in Spain.

If nothing else, her fancy schmancy school had taught her how to write a good, formal letter – the clothing for all sorts of intentions.

As you can imagine, while our meeting was hard for you, it was even worse . . .

She scrubbed that last word out.

. . . more challenging for me. I am afraid that I quite disgraced myself, both by my behaviour in front of you, and by the way I took my leave. I am truly sorry.

As Peg drafted, she had her legs, toes and eyes crossed. The language was coming out stiff and wrong, like a Victorian novel, but it seemed to fit the occasion.

I have thought long and hard about this.

It was descending into cliché. But what could she do? Wasn't the position she was adopting – that of the contrite daughter – something of a stereotype in itself? She stopped and pressed her fingertips against her eyelids, screwing her cheeks up into her palms. It certainly didn't reflect the complexity of her actual stance.

How *did* she actually feel? Shocked? Dismayed? That wasn't it. Because despite his little-man-with-a-big-chip-on-his-shoulder unlikeability, bizarrely, something in her understood Raymond. She felt sorry for the suffering and isolation brought on him by the things he had done in the past, his mistakes.

If he *had* done those things in the past.

She also pitied him because his sister hated him so.

Yet, on top of all of that, still she despised him.

If only he hadn't been such a twat when they met.

I have thought long and hard about this and, if it's still going, I would like to take you up on your offer of help.

There, she had said it. The pact was made. She hoped he was as blind as she suspected. She hoped he wouldn't see that there was no way the real Peg would write those words. The Peg without the ulterior motive.

But then, what did he know of the real Peg?

I won't ever bring up the past again, and I will play by your rules. I am sorry to have caused you any upset and I would like us to move forward together.

Because, with him living all the way over in Spain, how often would she actually have to go and see him face to face? It would be easy to pretend to be dutiful from a distance. Then she could divert the funds to sorting out Doll's problems. She took a deep breath and forged on.

My immediate problem is that I've got myself into a bit of financial difficulty, as it happens. I owe about seven thousand pounds on various bank accounts and credit cards. Can I, as your daughter, ask you to help me out? It would be great to be able to make a fresh start.

Was that too bald? Or could she get away with it? Peg thought perhaps she had better sleep on it. Slipping Raymond's business card between the pages to mark her place, she closed her notebook, sat back and looked at the Gordon's Gin box full of photographs.

Why did Jean react like that to the pictures of the blonde woman?

What was she trying to hide?

It was more than likely that she had been trying, in her own clumsy way, to protect Peg from photographs of her father with his arm round someone other than her mother.

Her reaction had been on the strong side, but then Jean was like that. Hemmed in by her own flesh, her world had contracted so much that the slightest thing – a spilled cup of tea, or burned toast, say – took on apocalyptic importance.

Peg leaned forward, pulled the Gordon's box towards her and looked in it for the wallet with the other pictures of the blonde woman. She thought she had put it back on the top, but it wasn't there. She rummaged down into the box, but came up with nothing. In the end, she tipped the whole boxful of photographs out on the floor and went through them carefully. The wallet was nowhere to be found.

Frowning, Peg scooped everything back into the box.

She sat back on the settee, closed her eyes and scratched the material.

The sound of the gas fire began to throb as if someone were playing with the volume. Like in a film, she saw a little boy push a baby, fat-bottomed in terry nappies, off a steep dock wall into the murky tidal Thames. She heard head meet stone then body meet water, then the desperate splashing of a child trying not to drown. Then the image cross-faded to Raymond, moving a pillow to cover her mother's beautiful face, holding her brown hand down in his own pasty fingers as her life ebbed away. In both scenes, Peg tried to see her father's face, but the focus kept slipping away. He was there, but she didn't know *how* he was there. Then his arm grew, like a snake uncoiling, and wrapped itself round the blonde woman. Then the two of them, Raymond and the blonde, turned to her and pointed.

Peg's eyes shot open.

These were scenes she couldn't have witnessed, but they were so bold, so vivid, she saw them as if she had been there. How could she be sure that the memories she was recovering weren't also imagined?

How was she going to find out the truth?

Did she really *have* to find out the truth?

Perhaps she should just give up. Take the money and run. Then let it all lie.

But with what she knew now, how could she?

She pulled her parka from the back of the dining chair, tucked it over herself, and curled up on the settee.

The thing was, she had a niggling feeling she didn't know the half of it.

Twenty-Two

SHORTLY BEFORE MIDNIGHT, PEG WAS PULLED FROM SLEEP BY the buzz of her phone. She blearily held the screen up in front of her and saw that it was a text from Loz.

Gr8! Got last train! Gets n @ 1.30. Drexons?

Excited and dismayed in equal measure – she hadn't been expecting Loz till the morning, and needed to prepare the bungalow for her arrival – Peg texted back.

I'll be there Xxx

She spent the next hour sorting out the bungalow. Part of her felt embarrassed that, like some sort of suburban housewife, she would feel shame at Loz seeing the state of the place. But she was powered on by the truly cat-piss-rich stench of the bathroom, which invaded the rest of the house. Peg had always thought it was down to the greasy toilet and the soiled floor around it. She had only been able to stage quick and rough clean-ups when she visited in the past – if she stayed longer than her allotted five minutes in the toilet, Doll would be banging at the door asking her if she was all right in there. So, to avoid cross-questioning on the state of her bowels and force-feeding of laxatives, she had never given it the thorough clean it needed.

Now was her chance, so she scoured the bowl and the floor, threw away the mouldering toilet brush and scraped the dust from the pipe behind the toilet. But even after all this, the smell persisted.

Then she opened the cupboard under the sink.

It seemed that Doll had used incontinence pads, which was news to Peg. And after they were soaked she had thriftily hung on to them, stuffing them into this cupboard so tightly that when Peg opened the door, she was presented with a piss-stiffened papier mâché wall.

With rubber gloves on, she gouged the mess out, bagged it up and put it out the back. Then, after filling another sack with the contents of the bathroom cabinet – enough out-of-date pharmaceuticals to stock a small chemists' shop, empty shampoo bottles, rolled and squeezed toothpaste tubes, dog-ends of soap, threadbare flannels and used cotton wool balls – she bleached every surface.

A little late, and with bleach fumes still stinging her nostrils, she rushed down to the station to meet Loz. The air was even more brittle with cold than it had been the night before, and, when she got there, the icy platforms were deserted and the ticket barriers open.

Peg wandered onto the platform and sat in a frosted glass alcove, sheltered from the sharp, bitter wind. An almost inde-cipherable announcement apologised that, due to a signalling failure, the train from London Victoria, due in at one thirty, was delayed by twenty-five minutes.

She hunkered down into her parka and listened to the sound of the sea, carried inland by the wind. The delay, the cold, the sodium-yellow light and bitter, metallic tang of the station could have pulled her spirits down, but excitement at the prospect of seeing Loz buoyed her. It had been two long days and, even though they were now just over a year into their relationship, her stomach still turned over and the world seemed a little lighter at the thought of her girl. Limerence, it was called. She had found the word in a self-help book.

At last the lights of the train approached, first silently, then, as the engine drew closer, the sound of wheels on rails carried over the night air, swishing in time with the distant sound of the waves. Five seagulls rose from the tracks like grey ghosts, calling into the night sky. And then the train was there, slowing, screeching past Peg and drawing its caterpillar of near-empty carriages to a halt on the platform, showing her the squashed face of a lolling drunk home from a night on the town, his eyes shut, his skin yellow where it pressed against the grimy glass. For a second Peg worried that he might have missed his stop and wondered whether she should jump on and shake him awake. But then she remembered that – to use one of Loz's favourite phrases – it wasn't her problem.

She looked up and down the platform. No one was getting off. Peg hurried along the length of the train. Perhaps Loz, too, had fallen asleep. But then the doors beeped and there she was, stepping out of the final door, her hair dishevelled, her long unbuttoned duvet coat almost sweeping the concrete ground.

Peg ran to greet her. With a smile on her face as wide as the train, she swept her into her big, strong arms and there they stayed as the train exhaled and beeped, then slid its doors shut and pulled away into the night.

'Nearly missed the stop, I was so taken up in this.' Loz held up a paperback, one of her true crime books.

'God how I've missed you,' Peg said fondly, wrinkling her nose at the gory cover of the book and doing up the top buttons of Loz's coat.

'Me too you,' Loz said. She stood back, holding Peg's face in her hands. 'I'm so excited to see the place that made you.'

'Don't get your hopes up too high. Come on. Let's get you home.' She took Loz's big rucksack from her and hauled it on to her back. 'Jesus. What you got in here?'

'Stuff for me for a couple of days,' Loz said, hoisting a bulging cotton shopper onto her own shoulder. 'And I thought you'd need some more clothes, too. And some books. You left in such a rush. Can we go your seafront way? I really want to see it.'

As they walked down towards the water, Peg told Loz about the letter she had drafted to her father, asking him for money.

'Quite right too. He owes you everything, Peg.'

'It's not for me though, remember. It's for Nan.'

'Whatever. Screw him for everything he's got. Bastard.'

They walked hand in hand until they reached the sea. The moon, just on the wane, hung like a great ball in the sky, streaking silver across the water, outlining Loz's pale cheekbones as she stood and took it all in.

'Gorgeous,' she said. 'Just how I imagined it. Just breathe in that salty air.'

'That salty, shitty, muddy air.'

'Nicer than Leicester Square at chucking-out time though. Can we stop for a minute? Catch our breath.'

They sat on a park bench on the shingle, facing the sea. It

was dedicated to a Florence Ivory, who had loved the view.

'So you've got a picture of your mum, then?' Loz said.

Peg reached in her bag for her red book and slipped out the article with the photograph.

'She's beautiful,' Loz said, holding the paper out in the moonlight. 'Got your eyes, see?' Then she bent to read the article. '"Tragic Wife Mercy Killing". Jeeze. Still, in some cases it's a mark of love. My *oma* keeps going on about wanting Naomi to take her to Zurich.' She hunched her shoulders and assumed an exaggerated Yiddish accent. 'Ven my mind goes, I vant you to throw me to the dogs.'

'But Jean says Mum *didn't* ask Raymond to help her die.'

'No way.' Loz's eyes grew wide.

'She also said that Keith didn't fall off the dock: Raymond pushed him.'

Loz blew out her cheeks.

'I'm not sure what to believe, though. It seems like she just wants to make him out to be totally evil. And then I showed her these photos and she acted really weird.'

'Photos?'

Peg told her about the pictures of the blonde, and how Jean had reduced them to paper snowflakes. 'I suppose she doesn't want me to hear about my father being unfaithful to Mum.'

'But she doesn't mind telling you that he killed her, and his baby brother?'

Peg stood up. 'Can we start walking again? It's bloody freezing.'

Loz took her arm and, as they carried on along the seafront towards Tankerton, Peg bit her lip against the cold and looked at the waves folding and unfolding on the shingle. It was an unusually high tide, and the water was practically lapping their toes.

She stopped and pointed out to sea. 'That's where The Street is,' she told Loz. 'You can't see anything now, but we'll come back tomorrow at low tide and we can walk out.'

'I look forward to it.' Loz leaned against her.

'There were other photographs of the blonde girl. I wanted to show you them,' Peg said. 'See what you thought. You're so good at reading people. But I seem to have lost them.'

'They've got to be somewhere.'

'They'll turn up. Eventually. There's a lot of stuff, though, and I've been shifting it around all day. They could have got buried anywhere. Or I might have thrown them out by mistake.'

As they rounded the curve that took them to the bottom of Tankerton Slopes, they were met by the deep bass-thrum of a sound system, underscoring barely-broken-voiced boy laughter and drunken girl-shrieking. Over on a shingle bank, a gathering of the local youth were dancing in front of a bonfire, squeezing what fun they could out of the cold night. As Peg and Loz drew closer, the unmistakable musk of skunkweed wafted towards them.

Peg had to think for a few minutes to place when she had seen the detritus of an earlier party at this same spot. It came as quite a shock that it had been just that morning – that only a day had passed since she was last here.

'Oy, batty boy!' A young male voice squeaked up at them from the beach. Peg instinctively broke away from Loz.

'Sling your hook, knob parcel,' Loz called back, pointedly taking Peg's arm again. A flock of boy laughter rose from the shingle, but to Peg's surprise and relief, it was not followed up by any action.

'Twats,' Loz said, and, Peg's cheeks burning, they headed up The Slopes towards Tankerton.

* * *

'So this is it,' Loz said, standing at Doll's front door. 'The Famous Bungalow.'

'And Aunty Jean's down there,' Peg pointed to the back of the building.

'It's like going back to the nineteen fifties.'

Peg let them in, and Loz stood in the doorway, sniffing the air, which was still pretty thick with bleach. After the cold night, the stifling warmth and the bright fluorescence of the hallway – Doll and Frank had never gone in for atmospheric lighting – made Peg feel so weary her legs could barely hold her.

'Crazy colours,' Loz said, as Peg showed her round.

Peg had never noticed it before, having grown up with the decor, but seeing it through Loz's eyes, the combination of the many swirls of orange, turquoise and purple in the place was quite remarkable.

'And so much stuff!' Loz said, going into the kitchen and peering into a tall cupboard completely crammed with mismatched plates of all colours and sizes.

'There's still loads to do. But you should have seen it before I got started.'

'Poor old lady. Fancy living like this.'

'It's not so bad. It's what she's used to.' Peg twisted her fingers together. Loz was inadvertently hitting a lot of very sensitive buttons, making her feel scrutinised, on the defensive. 'But it's got to change now; she's got no choice.'

'Is it all right if I move these?' Loz said. Most of the kitchen worktop was invisible under a crowd of badly washed empty jam jars and plastic food containers Doll insisted on keeping for some hypothetical future batch-cooking and jam-making session.

'Hang on a sec.' Peg fetched a couple of carrier bags from

the cupboard, filled them with the junk from the worktop and put them by the back door to join the rest of the recyclables in the morning. Loz took a cloth from the sink, wiped the newly cleared space and put her cotton shopping bag down there.

'Fancy a nip and a nibble?' She pulled out two bottles of vegan-friendly Bardolino, a couple of Jiffy bags full of the spiced nuts that were Seed's signature snack and a foil-wrapped slab of what she revealed to be the chocolate nut torte they made that Peg sometimes actually had dreams about.

'Loz! You didn't nick it, did you?'

'So what? They pay me rubbish and I work my arse off. So why shouldn't I just top it up a bit?'

Peg looked at Loz, her mouth open.

'Careful, or you'll catch flies. Now then,' she said, searching in the kitchen cupboards, 'I can see the cake stands and the vintage electrical appliances with the fraying cables, but where are the wine glasses?'

'In the lounge. In the cocktail cabinet.'

'Ooh. A cocktail cabinet.' Loz grabbed the bottles and bags and swept through to the lounge. Peg followed.

'Oh how super!' Loz said in a clipped vintage BBC voice as she lowered the foldout table to reveal the mirrored interior of the cabinet. 'And it lights up too!' She picked up the flock Babycham faun that stood guard over Doll's rarely touched sherry, gin and Martini bottles and kissed it on the nose. Then she pulled out some flamingo-shaped plastic cocktail stirrers, and the drinks mats. 'Are these from Raymond's club? Classy.'

Peg looked at the dust-swathed bottle of Doll's potato wine in the cabinet and, with a flash of yearning, remembered her grandfather handing her a taster in a small liqueur glass. It was Christmas, and Jean and Doll laughed heartily as she tried it and made a face.

'We'd best rinse these out before we use them,' Peg said, pulling herself back together. She picked out a couple of dusty wine glasses.

'Are you OK?' Loz followed her through to the kitchen. 'Did I say something wrong?'

'No.'

'You think I'm being snitty, don't you?'

'No.' Peg rinsed the glasses carefully, then smiled up at Loz. 'Yes you do.'

Peg shook her head.

'I'm sorry,' Loz said, following her back into the lounge. 'I'm sorry. I didn't mean to upset you. I'm just a little excited to be here, that's all. And all this –' she gestured at the wall clock framed by wrought-iron curlicues, the canvas-effect Tretchikoff Chinese Girl print, the collection of precious Franklin Mint porcelain figurines that Doll used to let Peg sit on the settee and hold, one by one, over a velour cushion. 'We'd be laughing at it if we found it in, say, the Golden Hind.'

The Golden Hind was a pub just round the corner from Loz's parents' immaculately tasteful house, which Peg and Loz used as a decompression chamber after a visit. It was run single-handedly by Daphne, a buxom, beehived blonde of at least sixty, whose eyelids were so heavy with mascara and eyeliner that Peg always wondered how she managed to hold them open. Her saloon bar was festooned with silk flowers, cute china animals and pictures of big-eyed little boys pissing in the gutter, worked in fluorescent paint on black velvet. Loz and Peg had spent their first evening there together giggling into their lager. The Spanish dancer loo-roll holder in the pot-pourri-scented 'little girl's room' had nearly finished them off.

'But this is different, Loz,' Peg said quietly, looking down. 'This is where I come from.'

Loz stood there for a moment and her spikiness melted away. 'I know.'

She stepped forward, took the glasses from Loz's hands and replaced them with her fingers. 'And I'm sorry. I love it because I love you. I'm feeling nothing but love here. Come on.'

It took Peg one minute to melt, gratefully, into the one place she wanted to be more than anywhere else in the world. Wherever she was, if Loz's arms were there, she was at home.

As Loz led her to the settee, the intercom buzzed briefly. Peg froze for a second.

'What's that?' Loz said.

'Aunty Jean. She might need me,' Peg said, hoping it wasn't another curry explosion. She listened for a couple of beats but nothing followed. Jean was unlikely to be wanting anything at two in the morning. For all her difficulties, thanks to the Guinness, some blue torpedo-shaped pills and a machine that helped her breathe through sleep apnoea, she generally managed to remain unconscious the whole night through.

'It must be playing up,' Peg said. 'It's getting on a bit. Gramps must have put it in over twenty years ago.'

'Now, where were we?' Loz said, as she pulled Peg towards her and worked her hand inside her T-shirt.

Then

MY SCHOOL YEARS WEREN'T ENTIRELY FRIENDLESS. THERE WAS a brief interlude when I was about eight, with a new girl called Philippa Burrell.

Phil was so skinny she was almost see-through. She also had a big hairy mole on her left cheek like a splodge of beard. Because she was even odder than me, she stepped neatly into my place at the bottom of the classroom pecking order. I was therefore able to offer her the understanding hand of friendship, which she was only too glad to grab.

Our tormentors called us Laurel and Hardy, or Mole and Wog.

I'm not sure that we liked each other, really. She pinched me too much. And she was always fainting, and I was pretty certain she faked it at least half the time.

But I suppose I was grateful for any friendship.

It was doomed, though, of course.

This is a quarter-way through the spring term.

Phil has been told that her parents are going away on business so she'll have to stay at school for half-term.

She throws herself down on her bed.

I don't think she's crying. She's just very, very still.

'They hate me,' she says into her pillow. 'If I was a pretty round blonde girl, they'd take me with them and show me off. I don't want to stay here all on my own with just Uma for company.'

Uma's parents live in Hong Kong, so she only goes home for the summer. She's got the stinkiest breath you can imagine, so, although she's actually slightly above us in who to pick on, we make ourselves feel better by looking down on her.

So I go: 'Come and stay with us for the hols!'

Phil lifts her head from the bed.

'Seriously?'

'Seriously.'

She leans over and gives me a sharp, hard pinch which I think means she likes the idea.

At first Nan isn't too keen when I call and ask her, but when I beg, she gives in.

'She'll have to sleep on your floor,' Nan says.

I say that's fine, because we're used to sleeping in a dorm together.

'And she'll have to take us as she finds us.'

'Of course,' I say.

I'm twitching with excitement as we stand under the school portico waiting for The Car.

For the first time, I am bringing a friend home with me for the holidays.

* * *

The Car is one thing I remember clearly. It took me to school at the beginning of each term and returned me to Tankerton at the end. I didn't ever wonder about it at the time – it was just one of those things that happened. But of course, it was paid for by my father, and Wayne the driver, a big man with a shiny suit and no hair, was his man.

Keeping an eye on me for Raymond, of course.

Of course.

When Wayne swings the big shiny Car up the gravel roundabout in front of our school, Philippa takes one look at him and pulls a face.

'Who's *that*,' she says.

'Wayne.'

She shudders and I look down and see that she has goosebumps on her arm. I think for an awful moment she's going to faint, but luckily she decides not to. Wayne jumps out of The Car to hold the back door open for us and we clamber in to the wood-and-leather inside while he puts our suitcases in the boot. Philippa sniffs, wrinkles her nose and looks at me, but I like the smell of The Car. It's coconut, and mint from Wayne's Polos that he keeps on the shiny wooden table thing between the two front seats.

He climbs in and as usual turns to me and gives me a little salute.

'Morning milady,' he says in his boomy voice. 'And where shall it be today?'

I pretend to um and err and then I say, 'Tankerton, please, Wayne.'

'Right you are milady,' he goes. He turns and starts the engine, and I try not to look at his oily brown scalp and the bristly rolls of fat at the back of his neck.

We roll along the long, gravel driveway that leads from the school to the road and I turn to look through the back window. It's such a grand building, all tall columns behind a misty mile of green, mole-hilled park. It reminds me of the house in *The Secret Garden*, or the one in *The Water Babies*.

It's a world apart from where we're going. But I prefer it at Nan's, which is home and where I'm really and truly looked after.

We drive up through Sussex and onto the motorway. Philippa hardly says a word. She just sits back and looks out of the window like a sick child. In the end I give up trying to talk to her and pull out the *Beano* and a packet of Fruit Pastilles which, as usual, Wayne's put in the back pocket of the seat in front of me.

'And here we are,' Wayne says.

I don't know if it's his voice or the stopping of the car that wakes me. But then we are out, and he's carrying our suitcases into the bungalow. Nan hurries across the front lawn in her pinny to give me a hug.

'Hello, Meggy lovey.' She puts her hands on my shoulders, which she almost has to reach up to do these days, and takes a look at me. 'I should find out what they're feeding you at that school of yours and try some for meself.'

She turns to Philippa, who is standing on my left. 'And this must be—' but she is caught short by the sight of Phil's mole as she turns to face her. 'Oh dear,' Nan goes. 'You *poor* little girl.'

As Nan brings her hand up to the mole and touches the hairs, I see Phil's mouth working, her little round mouse eyes falling back into her bony face.

'I might be able to help you with that,' Nan says. 'I'll see what I've got in the house.'

'Cheerio then, miladies,' Wayne thunders as he crosses the lawn towards the car.

'How many times do I have to tell you? Use the path,' Nan says, her hands now on her little hips.

'Lovely to see you too, Mrs T.' Wayne salutes her like a soldier, and swings himself into the car.

Nan just lifts her shoulders a little and rests her head on one side, watching as he pulls out along the road.

'Come on then, you two. Let's see what we can find you to eat!' Nan says, and we follow her into the bungalow. As usual, she has pulled out the dining table so it fills her lounge and it's groaning with mounds of sandwiches, sausage rolls, rich and livery galantine and, my favourite, Nan's chocolate cake, which is so gooey it's almost a milkshake instead of a cake.

'Sit! Sit!' Nan says, pulling out a chair and nearly pushing Philippa into it.

'Shouldn't we say hello to Aunty Jean first?' I say. That's the way we normally do it.

'Poor Jeanie's having a snooze,' Nan says. 'She's had a bit of a chest recently. Now then, Meggy, don't forget to be the hostess.'

She disappears to the kitchen, leaving us alone with all the food.

I run round the table, grabbing things and piling them on two plates. I put one down in front of Philippa and take mine to my seat at the other side of the table. I'm pretty hungry after the long journey. It's only when I reach across for more that I realise that Phil still has everything on her plate.

'Tuck in,' I say.

'Not hungry,' Phil says. It's the first thing she's said since we arrived, and her voice is tiny, her arms drawn round herself and her shoulders all hunched up.

I shrug and put some more stuff on my plate.

For a short while, the only sound in the room is my munching as I work my way through my second plateful. Then Nan bursts through.

'How's it doing, girls?' she says. Then she sees Phil's untouched plate. 'What's the matter, Philippa?'

'She said she's not hungry,' I say, through a mouthful of sausage roll.

'Oh, but you've got to eat,' Nan says. She grabs a sausage roll and holds it in front of Phil's mouth.

'Go on,' she says as Phil just sits there, looking at the food in Nan's hand.

'I can't,' Phil says.

'Course you can,' Nan says.

'Go on, Phil,' I say.

'I don't like sausage rolls.'

'Well try an eggy sandwich then, girl,' Nan says, popping the sausage roll onto my plate. 'You've got to eat something.'

Phil reaches out and curls her bony fingers round a sandwich, lifting it as if it weighs ten tons. She puts it up to her mouth and slowly opens her lips to let the tip of the corner in. She bites it, frowns and chews slowly. Then she puts the rest of the sandwich down. Nan eyes her like a cat watching a sparrow.

Then, as if it were the biggest lump of stuff in the world, Phil swallows the bit of the sandwich. Almost immediately, she grasps her stomach and closes her eyes.

'May I be excused, please, Mrs Thwaites?'

'Oh, call me Nan,' Nan says. 'I don't hold with all that Mrs bother stuff. You want to get down?'

'She wants the toilet,' I say, interpreting our school language for Nan.

'Oh yes, dearie. Show her the way, will you Meggy? There's a good girl.'

I go into the hallway and point towards the bathroom. Phil only just makes it in time before she is sick.

'Nan! Nan!' I call. 'Philippa's poorly!'

'Oh no,' Nan says, coming out to the hallway and barging past me to find Phil crouching over the toilet retching green stuff up. Nan grabs Phil's hair and holds it back, then rubs her on the back, helping her up with the last bits. She's great when you're being sick, Nan is.

'Get a glass of water, Meggy,' Nan says. 'And the Dettol, a bucket and a roll of kitchen towels.'

I do as I'm told and when I come back with the supplies, Nan is sitting on the toilet, with Phil on her knee, holding her close. I feel a sudden stab of jealousy and wish it was me that had been poorly, not Phil. Nan reaches out for the water and, after a bit of cleaning and dabbing and wiping Dettol round the toilet, we go back to the lounge, where the smell of the eggy sandwiches makes Phil retch.

Nan dips into the kitchen and comes out with a tube of lavender air freshener, which she sprays round the room. Then, out of the blue, the buzzer goes off and Phil jumps out of her skin.

'It's only Aunty Jean's buzzer,' I say, laughing.

'Hello?' Aunty Jean's phlegmy voice sounds down the buzzer. 'Is that my favourite girl back, then?'

I jump off my chair and excitedly put my mouth up to the buzzer. 'Hello, Aunty Jean!' I yell.

'Ooh, volume down a bit, girl,' she says. But I can hear the laugh in her voice.

'You don't need to stand so close, dearie,' Nan says, putting her arm round me. 'Shall we go in and say hello?'

I look at Philippa who still hasn't lost the shocked face she had when the buzzer first went off. 'Come on, Phil,' I say. 'Aunty Jean's a barrel of laughs.'

Like a little lost ghost, Philippa slips off her chair. I take her cold, dry hand and we follow Nan, who has piled up a big plate of food for Aunty Jean, out of the back door, down Nan's slope and up Aunty Jean's. We open the back door and, almost instantly, Philippa starts coughing. It's probably because of the smell of Aunty Jean's cigs, but that's what it's like in her extension, so that's that.

'Now then,' Nan says in a low, serious voice to Philippa. 'My daughter is handicapped, so you'll have to take her as you find her, I'm afraid.'

'Where's my favourite girl?' Aunty Jean calls and, forgetting that I am supposed to be the hostess and taking care of my guest, I drop Philippa's hand and rush through to the bedroom and throw myself on top of her, which makes Lexy hiss and fluff up and jump off the bed. He hates sharing Aunty Jean.

'Oof, have a care, dearie,' she says, opening her bare fleshy arms to give me a big, big hug. I am lost in her giant soft bosom and her smell of cigarettes and chocolate, mixed with the Sudocreme that Nan and I rub in her skin to stop it from breaking.

'And who is this little girl, then?' I hear Aunty Jean rumble from underneath the nylon frill of her nightie.

I look up and see Philippa cowering in the doorway. Nan is trying to coax her into the room, but she's having none of it.

'Come and sit here, dear,' Aunty Jean says, moving a kidney dish with some used bits of cotton wool in it from the other side of her bed to clear a space. Philippa doesn't move. It's like she's just turned herself off.

'Come on, Philippa,' Nan says in a whisper that's loud enough for everyone to hear. 'Don't be rude, now.' She takes Phil by the arm, leads her round the bed and pushes her down on to the eiderdown. Phil is stiff and stick-like. She just perches there, as far away from Aunty Jean as possible.

'I brought through a snack for you, dear,' Nan says to Jean as she hands her the plate.

'Lovely. Thank you, Mummy.' Aunty Jean takes a slice of galantine and pops it into her mouth.

'Now then, I want to hear all about school,' Aunty Jean says. She lights a cigarette, then I snuggle in to her side and begin to tell her the good bits. Every now and then, I try to involve Philippa. I say, 'Didn't we, Phil?' and, 'Don't we, Phil?' and she nods. But I'm not really enjoying having her there on the edge of Aunty Jean's bed.

Also, she'll know that I'm not telling everything about what goes on at school, and I'm scared that if she says anything it's going to be something like, 'Remember when we were pushed into the pool with all our clothes on and your watch got ruined.' Or 'But that girl you're talking about as if she's our friend puts chewing gum in your hair.'

I don't want Aunty Jean and Nan to worry about me at school. Goodness knows they have enough on their plate as it is. That's what Nan says whenever any sort of trouble happens. I don't want to make them worried. I want to be able to come home and just be happy.

Later, when we're back in the bungalow watching *Blue Peter*, Nan comes in with a tube of something and a plastic spatula.

'I said I could do something about your poor face,' she says to Philippa, squeezing the tube so a big dollop of cream lands on the spatula.

Philippa's hand darts up to her mole. 'But Mummy says I mustn't touch the hairs,' she says. 'If I don't touch them until I'm twelve, I can have them taken right off forever with lasers.'

'Is that a kind thing to do to a girl?' Nan asks me. 'Making her go around all those years with an ugly thing like that on her face?' I shake my head, although, to be honest, I'm more interested in the *Blue Peter* Canada expedition.

Then there's this struggle and I see that Nan is somehow using one hand to hold Philippa's hand away from her face and keep her head still, while using the other to smear the cream thickly over the hairy mole.

'Now you mustn't touch the cream,' Nan says, 'or you might burn your fingers.'

I wonder how it can be on her face if it would burn her fingers, but I don't say anything. Nan knows what she's doing.

'I'll just do the kitchen floor, then it'll be time to get that cream off. And tomorrow I'll show you a thing or two to do with make-up to hide the mole. You're about the same complexion as Jeanie, so we'll use her foundation.'

While Nan is in the kitchen, Phil and I don't say a word to each other. We're sitting with the whole settee between us.

Then Nan marches in with a little bowl of water, the spatula and a flannel, and she scrapes the cream off and I get a little closer to watch, because it's really interesting. The cream comes off really disgustingly mixed up with lots of little black hairs.

Philippa doesn't struggle, or even move, particularly, but she is crying.

'There, girl,' Nan says, dabbing at the now-hairless mole with the flannel. 'Miles better. Now I think someone deserves a little treat for being such a good, brave girl.'

'I'm a good, brave girl, too,' I say, and Nan ruffles my hair and says that of course, she never forgets that. She bundles everything into the bowl and goes back out again.

'My mum will kill me,' Phil says. And then she goes, ever so quietly, 'I hate your nan and I hate your aunt and I hate you.'

I don't understand. Nan was only trying to help.

'Now then,' Nan says, coming back in with the sweetie tin. 'Who's for a little something?'

In the night Phil wets the bed. Then in the morning, she calls her mummy on this phone number she has for emergencies. She has a word with her mummy, then asks Nan to have a word with her. Nan comes away from the phone with her lips all tucked in and fusses around making sure Phil is all packed up. By ten o'clock, before Nan even has a chance to show her what to do with Aunty Jean's foundation, a taxi arrives and Phil is taken back to school to stay there for the rest of the holidays.

'Well, she was a bit of a drippy Dora,' Nan says, as we watch the taxi turn the corner onto the main road.

When I go back to school, I realise that Philippa is now best friends with Uma. They don't talk to me. Once, when they're walking together in the playground with their arms round each other and I ask them if I can play and they say no I can't, I really feel like smashing their heads together.

But, mostly, I'm OK with it.

I didn't ever really like her, anyway.

Twenty-Three

PEG WOKE WITH A BLINDING HANGOVER, FEELING ROTTEN. SHE wasn't much of a drinker, but if anything she'd call herself a beer girl. Red wine didn't suit her at all. Loz had allayed her initial qualms about getting up to anything in Doll's lounge with a third glass of Bardolino, and it was not until pale dawn had started creeping through the curtains that they finally crawled up the ladder to the little bedroom. Once there, they curled up tightly together on the narrow single bed and fell into the kind of deep sleep that only the completely satiated – or the utterly deluded – can ever know.

But Peg found herself alone when she woke. She could hear Loz banging around in the kitchen, singing along badly to a Fleet Foxes track. Led by a sour smell of burnt-on animal fat mixed with something more delicious – eggs in butter perhaps – Peg gingerly swung her feet on to the Spice Girls rug and climbed down to the kitchen where Loz was busy at the stove. Beside her were her portable iPod speakers, which she must have brought with her. It didn't suit Loz to be without musical accompaniment while she worked.

'Get back to where you belong, woman,' Loz said. 'I'm making you breakfast in bed and you'll spoil it if you get up.'

Picking up her bag, Peg obeyed. She climbed back into bed, pulled out her notebook and read through the letter she had drafted to Raymond the night before. It would do, she thought. It was worth a punt. When she was allowed to get up, she'd go down to the Internet café in the shopping street, type it up and email it from there.

Later, when they were enjoying freshly brewed coffee – wine, snacks and chocolate nut torte weren't the only gifts that had been borne to Tankerton from the Seed larder – Loz said that she hadn't been able to sleep in the single bed.

'I mean,' she said. 'It's all right for kids, but we're big girls now. I like my space.'

Peg knew this. She also knew that Loz was used to a double bed – her large attic bedroom at her parents' house, the scene of many proudly related schoolgirl conquests, had an American-sized king, all covered in fake fur throws and cushions made from old Persian carpets.

'I've looked in Doll's room and she's got a lovely big double.'

'But it's total chaos. I haven't even started sorting it out in there.'

'If we put our minds to it, I bet we can get it clear by tonight. We'll be much more comfortable in there.' Loz leaned forwards over the breakfast tray and put her hand on Peg's cheek.

'I don't know,' Peg said, rubbing Loz's hand between her cheek and her shoulder, like a cat.

'Oh, come on, Peg. We're grown-ups doing a good job here.'

'But . . .'

'Doll won't ever know, if that's what you're worried about.'

Which, of course, *was* what Peg was worrying about.

'And we don't have to *do* anything, if that's your concern.

We could just have a couple of nights' well-earned rest after working our arses off.'

'I know.'

'You're being a bit pathetic, old Peg.'

'I know.'

When she was dressed, Peg went through to check on Jean. She had decided it would be better to wait until the afternoon to introduce Loz. Jean wasn't a morning person, and seemed to be in a particularly foul state of mind today. Then she went down to the otherwise empty Internet café and typed out her email to Raymond, grateful that the qualms she knew she had about asking him for money couldn't really make it out of her wine-fugged brain.

Saying a little prayer, she hit *send*.

'Done!' she said, slipping back into the bungalow and marvelling at the kitchen transformation Loz had worked in the hour or so she had been away.

'It's so absolutely the right thing to do,' Loz said, slipping the last piece of washing-up onto a full draining board. 'Hey, I tracked down that death smell. Did you catch it when we came in last night?'

Peg shook her head.

'Well, anyway, it was coming from the fridge, so I had a root around and found an old chicken breast on its way to hell, stinking even through its plastic wrapping. It was two months past its sell-by date.'

'Ew,' Peg said.

'So then I went through the whole fridge and almost everything had to go. There was a bottle of milk that was literally solid, and some butter that had this, like, thick orange leathery skin. I got excited for a second, thinking I'd discovered a new ingredient, but after a whiff of it I changed my mind. And there was a pack of fish fingers in the ice box that was twelve years out of date.'

'She used to buy them for me when I was little.'

'Oh God, sorry. I threw them out. You didn't want to hang on to them for a souvenir, did you?'

'Do you want me to dry this lot up?' Peg said, taking a fresh tea towel from the newly gleaming row of hooks by the back door.

'Yes please. But let's not put away till we've tackled the cupboards.' Loz looked round at her, her eyes gleaming. 'It's going to be a challenge all this. I love a challenge!'

'Yep.' Peg fiddled with the tea towel, twisting it round her finger.

'What is it?'

'I don't know.'

'Yes you do. What's the matter?'

'It's just, well, this was my world, and I've let you in on it.'

'And that's a good thing, no?'

'Yes. Of course it's a good thing. It's just that everything's changing. It's going to take me a bit of a while to adjust, that's all, I suppose.'

'I'm sorry,' Loz reached out and took Peg's hands. 'I'm such a steamroller. I just get a bit carried away, as you know.'

Peg nodded and sniffed. She felt weepy again, like a big lump of a girl.

'Tell you what,' Loz said, squeezing her hands. 'I'm going to try to be a bit more sensitive to your feelings, a bit more delicate. But you've got to tell me. If I'm being an arsehole, you've got to let me know. Sometimes I can't see it myself.'

'Sometimes!' Peg said, smiling. She bent down to kiss her.

* * *

Peg found some rubber gloves and two of the faintly clinical pinnies Doll always wore around the house. Suitably protected, they set to work on the mounds of clothing in the bedroom, textile records of everything Doll had worn over the past couple of years. As the piles had grown, she had maintained that it was easier to find things like that, rather than putting them away. But it had got so out of hand that parts of the room had become impassable and she was reduced to re-using the same few things over and over, until they were stiff with wear.

Added to that were the empty pots of face powder and cold cream, and the boxes and boxes of broken bits of jewellery – twenty-four carat gold mixed with brass, plastic beads tangled round real seed pearls – and more of the ubiquitous piles of old newspapers and bags of scarves, underwear and old shoes.

'Wow,' Loz said, peering into a bag of Commonplace Books. 'What are these?' She pulled one out. 'Some of these have been burned round the edges.'

'Don't!' Peg cried, grabbing the book before Loz could open it. 'They're Nan's Commonplace Books.'

'Her what?'

'They're private. Like a diary.'

'Can't we just peep?'

'No! How would you like it if you kept a diary and I read it?'

'But I don't keep a diary. And even if I did, I haven't got anything to hide.'

'Nor's Nan. But these are private. So please don't look.'

Loz sighed. 'OK then.'

'Promise?'

'Promise.'

'We'll just stack them up in the shed, where they should have stayed all along.'

It was incredible how quickly things progressed with Loz and her music around. By midday, they had cleared all the mounds of clothes into three piles on the lino bedroom floor: one to be cleaned, one for the charity shop and one to be thrown away.

'Should we make a mending pile?' Peg asked.

Loz just looked at her with one eyebrow raised. She was far more ruthless than Peg, who, every time she picked something up, had Doll in her head, running through the arguments for keeping it.

It was far easier to be an outsider.

Finally, the floors and surfaces were cleared and the bed stood stripped and airing.

'It looks so bare now,' Peg said.

'It's the lino floor. Weird for a bedroom,' Loz said.

'Nan said it was easier to keep clean – back in the days when she did a lot of cleaning. Aunty Jean's got the same flooring throughout her extension.'

Loz raised her other eyebrow. 'Shall we get on, then?'

They were bracing themselves to tackle the last area in the bedroom: two large wardrobes.

Peg nodded.

'Five, four, three, two, one,' they counted together.

They pulled open both sets of doors and, from Peg's side, a load of old medical supplies tumbled out.

'Jesus, there's enough here to start a hospital,' Loz said, sifting through the incontinence pads, plastic disposal bags, changing mats, medicated talc, syringes, rubber tubing, latex gloves and disposable sick bowls.

'All well past their expiry dates,' Peg said, examining a pack of scalpel blades. 'She used all this stuff to look after Aunty Jean. She used to be a nurse, you see. Liked to do it properly.'

'Where did she get it all from?'

'I don't know. I think the hospital sent it. There were deliveries every month. The same man, I remember. He used to give me a lolly when I helped him carry the boxes in.'

'Hey,' Loz said, rubbing Peg's shoulder. 'That's a clear memory.'

'I've a feeling there's plenty more like that, just on the verge . . .'

'It's all coming together, isn't it?'

Peg didn't know about that. It felt more like it was all falling apart. But she nodded and smiled, anyway.

They bagged all the medical stuff up and hauled it out to the back garden.

'Such a waste,' Peg said, looking at the mound of rubbish they were going to have to get to a tip.

'Not if you think that we're dealing with a lifetime of not throwing anything away. It's just a bit of catch-up.'

They went back and hauled the clothing from the wardrobes, dumping it in piles on the bed. Doll's nurse uniform was in there, clean and ready to wear, hanging under a professional cleaner's filmy plastic bag.

'I don't know where to start with all this,' Peg said.

'Some of this stuff is pure seventies,' Loz said, pulling on a salmon-coloured Crimplene coat with navy-blue piping and frogging that fitted her perfectly in her Doll-like tininess. 'We could set up a stall in Camden. Make a killing.'

'Or we could put it in the charity pile.'

'I suppose now we're going to rake in Daddy's dough, we don't need to worry about cash.'

'It's for Nan, remember? I don't want anything to do with it.' Peg shook out a floral nylon blouse with white stains in the armpits.

'We'll stick by your principles, girl. All the way to debtor's jail.'

'Oh shut up and get on with it.'

'Ooh,' Loz said. 'Fierce.'

They sorted through the clothes until Doll was left with just five coats of varying weights and ten each of jumpers, skirts and what she would call slacks. The rest were stuffed into bags.

'Oxfam,' Peg said.

'PDSA,' Loz countered.

'Really? Pets over people?'

'Have you seen what people *do* to each other?'

'I don't care. It's Oxfam or nothing.'

'Whatever. She's your nan, I suppose.'

'Yes. She is.'

Peg climbed on a chair and handed down the dust-encrusted boxes piled on top of the wardrobes.

'Phew,' Loz said as she set down the final one. 'How long have they been up there?'

'Years. Gramps must've put them up there. Nan could never manage it. She's too tiny.'

'Look,' Loz said, blowing the top of the box clean. 'It says *Raymond* on it.'

'And this one's got *Jean* written on the top. And, oh God, this one says *Keith*.'

'Naomi's got a box like this for each of us,' Loz said. 'Keeps them in the attic.'

Peg checked the other boxes, but there wasn't one for her. Perhaps back in the Farnham house there was one, made by her mother for her, and left forgotten in a dark corner of the attic.

'I don't know if we should open them,' she said.

'Course we should,' Loz said, undoing the Raymond box. Unable to hold back, Peg peered in.

'Hard to think of him in these,' she said, holding up a tiny pair of bootees that had probably been crocheted by Doll in the pre-arthritis days. She put them to one side and opened a slim cardboard box to reveal a crispy, papery thing, and something that looked like a withered worm. As they met the air, they seemed to sigh and shrivel.

'Ew. What's that?' she said.

Loz bent forward to inspect it. 'It's a caul – the skin thing that goes round the foetus in the womb. Some babies are born with it intact, and if you keep it for them, they'll never drown. And that's his umbilical cord,' Loz said, calmly, pointing at the worm thing.

Peg nearly dropped the box. 'How do you know?'

'Naomi's got mine. She showed them to me on my eighteenth birthday.'

'You're kidding.'

'Nah. Honest. And look,' Loz held her hands out and took a bow. 'Undrowned! She's also got my little sister, who was stillborn at twenty-two weeks, in a jar.'

'Is that allowed?' Peg said.

'Clearly it is. Although, even if it wasn't, if Naomi wanted it . . . Well, she knows a few strings and how to pull them.'

Peg shuddered.

'What else is in there?' Loz said, peering into the box. Peg pulled out a sheaf of papers – glowing school reports, gymnastics, and school prize and music certificates.

'He was her golden boy,' Peg said. 'She doesn't talk about him much, but when she does it's always "My Raymond" this, and "My Raymond" that. He couldn't do a thing wrong in her eyes.'

'So sad,' Loz said.

The next thing to come out of the box was a small tan

leather photograph album with whipped edges. There, held on by faded photograph corners, was the baby Raymond in black and white, all fat and dimpled, in a knitted suit, smiling up at the camera as he sat on a checked rug on a sun-dappled lawn. There he was, a little older, with a walking trolley full of bricks and his big sister behind him, her arm encircling his shoulders in a way that reminded Peg of how he had stood by the blonde woman in the torn photographs.

'And there's Keith,' Peg said as she turned the page.

'If looks could kill,' Loz murmured as they both studied the picture.

Taken at an early meeting between Doll's two eldest and her new arrival, it went some way to backing up Jean's story about the baby and the dock and the stone. Bespectacled and plaited, Jean sat holding her newborn brother, beaming at the camera. Raymond, however, stood a little aside, staring at Keith with a level of malevolence, which, without the benefit of hindsight, must have caused some amusement at the time.

'The usurped prince,' Peg said.

'But then again there's one of me and Rach, taken in the hospital just hours after Mum had her, and I'm looking at her just like that. But I never killed her.' Loz shrugged. 'Never even felt the urge that strongly.'

'You put things so baldly sometimes.' Peg turned the pages. There was Raymond, all brushed and smart in his school uniform; there he was in probably his first suit, and there he was older, standing by a white Jag.

'I just tell it how it is, babe.' Loz caught a picture as it fell out of the album, the glue on its corners having given up. 'Who's that?' she said, frowning at it.

Peg peered at the picture and frowned. 'God, it's that girl. The one whose photos Jean tore up. And that's Dad next to her, of course. Why's Nan got that in there?'

'Let me see,' Loz said, taking the photograph and holding it to the light. She suddenly shivered.

'What?'

'Someone walking over my grave,' Loz said, smiling at Peg. 'I thought— oh, nothing.' She frowned at the picture. 'Pretty girl, though.'

'I'd hardly have thought she was your type.'

'Clearly Raymond's though. Look at him all Brylcreemed in front of his fancy Jag, his hungry arm round her.' Loz made a face.

'Poor girl.'

'And her in her smart little zigzag coat.'

They both jumped as the sharp sound of Jean's buzzer cut through from the lounge, followed by her amplified coughing and gasping for air, the click and whoosh of a cigarette lighter, and an impatient exhalation.

'Meggy? Meggy? You there?' Jean's voice boomed, distorted by a ringing feedback. 'I've dropped me book.'

'It's time to meet Jean,' Peg said. 'Brace yourself.'

Twenty-Four

'THANK GOODNESS YOU'RE HERE,' JEAN SAID. 'I HAVEN'T SEEN anyone since the morning.'

'Hasn't Julie been in to give you lunch?' Peg asked.

'Oh, *she's* been in of course.' Jean gave a dismissive shrug. 'But no one else.'

Without acknowledging Loz, who was standing right beside Peg and clearly trying very hard not to stare, Jean looked back over at the TV, where a woman sat weeping, mascara coursing down her cheeks, while a man wielding a microphone on a long stick like a lion-tamer's whip appeared to be telling her off.

'She's a dreadful mother, that one,' Jean said, waving her cigarette at the larger of the two women. 'She had three children by this lovely kind fella, then walked out and left them all while she shacked up with some fat lezzer.'

'Perhaps she wasn't happy with her family,' Loz said.

Jean looked at Loz as if she were some sort of escaped animal. 'Family comes first. Always. I dropped my book, Meggy. Pick it up, will you? There's a dear.'

Peg reached down and picked up the copy of *Take a Break* that had slid to the floor by Jean's bed. 'This is Loz, Aunty Jean. My friend. She's come to stay and help me out a bit.'

'Hello.' Loz stepped forward and held out her hand.

'Pleased to meet you,' Jean said, through pursed lips, keeping both hands firmly on her magazine. 'I hope there's enough space for you both through there in Mummy's home.'

'It's fine, Aunty Jean.'

Jean looked gloomily at the TV where a bigger woman was being ushered in. She embraced the crying woman, then turned to have a few bleeped-out words with the microphone man. The audience howled.

'That's the filthy fat dyke,' Jean muttered, her eyes on the screen. 'Disgusting.'

Peg shot a glance at Loz, who stood out of Jean's sightline, watching.

'Would you like a cup of tea, Aunty Jean?' Peg said.

'Yes please, dear. And some of that walnut cake the girl bought from the supermarket today. I prefer home-made, but as no one's making cakes round here any more . . .'

'I can make a cake for you if you like,' Loz said.

'What do you know about it?' Jean said, shooting her a look.

'Loz is a chef, Aunty Jean.'

'Well, I don't know about that, I'm sure,' Jean said, settling down into her chins and returning her attention to the TV.

'Loz, do you want to come and give me a hand?' Peg said, gesturing with her eyes towards the kitchen.

'It's OK, Peg.' Loz drew up a chair at the side of Jean's bed. 'I'll stay here with Jean. I love this show.'

Jean looked at Loz sideways as she settled down beside her.

* * *

Peg was just putting a big slice of the shop-bought cake on a plate when she heard Jean yelling forcefully in the bedroom.

'*Where in the name of God did you find this?*'

She dashed through and found Jean holding Loz by the wrist. On the bed in front of them lay the photo of Raymond and the blonde.

'She's poking her nose into our family affairs,' Jean snarled to Peg. 'You've let her root and nose about in our private business.'

'I was just showing Jean what we found next door,' Loz said, her eyes wide.

'It's Miss Thwaites to you,' Jean snarled.

'I'm sorry if I offended.'

Peg sighed. Loz *knew* Jean had torn up the other photos of the girl. She *knew* she had some sort of issue with her. What was she playing at?

'Where did she find this?' Jean grabbed the photo and pushed Loz away.

'In some boxes on top of Nan's wardrobe,' Peg said.

Jean's eyes bulged and a vein throbbed on her forehead. 'I told you not to go nosing around in Mummy's stuff,' she said to Peg.

'I just wondered who that girl might be,' Loz said again.

'Get her out of here,' Jean said, her voice suddenly low and hoarse. 'Get that filthy pervert out of here.'

Peg gasped.

'Don't think I don't know what you're up to in there,' Jean said, pointing at the wall between Doll's part of the bungalow and her own. 'Don't think I was born yesterday.'

'But Aunty Jean—' Peg said. This was all going so horribly wrong.

'Do you want to kill your nan? Is that it, Meggy? What do you think she'd do if she found out?'

Loz stepped forward. 'I can assure you, Miss Thwaites, that nothing whatsoever is "going on" next door except a lot of clearing up and cleaning for Doll's return. We're working really hard.'

Peg looked at Loz, who remained inscrutable. Jean's mouth opened and closed, opened and closed like that of a big old carp.

After a long, painful pause, Jean finally turned and faced Peg.

'I thought I said I wanted that out of here,' she said, pointing at Loz.

'I'll be glad to go,' Loz said. 'See you next door, Peg.' She put her hand on the back of her head and kissed her full on the lips.

'Well!' Jean said when Loz had left. 'I've never seen anything like it. What on earth were you thinking, bringing that into our house?'

'She's my friend, Aunty Jean.' Peg felt an unaccustomed whorl of anger threading in her belly. She wanted nothing but the best for Doll – she structured her whole life around her. To be accused of purposefully setting out to harm her was too much. 'I wish you wouldn't be so rude to her.'

'It was her doing the upsetting, if I remember rightly,' Jean said, wobbling her head on her shoulders so that her cheeks quivered. 'Showing me this.' She picked up the photograph and tore it down the middle.

'Don't!' Peg snatched it from Jean's grasp.

'What are you doing?' Jean said, reaching for the photo with surprising force and yanking herself to a sitting position – the first time Peg had seen her do so for years. Peg leaped back, the two parts of the picture between her fingers.

'I – I want to keep this,' she said to Jean.

'Give it here!' Jean tried to reach out again for the photograph.

'No. I want to keep it. It's a picture of my dad.'

Peg was surprising herself. This was the first time she had ever, ever, openly defied her aunt. But, if she wanted to find out more about why both Loz and Jean had reacted to the photograph in the ways they had, she needed to hold on to it.

'You don't know what you're getting into with all this,' Jean snarled. Then, unable to hold herself up any longer, she thumped back against her pillows, blasting up a cloud of fetid air and making the whole room shudder.

'Oh. Oh,' she moaned, closing her eyes. 'Meggy. What's happening to you?'

She stayed like that for a few uncomfortably silent moments, shaking, until Peg noticed that there were tears in her eyes.

'What is it?' Peg carefully put the two pieces of the photograph down on top of Jean's medical supplies cabinet, well out of her reach.

She suddenly felt a wave of pity for her aunt. Loz had, typically, dive-bombed from her wide world into Jean's stagnant pool. What had she been thinking, showing her the picture? But Peg knew it wasn't Loz's fault. It was her own, for even thinking that these two parts of her life could meet without friction.

'What is it, Aunty Jean?' she asked, drawing up beside her and curling her fingers over her hand.

'It's just,' Jean said, catching her breath between sobs. 'Could you get me my mask, lovey?' She patted Peg's hand with her fat, soft palm and smiled at her between sobs.

Peg reached over for the plastic contraption and fitted it over Jean's mouth and nose. Holding tight on to Peg's hand, Jean breathed in and out until she could do so normally and her chest stopped shuddering. Then, at last, she spoke, the mask still clamped over her face, muffling her words and accompanying them with the sound of the oxygen tank hissing on every in-breath.

'It's just I don't want your daddy to get into any more trouble,' she said, looking at Peg.

'But you said he was evil, though, that you don't get on,' Peg said, reaching for a tissue and dabbing Jean's face, trying to smooth out the mascara that had run down her cheeks and round the edge of the mask like a child's felt-tip outline. 'Why would you protect him if you don't even like him?'

'Oh Meggy. It's him doesn't like me. I embarrass him. Even before I was big. I don't know why. Perhaps because I know about what really happened with Keith. But he's my little brother, Meggy, and what can I do? I've got to look out for him. Because his going to prison for your mum – well, that nearly killed Mummy. The shame. What I told the police and the court turned him into a hero, and that's what saved it all. And *she's* what's important here: Mummy. She is a saint. She's lived through so much, put up with so much, looked after me all these years.' Jean took hold of Peg's hand and looked at her with fire in her eyes. 'I would do anything to save Mummy.'

'And that's why you tore the photographs up?'

Jean took her hand from Peg, closed her eyes, crossed her arms as best she could in front of her and nodded her head slowly.

Peg watched her aunt. It had been an impressive performance, but she didn't believe a word. She had no idea what it was, but Jean was clearly still hiding something.

The only sound in the room was the oxygen hissing and stopping, hissing and stopping as she lay there like a resting corpse.

A worryingly long time passed.

Then, just as Peg was wondering if she had fallen asleep, Jean opened her eyes. As if nothing had happened, she lifted her mask from her face, lit up a Marlboro, inhaled and exhaled, and turned to Peg.

'Where's that walnut cake, then?' she said.

'What the hell were you doing back there?' Peg asked, storming into Doll's bedroom.

'Sorry,' Loz said. 'It's just something's not right about that blonde girl.'

Peg was unable to disagree about that, but before she had a chance to compose her thoughts, she noticed the cleared state of the room.

'Where's all Nan's boxes?' she said, looking around. Loz had somehow unearthed a scented candle, which was burning on the dressing table, and there were fresh sheets and blankets on the bed.

'I put them in the shed. I didn't nose in all the precious stuff, or anything,' she said quickly. 'But look. Before you carry on being cross with me, look at this.' She handed Peg a key. 'I found it when I was scraping the dust off the top of the wardrobes. It must've been tucked underneath the boxes. Does it mean anything to you?'

Peg looked at the key. Attached to it was a label with *Heyworth Court* written on it. 'Nope. No idea what or where that is.'

'Your nan must, though. That's her writing, isn't it?'

'We're not going to start on her, Loz.'

Loz held up her hands.

'And that was out of order, sneaking that photo on Jean,' Peg said.

'Makes you wonder, though, eh? The way she reacted.'

'Why though? Why did you do it?'

Loz narrowed her eyes at Peg. 'I've seen that girl before.'

'What do you mean?' Peg pulled the two rescued pieces of the photograph out of her back pocket and pieced them both together.

'I think she might be this girl who went missing,' Loz said, pointing at the blonde's face.

'What?'

'I think there's a bit about her in one of me books.'

'That's just ridiculous.'

'It might be. But it might not be. I've got a pretty good memory for faces. And that coat's pretty distinctive, too. And if it *is* the same girl, then perhaps Raymond has an idea what might have happened to her. Or Jean might. Why did she tear it up if she doesn't know anything?'

'Jesus, Loz,' Peg said, rubbing her eyes. She didn't like the way Loz was trying to turn her family into a chapter of one of her idiotic books. 'Aren't you just getting everything out of proportion?'

'Possibly. But what if I'm not? Wouldn't it be great if we could find out the truth?'

Peg didn't know. She thought she preferred it when she hadn't known anything. 'Look,' she said, attempting to change the subject. 'I've got to go and see Doll soon. Do you want to come?'

'Do you think she'll want to have a pervert like me in the same hospital as her?' Loz said.

'I'm sorry about Aunty Jean,' Peg said.

'It's all right,' Loz said. 'She's quite a handful though, eh? And what is it she's hiding, then?'

'I really haven't the faintest idea,' Peg said.

She did, but she wasn't going to admit it, not even to herself.

Twenty-Five

'DO YOU THINK IT'S A BAD OR A GOOD SIGN THAT DOLL'S NOT only recognising people she knows but also people she's never met before?' Peg asked, as she and Loz rode the train back from the hospital to Whitstable.

Although still a little confused about where she was, Doll had been in fine spirits in her more comfortable, sectioned-off private room – so fine that she greeted Loz as if she were an old friend.

'That was a nasty turn you had, dear, wasn't it? I thought we'd lost you,' she had said, grasping Loz's hand. 'I'm so glad to see you're all better now.'

'Oh yes, I'm all good,' Loz had replied, smiling.

'It's a good approach to life, though,' Peg said as they slipped past the charmless Kentish bungalows that lined the railway track. 'You'd never run the risk of offending anyone.'

'You'd fuck with their minds though, making them wonder when they actually met you before,' Loz said. 'Though it's nice to be welcomed by one branch of your family. Even if it is the la-la one.'

'I'm just worried that she's doing so well they'll have her out before we've got the place clear for her.'

'Glass half full as ever,' Loz said, tapping Peg on the thigh.

'Can we go into town and pick up some ingredients for supper?' Loz asked as they stepped from the train onto the chilly platform at Whitstable. 'And something for that cake I said I'd bake for Jean.'

'What, like rusty razor blades and rat poison?'

'Oh don't. The poor woman needs feeding up.'

Peg kissed Loz on the nose, grateful that she'd taken Jean's rudeness so lightly. 'We can stop off at the library on the way. I need to see if Daddy's got back to my crawling message.'

It was a cold, late afternoon, further sharpened by a bitter wind whistling down the deserted street. The library, a functional 1960s building, was tucked off the road behind an unlovely concrete forecourt. But inside it was festooned with Christmas decorations and brimming with people – young mothers curled up on beanbags, reading to fractious, teatime toddlers; elderlies looking at books and escaping heating bills and loneliness. A deskful of younger secondary schoolchildren struggling with their homework brought a clear memory to Peg of coming to this same library to work on a school project during the holidays, escaping the bungalow's TV noise, cigarette smoke and medical smells.

It was her first memory where the bungalow was something other than a place of refuge to her, and, while Loz smiled wryly at her, she noted it into her voice-recorder, just in case it was useful later.

She went over to one of the busy checkout desks and waited until the librarian was free. She showed her work identity card and explained their situation. Without a moment's hesitation, the librarian gave them each a membership card so they could use the Internet.

'What an influential girlfriend I have,' Loz said, as they crossed the room to the computers. 'She can get me my heart's desire.'

'If it's in a library, it's yours.'

They set themselves up on the only two free computers – one at each end of the long bank of terminals. Logging on to her webmail, Peg was surprised to find that she had indeed received a reply from Raymond. It was brief, but it said what she wanted it to say:

> *Glad youv seen sense girl. Your apologys aceppted. It was tough for both of us, meeting like that. Lets say bygones be bygones. Give me your bank details and I'll see your OK. Hope your coming this way soon. Paulie talks about his big sister lots.*

The fish had bitten.

Peg replied with a formal thank-you and her sort code and account number.

'Dad's sending me money,' she said, as she went over to Loz, who appeared to be engrossed in something on her screen.

'That's great.'

'I'll be able to pay for Nan's hospital room, and we can fix the roof, get the electrics overhauled.'

'Brilliant.' Loz didn't seem able to pull her eyes away from her computer monitor.

'What are you looking at?' Peg pulled over an empty chair and sat beside Loz. Then she looked at the screen. 'Oh no,' she said.

There, smiling up at her from a web page, her blonde hair whipped by the wind as she stood by the Thames, Tower Bridge looking like it was growing out of her head in the background, was a young blonde woman in a zigzag-patterned coat. The word UNSOLVED was written over her photograph in red, as if it had been rubber-stamped.

'Mary Perkins. It's her, isn't it?' Loz said. 'Unmistakably. They call her a "party girl". I hate that, as if women bring it on themselves by going out and having fun.

'Look,' she went on. 'The coincidences come thick and fast. She grew up right here, in Tankerton, but had moved to London a few months before she went missing. And guess where she worked? Club by the name of Flamingos.'

Peg thought of the photograph of Mary and Raymond at the club doors.

'She was last seen in February 1992, walking on the docks east of London Bridge. Wasn't that where you said little Keith died?'

'I'm sure lots of people have died there. It's a place with water and high drops in the middle of a big city.'

'But your dad obviously knew her. Perhaps he can shed some light on what happened to her?'

'The deal I have to take on for Raymond's money is that we don't talk about the past.'

'So he's buying you off,' Loz said.

'No, but—'

'Or Aunty Jean's made you feel all dirty about nosing around and you're just being good little girl Meggy and doing as you're told.'

'But—'

'You're a grown-up now, Peg, and if you think something's off, you should follow your instinct. I mean, what right have

256

either of them got telling you what to do or think?'

'It's not like that.'

'Yes it is.'

'Could we keep it down a bit, please, girls?' the librarian had appeared at their shoulders and was standing over them, smiling but firm.

'Yes. Sorry,' Peg said.

The woman left and Peg stared at the screen in silence, feeling big, soft and blurry.

Loz scrolled down the page. For a second Peg thought she glimpsed something – a hunger – in her expression. The part of her that liked to read that creepy, exploitative stuff about real girls being ripped to pieces by real murderers was really enjoying this.

'Ugh,' Loz said. 'It says here that although initially she vanished without trace, they did eventually find something. Listen to this:

'"Three months later, poor Mary's head – and only her head – was found by a beachcomber on The Street, a spit of shingle that protrudes into the Thames Estuary right by her home town of Tankerton, Kent".'

'I know that story!' Peg gasped. 'That was Mrs Cairns's son. Colin.'

'Mrs Cairns?'

'You know, Nan's nosy neighbour. Her son was that beachcomber.'

Loz looked at her. 'It's getting really close to home, isn't it?'

'Colin found the head and the police arrested him.'

'Arrested him?'

'Or took him in for questioning. I'm not too clear on the details. In any case, he was a bit simple. The shame was too much for him and he hanged himself in the cells.'

Loz frowned. 'When did they move down here?' she asked Peg.

'Who?'

'Doll and Frank and Jean.'

'When I was two. So, what, 1990?'

'So Raymond would have known the area by '92. He would have come down here and visited. Perhaps with you, too,' Loz said, moving the cursor around the web page. 'I'm printing this lot off.'

'What is this website anyway?' Peg said.

'It's connected to this book I've got called *Unsolved*, about people whose disappearances are still a mystery. Any new information that's come up since publication can be found on here. Look.' Loz clicked on the home page, which showed a grid of photographs of faces, some colour, some black and white.

Peg's eye was drawn to one of the colour pictures. Her stomach clenched as she looked at the school portrait of the sharp-featured, red-haired girl in the blue blazer and striped tie. 'Who's that?' she said, her voice barely audible.

Loz clicked on the picture and, as the larger file slowly unfolded on the screen, Peg stopped breathing.

'No!'

'What?' Loz said, looking up at her.

'She's the girl from my school.'

'What girl?'

'There was a photo of her in the Gordon's box back at Nan's. I thought it had got there by mistake, but . . .'

'Are you sure?' Loz bent closer to look at the picture. Her nose was practically against the screen.

'What's her name?'

Loz clicked the info button. '"Anna Thurlow. Pupil at thirty thousand pound per year St Wilfrid's school, Wiltshire." Thirty grand? Jesus.'

Peg put her hand over her mouth. Seeing the name of the girl was like a punch to her stomach.

'"Vanished from the £3m family home in Hampshire during the summer of 2000 . . ." Shit, Peg. And her picture was in the same box as the Mary Perkins photos?'

Peg nodded.

'And you knew her?'

'I think so. I don't know, Loz.'

Loz pressed *print page*.

Anna Thurlow, Anna Thurlow.

Peg ran the name over in her mind, but the pathways to understanding why it so shocked her were buried.

'Can't we forget about all this?' she asked Loz as they crossed the library to the printer. She could hear the shake in her own voice.

'I think the answer to that is no, Peg. Two missing girls in one box?'

'What's that?' Peg asked her, pointing at a map on top of the pile of paper Loz pulled out of the printer tray.

'Heyworth Court.'

'Eh?'

Loz took the key and label from her back pocket. 'There's only one Heyworth Court in the whole of the south-east, and it's a block of flats in London SE1.'

'Fuck.'

'Day trip for tomorrow, I reckon. Don't you?'

Anna Thurlow, Anna Thurlow.

Peg regretted ever getting Loz involved in all this. With her love of a mystery, she was getting carried away, making too many connections based on the flimsiest of evidence.

It was beginning to look dangerous.

Peg had so wanted to find out the truth. But now she wished she was back where she had started – knowing nothing, and suspecting no one of anything.

And then she remembered why the name Anna Thurlow was so familiar to her.

Then

ANNA THURLOW WAS THE GIRL WHO MADE MY LIFE HELL.

Breathe.

I can feel the shame now.

Of all the tricky moments during my days and nights at school, the worst was being in the changing room after gym when Miss Humphrey, our foghorn-voiced gym teacher made us pull our leotards right off our sweaty little eight-year-old bodies – we weren't allowed to wear underwear – to take a shower.

She said if we didn't we'd make the whole school stink to high heaven all afternoon.

It was open season on Margaret Thwaites.

'Boing,' goes Anna Thurlow, the girl who because of the alphabet has the peg next to mine. She springs her index finger from behind her thumb, sharply flicking my breast bud, the only curve, apart from my own buttocks and hips, in the otherwise flat-chested room.

I try to ignore her as I edge towards the shower, my hands held tight in front of me, but it's too late.

'Look,' Anna says, too quietly for Miss Humphrey to hear, but loud enough to share with the four or five girls between me and her. 'Margaret's got hairs on her bum.'

'Erk,' one of the others says, and they all look at my offending area like it's somehow diseased. Which it might as well be, so freakish is it in someone of my age.

Nan told me when she ran me a bath the Christmas before this that some girls mature very early and, although she couldn't vouch for my mum, Aunty Jean was certainly fully developed by the age of ten, and that I reminded her of her in so many ways.

While I'm ambivalent about Aunty Jean now, I loved her with all my heart when I was younger.

But, even back then, I remember not finding this a particularly comforting thought.

Twenty-Six

PEG KNEW SHE APPEARED PREOCCUPIED AND SULKY IN THE Spanish delicatessen Loz had swooped on in Whitstable High Street, but she lacked the art to conceal it. After all that in the library, she just couldn't drum up much enthusiasm for the lovely olives and the gorgeous Manchego and membrillo.

Loz, on the other hand, seemed only to have drawn energy from her discoveries.

'I'd *love* to meet Raymond,' she said as she added peppers and rice to the pile of things on the counter that she wanted to buy. 'Ask him some questions about those missing girls.'

'I don't know . . .' Peg said, hanging back, leaning against a row of wooden shelves stacked high with fiercely expensive but insanely beautiful tins of tuna.

'Oh, I'm sure it would be all wrong and it'd all end in tears. But just think.' She turned to Peg, her eyes shining in the dimly lit shop. 'Just think. If he did it and we found him out.'

'For God's sakes, Loz. He's my father.'

'Myra Hindley's brother-in-law shopped *her*, you know.'

Wincing at the total – carried away, she hadn't looked at the prices – Loz paid and piled her shopping into the string bag she always carried with her.

'It's probably all just coincidence,' Peg said, opening the door for Loz. They stepped outside onto the narrow pavement. 'There's probably some really rational explanation.'

Drawing their coats tight, they set off up the dark hill towards Tankerton. The end-of-day traffic was still quite heavy, and moving much faster than it should in a town. A white van cruised past them, slower than all the other vehicles. The driver, who looked over at them as he passed, was bald, big and black.

'What?' Loz said, feeling Peg shudder next to her.

Fearing that she would only add material to Loz's dramatic construct, she said nothing. But the very presence of that white van reinforced her sense that the rational explanation behind photographs of two missing girls turning up in the same box at Raymond's mother's house was not one she particularly wanted to confront.

Just how closely *was* Raymond watching over her? And had he always been quite so attentive?

She knew now that all through the years she thought he had deserted her, he had in fact been keeping tabs.

But just how much did he know?

For example, did he know about what Anna Thurlow did to her?

'I wonder what the police would say if we told them what we've found?' Loz said, cutting across Peg's thoughts.

'You're kidding, aren't you?'

'Let's go and visit this Heyworth Court first.'

'We're not going to the police, Loz.'

'What if it was your sister, though, that had disappeared, Peg? Or your friend? Or *me*? If we have any information that we think would be useful to the police, then we have a duty to take it forward.'

Peg sighed and looked away. All she could think about was what it would do to Doll. 'We'd be wasting their time. It's only because we've nosed around in a couple of boxes that we shouldn't have. You're putting two and two together to make five.'

'I'm surprised at you, Peg. I always thought you were the Little Miss Moral in this relationship.'

By the time they had lugged the ingredients for a fine vegetarian paella back to the bungalow, it was gone seven. Julie's little car was parked in the driveway, and the usual easy-listening music and complaints seeped with the Marlboro smoke from Jean's extension.

Peg opened the door to the bungalow and they were met by a stink that, disappointingly, despite all their work, seemed to be worse than ever.

'Ugh. It's as if we've made no impression whatsoever in here,' Loz said, wrinkling her nose.

As Peg flicked on the hall light, a dark shape flew out of the bedroom, across the hallway and bowled into the kitchen, where it barrelled into something clattery.

'Lexy?' Peg said, following it through. The cat cowered by the door, scratching as if it were trying to dig its way out. 'Poor thing,' she said, unlocking the back door to let the panicking creature make its escape. 'How on earth did he get in here?'

'Jesus Christ,' Loz said from the bedroom. 'Come and look at this, Peg.'

'Oh God,' Peg said, then she retched in the doorway. The cat had emptied itself, from both ends and, from the look of it, quite violently, all over Doll's bed. The stench was overwhelming.

'We must've locked him in,' Peg said, covering her nose with her hand.

'Did we? I don't think we did, though,' Loz said.

'So how did he get in then?'

Through the partition, they heard Jean howling angrily at poor Julie's efforts to care for her.

Peg looked over at Loz, whose eyes were fixed on the wall as if she could see through it, her mind working overtime, spinning connections out of loose strands.

None of this was healthy. None of it at all.

Then

It's history and we're learning about the Great Fire of London. There's a lot of giggling going on behind me whenever Miss Grey turns her back to write something on the blackboard.

Don't think I can't hear it, because I can.

I sit at the front, on my own in a double desk, because it's safer.

Miss Grey turns to write '1666' on the blackboard, and 'Thomas Farriner', which is the name of the baker who left his oven on and caused the Great Fire. We're supposed to copy it all down in a list of things to remember for a test at the end of the week.

As I curl myself round my exercise book, I feel something light hit my back. This is followed by a snigger, which causes Miss Grey to turn and give the class one of her Looks. I wait for her to turn back to her writing before, without looking anyone in the eye, I turn and reach down to find the thing that hit me.

It is a crumpled-up ball of paper. I put it in my lap, smooth it out and see that it is a drawing of me with no clothes on. In the drawing, I have massive breasts that hang to my waist, long pubic hairs that reach to my knees. I have a puddle of something wet on the ground between my legs and snot hanging from my nose. The artist has also thought to give me a massive Afro and, as a final gesture, I have a bone through my nose, like a cartoon cannibal. Just to avoid any confusion, the picture has been labelled TRUE PORTRAIT OF MARGARET THWAITES.

I try to hold back the coldness it makes me feel by squeezing my shoulders in really tight. But this tiny, tiny movement is still noticed by those behind me, and another ripple of snorts passes back through the room, led by – I can hear her – Anna Thurlow.

'I WILL NOT HAVE THIS,' Miss Grey turns and tells the class. Behind me I feel the weight of twenty pairs of lips being pressed tight in against one another as they all turn silent.

I could tell. I could tell Miss Grey what she is doing to me. But I won't do it. Because that will only make things worse in the long run and I know if I keep my head down and my mouth shut this won't last forever.

She'll move off to a new target and I'll be left on my own, in peace.

I hope.

Twenty-Seven

THEY CLEARED AND AIRED THE STINKING BEDROOM, THEN ATE what they could of Loz's paella. In Peg's case, this wasn't a great deal: a creeping nausea seemed to be replacing her appetite, and not all of it was down to the cat mess.

She showed Loz the photograph of Anna Thurlow, and told her about the bullying and how it had felt to be on the receiving end.

'Poor you,' Loz said.

'Poor her,' Peg said, looking at the girl in the photograph. 'She was only a kid. She probably didn't even know how much she was hurting me.'

'Someone thought she deserved to die for it.'

'We don't know she's dead.'

Loz snorted.

'And what about it being a random abduction?' Peg went on. 'Or something completely unconnected to me? Eh? You just have to keep on making up these stories, don't you?'

'So why was her photo in the same box as Mary's?'

'For God's sake. It was probably sent to Nan by mistake,

instead of that one.' Peg pointed at the silver-framed school photo of herself on the bookshelf. 'She must've just forgotten to send it back.'

'Now who's making up stories?'

While Peg glowered on the settee, Loz sat at the table with her computer printouts and Frank's old London *A to Z* and worked out that, according to information supplied by the *Unsolved* website, Heyworth Court was about three streets away from where Mary Perkins's bedsit had been. It was one page after the green-biro-marked Flamingos and, from the address Frank had written under his name on the inside front cover of the *A to Z*, also just four streets in the other direction from the house where he and Doll had brought up Raymond and Jean, and where they had remained until they moved to Tankerton.

'All quite cosily tucked up together, aren't they? We can visit the other places too,' Loz said, poring over the map like a tourist planning a holiday. 'And then, perhaps next week, we can go to Hampshire and check out Anna Thurlow's parents' house.'

Peg tried to object but was faced down by Loz's own sense of the rightness of her quest.

This turned out to be the warm-up to the row which fully erupted when Peg told Loz that she really couldn't sleep with her in Doll's bed. The cat business had made her mind up, as if it were some sort of sign to confirm that she shouldn't.

'You're welcome to come up to my room and share the bed there, though,' she said.

'For God's sake, Peg.'

'It just doesn't feel right, not in Nan's bed.'

'What? Worried that Aunty Jean might somehow find out?'

'No—'

'Is Meggy worried that she might upset her aunty?'

'Don't be so fucking nasty, Loz.'

'I'm not being nasty. You're putting your aunt's homophobia before me. What about how I feel?'

'It's not like that—'

'She called me a filthy pervert!'

'She didn't mean it. She—'

'Oh go upstairs and sleep in your little-girl single bed,' Loz said and, slamming Doll's bedroom door, barred Peg from any further argument.

So they spent the first two hours of the night apart until, unable to sleep and feeling wretched, Peg tiptoed down the ladder and crept in beside Loz, curling herself against her back.

'I'm sorry,' Loz murmured. 'You have to tell me to shut up sometimes.'

'Shut up sometimes,' Peg said, kissing the base of her neck and cupping her small breasts in her hands.

'But we mustn't,' Loz said, turning in her arms to face her. 'What would Aunty Jean say?'

'Fuck Aunty Jean,' Peg said, kissing Loz and pulling her full against her.

'Naughty Peg. Naughty, naughty Meggy.'

The air of détente had carried them through breakfast and on to the train, where Loz's manic certainty that they were going to find the lock for the key clashed badly with the sulk that had descended upon Peg when the reality of what they were actually doing hit her.

Half of her was annoyed that Loz was taking them away from the far more important work of clearing the bungalow to engage in what would more than likely be a futile, needle-in-haystack exercise.

The other half hoped that it *would* be a futile, needle-in-haystack exercise.

In her excitement, Loz almost dragged Peg down the slope from the platform at London Bridge Station. Map in hand – this was unfamiliar territory beyond the occasional Loz-led foodie foray into Borough Market – they set off on foot for a mile or so south. They passed through the renovated, Shard, City pied-à-terre areas of Southwark – which, apart from certain bits of Chelsea and Knightsbridge, contained some of the highest priced property in London – down into the grittier segments of the borough, which, even with the fat cats to the north, earned it a place among one of the most deprived in London.

This was a London of buildings that look derelict but which, on closer inspection, bear signs of habitation. Of groups of boys hanging with fierce-looking dogs, of sharp-faced, thin women, hurrying along litter-strewn pavements, off to meet some appointment or other to stop the gap between body and soul. Of thirteen-year-old girls pushing buggies containing sticky, dummy-stopped babies, each of them deserving a better start in life.

As they moved through these streets, even Loz modified her customary, I-know-all-this swagger, so that she moved with an energy more like Peg's.

'We're nearly there,' she said, sneaking a peek at the *A to Z*, which, not wishing to appear like an outsider, she had hidden in her bag. 'Next street.'

They turned a corner and came to a boarded-off area stretching an entire block. In between impressively wrought graffiti, signs declared that this was the work of Southwark Council, who, with an interminable list of private contractors, was 'Bringing You a Brighter Future'. A series of obscenely altered developers' visualisations showed a 'before' of a grim tower block replaced by an 'after' of low-rise, low-impact housing with happy children enjoying safe-surfaced playgrounds and plentiful, crudely drawn penises.

'Fucking brilliant. They've only knocked Heyworth Court down,' Loz said, leaning against the hoarding, as if she had walked five thousand miles to discover this.

A wave of relief passed through Peg.

Loz ripped the key out of her pocket and looked at it as if it had slighted her. 'I suppose if there had been anything incriminating inside the flat, there would have been something in the news about it when they knocked it down. So let's find out when they did it and look it up in those online archives of yours.'

'What did you expect to find?'

'I dunno. Bloodstains? A mummified corpse? Something under the concrete?'

'You read too much of that crap, you know. Life's not like that.'

'It is though, Peg.' Loz looked at her with immense seriousness. 'That "crap" is *all about* real life.'

'You're too gullible.'

'Ha! You're a fine one to talk.'

'Don't be cruel.'

'What a fucking disappointment.' Loz kicked the ground.

'What do you want to do now?' Peg said, leaning back against the hoarding next to Loz and squinting up at the heavy grey sky that loomed over them, threatening snow.

'Might as well walk round the block,' Loz said. 'Then we'll go and get some lunch up Bermondsey Street. But I've lost me enthusiasm now.'

Good, Peg thought.

They followed the hoarding along the street. Every ten yards or so, peepholes cut at varying heights allowed passers-by to see what was going on inside. All that remained of what had once been the tower block was a big hole in the ground. There were no bricks, no leftover girders, no materials whatsoever to suggest that a building had once stood there full of lives, families and secrets. The machinery that had dismantled it had also been removed, leaving just a void. The only sounds were of distant traffic, an eerie, echoing dog bark and the occasional train rumbling along the tracks criss-crossing the area.

For the middle of one of the largest cities in the world, it was a pretty empty place.

Still following the outline of the site, they turned down a side street until they came to a driveway. Boarded up on either side, it led deep into the centre of where the building had once stood.

'Let's go and get lunch,' Peg said, trying to pull Loz away.

'No. Let's investigate.' Loz shook herself free and set off along the drive. Reluctantly, Peg followed, tripping over the rutted tarmac and trying to avoid the icy puddles of muddy rainwater that lurked in the potholes.

The track led to a long, narrow cul-de-sac lined with rusted garages on one side and a high wall on the other. Defying the season, weeds and saplings sprouted among the buildings, reclaiming territory long lost to council developers.

The garages looked disused except for one right in the middle of the row, where an old dustbin with holes punched in it stood burning rather desolately by an open door. Inside, someone was using a noisy power tool, grinding metal on metal.

There was something about this deserted urban space that made Peg feel uneasy. *Gave her the collywobbles*, as Doll might put it. She put her hand on Loz's arm. 'I don't like it here. Can't we just go?'

'Just give me a minute,' Loz said. She crossed over to the open garage. 'Hello?' she called into the darkness inside.

'Arseholes,' a voice grumbled from within. Then the grinding noise stopped.

After a couple of moments, a wiry, weather-beaten man came to the garage door. Framed by the filthy earflaps of a Russian army hat, his face was as grimy with engine oil as the overalls that hung from him. A yellow roll-up dangled from his lower lip.

'What the fuck do you want?' he said.

'Hi,' Loz said. 'We were just wondering what this place is.'

'You from the council?' the man said, narrowing his eyes and drawing on his cigarette so that his cheekbones protruded, skull-like, from his face.

'Do we look like it?' Loz said.

The man shrugged and threw his cigarette on the ground.

'Why are these garages here?' she asked him.

The man's lips parted slightly, revealing black gaps between yellowed teeth. 'Why is anything here?'

'I mean, why are the garages still standing, if the building's been knocked down?'

'Tory bastards sold them off in the eighties. So they're all privately owned. There's leases still to run out and the owners want too much money for them. Council don't have a leg to stand on.'

'Ah.' Loz pulled the key from her pocket again and held it out. 'Do you know if this might fit one of the garages?'

The man took the key and held it far from his eyes to read the label. 'Looks like it.'

'We thought it was for a flat.'

'Nah. That's not a fucking house key, is it?' he said, waving it in front of her. 'Where'd you find it, girls?'

'We were clearing out her nan's bungalow,' Loz said.

'Did she own the garage, God rest her?'

'Oh, she's not . . . She's only in hospital,' Peg said quickly, from behind Loz. Something in her still wanted to run away from this place.

'Sorry, my mistake. What I meant was if she owns it, it might be worth a bob or two to her,' he said. 'With the council being desperate and all that.'

'I don't know if it's hers . . .'

'What's the lady's name, then? I've had this,' he gestured to the garage behind him, 'for forty-odd years. Might be able to find the right one for you.'

'Thwaites. Dorothy – or Doll – Thwaites,' Peg said.

The man frowned and stuck out his lower lip. The cracks and creases in his skin reminded Peg of badly tanned leather.

'Or you might know Raymond, her son?' Loz chipped in.

The man removed his hat and scratched his mostly bald head, as if encouraging blood to his brain. Peg noticed that, deep within his grizzled face, there was some warmth in his sharp grey eyes.

'That rings a bell,' he said at last. 'Shortish bloke? Sharp dresser? White Jag? With the little old mum and the fat sister?'

'That's them!'

'You're not the pigs are you?'

Loz laughed. 'Nah, Raymond's her dad.'

'You're having a laugh. He never struck me as the dad type.'

'Me neither,' Peg said.

'Ah.' The man nodded at her. 'Bit of a flash fucker, wasn't he. Must've been the same age as what I was, but he had the suit, the Jag.'

'He's in Spain now,' Peg said, as if this somehow explained why they might be wanting to nose around in his garage.

'Lucky fucker. If there's one place I'd be if I could – other than here, of course – it'd be Spain. Love it. *Y Viva España* and all that shit.' He hinted at a matador pose by slightly raising his arms.

'There's Spain and there's Spain,' Peg said, thinking of the stifling acres of marble at her father's house and the stench of the cesspit.

'Can you show us which garage it is?' Loz said. 'I'm Loz, by the way. And this is Peg.'

'Parker,' the man said, holding out an oily hand. As he moved, he gave off the smell of diesel. 'Arseholes, it's fucking cold today, innit? Fancy a cuppa in a bit?' He motioned to his garage.

'That'd be lovely,' Loz said.

'I'll get the kettle going, then, girls. Hold on a tick.' He dipped inside.

'I don't want to do this,' Peg whispered to Loz.

'Course you do.'

'I don't. I—'

'Well now. Let's see if I can remember.' Parker hobbled back out and led them down the row of garages. He had a pronounced limp, and it seemed to be an effort for him to walk. Talking, however, came quite easily to him.

'Most of these units are empty now. There's only a few come down here these days. Mind you, not that it was ever Piccadilly Circus. Most people originally got the garages with their flats – well, mine came with my old mum's, God rest her – and used them to store the tat they couldn't fit indoors. Cars was beyond most of them. But your dad was separate. He never lived in the block. Not really the council type, was he? Now then.' He stopped in front of the very last garage, tucked away almost right against a wall that marked a dead end. 'This is the one.'

Peg and Loz looked at the garage door. Once white, like all the others, it was now almost entirely rust and graffiti.

'I don't think we should do this,' Peg said to Loz. She turned to Parker. 'Do you know what he kept in there?'

Parker shrugged. 'I didn't used to be down here quite so much back then. He never kept his Jag in it, though, mind. Nor would I leave a nice motor like that down here. Didn't he have some club somewhere?'

'Flamingos,' Loz said.

'Something like that. Well, I think he used this place for storage, if you know what I mean. Goods that needed to be out of the way?'

'Stolen?' Peg said.

Parker shrugged. 'Me, I never ask too many questions.'

'When did you last see him down here?'

Parker frowned and rubbed the back of his neck. 'Years back. I was away on tour mostly, but I saw him around from time to time back in the day when I was on leave. Till about the nineties, I suppose. I just saw the mum and the sister after that.'

A kettle whistled from inside his unit. 'Got a pot of tea to make,' he said. 'That's the one though.' He banged the garage door.

'You ready?' Loz said, after he had shuffled away.

'It's just storage,' Peg said. 'If Aunty Jean and Nan used it, it's probably just more of the same old stuff we've been clearing out of the bungalow.'

'Yeah,' Loz said, not altogether convinced. 'It'll only be some old pop socks and bags of sweet wrappers.'

'Shall we not bother?'

Loz rolled her eyes. 'I can't let this lie, Peg. Not until I've got to the bottom of it.'

Peg kicked a can that was lying on the ground, skittering it across the crumbled tarmac. It was pointless to object.

'Better get it over with, then,' she said.

Loz fitted the key into the central lock of the up-and-over door.

'It's the right one,' she said, looking at Peg excitedly. She turned it, then grasped the handle and tried to twist it open, but the door didn't move.

'Can you give it a go?' She stood aside for Peg, who took the handle in both hands and tried with all her strength to turn it.

It wasn't moving.

'Mr Parker! Mr Parker?' Loz called, running back to the open garage.

He came back outside with a large, grimy tray of tea things. 'It's just Parker, love. What is it?'

'We can't get the garage open.'

'They can be a bit tricky.'

He put the tray down on top of a big tyre, turning it into a sort of table, and limped over to where Peg was still battling with the door. Leaning on it with one hip he lifted the handle and twisted it at the same time.

'It's not going anywhere, girls.'

'Have you got any oil?' Loz said.

'Oil won't do the trick.' He was squatting down, feeling along the bottom edge of the door. 'Look.'

He held aside a tuft of grass to reveal another lock. Then he stood and pointed up under the lintel.

'Some kind of rack bolt top and bottom. You'll need at least one other key to get into here.'

Loz and Peg stood and looked at the door. A giant Airbus

passed by overhead, its booming engine so close it made the metal garage doors rumble.

'Have you got any tools we could use to get it open?' Loz asked.

'Nah, mate,' Parker said, putting his hands up. 'I've got the council watching my every move so they can get me. I'm not doing no breaking and entering.'

'But it's her nan's garage,' Loz said. 'Or her dad's, at any rate.'

'And so it's not hers. You bring down her nan or her dad and, right as rain, I'll help you get in there, but until I see them, and paperwork proves they own it, I'm not doing nothing. Now, if you don't mind, I'll go and pour out that tea. Don't want it to get stewed.'

'Fuck.' Loz moved into the alley that led between the garage and the end of the driveway, testing its walls with her fingers as if they might somehow give way.

'Let's just have a cuppa with Parker, then we'll go and get something to eat,' Peg said as Loz disappeared round the back of the row of buildings. She pulled the key out of the garage door and put it in her back pocket.

Alone for a moment, she was suddenly aware of the fact she had been there before, on that very spot. A dull nausea filled her belly, and sharp prickles ran down her spine.

She really wanted to run away.

'Peg! Come and see!' Loz called.

Keen not to be on her own for a second longer, Peg picked her way through the mud and weeds to join her in the alley.

'Look,' Loz said.

Each of the garages had a small window at the back. Not big enough to climb through, they were presumably designed to let in a little light and air. Loz was leaning on the one at the back of the family garage, prising apart a makeshift fence of barbed wire, trying to see through the filthy, wired glass.

'Is that some sort of table?' she said, stepping back to let Peg have a look.

Peg pressed her face to the window, cupping her eyes with her hands. All she could see was a murky collection of shadowy shapes. 'Could be. Or a bed or something.'

She shuddered.

'Shit. I wish we could get in.' Loz kicked the concrete garage wall.

'Well we can't.' Peg said. Then she saw the gash in Loz's palm. 'What's that?'

'Oh bollocks,' Loz said. 'It's so cold I didn't notice.'

'Must've been on that barbed wire. Looks nasty,' Peg said, bending to examine it. 'And there could be all sorts of bugs in it, with all that rust.'

'Girls!' Parker shouted. 'Tea's mashed.'

'D'you think he's all right?' Peg asked Loz.

'Yeah,' Loz said. 'Harmless.'

The blood was running down Loz's arm, dripping onto the icy ground. 'We need to get that seen to. Perhaps he's got a first-aid kit,' Peg said, trying to disguise the fact that, despite all the medical training she had received from Doll, something about the sight of that wound in this place made her feel as if her knees were about to give way.

Loz raised an eyebrow at Peg.

They squeezed along the alley and returned to Parker's garage, where he had placed three variously dilapidated folding chairs round the dustbin, which was newly blazing with wood from a pile of broken-down pallets.

'Casualty?' he said, pointing to Loz's hand.

'You haven't got a plaster?' Peg said.

Parker took Loz's hand and examined it. 'Sit down girl,' he said. Then, handing out the tea and biscuits, he disappeared inside his garage. A few minutes later he emerged with a camouflaged canvas shoulder bag emblazoned with a red cross. He knelt at Loz's side, opened the bag and, after pulling on a pair of disposable gloves identical to those Peg and Doll used when caring for Jean, he cleaned Loz's wound with a sterile wipe.

'It could do with a stitch,' he said, once he could see the extent of the cut. 'But my suturing material's expired and I'm not taking any risks. I'll give it a couple of paper stitches and bandage it instead. Should be fine. Have you had a tetanus jab recently?'

Loz nodded.

'Good. I could've helped you out there, but no need then.'

Peg watched as he worked on Loz's hand. He was good. As good as Doll, she thought. Professional. She felt safer over here, away from the other garage.

'How do you know all this?' she said.

'Army medical corps,' he said. 'Nineteen eighty to 1995. Active service in Falklands, Gulf and Bosnia. Retired with knackered leg, fucked-up lungs and buggered sense of smell due to gas inhalation. I done my fucking time all right.'

'Your old man's sister got fat, though, didn't she?' Parker said, once Loz was bandaged and they were settled in front of the flaming dustbin with cups of tea.

Peg looked at him. 'You mean Aunty Jean?'

'Yeah. I suppose she's your aunt then.' Parker nodded, cradling his mug between oily fingers. 'She used to be not such a bad looker when she come down here back in the days when there was the flats and that. She used to boss your dad about

282

something rotten. But when she come down a couple of years ago, I couldn't believe the size of her.'

'A couple of years ago?' Peg said. 'But Aunty Jean's not been out of bed for over ten years.'

'Is that so? Let me think now, I still had the flat then, so it must've been before 2002. Not a couple of years, then. Oh yes. I remember her not taking kindly to my dog, and he went in 2001, God bless him. So it must've been around 2000. More like twelve or thirteen years, in fact. Time flies when you get old like me, girls.'

Peg frowned. 'What was she doing down here?'

'It's all coming back now,' Parker said, rubbing his nose between his thumb and fingers. 'Here, give us that key again.'

Peg reached into her back pocket and handed the key to Parker.

'Where'd you say you found it?' he asked her.

'On top of a wardrobe at my nan's. Under some boxes.'

'She was trying to get into the garage. That's right. She'd lost a key. Must've been this one, then. Quite upset about it, she was. She'd heard about the plans for the flats and was worried they was going to knock down the garages as well. Said she had some stuff in there she wanted. She was quite aerated about it. He must've hidden it on top of the wardrobe, then.' Parker nodded to himself and handed the key back to Peg.

'What do you mean? Who must've hidden it?'

'Her dad. She kept on going on how her dad had hidden the key and wasn't letting her have it. Memorable, that: all that temper in someone so large. Fucking scary.'

Loz had not said a word through all this, but Peg could see that she was working on something as she drank her tea and stared into the flames, nursing her hand, listening to their conversation. At last she looked up at Parker.

'Are you here a lot?' she asked him.

Parker leaned forward and cupped his hand to his mouth. 'Don't let on, girls, but . . .' and he got even closer to them and whispered, 'I'm here all the time. I live here. I grew up in them flats, and when they pulled them down I didn't want to go nowhere else. Didn't want to be rehoused somewhere out in fucking Medway or something. So I just sort of moved in here. Keep an eye on the place, like a sort of unofficial security guard I suppose.'

'Don't you get scared?' Peg asked. 'Down here on your own at night?'

Parker laughed. 'I can take care of myself, girl. I've been in a lot worse situations.'

'Will you do us a favour?' Loz said. 'If you see anyone come down to look at the garage, will you let me know?'

'Leave it, Loz,' Peg said. 'Who's going to come down here out of the blue?'

Loz shrugged. 'It's just a hunch. With all the mud being stirred up. You never know. Will you, Parker? We might find out who's got that other key.'

'Course, girl. Give me your number.'

Loz scribbled her phone number on a blank page at the back of a gory crime book she had in her bag, tore it out and handed it to Parker, who received it with great seriousness.

Later, they found Mary Perkins's bedsit and Doll and Frank's old house, but they were just anonymous Victorian terraces on unremarkable South London streets.

'Shall we knock on the door?' Loz asked as they stood outside the old family home. 'Ask if we can take a look around?'

'Do you want to be taken for a complete lunatic?' Peg said.

Loz shook her head. 'S'pose you've got a point.'

They headed back to London Bridge, Peg quietly wondering what it had been about the locked garage that had made her whole body reel.

If only she could put her finger on it . . .

But she didn't mention a word of this to Loz.

That would have been like pouring petrol on a fire.

Then

HERE COMES ANOTHER ONE.

I don't like these.

I wish I couldn't remember them. I've tried to think of something lovely, but I just seem to be stuck in this groove now. This school-was-hell groove.

It's later now and, after an evening lurking in a carrel at the far end of the library – my favourite hiding place – I use the bathroom last and put my nightie on in the toilet stall. Then, careful to avoid everyone's eye, I walk the length of the dormitory to get to my bed, which is the last of all twelve.

I pull the duvet back and climb in, ready to bury myself for the day. But as I do so, I hear the snort again, like a room full of stupid dogs with bones stuck in their throats, and I realise that my bed is not as dry as it should be. In fact, as I lie down, it squelches with the dousing of a good jugful of cold water. I continue to settle myself down though, as if nothing is amiss. I refuse to allow them the satisfaction. The cold water seeps into my skin, stinging me.

From the shelter of my covers, I take a look behind me at the other beds and they are all shaking. Not with cold like me, but with laughter as Miss Elliott comes to turn the lights off and tells everyone to calm down.

Ugh.

Twenty-Eight

BY THE END OF THE FOLLOWING DAY, AND AFTER A LOT OF HARD work, they had the bungalow pretty much clear, and, as Mrs Cairns informed Peg when she went out to get a pint of milk, the pile of rubbish in the garden almost entirely covered the overgrown lawn.

Peg visited Jean several times, but Loz, in her endless speculations about what was in the garage, had decided that they had to keep everything level with – and here she had dropped into an imitation of Parker – 'your old man's fat sister'. She declared that no mention of keys, garages or missing girls was to be made to Jean, and, to keep her sweet, she wasn't going to join Peg on her trips to her bedside.

Peg felt relieved on all counts by this.

'Best I don't get within earshot,' Loz said, as they scrubbed out the newly cleared kitchen cupboards. 'You know what a blunderbuss I am. I can't be relied on to keep my trap shut like a good little girl.'

'Like me, you mean?' Peg said.

'I never said nothing.' Loz smiled, sat back on her heels and held her hands up in the air.

But even Peg found it hard not to ask about the garage. And Jean didn't make it any easier by subjecting her to a grilling about their trip to London.

'Something came up at the restaurant,' Peg said.

'So why did you have to go too?' Jean said, flicking off the TV with the remote and turning to face her.

'Um, it was a good friend's birthday, so I—'

'But you've got to sort things out for Mummy! Isn't that more important than gallivanting off to London? I suppose you saw that demonstration, then?'

'Demonstration?'

'Yes, that student thing. Running battles all the way down Oxford Street they said on the telly. Dreadful. I don't know where all the respect's gone. That girl's restaurant is in Soho, you said? You must've passed it on the way.'

'We must've just missed it.'

'But you were there at lunchtime, you said? It was right over the middle of the day.'

'Oh, we were inside most of the time.'

And so it went on, Peg proving what she already knew – that she was rubbish at lying – and Jean, with apparently innocent questioning, managing to drive her into a corner. It was clear she thought Peg was up to something. It was as if now she had cottoned on to the true nature of her relationship with Loz – and Peg was sure that this was the case, although of course there would never be the chance of a conversation about it – Jean had labelled the two of them as entirely suspect.

And who was to say they weren't? Peg *was* lying to Jean – something she realised she had never done before. She might in the past have omitted a few facts just to keep her sweet, but to tell her things that were actually untrue . . . Well, this was something new.

Payback time, perhaps, for all the lies she now knew she had been told?

Or just a sign of how low she was sinking?

If Peg had felt without edges before all this family mess began to reveal itself, at least she could have said back then that she knew what goodness was, and that some part of the way she led her life contributed to the stock of it in the world.

Now she wasn't so sure about anything.

And something indefinable continued to gnaw at her, making her feel sicker and sicker, as if she were really ill, as if she had some sort of cancer growing inside her.

When Peg went out later to get another pint of milk – they were fuelling themselves with endless cups of tea – she also stopped at a cashpoint. With a sinking feeling she saw that her balance, which rarely stretched beyond two figures, now showed that she had eight thousand pounds in her account.

Raymond had come through pretty efficiently.

Good old Raymond.

The first thing she and Loz decided to spend the money on was getting rid of the rubbish in the back garden.

'I'm looking for a *woman* and a van, really,' Loz said, flipping through the fat *Yellow Pages* she had on her knee.

The day's work done, they were sitting with a bottle of beer each in Doll's newly pristine and slightly antiseptic lounge.

'Does it really matter who's driving, so long as we can get all that shit carted away?' Peg said. The pile of bulging bin liners had turned the back garden into a small-scale municipal tip, and, as Mrs Cairns had informed Peg that morning, something needed to be done 'before the rats move in'.

'Here's one,' Loz said. '"James and Daughter. No job too small".'

'Perfect. Tell me the number,' Peg said, pulling her phone from her pocket. But just as she was dialling, Doll's house phone rang – the first time Peg had heard it doing so since she had moved away to London.

'Hello?' she said cautiously.

'Can I speak to Ms Margaret Thwaites, please?' the rather camp young male voice at the other end asked.

'Speaking.' She had no idea why someone like that would be calling her at the bungalow and asking for her by her horrible full name.

'My name's Jamie. I'm calling from the Kent Hospitals' Trust. I'm afraid—'

'Nan!' Peg gasped, her heart lurching.

'Ooh, no, sorry. It's not bad news. Well, not really. Not that sort of bad news. In a way it's the reverse. Well, I'm afraid we've had a bit of a Norovirus outbreak on the ward Mrs Thwaites is staying on at the moment.' He made it sound like a hotel room, and that Doll was there on some sort of mini-break. 'And we've no choice but to shut down for a deep clean.

'Mrs Thwaites has been looked at by our discharge team and, in view of pressure on beds, she has been assessed as capable of returning to her home which is, due to the level of infection present in the ward, the best place for her to be.'

'Oh,' Peg said. 'Well. That's great news.'

'What is it?' Loz said, as Peg put the phone down after Jamie had finished running through the arrangements for Doll's return.

'She's coming home,' Peg said, buoyed by the absurd hope that things could return to normal. 'Nan'll be home tomorrow.'

Twenty-Nine

AT MIDDAY THE FOLLOWING DAY – A DAY SO COLD THE FOG AND frost still hung in the air like a freezing blanket – the ambulance appeared.

It was an hour earlier than expected, turning into the driveway just as Peg returned from walking Loz to the station; her three days' leave had expired and Cara had called that morning to beg her to come in early, as yet more staff were off sick.

'Are you sure she should be coming home?' Peg said, as the paramedics – a cheery, plump-cheeked woman who introduced herself as Sue, and her co-worker Don, a tall man with an Elastoplast under a half-closed bruised eye – slid Doll out of the back of the vehicle. As they put up the sides of the wheeled stretcher to move her in to the bungalow, the old lady remained fast asleep, her skin ashen, her breath coming in small rasps, sending feeble puffs of steam into the thick, icy air.

'Believe me, darling, she's a million times better off here,' Sue said.

'Don't quote me,' Don said in a voice that matched his

gloomy demeanour, 'but they've already lost five to the bug, and there's twelve more in intensive care.'

'Too much information, Don.' Sue shot him a warning look, then turned to Peg. 'Don't worry, dear. Mrs Thwaites is just a bit dozy. They gave her a little something to keep her calm for the journey.'

'Didn't she want to come home?' Peg said.

'I should say not,' Don said. 'She put up quite a fight.' He gestured to his eye.

'She did that to you?' Peg was astonished. Doll couldn't harm a fly.

'She was just a bit confused,' Sue said. 'They get like that.'

They wheeled her to the front porch, where they realised they had a problem. There was not enough room to turn the dogleg to get to the front door.

'We'll have to get her up, put her in a seat,' Don said.

'I'd rather not. Is there another way in?' Sue asked.

'We can go in through her daughter's extension,' Peg said, thinking of the wide corridors and the one-way door into Doll's lounge. 'I'll just go and check with Aunty Jean.'

'Don't keep us hanging around out here too long though, love,' Don said. 'It's brass monkeys.'

'I'll get another blanket for her,' Sue said, heading back to the ambulance.

Peg got the key to Jean's back door and quietly let herself in, in case her aunt was sleeping. The hot, dry air of the central heating almost sucked her in out of the cold. A chipper voiceover from some reality TV show jeered at high volume from the bedroom, but Jean tended to keep the telly on all day long, dozing through it at intervals, so this didn't necessarily mean she was awake.

'Aunty Jean?' Peg called softly, but there was no reply. She tiptoed through to the hallway and peered through the half-open bedroom door.

'Naughty Lexy,' Aunty Jean scolded. She had thrown her bedcovers off and, to Peg's astonishment, with her tent-dress riding up so that it displayed the wide, pinkly mottled expanse of her buttocks, she hauled herself up in the bed and rolled over so that her head was at the foot end.

Reaching out with her grabber, she righted a pelican figurine that had been knocked from its watchful position on her dressing table.

'The poor pellies don't like to be upset, naughty pussy cat,' Jean said, dragging herself even further to look under the bed where Lexy must have taken cover. In doing so, she exposed yet more rippling regions of flesh.

Stunned, Peg backed silently away, retracing her steps to the kitchen.

Jean could barely prop herself up in bed, let alone swing her body round like that.

Peg's cheeks flushed with anger at the thought of poor Doll knackering her back hoisting her daughter up and down, doing things for her that she could, from the evidence she had just seen, quite clearly manage on her own.

In Peg's eyes, this removed every last shred of credibility from Jean. She was going to watch her like a hawk.

She was going to watch her with Loz's eyes.

She opened and slammed the back door and called her aunt again, as loudly as she could.

'Is that you, Meggy? I thought you said you were going to the station with that girl. Can you stay there just a mo, dear, please?' Jean called breathlessly. 'OK, I'm decent dear,' she said after the amount of time Peg reckoned it would take to nimbly swing herself back and cover herself up.

Peg stuck her head round Jean's bedroom door and forced a smile. Her aunt lay back on her mound of pillows, rather pinker than usual. Her arms flopped at her sides, and, without moving her head, which she was making out was too much effort for her, she looked sideways at Peg.

'Has that "Loz" gone, then?'

'Yes.'

'I hope Mummy never finds out.'

'What do you mean?'

'You know darn tooting what I mean.'

Peg chose to ignore Jean. She needed to focus on getting Doll inside, out of the cold.

'She's back.'

'Eh?'

'Nan. She's back. They came early. Is it OK if they bring her through here? They can't get the stretcher thingy through her door.'

'Of course dear,' Jean said, her voice weaker than it had been, resuming its invalid character. She pulled the bedcovers up to her chin.

Peg went outside, where Sue and Don had wrapped Doll up in a couple of spare blankets. She led them to Jean's door and they wheeled the stretcher through the hallway.

'Mummy! Mummy!' Jean called feebly from her bedroom. At the sound of her daughter's voice, Doll's eyes shot open.

'Jeanie?' she said. 'Is Jeanie come to visit?'

'We're at home, Nan,' Peg said, leaning forward to stroke her tiny, wrinkled forehead.

'Home? Let me see her?'

'Is it OK if she goes in to see her daughter?' Peg asked the ambulance people.

Don, who was at Doll's head end, looked at Sue, who was at her feet.

'Bless her,' Sue said and nodded, so they pushed her into Jean's room.

'Ooh!' Don said, as he caught sight of Jean. Sue flashed him another of her looks.

'Mummy,' Jean said, reaching out a puffy hand for her. 'Oh Mummy.'

Doll pulled her own hand out of her tightly tucked-in sheet and took her daughter's fingers. 'Ooh, Jeanie. How are you doing, darling? I missed you so much.'

'Not so bad, Mummy,' Jean said, her chins quivering. Doll struggled up on her stretcher so that they were close enough to kiss.

Sue smiled at Peg, her eyes moist.

'Now, don't you go and start frightening me and Meggy again, will you, Mummy?'

'No dear,' Doll said. 'I try not to frighten anyone. I keep it nice and safe.' Her tiny hand, contoured with loose wrinkled skin like an old map, rested on the fleshy plane of Jean's cheek. 'Don't worry about me, dears. I'll be up and about in no time and we can send the girl packing and I'll be looking after you again like I always have.'

'Of course you will, Mummy.'

Peg glanced up at Sue and Don and gave a little shake of her head. She didn't want them to start thinking she was about to let that happen.

Eventually, they prised Doll away from Jean and wheeled her through the one-way door into her part of the bungalow. Heading in first, Peg spotted the photograph of Doll with Raymond, Jean and Keith still propped up on the bookcase. Cursing herself for her oversight, she turned it face down to avoid upsetting Doll.

But upset was not entirely avoided. As the partition door swung shut behind her, Doll pulled herself up on to her elbows.

'I thought we were going home?' she said, outraged, her voice at full pitch. 'What place is this? Where have you brought me?'

'We *are* home, Nan,' Peg said, taking her hand. 'This is your lounge. We had to clear it up a bit so that your carers can look after you properly.'

'Who the fuck are you?' Doll roared, snatching her hand away.

'Sorry,' Peg said to Sue. Despite the fact that she knew Doll would take the clean-up badly, the hostility of her reaction stung her.

'Oh don't worry,' Sue said. 'Change is so hard for them, isn't it? We'll get her tucked in and calm her down.'

Peg led them into the bedroom, where, looking around in horror at her rearranged room, Doll was transferred into her own bed.

'There we are, Mrs Thwaites,' Don said, arranging the sheets for her. 'Back home.'

'Tell that to the ceiling,' Doll said, looking away.

'Perhaps we could have a word?' Sue said, unhooking a bag from Doll's stretcher and leading Peg back into the lounge. 'These are her medicines and instructions on what she needs to take when.' She handed the bag over. 'And the district nurse will be in tomorrow as soon as she can to settle Mrs Thwaites in. There's some leaflets in there to give you some pointers on diet and hygiene.'

'How much longer till we get the carers set up?' Peg asked, feeling a little overwhelmed by what was being asked of her.

'I'm afraid I have no idea. That's really a matter for Social Services. This is just an emergency measure. And I've got another five patients like your grandmother to get to their homes this afternoon.'

'Oh yes. Sorry. I didn't mean to keep you.'

'She's all settled.' Don wheeled the empty stretcher back into the lounge.

'We'd better get a move on,' Sue said, taking the front of the stretcher. She went to the door in Doll's lounge wall that led back to Jean's part of the bungalow, but it had swung shut and she couldn't open it.

'It's one-way only,' Peg said. 'I'll go back through Aunty Jean's and let you through.'

Peg let herself once more through Jean's door.

'Pretty grim, eh?' she heard Don say from Jean's bedroom.

'It was quite touching though, when the old lady kissed the fat one,' Sue said.

'Fat one,' Peg heard Jean mutter. 'She's no stick insect herself.'

Despite feeling that she was doing too much creeping around behind her aunt's back, Peg tiptoed once more to Jean's bedroom door. Sue and Don weren't in there, of course. There was no way they could have got through the interconnecting door. But Jean was there, sitting upright in her bed, eating a bar of chocolate and holding the white box of the intercom to her ear as if it were a big telephone, listening in to what was going on in the lounge.

Peg wobbled as her mind raced back over what she and Loz had said and done in Doll's bungalow, thinking they were alone, unobserved. Had Jean heard it all? Shame stung at her cheeks.

That's why she hadn't been believed about the trip to London – Jean had known what they were doing. She might even know of their suspicions about the vanished girls, and that

Peg had gone behind her back and accepted Raymond's money.

Peg quietly went back to the interconnecting door between Jean's hallway and Doll's lounge and, as noisily as possible, opened it and greeted the ambulance people.

What the hell was Jean playing at?

Thirty

'I'M SO GLAD SHE'S BACK,' JEAN SAID.

Having made sure that Doll was tucked up and fast asleep, Peg sat drinking Guinness with Jean and biting her tongue.

'How long are you going to stay with us, Meggy?' Jean asked, as she helped herself to another mini sausage roll from the stacked plateful she had made Peg fetch in from the kitchen.

'I'm going to see if I can get another week off, until we get Nan's carers sorted. And I could commute for a bit if it came to it.'

'Oh, you don't need to do that. We'll be back to normal in no time. Really Meggy, there's no need to stay next week as well.'

This independent stance was an interesting new tack for Jean to be taking. Peg decided to hold her cards firmly to her chest. Whatever Jean's game was, she needed to do what was best for Doll.

'But Aunty Jean, they said she'll need almost full-time care, and she shouldn't really be out of hospital. It was only because of the bug they let her out.'

'You're such a caring girl,' Jean said. 'You've always been like that.' She smiled, reached forward and patted Peg's hand.

Peg forced a smile.

'We're so alike, you and me. Both rebels,' Jean went on.

Rebel was so far from how Peg thought of herself that she almost laughed.

'We go our own way, do our own thing. A touch of the wild we've both got. I'm sorry if you think I was judging about you and that girl, Meggy.'

'I didn't think that, Aunty—'

'Yes you did. You've got to live your life the way you see fit. Live and let live, that's what I say. It was just I was all sixes and sevens about Mummy being poorly and what it might do to her if she found out, but of course she doesn't have to find out or know anything, does she, Meggy?'

Jean's fingers were now clasping Peg's wrist tightly; her eyes fixed Taser-like on her.

'Of course not, Aunty Jean. I'd never dream of it.'

'Because it would kill her, you know. And you wouldn't want responsibility for that.'

'No.'

Peg retrieved her arm and took a swig from her glass, shuddering as the bitter liquid slid down her throat. And, in that moment, her mouth opened, the words just spilled out, and she showed the first of her cards.

'Does Heyworth Court mean anything to you, Aunty Jean?'

Like a flick knife opening, Jean turned to face her. 'Heyworth Court? Where did that come from?'

'It was on a key. On a label on a key we found under some boxes on Nan's wardrobe.'

Two vertical furrows appeared in the flesh on Jean's forehead as she appeared to be racking through some sort of mental filing system – Peg wondered if it was memory, or tactics. Eventually, she looked coolly up. 'Nothing. Heyworth Court means nothing to me.'

'And Mary Perkins. Have you ever heard of Mary Perkins?'

Jean nodded, her eyes on Peg. 'Of course. She was that poor girl from down the road. The one whose head that Cairns weirdo found on the beach. I'm sure he done it, you know. He was a right odd one, that one. Beachcombing. I'll believe that when I see it.'

'It was her in one of those photos I showed you. The photos you tore up.'

'Well, I don't know about that,' Jean said, pushing a curl back on top of her head. Peg thought she could make out a sheen of sweat on her upper lip. It felt wrong, but she was enjoying watching her aunt squirm.

'She was standing next to Dad in the photo.'

Jean scowled and shook her head. 'Means nothing to me.'

'What about Anna Thurlow? Does that ring any bells?'

'Who?'

'She went to my school. Went missing during the summer holidays twelve years ago.'

'How horrid, dear. Never heard of her, I'm afraid.'

'But I was at the school at the time. You must've heard about it.'

Jean pursed her lips and shook her head. Then, after a pause too brief for Peg to say anything else, she licked her bloated lips and went on. 'Now listen, Meggy. Like I was saying. You really shouldn't stay any longer than the end of this week. We're all right now, me and Mummy. We've managed all these years, and there's nothing to say we can't keep on managing.'

'I was thinking,' Peg said innocently. 'That intercom thingy Gramps put in. Does it still work well?' She reached over and picked it up from Jean's bedside table.

'You've seen how I can still call through if I need you or Mummy, haven't you?' Jean said, reaching out and grabbing it away from Peg.

'I mean, if it needs fixing or replacing, then let's do it. You see, Dad's given me some of that money.'

Jean gasped and put her hand to her face, but it was a phoney reaction, carried out a beat too late.

She knew. Of course she knew.

'And I want to use it to help you and Nan out,' Peg went on. 'So that you *can* go on like you did before.'

Jean said nothing, so Peg felt compelled to continue.

'As much as possible, I mean. With a bit of help and equipment and so on. Like grab bars and alarm cords and lifting aids. And possibly a live-in carer for Nan.'

Peg couldn't think of anything else to say to fill the silence that radiated from Jean. So she stopped, and watched her closely for some sort of reaction.

'He's giving you money to look after us?' Jean said.

'Not exactly, but—'

'He's paying you off,' Jean said, a smile slowly creasing across her face, balling her cheeks up so they were the size of grapefruits.

'You could see it like that,' Peg said, shrugging. 'But—'

Jean cut in on Peg, her voice low and urgent. 'You be careful, girl.'

'But I'm putting it to good use round here, on you and Nan. I don't want a penny for myself.'

Jean muttered something indistinct under her breath.

'Sorry?' Peg asked.

Jean just looked away. It was as if she hadn't yet decided how to react.

'So shall we get a new intercom installed? Perhaps something two-way so that you can listen in on Nan, make sure she's OK?' Peg knew she was pushing it, but Jean's balloon of a face was unreadable.

'I think this one can do that,' Jean said, fiddling with a button on the front of the intercom. 'I'm not sure how, though.' She eventually put the thing down on the bedcover, apparently having failed to make its surveillance mode operate.

'In any case,' she went on, folding her hands one over the other. 'Even if Mummy did get into trouble, what could I do? I'm stuck here in this bed. I'm useless. Oh Meggy, don't get old or disabled. Cherish your youth and the fact you can do exactly what you want when and how you want. Don't end up like me.' Jean gave her a pleading look that might have been created for a small Disney animal.

As she sat there beside her mendacious aunt, nursing a glass of Guinness, a drink she had never liked, whose bitter taste actually made her feel ill, the idea that she was in a position to do what she wanted seemed almost laughable to Peg. She was in fact trapped: bound to a life defined by duty and secrets.

It had all started to seem never-ending and overwhelming to her.

Then

AT SOME POINT, I THINK IT WAS WHEN I WAS JUST ABOUT NINE or ten, Gramps took up fishing. He'd take himself off before anyone else was up, slipping out of the back door with his tackle and a pile of sandwiches he'd made himself.

He wouldn't come back until my bedtime, or even later, so I saw him less and less. On the very greyest, wettest days, when water bucketed out of the pewter sky, he'd go and sit in his shed, not even coming out for tea because he had this little primus stove and kettle down there.

One day, I don't remember when exactly, I came downstairs to find Nan standing in the kitchen, her arms crossed, staring across the rain-streaked garden at the light in the shed window.

'Oh,' she says, jumping when she hears me. 'Oh Meggy, you nearly gave me a heart attack.'

'Why's Gramps never around any more?'

'Oh, he's got hobbies, dearie, never mind about that.'

* * *

Later – or perhaps it's another time altogether – Nan's round doing Aunty Jean's hair. This takes a long time, because she likes it set just so.

I remember now. It is a different time altogether, because I'm poorly. I'm upstairs in my bed and my head is all woozy with a fever, despite the medicine Nan gives me. And it's not raining. It's the summer and it's really, really hot, so Nan has left my attic trapdoor open to keep my temperature down.

There's a burned smell in the air, but it's something extra to the normal cigarette smell of the bungalow. Somewhere inside my head I know what that smell is about, but I can't place it now . . .

I hear the back door opening and shutting, and Gramps softly calling Nan's name.

'Dolly?'

There's no reply because, like I said, she's round in Aunty Jean's.

I'm just about to call down and tell him this when I hear the whir of the dial on the phone.

It's the old phone, not the cordless. It lived on the phone table in the hallway, just under my trapdoor, until it finally broke down about the time I moved away when I was eighteen.

'Er, hello?' I hear Gramps say. 'Is that you? It's me.'

There's a silence while he listens to what the other person says.

'Yes, yes. I know. I'm sorry,' he goes. Then after a moment, he says, 'Archer. I got your number from Archer. No. No, don't. It's not his fault.'

There's another pause. Then he speaks again.

'That's exactly it, though. It's got dreadful. It's got out of hand and it's got to stop.'

His voice has got really low now, and all I can hear is mumble, mumble, mumble. I get bored and I open *Alice in Wonderland*. But then Gramps raises his voice.

'I don't know what to do though. Meggy's ill because of it, and I—'

I prick up my ears at the mention of my own name.

'I tried to burn them, and I hid the key where no one'll find it. But I need you to—'

Then he listens again, but it isn't long before he blusters out, his voice all agitated and a bit whiny, like I've never heard him before. 'I *can't*, son. She—'

At that moment the back door opens and slams shut and I hear the clip-clop of Nan's furry slippers with their little heels.

'Frank?' I hear her say. 'Who are you on the phone to, Frank?'

'No one, Dolly love,' he says. 'It was a wrong number.'

I hear the ding of the phone being replaced on its hook.

'You're not looking too good, Frank,' Nan says. 'Are you sure you're all right, dear?'

'Nan,' I call down. 'I can't sleep.'

'Hold on a tick, darling.'

And after a couple of minutes she's there, climbing up the ladder to my attic with a story in her mind and my sniffy blanket in her arms.

I'm not sure about this one. I was ill. I had a fever.

Perhaps I dreamed it.

Perhaps I'm just making it up.

Perhaps I'm making *all* of this up.

Thirty-One

'IT'S SO GOOD TO BE BACK HOME, EVEN IF IT IS ALL EMPTY AND bare,' Doll said the next morning as she lay in her bed. 'I do wish I could sit up in my chair in the lounge.'

So, surprised at how little she weighed in her arms, Peg carried her through and they sat in front of the gas fire, Doll in her old rocker, Peg nails bared to the settee. They were waiting for the district nurse, who had rung earlier to say she would be round before twelve.

'This is a lovely biscuit. You're such a clever girl, Jeanie,' Doll said as she tucked into the walnut cake Loz had cooked for Jean before she left, but which hadn't reached her because Peg decided that her aunt neither needed nor deserved something quite so delicious. 'I feel a bit naughty having this though.' Doll giggled, nodding to the sweet sherry Peg had poured her. 'Before the sun's gone down.'

'Nan,' Peg said, wondering if Jean might be listening in to their conversation. 'Do you remember anything about a girl called Mary Perkins? Lived round here and disappeared?'

'Mary Perkins? Let me think. Oh yes,' Doll said, wiping a crumb from her mouth. 'Her mum lived round the corner, just here. Such a lovely girl. A friend of Jean's she was.'

'Wasn't she a friend of Dad's?'

'Raymond? No. No. He never knew no Mary Perkins.'

'Didn't she dance in his club, though? Flamingos?'

'Flamingos. Oh, it's ever such a nice place, Meggy. We must go there again one day.'

'So Dad must've known her.'

'I don't believe he did, dearie.' Doll patted her hair, her milky-rimmed eyes focused inwards. 'She got into trouble, that Mary Perkins. Up the spout they said. Well they all did, didn't they? The floozies. Such a pity what happened to her,' she said, frowning. 'Dreadful.'

'What did happen to her?'

'She got got, didn't she? Got cut up into pieces and thrown in the sea. It was in the papers. Didn't they lock her up first? In some sort of outhouse? And then Frank found out and it all went—' Doll's voice drifted off and she clamped her mouth shut.

'What, Nan? What sort of outhouse? Where?'

'It was . . . Let me see now . . .' Doll's little fingers trembled, brushing her forehead as if trying to pick up the layers of her memory. 'Oh!'

'Who found out, Nan?'

'She were no good, though. She'd have brought shame, you know.' Doll looked once again at Peg, nodding her head as if this were a complete wonder.

The doorbell rang and, startled by the noise, Doll shrank into herself, balling her hands up and biting her thumbnails.

'Don't worry, Nan. It's only the district nurse,' Peg said, twitching the net curtain to check on the door.

She had wanted to ask about Anna Thurlow, but it was probably better to leave it for another day.

Doll looked quite upset.

'Someone's been having a big clear-out,' the nurse said as she bustled through the front door. 'Judging by all those bin bags in the back garden.'

'It's probably best we don't mention all that,' Peg whispered. 'She's not too happy that we've got rid of loads of her stuff.'

'OK,' the nurse boomed. 'Mum's the word.' Then she moved straight through to the lounge and opened her arms wide. 'Well then, Mrs Thwaites. How are we doing, then, my love?'

'Who the fuck are you?' Doll said. 'And what bin bags?'

Doll was exhausted after the nurse's visit, so Peg carried her back to the bedroom, where she immediately fell asleep. Julie was next door with Jean, so Peg asked her to keep half an ear out for Doll while she went out to get some food in.

'I'm only here for an hour, I'm afraid,' Julie said. 'I've got to get to my next lady.'

'If I'm not back before you leave, just go, I won't be long after you.'

Julie raised her eyebrows, but nodded her head.

Peg decided to go right into Whitstable, trundling Doll's shopping trolley along the beach route. The fresh air was very welcome after almost twenty-four hours cooped up in the bungalow, but she had to step briskly to keep the cold from pinching into her. The tide was out and the sea completely invisible, shrouded by a freezing fog.

She pulled out her phone and called Loz. She didn't say anything about the intercom, nor Jean's strange mobility or

Doll's odd reaction when asked about Mary Perkins. She needed to work out for herself what was going on before she let Loz's speculation machine loose on it all. She did tell her about her decision not to give Jean the cake, though, and Loz laughed until she choked.

'Parker rang,' Loz said when she had recovered.

'And?'

Loz put on a gruff voice. '"Just checking in, girly. Nothing to report. But, in the meantime, would you like to join us for tea again?"'

'Sweet bloke.'

'Yes, he is, isn't he? Here, Peg?'

'Yep?'

'You couldn't ask Mrs Cairns a bit about her son, could you?'

'What? No way.'

'Thought you'd say that.'

'Why'd you even ask?'

'I want to find out more about Mary Perkins. All I've got is that printout from the *Unsolved* website, and old slave driver here won't let me out of the kitchen. We're down to five now. Everyone else has got the flu.'

Peg sighed. 'I could go to the library, I suppose, and look up the local paper archive.' She felt she needed to provide Loz with some sort of kindness, given that she was concealing so much from her.

'Would you? It's just I can't get it out of my head, and there's nothing I can do here.'

'Yeah, yeah.'

Peg got the supplies in, then decided to spend some of Raymond's money on a small plastic Christmas tree which lit up when you plugged it in. She also bought an armful of tinsel and a real holly wreath, to make the place look seasonal. She knew Doll had a box of Christmas decorations – she had always pulled out all the stops when Peg was younger. But they were stored in the shed, and it had only just occurred to Peg that she had put over twenty full boxes of stuff in front of them. As money was no object now, she enjoyed the never-before-tasted freedom of spending a little to make life easier, glad she could treat Doll.

On her laden way back from the shops, Peg stopped in at the library and asked the librarian about the local paper archive. She was guided to a local history reading room, where she parked her shopping and positioned herself at a large, pale wood table. The librarian hauled out a pile of beautifully bound sections, one for each of the six months from February 1992. According to the *Unsolved* website, Loz had said on the phone, Mary went missing on the second of that month, which was a Sunday.

'We had a very keen local historian working here at the time,' the librarian said, as she and Peg admired the hardback covers. 'She made sure they could withstand fire, flood and famine. Now are you sure I can't get you anything else?'

'Thank you – I've got plenty to be getting on with here.'

'Just whistle if you need anything.'

The librarian left, leaving a scent of tea and patchouli in her wake, and Peg – aware that, in her eagerness to please Loz, she had taken on a rather lengthy task for someone who had just popped out for an hour or so – set quickly to work.

The first mention was four days after the date Mary went missing. The brief article said that she had last been seen that Sunday night in Flamingos.

'She seemed upset,' fellow hostess, Carleen Peters, 29, said. 'But she kept herself to herself and never opened up to us.'

So Carleen had known Mary. Peg made a quick note of this. She wondered what else she might know. When the time was right, she thought perhaps she would pay her another visit.

Mary's flatmate, attractive brunette Claire Watkins, 20, said: 'I haven't seen her since the Friday before she disappeared, although I didn't think anything of it over the weekend. She often stayed away overnight.'

'We haven't seen her for over a month,' Mary's mother, redhead Gina Perkins, 53, said from the family home in Tankerton. 'But she's a good girl and always phones home every Monday. When we didn't hear from her this week, we knew something was wrong. It's just not like her.'

The alarm was raised when she didn't turn up for work this Tuesday. 'We're always on time,' Peters said. 'We're fined if we're even a minute late for work.'

The article said that Mary had been twenty-two when she went missing.

The same age as me, Peg thought.

She noted down the details for Loz – apart from the part about Carleen, which she added to the store of things she was keeping to herself for the time being.

Quickly, she worked through the next few volumes. There were a couple of tiny pieces reporting that there had been no more news. Then, when Peg got to Monday twenty-fourth of April 1992, a headline screamed at her.

This was two months after she had gone missing. The story, which covered pages two and three of the paper, had been instigated by Mary's parents, who felt that the police had given up on their only child. There were touching descriptions of what a loyal and hardworking daughter she had been, and a spread of photographs of her – as a heartbreakingly pretty little girl in knee socks and puffy-sleeved dress feeding pigeons in Trafalgar Square; as a studious-looking schoolgirl, and as a striking young woman in a bikini by a swimming pool. In all the photos she looked so solid, so alive.

Peg took photographs of the pages with her phone. As she did so, two details caught her eye in the swimming-pool photograph and made her pause. It had been difficult to tell at first glance, because the black and white images looked as if they had been screened through a colander. But on closer inspection, behind the smiling girl in the bikini – was that a bit of a flirt in the way she looked at the camera? – she could just make out the shape of an inflatable killer whale in the pool.

But it wasn't any inflatable killer whale. Peg knew it had been hers. She could still feel the slippery rubber of its handles as she tried to ride it in that pool. She remembered screaming with laughter as Raymond splashed around beside her, trying to upend her into the water.

For the first time, she remembered being with her father as a child.

Having fun with him.

She also recognised an enclosed wicker sun lounger in the background. That sun lounger had lived at the side of the swimming pool of the house she spent her first six years in near Farnham. She could remember lying inside it on a hot day, her nose pressed against the sun-cream-scented canvas cushions, the spots of sunlight speckling her through the holes in the wicker.

So here was Mary Perkins standing by her parents' swimming pool. It was probably Raymond she was smiling at while she posed there all lush and young in her bikini.

Peg allowed herself to breathe for a moment, to let this sink in. Had she been there, too? And where was her mother when this photograph had been taken?

Suzanne. For a second, Peg felt a flush of rage towards the young woman so brazenly flaunting herself in Raymond's family home, heedless of how she could fuck everything up for herself and her mother.

Bitch, she thought. And: *you had it coming.* And: *you deserved it.*

Shocked at herself, she closed her eyes and calmed her breathing.

Then she had to plough on. Julie would have been long gone, and Doll and Jean would be on their own. Skimming as quickly as possible, she got to the fourth issue of the May volume, which started with a page of headline:

LOCAL BEACHCOMBER MAKES GRUESOME DISCOVERY ON THE STREET

Then, four days later, the same photographs from two weeks earlier were reproduced on the front page, under the banner:

STREET HEAD IS MISSING GIRL MARY

That was it, then, Peg chided herself. No one deserved that ending.

She quickly photographed the final article, a gory description of what poor Colin Cairns had found. Then she grabbed the shopping trolley, tucked the Christmas tree box under her arm and half-ran up the hill to Tankerton, taking the quicker, main-road route. As she panted along the pavement – she was a long way from being anything like a jogger – a maggoty thought burrowed into her brain.

In all the pages she had worked through at the library, not once had Mary's disappearance been linked with an outhouse, nor had any mention been made of her being in 'trouble'.

But Doll had been very clear on both points.

Doll knew things that the press didn't.

How was that, then?

Peg quickened her pace. She needed to get back to Doll and, very gently, find out what else she knew.

And, more importantly, how she knew it.

Thirty-Two

AS SHE TURNED THE CORNER INTO DOLL'S STREET, A SNOWFLAKE fell onto Peg's eyelashes.

She was glad she had bought the Christmas decorations. They would make the bungalow feel fuller again, and perhaps that would make Doll happier about all her stuff being cleared out, which in turn might make conversations about outhouses and fallen women and lost schoolgirls a little easier.

But she also thought she might give it a rest for a bit. She might ask Loz for a truce on her investigations until December was over. She just wanted to make it lovely for Doll. With her growing dementia, this could, after all, be the last Christmas she would be aware of. To delve into the subjects of Raymond and the girls and all the Jean business could dirty the holiday for the whole family.

The truth had waited long enough – a couple more weeks wouldn't make much difference.

Peg tugged the shopping trolley the last couple of hundred yards along the road, worrying about the food she had bought. She had got in what she knew Doll liked to eat – Heinz tomato soup, pink ham with yellow breadcrumb-speckled fat, white sliced bread, proper butter, Branston Pickle, and Cheddar so mild it only had a passing resemblance to cheese.

But all the time in the shop, she imagined Loz nagging in her ear about good nutrition, asking her why there were no fresh fruit and vegetables in her basket. Her internal riposte was that because Doll ate so little, what she did put in her mouth had better be calorie-laden enough to keep her tiny frame going. Even Loz would struggle to wear down Doll's toddler-force intolerance for new foods. She'd had nearly ninety years of practice, after all. Peg worked herself up into quite a lather with this argument, until she realised that she didn't actually have to have it. That, in fact, she, Peg, was in charge and not Loz, who was tied up at work for at least a whole week.

She tried not to acknowledge how much relief this thought brought her.

'Hi Nan, I'm back!' she called as she let herself in through the front door. Kicking off her boots, she wheeled the shopping trolley through to the kitchen, and put the kettle on. Julie had left a little note on the Formica breakfast table, saying that she had come in and checked on Doll several times while she had been in 'doing' Jean, and all that time she had been sleeping like a baby. She added that she had plated up a ham and salad tea for her for when she woke up and left it in the fridge.

Blessing Julie, Peg poured two cups of tea and sliced two pieces of pink and yellow Battenberg cake and put them on the best plates on a tray.

'Nan? Are you awake? I've got us a nice cup of tea here,' she called as she carried the tray along the corridor.

She turned into the bedroom and stopped in her tracks, the tea ricocheting around the edge of the mugs, slopping over the dainty slices of cake.

Doll's bed was empty, the sheets flung back, the pillow dented and decorated with a few strands of hair where her head had lain. Peg dumped the tray on the dressing table and dashed through to the bathroom, which was empty, then the lounge. Doll wasn't there either – her chair was as empty as it had been when she was in hospital.

Wobbling with panic, Peg buzzed through to Jean.

'Aunty Jean? Can you hear me?'

'Yes dear,' her voice crackled through the silver mesh on the front of the box. 'Is everything all right?'

'Do you know where Nan is?'

'Isn't she in her bed?'

'No.'

'The girl went through to check on her before she left, and said she was "sleeping like a mouse". That's what she said. I thought it was a bit of an odd thing to say, myself.'

'She's not here, Aunty Jean. She's not in the bungalow.'

'But have you only just got back?' Jean said. 'Where on earth have you been?'

'I've been getting some food in,' Peg said, her voice trembling.

'You took a hell of a long time about it, Meggy, didn't you? She must've gone out looking for you. She could be in Seasalter by now, the time you've been. You'd better get out there and see if you can find her.'

As Peg put the intercom down she caught sight of the picture of Doll with Raymond, Jean and Keith, which she had turned over on the bookshelf. It was on the floor, face up, exactly where it would have landed had it fallen from Doll's shocked fingers.

'Oh no!' Peg gasped.

An image flashed through her mind: Doll, wandering along the seafront in her slippers and nightie, cold, scared and lost, perhaps looking for Keith, not knowing who she was or where she was heading. And Peg knew it was all her own fault.

She dashed through into the hallway and pulled her boots back on. Then she ran out of the front door and into the street, where she paused, bouncing indecisively on her toes. Which way would Doll have taken? Down the hill towards the sea? Or the other way, towards the shops?

Peg looked up and down the street, but there was no sign of her grandmother. It was pointless to take off in any one direction. She could have gone anywhere. The snow was falling quite thickly now, and for one disorienting second the sight of it settling on the ground gave her a childlike thrill.

She shook herself to her senses. Doll was gone, and she needed to do something quickly to find her.

The sensible thing to do would be to call the police. She let herself back into the bungalow and picked up the phone. But some innate – inherited? – mistrust of the law made her hesitate. And anyway it would be better to see first if Jean had any more detail to add to what had happened while she was away.

Peg let herself out of the back door. As she negotiated the ice-slippery slope down to the back garden, she noticed that something was awry on top of the pile of bin bags on the back lawn. At first she thought seagulls had got to them and pulled out one of Doll's old nighties.

But then she realised the horror of what she was looking at.

'Nan!' Peg yelled, and ran to her, stumbling over the bags, cutting her leg on something metal, rusty and protruding. She reached the old lady and turned her over, checking her throat for a pulse.

But there was none.

Doll's eyes had rolled back to show only their whites, while snowflakes landed in her open mouth as if she were catching them on purpose.

'No, Nan, Nan,' Peg said, putting her head to the old lady's chest. She looked down at Doll's hands, which had already stiffened, something in their clasp. Peg prised the fingers open. Doll had been holding onto the wallet of photographs of Mary Perkins. The wallet Peg had thought she put back in the Gordon's Gin box, but which had somehow got thrown away.

Doll had come out here to look for them. Peg's questioning had stirred her up and she had come out here, into the icy cold back garden, to dig through all these bin bags until she found the photographs.

She had been doing this while Peg had been cocooned in the warm, dry library.

Weeping tears of guilt and regret, Peg clasped the birdlike body of her grandmother to her. With shaking arms, she picked her up and carried her indoors, where she gently laid her out on her bed. Then, in a daze, she finally called an ambulance.

'I think my nan's dead,' she said, choking into the mouthpiece. She gave the address and some details, then lay down and held Doll's body, hoping that she might find a thrum of life, or a hint of warmth.

Within what must have been minutes she heard the siren as an ambulance approached. At the same time as she heard the doorbell, the intercom buzzer sounded in the lounge.

'Meggy? Meggy? What's going on? Why's there an ambulance?'

She had completely forgotten about Jean.

Thirty-Three

AS SOON AS THE PRIVATE AMBULANCE HAD DRIVEN DOLL AWAY, and the doctor who certified the death had also sedated a distraught and hysterical Jean, and a sympathetic policewoman had taken a statement from Peg 'as a formality', Peg sat down in Doll's old chair and left a long message on Loz's phone, telling her the news. She found she was shivering, even though she had wrapped herself in a blanket and turned the gas fire up high.

She tried to look at the booklet the doctor had given her: *What to Do When Someone Dies*. But she couldn't focus her eyes or her mind.

Then she called Raymond in Spain.

'Oh,' he said, his voice as flat as Whitstable low-tide mud. 'Oh.'

'The doctor says it was probably a heart attack, but we've got to see if the coroner wants to do a post-mortem.' Peg fiddled with the curly wire on Doll's phone and rocked herself in Doll's old chair. She felt tiny.

The idea of her grandmother being cut up and taken apart

made her feel ill. The arms that held her when she was tiny and needy cut to bits. The breast she used to lean her head against sawed open.

'Right,' Raymond said.

'It's my fault,' Peg said, in a small voice. The impersonal nature of the phone, and the physical and emotional distance she felt between her father and herself made the whole business feel like a confessional.

'What do you mean it's your fault? Come on, girl.' His voice had a new softness in it, something she wouldn't have thought possible when she met him face to face. 'They sent her home early from hospital. She was old, she was poorly.'

'I shouldn't have stayed out so long. And I was asking her too many questions. I confused her. I upset her. I drove her to it.'

'Questions?'

Peg sighed. To Loz, this would present an opening. But Peg knew that she couldn't go down that route. What did she have to go on, anyway? Just a couple of photographs, which at the very worst showed that Raymond had been having an affair while married to her mother, which hardly made him unique amongst men.

What else was there?

Nothing but the dramatic storytelling of a bed-bound fantasist and a forgotten family storage facility. It amounted to nothing – except to Loz, who shared with Jean an extraordinary ability to wind a couple of random facts into a cut and dried case.

'Oh you know,' Peg said at last. 'The kind of questions I was asking you. About the past.'

It was Raymond's turn to sigh. In the background, Paulie splashed and laughed in the pool, calling to his father to join him.

'Hold on, darling,' Raymond said to his son, muffling the receiver. 'Daddy's on a call.' Then his voice came back into focus. 'You're too hard on yourself, Margaret. You said yourself when you come over here you was worried about her, that you didn't think she had all that long left.'

'Yes.' Peg swallowed back the tears. She was amazed that he had taken in so much of what she had said to him in Spain.

'Is that sister of mine making a stink?' he went on.

'She was very upset. Hysterical. But the doctor's given her some pretty strong pills. She's worried about what's going to happen next, though.'

'I'm sure she is. Well, I'm not going to let you be lumbered with all that.' Peg heard the click of a lighter and an exhalation so slow and thoughtful she could almost smell the cigar smoke.

'Daddy!' she heard Paulie shout and splash in the distance. 'I'm *bored*.'

'Hold on a minute, darling!' he called to his son. 'Look, Margaret,' he said at last, his voice low. 'I can help you out now.'

'What do you mean?'

'I'll put my brief in touch,' Raymond said, either not hearing or ignoring her question. 'Bloke by the name of Archer. And I'll sort that aunt of yours out too. She can't stay there now Mum's gone—' His voice caught a little on his last word, like a scratchy woollen, snagged on a rusty nail. 'We'll have to work out where to put her. Now then, are you all right for money, girl?'

Peg sniffed.

'You loved your old nan, didn't you?'

'Yes, of course,' Peg said, tears tumbling from her eyes again. 'She looked after me.'

'She was a great looker-after, my old mum,' Raymond said, his voice small, gruffly on the point of breaking. Then he seemed to rally, as if having told himself to pull himself together. 'Look. I want you to sort out the sending-off you want for her. What you think she deserves. Bury her good and proper, money no object. Get them to send all the bills to me, and as soon as you've got a date, let me know. There's some invitations need to go out, people need to know.'

'Are you going to come to her funeral, then?' Peg said.

'Nah, girl. Can't do that.'

'Why not?'

'Never you mind. But when it's all over, I'll get in touch, and we can take it from there.'

'But—'

'Look, love. Don't try to change my mind. Don't waste your breath. And if you're still worried about me getting "closure",' – she could hear a faint, incongruous sneer in his voice – 'I've had all the "closure" I need. Let's just leave it at that. And Margaret?'

'Yes?' Peg sniffed.

'I know you're in bits about your nan passing away. But remember – she was old, she wasn't so good. An end can be a beginning.'

His tone was that of a man cut free.

'Perhaps it's because he felt too ashamed to face her when she was alive,' Loz said when she finally called back towards the end of her shift, and after Peg had cried again and been comforted. 'With all he did.'

'You're not still on about that? Look, so he had an affair with Mary Perkins. So what?'

'And what about Anna? Why were the pictures of two seemingly random missing girls in the same box?' Loz had to raise her voice against the sound of an un-silenced motorbike farting down the road at the end of the Seed kitchen staff's smoking alley.

'I can't believe Raymond's a killer.'

'He killed your mum . . .'

'That was different. That was a mercy killing. She wanted to die.'

'But Jean said—'

'Jean's a fucking liar.'

'Peg!'

Peg screwed her eyes shut and shook her head. 'Look, Loz. Can you please just leave it. Just for a bit? My nan, who was like a mother to me, has just died. Give me a break.'

'OK, OK, I'm sorry,' Loz said. Peg heard her put her hand over the mouthpiece of her phone, and the muffle of her voice as she said something to someone. 'Shit Peg, I've got to go. She's only squeezed in an unbooked party of eight. Listen, love, don't let it get on top of you and if you need me, I'm here. I'm going to keep my phone on vibrate while I'm working. And I'm going to try to get another couple of days off.'

'OK then. Good. Thanks,' Peg said. 'Love you.'

She put the phone down and sat there for a long time, rocking herself in Doll's chair, the gas fire hissing at her side. She must have fallen asleep eventually, because the next thing she knew dawn was spreading its grey cold light in through the net curtains and Julie's little car could be heard drawing up outside.

Peg pulled herself together and braced herself to go out and tell her the news.

Thirty-Four

PEG PASSED THE FOLLOWING DAYS IN A NUMB HAZE, FOR THE most part with a phone clamped to the side of her face. To her relief, the coroner had decided that no post-mortem was necessary – Doll was elderly and showed all the signs of having died from a heart attack.

A white van turned up to take the bin bags away from the back garden. Peg saw it driving away as she returned from a long, dazed walk along the seafront; she supposed Loz must have made that phone call to the women and their van, James and Daughter, for whom no job was too small.

At least, she hoped that was where the white van came from.

Raymond's solicitor Mr Archer called. In a voice that sounded like he was in an authentically detailed BBC Dickens adaptation, he told her that yes, he had indeed taken instruction from Mrs Thwaites, having drawn up her will for her 'some time ago, I have to add'. He had a copy lodged in his office if she cared to come up 'at your earliest convenience' to view it.

The next phone call was from a local reporter, a woman with a high-pitched nasal voice and mud-thick Kentish accent, who clearly thought she was on to some big scandal about Doll having been released from hospital early.

'I'm not into blame,' Peg said simply. 'It could have happened any time, and anywhere. Please leave us in peace now.'

She put the phone down and looked at her reflection in the salty drizzle-crusted window.

Peace. It felt like anything but that.

The bungalow seemed far emptier than it had when Doll was merely away in hospital. It now felt evacuated, sucked of its soul. Like it had nothing to do with anyone any more.

When she told the journalist that she wasn't into blame, Peg hadn't been telling the whole truth. She could stand in front of a mirror and point the finger in exactly the right direction. If she hadn't been so bent on finding out about Mary Perkins, if she hadn't asked all those questions, if she hadn't cleared out all the things that were important to Doll and piled them up in stinking bin bags in the back garden, if she hadn't stayed out far longer than she had intended, putting together some sort of spurious case against her father just to keep her girlfriend happy, if she hadn't left that damn photo with Keith in it out for Doll to find . . .

If she hadn't done all that, her grandmother would still be alive.

She called Marianne, who begrudgingly granted her two weeks' compassionate leave, as was council policy.

'It's not normally extended to grandparents,' she said, and Peg could hear her beads clatter as she made some exasperated, expansive gesture. 'But in your case, since your grandmother brought you up, I suppose I haven't got a leg to stand on.'

'Thank you,' was all Peg could say.

In between covering herself in guilt and carrying out the set of tasks dictated to her by Doll's death – including a very different, final sorting of her belongings which involved a deal of regret at what she had discarded during the first clear-out – Peg spent a good deal of time with Jean, who had descended into a near-catatonic state. All of her former vigour seemed to have solidified into her flesh and they sat together, watching TV, snacking on high-fat, low-nutrition comfort foods and drinking beer. Peg even once joined Jean as she smoked, but, unused to the smell and taste from a user's point of view – as opposed to that of a passive recipient – the cigarettes brought her scant comfort. All they did was make her feel as ill as she thought she deserved.

'You won't desert me, will you Meggy? Mummy was all I had,' Jean said one evening.

'Of course not, Aunty Jean. Of course I won't,' Peg said. Then, feeling the need to change the subject, she got up. 'Can I get you another slice of cake?' she asked as she moved to the bedroom door.

'You're a good girl, Meggy,' Jean said.

She finally read *What to Do When Someone Dies* and realised that she had to appoint an undertaker. So, on the third day after Doll's death, she visited the first funeral parlour she came across in the main Tankerton shopping street – she later discovered there were five, a fact she had failed to notice all those years she had passed them on her way to the beach, or the sweet shop, or to the station to return to London. The proprietor Mr Watkins said he would be happy to take Doll as soon as the coroner released the body, and did her grandmother have any preferences as to service, or to cremation or burial?

Peg had no idea. She knew Frank had been cremated and his

ashes scattered on the sea. She supposed, therefore, that this was what Doll would have wanted for herself.

'Does it say anything in her will?' Mr Watkins asked. He was a small, round, glossy man without a crease on his body or his lustrous suit. He had, she noticed, obscenely clean fingernails tipping his fat fingers, as if he were constantly scrubbing them after delving around in the entrails of corpses.

She couldn't imagine it was actually like that. Not really. But he did have a set of staff-only stairs leading down from his deeply carpeted 'Bereavement Consultation Room' into some sort of basement, and it did make her think that she didn't want Doll's little body to end up down there on some slab, touched by those hands.

'I'm seeing the solicitor tomorrow,' Peg said, sitting on her hands to stop them from touching the glass ornaments that bedecked his vast, reproduction mahogany desk. They were too shiny, and she would leave her greasy fingerprints all over them and ruin them.

'Well, there's no hurry,' Mr Watkins said, resting his poached-egg chin in his frankfurter fingers. 'We embalm our clients, and have full refrigeration facilities.'

'Embalm?'

'We always embalm – unless you have any religious objections?' He smiled and raised a shiny eyebrow at her.

Peg shook her head.

'Now then,' he said, rummaging under his desk near his groin and producing a glossy brochure, 'Perhaps you'd like to view our range of caskets? Please take this, with our compliments.'

On her way home, Peg took a long detour along the seafront, clutching the leaflets to her chest in freezing, mittenless hands.

As she walked, she searched the shifting slate of water for

absolution. Or, at any rate, for some sort of guidance. But it just sat there, unyielding.

As she approached the bungalow, a photographer surprised her, pushing his camera up into her face. Behind him, a woman with a fur hat pulled down over her ears readied a voice recorder exactly the same as the one Peg had her hand on in her pocket.

'What?' Peg said, as the flash fired in her face, leaving her with nothing but blackness for a few seconds.

'How does it feel to lose your grandmother to health service cuts?' the woman demanded, practically thrusting her digital recorder into Peg's mouth. Peg recognised the voice immediately: it was the reporter who had called her the day before.

'How does it feel to be an obtrusive, insensitive cow?' Peg said, feeling a slick of disgust ooze through her, as she swept past and slammed the door in her face.

'You would've been proud of me,' she said to Loz.

Safely inside the bungalow, she had shut herself in the kitchen with the radio on, in case Jean was listening in on the phone call.

'You've stolen my chutzpah,' Loz said. 'And I've gone all weedy.' She sounded weary.

'What's up?'

'Well, I want to support you through all this, so I went to Cara and told her that I needed to take time off, and do you know what that tight bitch said to me? She said "I'm terribly sorry, Loz",' Loz imitated her boss's flat and wide Australian accent, '"But I have a business to run, it's the busiest time of my year, and I have to draw the line somewhere or I'll be letting people off because their kid sister's gerbil passed away."'

'That's awful,' Peg said.

'Too bloody right it's awful. I'm going to see if it's also discriminatory. I mean, she probably wouldn't be so outright objectionable if you were my fucking *husband*.'

'God's sake, Loz. Cara's the biggest dyke out there. She just needs you in the kitchen. And, anyway, there's nothing you can be doing here, not really. I'm fine.'

'You don't want me there.'

'I *do*.'

But Peg realised that Loz was right. She would far rather just get on and do things quietly on her own. It was her duty, after all. Her atonement.

'But I don't want you to feel bad because you can't be here. Save up Cara's goodwill for the funeral. *That's* when I'll need you.'

'I hate to leave you on your own, though.'

'Shhh.'

Peg made herself a cup of tea and settled down on the lounge settee with the casket brochure.

There were a few 'green' models that she would have liked to have chosen for herself – a willow basket with a Yorkshire wool shroud looked particularly appealing. But she knew that Doll would have thought such a thing odd. So, bearing Ray's instructions in mind, she chose a top-of-the-range model, called The Imperial, 'crafted from' solid poplar with brass fittings and white satin padded interior. It was two thousand pounds, but Doll deserved it.

Her decision made, she closed her eyes and imagined herself lying in her willow casket, wrapped up in her woollen shroud. The image was strangely comforting.

Thirty-Five

THE NEXT MORNING, PEG WASHED HER HAIR FOR THE FIRST TIME since Doll died, put on her clean jeans – which she noticed were tighter since she last wore them at work, what with keeping up with Jean's comfort eating – and set off up to London for her meeting with Mr Archer.

She felt odd, after a couple of days spent absorbed by the silence of the bungalow and the vastness of the grass, shingle and mud of the estuary, to be part of the pale and weary commuter crowd disgorging onto the platform at Victoria Station.

Mr Archer had suggested a nine o'clock meeting and now that money wasn't such a pressing issue and the early train no longer unaffordable, Peg readily agreed. She had never been in the station at morning rush hour though, and found it unbelievable that people were willing to put up with such daily discomfort. She had been forced to stand for the entire journey and, at the other end, sweating in her winter padding, she had to cram into a stoical English crowd of commuters reading papers and checking smart phones as they waited for London

Transport staff to allow them in batches into a packed Tube station.

She felt like a lumpy, confused child, lost in a world of grown-ups who knew what they were doing.

Eventually she emerged from the underground at Leicester Square. Using Frank's old *A to Z*, she located the ancient court that housed Mr Archer's offices.

She arrived, out of breath, at his door, which was at the top of five flights of stairs.

'Mr Archer will be with you presently,' his over-groomed middle-aged secretary said, motioning for Peg to take an armchair. 'Could I fetch you a cup of tea, Miss Thwaites?'

Peg nodded. She had never visited a solicitor's office before and she wondered if jeans, even if they were clean, had been the right choice of outfit. But she had nothing else to wear – her only skirt, last worn at her interview at the library, was screwed up at the bottom of the wardrobe in her and Loz's bedroom. She perched on the edge of the uncomfortable chair and flicked through a financial journal on the coffee table in front of her.

The secretary bustled across the room in her sensible shoes and put a cup of tea down in front of Peg. Then she returned to her desk, put on some earphones and immediately began typing, clacking her long red nails on the keyboard.

Peg sat and waited, gnawing her cuticles. Apart from the secretary's typing, the only other sound was that of a large grandfather clock set against the wall opposite her, flanked by a couple of ancient oil paintings of country scenes. She felt about as out of place as she could possibly be.

Eventually, an intercom not unlike the one Jean used back in the bungalow buzzed on the secretary's desk. 'You can show Miss Thwaites in now, Miss Lunt,' a dufferish voice crackled from it.

'Certainly Mr Archer.' Miss Lunt rose – she was not the kind of woman who would merely get up – placed her feet in third position and clasped her hands in front of her. 'Would you care to follow me, please?' she said, eyeing Peg up and down as if she were somehow amusing.

She led Peg ten or so feet across the room and opened a creaking door. The tall stooped man inside stood, taking care not to bang his head on the slanted attic ceiling, and extended his hand towards her.

'Ah, Margaret. So good to see you again.' He smiled, showing weasel teeth below his hooked nose. Despite his wizened appearance, there was an avuncular kindness about him.

'Again?' Peg said.

'Ah. You wouldn't remember, but I met you when you were younger, at a party at your parents' house. You must have been about five, I think. It was before your mother – your father – ah.'

Unable to find the appropriate form of words to describe to a daughter her father's killing of her mother, he closed his eyes and tapped his fingertips together a couple of times, as if rewinding. Then, refocusing on her, he smiled and gestured to a chair in front of his beaten old desk. 'Anyway, my condolences on the passing of your grandmother. Do take a seat, my dear.'

'So how long have you been my father's solicitor?' Peg said, sitting down as directed.

'Oh, since the Flamingos days,' Mr Archer said. 'I assisted your father with the legal side of the business, and I suppose you could say that since then we've been, if you like, meshed. Inescapably so.' His eyes drifted to the casement window, where a pigeon stood completely immobile on a parapet, its pink eyes on them.

'You see,' he went on. 'There was quite a lot to take care of when he was absent. And now I look after the discreet interest he retains on the UK side of things.' Mr Archer swiftly picked up the file he had laid out on the desk and tapped it so that the papers inside it were straightened.

'Now,' he said, again stretching his lips into a smile, 'I believe you're here to hear the late Mrs Thwaites's will. So, time is money and so on and so forth. May I suggest we proceed forthwith?'

It appeared that Doll had made a joint will with Frank when Peg was a baby and had not touched it since. If Frank Senior predeceased her, then everything was left to Franklin Raymond Thwaites, who was instructed to provide for the care of her daughter, Jeanette Thwaites, and the welfare of her grand-daughter, Margaret Thwaites.

'Everything to Dad?' Peg said, a little stunned. 'Is that really fair on Aunty Jean?'

'I'm afraid it's what Mrs Thwaites wanted,' Mr Archer said, smiling kindly and handing the will to Peg. 'It says it quite clearly here.' He pointed to the relevant clause, closed his eyes, his eyeballs flickering behind their lids, as if to picture the scene as it had happened. 'If I remember correctly, there was some discussion about this point at the time, between Raymond and your grandparents. I believe your aunt has some health problems?'

'You could say that.'

He closed his eyes again and summoned the scene once more before opening them and speaking. 'I believe the consensus even back then was that she needed to be cared for and was not really capable of making her own decisions. It was put to your grandparents that, as a successful businessman, a man of the world, if you will, your father would be in a far better position to deal with the administration of the estate. He and myself are named here as executors.'

'And Nan owned the bungalow? Aunty Jean doesn't have any stake in it?'

'No. I'm afraid not. It all passes to your father.'

So Jean was about to have everything – her home, her future, her autonomy – handed over to a brother who despised her. It seemed horribly cruel, so unlike Doll, to have decided that for the daughter she doted on.

Peg wondered what sort of pressure Ray had exerted on her.

'And what about Paulie?' Peg said.

'Paulie?'

'Her other grandson. Dad's new child. She never met him.'

'That'll be up to your father,' Mr Archer said. 'As I said, this will was drawn up a long time ago. A lot of water has passed under the bridge since then.'

'Does it say what she wants the funeral arrangements to be?'

'She wishes to be buried.'

'But Gramps was cremated. I thought they'd both have wanted the same.'

'The will states they both wished to be buried.'

'But he was cremated,' Peg said. 'And scattered at sea.'

Mr Archer closed his eyes again. 'Yes. I remember now. Your grandmother was quite adamant that, despite what it says here, he wanted to be cremated. Since he'd moved to the coast, that had been his wish. She was most insistent.'

Peg frowned. 'Is it possible to change someone's will after they die?'

Mr Archer smiled and put his fingertips together. 'Nothing, my dear, is impossible in this world.

'Now then. Do you want us to take care of the funeral arrangements?' he asked, his voice less formal.

Peg thought of the white-satin-lined coffin. 'No. I'd like to do that myself, if that's OK.'

'Your father has instructed me to let you do what you want, so long as you adhere to Mrs Thwaites's wishes, as stated in her will.'

'Can't you ask him to come?' Peg said. 'She would have so wanted him to come.'

'I'm afraid, my dear, in most respects, your father is very much his own man. He will only do what he sees fit. And there are – ah – logistical challenges to be met regarding his re-entry to the UK.'

Peg looked gloomily down at the brown carpet. It had seen better days.

'It means a lot to you, doesn't it, my dear? His coming to the funeral.'

Peg nodded, her eyes still tracking the stains on the carpet.

Archer leaned forward on his desk and tried to catch her eye. 'Don't be downhearted, Margaret. I'll do my best to persuade him. How does that sound?'

Peg looked up. 'What about the logistical challenges, though?'

'Like I said, my dear. Nothing is impossible. Which brings me to the final item for our meeting.'

Archer moved the will to one side of his desk, revealing a large manila envelope, which he picked up and handed to Peg. 'Your father has instructed me to hand you this. If you have any questions about it –' he gestured to the envelope – 'or any other matter, please don't hesitate to get in touch. I am at your disposal.'

He smiled at her, then stood and opened the door to his office. Accepting this dismissal, Peg stood too, clutching the envelope to her chest. At the doorway, Archer shook her hand and passed her over to his secretary.

'Could you see Miss Thwaites out, Miss Lunt?'

'Certainly Mr Archer.' Looking at Peg with pursed lips and raised eyebrows, Miss Lunt rose again, opened the front door to the office and let her out.

Peg took the stairs two by two until she was at ground level.

The package Archer had given her burning a hole in her hands, she went into the first Starbucks she came across, ordered a green tea, then sat and ripped the envelope open.

Dear Margaret,

The letter inside said.

> *I no I haven't been the best Dad to you.*
> *& You was right. Im sorry I never saw Mum before she dyed.*
> *You no now what the will says. I'm going to put yr aunt in a home, she sucked Mum dry & Im not going to let her do that to you.*
> *Archer will deal with it all, so you dont have to do nothing.*
>
> *In the envelope is my gift, Margaret. Its all in your name. Archers keeping the deeds for you. The agent has the keys and is waiting for you to pick them up.*

Peg pulled out a smaller envelope. Inside were two pieces of paper. The first was a Bermondsey Street estate agent's description of a two-bedroom converted warehouse flat right by London Bridge Station, asking price seven hundred thousand pounds. The second was a copy of a direct debit instruction for three thousand pounds to go, from Raymond, into Peg's bank account every month.

Peg put all three pieces of paper down and grasped the edge of the table to steady herself. She closed her eyes as the crowded coffee shop whirled around her.

This was not what she wanted.

All she wanted, she realised, was for everything to be back to how it was before she had found out about her father, before Loz had got the scent of a real crime drama in her nostrils, before Doll had died. She wanted just to be happy with Loz, in their little flat, getting on with their lives.

Living their own lives.

But it couldn't be like that any more, could it? Here was the possibility of a new life for a new, harder Peg. And it was being handed to her on a plate, should she choose to take it.

But it was blood money. She was being paid to forget: to forget about how her mother died, to forget about all the lies that she had been told, and not to think about those two girls and how they might have gone missing.

She was being bought.

'Is anyone sitting here?' a Japanese girl asked her politely of the seat opposite her.

'No,' Peg said, her voice shaking. 'I was just leaving, anyway.'

She got up and stuffed the papers back into the envelope. Then she dipped out of Starbucks and down into the Tube station where, after just a moment's hesitation, she decided to head to Victoria, to catch the train back to Whitstable.

Let that estate agent hold on to the bloody keys.

Thirty-Six

'I'VE GOT TO BE THERE,' JEAN SAID, HER VOICE BAGGY THROUGH her tears. 'It'll kill me if I can't say goodbye to Mummy.'

Peg had handled Jean very carefully since she had discovered Raymond's plans for her. Her aunt was lost in a haze of grief, so the question of the future could wait until after Doll's funeral. While she knew that being moved out of the bungalow and into a home would be the end of Jean's world, Peg was relieved that the decision was out of her hands – something she couldn't be held to blame for.

'I'll see what I can do,' Peg said at last, squeezing Jean's doughy fingers between her own hands.

'But I can't even get out of bed,' Jean wailed. 'How am I going to get to the cemetery?'

Peg eyed her. She shocked herself at how glad she felt about washing her hands of her.

When did she become so callous?

Back at the library, Peg managed to locate a specialist company running ambulances built for obese patients. For a price, the company would take Jean from her bed to Doll's funeral, and, 'using a range of bariatric devices with our own trained, compassionate staff', transport her in a specially constructed wheelchair from the ambulance to the chapel and thence to the burial plot.

It had to be the first time Jean had gone outside for over ten years. Unless, of course, her levels of deception extended to that, too. From witnessing the agility with which her aunt scooted herself down her bed when she had thought no one was looking, Peg wouldn't have been terribly surprised if she had been sneaking out for regular strolls along The Slopes.

Peg reported back to Jean, to be met with more tears about not having anything suitable to wear and the shame of having to be transported by a specialist company. 'What'll the neighbours think? You might as well put me on a flatbed truck, Meggy,' she said, easing grey Marlboro smoke out through the gaps in her teeth. 'With a crane.'

Peg didn't tell her that, crane apart, this had been an early consideration before she had done her research.

She found a local dressmaker through a card placed in the newsagent's and asked her to make a black smock for Jean in a good wool crêpe, using one of the tent dresses Doll had made as a template.

'Better make it about half a metre bigger all round,' Peg said to the woman, who was barely able to conceal her astonishment at the amount of material she was going to have to use.

'Do you want a collar or anything?' the dressmaker asked.

'Let's keep it plain at the neckline,' Peg said, thinking of folds of flesh straining and spilling over fabric. 'Perhaps you can make a matching scarf or something?'

Peg spent the rest of the time leading up to the day liaising with Archer and the funeral directors over invitations, bills, and details. It appeared there would be quite a few elderly members of Frank's Masonic Lodge attending, and some distant cousins on Doll's side who Peg hadn't known about, let alone met.

The guest list extended to nearly forty, so Peg decided to hold a reception in The Worthington, a mock-Tudor hotel with good wide disabled access, within walking distance from the cemetery. Because of its position, the place was well versed in dealing with wakes, to the extent that the brassy landlady proudly showed Peg their three top funeral reception packages. Peg went for the 'Gold', which included teas and coffees, all drinks at the bar, ten assorted savoury canapés and five sweets. Because it had so roundly cornered the post-funeral market, The Worthington saw little other business, so was able to accommodate them at short notice even for an event just three days before Christmas.

'Sadly, people don't consider us when planning their seasonal festivities,' the landlady said, wrinkling her foundation into a wry smile as Peg paid the fifty per cent deposit. 'But we must be thankful that death goes on, regardless of the date.'

Peg was glad she didn't have to think about the cost of things before she agreed to them. She was beginning to see how money greased even the most challenging situations. Viewed in this light, the *fait accompli* Raymond had handed her with the flat and the income didn't seem quite so distasteful.

Since she didn't now have the ulterior motive of channelling it Doll's way, her initial plan had been to tell him he could shove it where the sun didn't shine. She had even drafted the message she was going to send him telling him to piss off, but had decided to sleep on it before going down to the library to send it. Three days later it was still waiting in her notebook, and her mind had been slowly changing.

Liberated from the binds of duty, she began to imagine what removing the need to make a living could do for her – and for Loz. She could go to university, as her father wanted her to. Or – a far more attractive prospect – she could help Loz get her restaurant off the ground. Money made all this possible, and the thought of a brighter future – albeit lodged firmly at the back of her mind until the funeral was out of the way – put a lightness in her step that otherwise would have been absent.

All she would owe Raymond was a promise not to mention the past.

How difficult could that be?

But still a sour taste stuck to her mouth, like she had eaten a curry and forgotten her toothbrush.

After careful thought, she took one of Doll's pinnies to the funeral parlour. The pinnies were the clothing she most closely associated with her grandmother, and she found the idea of her going into the ground dressed like that greatly comforting. The funeral director looked a little surprised as he took the powder-blue garment from her and held it up.

'Are you sure this is what you want?' he said.

'Yes.'

He formed his lips into a small, mouth-closed smile that verged on a smirk. 'It's quite plain, isn't it? Almost the same as my attendant wears.'

'Is it?' Peg said.

The new, hardened Peg.

Not returning his smile.

The night before the funeral, Loz came to stay. After a serious campaign of working double shifts, she had bagged two begrudgingly allowed days off.

She arrived with a suit carrier and a wheeled suitcase containing four bottles of champagne, a series of plastic containers full of Seed's vegan antipasti selection, a large chunk of nut pâté and some good bread.

'For our own private ceremony when all the cronies have trundled back to where they were hiding when she was alive,' she said, stacking the champagne in the fridge. She turned to Peg. 'Is he coming then?'

Peg shut the kitchen door. She'd rather Jean couldn't listen in on this conversation.

Even with her personal ambivalence towards Raymond, some deep-seated moral conviction made her feel that she should do everything she could to persuade him to come to his mother's funeral – for his own sake as well as Doll's. He had said in the note about the flat that he was sorry he hadn't seen his mother before she died. And she remembered his voice when she phoned him with the news of Doll's death. He had been touched. He was not emotionally uninvolved. He needed to say goodbye.

She had tried calling him several times and had sent him three emails with details of Doll's funeral, urging him to come. She had not mentioned the flat or the monthly income.

She couldn't understand why he was staying away. Guilt or shame shouldn't figure now he had no abandoned mother to face up to. If it was because he detested Jean so much that he couldn't bear to see her, surely the fact that he had total power over her now the whole bungalow set-up was coming to an end would somehow mitigate that? And, as for any legal obstacles to his returning to the UK, well, didn't Archer say that nothing was impossible?

But she had heard nothing from him in return.

'Please don't start, though,' she said to Loz, helping her by taking the antipasti out of the suitcase.

'I promise. I'm on my best behaviour. I'll be as good as gold. But is he coming, though?'

'No. He's not coming.' Peg stopped mid-task, the nut pâté in her hands.

'Put that down,' Loz said, holding out her arms. 'And come here.'

'This is the end of the road for my family,' Peg said, stooping to bury her face in Loz's shoulder.

They stood there like that for a moment, until Peg felt strong enough to draw away.

'It's not a tragedy, though. It's a liberation,' she said, smiling weakly.

'Almost convincing, Peggo,' Loz said. 'What'll happen with Jean? When she's in this home Raymond's going to put her in? How will that work out?'

'I'll visit her of course. But I won't be *responsible*. And that's how I want it.'

Loz looked at her through narrowed eyes. 'You could've fooled me.'

Peg avoided Loz's gaze. She wasn't up to one of her challenges. She decided at that moment not to mention anything about the flat or the money until after the funeral, when she would have a clearer idea of what she was going to do with her father's offer. There was no point in having an argument with Loz about it now, when she didn't even know herself where she stood.

The next morning, Peg got up early and put on the new black dress and tights she had bought from one of Whitstable's fiercely expensive boutiques.

'Sharp,' Loz said.

'Not so bad yourself,' Peg said, watching Loz button up an extremely well-cut jacket.

'I bought it for my interview at Seed, and it'll be getting more outings in the near future, unless Cara bucks her fucking ideas up and starts treating me more like a human being and less like a cooking machine.'

They went together to Jean's extension to cloak her in the new dress. It was a two-person job and Peg had given Julie the morning off so that she could come to the funeral.

'I'm not having that in here,' Jean said, pointing at Loz.

Loz raised one eyebrow at her, leaned against the door frame and folded her arms.

'Please, Aunty Jean. Can't we just have one day's truce? For Nan? We need an extra pair of hands if we're going to get you ready in time.'

From her pillow, Jean looked first at Peg, then at Loz.

'I suppose I haven't got any choice, though, have I?' she said at last. Grief seemed to have added another five stone to her. 'Well, get me up then.'

They used the air pillow to hoist Jean into a position where they could lift off her nightie. Peg kept half an eye on Loz, on her first encounter with Jean's bared flesh. With its folds and sores and stretch marks and blotched purple areas where networks of capillaries had burst under pressure from the fat around them, her body was far more blasted even than one would imagine from seeing her covered in her bed. Peg gave her aunt a quick upper-body wash, taking care to dry and powder underneath her flops of flesh.

'Give us a burst of that, will you, darling?' Jean said, nodding at a bottle of Miss Dior nestling among the ornamental pelicans on her dressing table. Peg had bought the perfume for her three Christmases ago, when she was feeling both flush on her first pay cheque from the library and guilty at having moved away from the bungalow. Jean had made a big fuss about how expensive the perfume was, and how Peg shouldn't have, and said she would only ever use it on special occasions. As far as Peg was aware, this was the first time she had opened the bottle. She took the lid off, and sprayed Jean's neck and wrists with it, momentarily masking the staleness of her shabby, hospital-like room with an incongruous whiff of glamour.

Peg and Loz slipped the giant black tent of a dress over Jean's head, taking care not to disturb the heated rollers they had put in for her. Loz was on her best behaviour, quiet and unobtrusive, simply providing help when Peg asked for it.

'It's too big,' Jean said, glumly pulling at the material.

'It hangs nicely though.' Peg arranged the yards of stuff. 'It's meant to be a loose fit.'

'Pass me my make-up and mirror,' Jean said.

Eventually, in the light-absorbing black of her new dress, with her hair pinned up into great billows, her features defined by rouge, blue eyeshadow, black eyeliner and deep red lips, and her skin softened and matted by a dousing of face powder, Jean looked strangely glamorous, like a blown rose. During the process of getting her ready, Peg had been taking and making phone calls to ensure that everything was on track – the priest was in place, the cars prepared, the reception all set up.

And then bang on the appointed hour the bariatric ambulance arrived. Two burly paramedics piled out of the vehicle and assessed the situation.

'Hello, boys,' Jean said, batting her eyelashes at them from the expanse of her face. For a second, Peg glimpsed the glamour puss from the early photographs: the Jean before the excess thirty stones; the Jean with the fiancé.

But the charm didn't work on the ambulance men, who were merely sizing her up to see what equipment they'd need to shift her. They nodded at her politely, then they went into the back of their ambulance and hauled out a double-width wheelchair that looked like it had been built with scaffolding rods. They also brought with them a sling hoist on wheels, which they used to lever the wincing and complaining Jean from her bed into the chair. The men were enormous, built like weightlifters, but still they found the process a challenge.

'Is my hair all right?' Jean asked Peg when they had finally installed her in the ambulance.

'It looks lovely, Aunty Jean,' Peg said, patting her hand.

'Your aunt is at the top end of our limit,' the driver said discreetly to Peg after he had closed the ambulance door on Jean. 'I'll let it go because of the circumstances. But we'll need to have a doctor's certification of her weight when we next move her. Health and safety.'

Peg turned to Loz, who was smiling and shaking her head.

'What?' she said.

'How did this family produce someone so wonderful as you?' she said.

Perhaps it was because they had spent the whole morning looking at Jean, but when Doll's flower-smothered coffin drew up outside in the hearse, it looked impossibly tiny. Peg and Loz climbed into the funeral director's shiny black Galaxy, and the three vehicles – hearse, car and ambulance – set off in slow-moving convoy towards the cemetery. A couple of neighbours had come out of their houses to watch. One woman crossed herself as the hearse passed.

Sitting in the back of the Galaxy, everything she needed to do accomplished, the enormity of her situation hit Peg for the first time. Here she was, on her way to bury the woman who had been a mother to her for seventeen years. Little Doll, who, through all those years, had given nothing but love, despite the losses and disappointments she had suffered herself. The activity of the past couple of weeks had kept Peg's feelings of guilt at bay, but now they came flooding back, making her feel dirty and useless.

The tears came. She took Loz's hand.

She only just managed to gather herself as the car swung up the tarmac path to the cemetery chapel. An inappropriately cheerful Christmas tree with lights and tinsel stood in the entrance, reminding Peg of the Christmases she had spent with Doll. The work her grandmother used to put in to make the day unforgettable was incredible: the wrapping of presents, the carefully constructed party games, the endless sweet and savoury snacks she prepared.

Peg and Loz waited by the ambulance as Jean, her oxygen hooked up to the back of the chair, was lowered to the ground. On its way from the lift platform to the ground, the wheelchair bumped and Jean shuddered.

'They're just bloody manhandling me,' Jean said, wincing. 'They're just bloody brutes.'

'Can I push her?' Peg asked the ambulance driver.

'I can't let you, I'm afraid. We're not insured to let our equipment pass into the hands of non-employees.'

'Oh no. Is that her? Mummy . . .' Jean sobbed, pointing at the coffin with one hand and bringing a tissue up to her mouth with the other.

The white-smocked priest, who had been greeting people as they arrived, rushed to open both chapel of rest doors to let Jean through. Loz and Peg followed behind.

Inside, seven dusty old men with red faces and shiny suits –

Frank's Masonic friends, Peg supposed – sat in a formal row towards the back, each holding his hat in his hands. They nodded at Jean as she was wheeled to the space cleared for her at the front. Sitting on his own in the back row on the other side of the aisle to the Masons, Archer acknowledged Peg as she passed with Loz, following Jean to the front. Like a strange bridal procession, the three of them – Peg, Loz and wheelchair-pusher – walked in time to the solemn recorded organ music, with Jean before them as their distorted bride. All the music was Doll's choice, as recorded in her will, along with her desire for no words to be spoken. Peg hadn't even considered that she might have been called upon to give a speech, so when Archer read this clause to her, she felt she had escaped an unforeseen hell.

A couple of neighbours sat at pews nearer the front of the chapel: Mrs Cairns, the woman from the post office in Tankerton High Street, and an Indian gentleman who, from the way he raised a hand as Jean went by, Peg supposed must have something to do with the Taj Mahal. Julie was there in a neat little black coat, and a small group of formally mournful-looking people – probably the distant cousins – occupied the front pew on the left side. Other than that, the tiny chapel was empty.

It was sad that there were so few people left to come to say goodbye to Doll. If Raymond had kept in touch, Paulie and Caroline would have been here – a whole new family to pay their respects. But then if Raymond had been around, Doll might even still have been alive, escaped from Peg's neglectful absence.

Poor Dolly. Poor Nan.

'Will you please stand,' the priest said, as the first bars of 'The Lord's My Shepherd' struck up. Jean shifted in her wheelchair to show that, even though she couldn't rise, she could pay her mother some respect. The congregation started to sing. Loz, whose strictly secular school had never once forced her to sing a hymn, mouthed along badly. Peg, who had endured daily religious assemblies at school, knew the form, but her voice caught on the pastures green and she couldn't go on. Loz put her arm round Peg, who laid her head on her shoulder, and wept.

As the song ended, Peg felt a chill on the back of her neck, as if a door had opened behind her. She lifted her head from Loz's shoulder and turned her tear-reddened eyes towards the back of the chapel.

There, at the back of the assembly, slipped in beside his lawyer, his eyes shielded by dark glasses, was her father.

Raymond had decided to turn up.

Then

I'M ON THE BEACH.

No, I'm on The Street and it's low tide and I'm quite a long way out. Perhaps it's the time the old bags asked me about my mummy and I said she was dead.

Anyway, if it was that time, the old bags aren't there any more, and I'm busy looking in a pool at this crab who keeps scuttling away whenever my shadow falls over him.

It's coming to the end of the day. I'm roasted, my head and my tummy ache and the beach is wiggly with heat. As usual, I'm slathered with sunblock.

I look up just to check Aunty Jean is still there in the trolley, and she is, sitting looking out to sea, or at me. It's hard to tell from this distance. A plume of smoke rises from her, straight up into the air because there's no wind at all, not even a little puff. It looks like she's on fire, but it's only her cig.

Something catches my eye. It's a big white car, rolling slowly along the prom towards her.

I can't see what make it is because it's too far away. I can't even hear its engine. But it's a really big, white car.

You can only drive along the prom if you're staying in one of the two houses down there. But the car stops a long way away from either of the driveways, a good long way before Aunty Jean, too. It just stops, and for a long time nothing happens. I nearly get bored looking.

Aunty Jean, who hasn't seen the car, waves at me, and I wave back.

I know this is her way of letting me know we should be thinking about heading back for tea, but I've got the car to be interested in now, as well as the crab.

A man gets out of the car, stands and stretches. He's smoking too, something too big to be a cigarette. A pipe, perhaps. Or a cigar?

A cigar.

Yes, even though I didn't know it at the time, even though I couldn't see it because he was too far away, I now know who it must have been in that big, white car, with that cigar.

It's not rocket science.

It's really hot, but he's wearing a pale coat and a dark hat, not a sun hat.

Slowly he walks along the prom, and he stops by Aunty Jean.

They seem to be talking to each other; though they're so far away I can't hear what they're saying.

It's just someone Aunty Jean knows, I think.

I check the crab. Thinking I have gone, he has come out into the sun again. I jump suddenly to one side to startle him and, very satisfyingly, he scuttles back under his stone.

I wish Aunty Jean could see this. It's so sad she's stuck up on the prom. I look up at her and now she seems to be arguing with the man. She's waving her finger at him, stabbing it into the air. The man has his arms outstretched, holding his hands out, as if he's trying to make a point.

I wonder if I should go and see what's going on, but I'm a bit scared of the man, and anyway it's Aunty Jean's business, not mine.

Then, blimey, she's pulling herself up, out of the trolley, and she has the man by the shoulders. She's pulling back her hand and it looks like she slaps him round the face. She then points at me and I look away pretending not to have noticed, pretending to be involved in my crab.

The next time I dare sneak a look at what's going on, the man is storming back to his car. He climbs in and slams the door and reverses it so quickly back along the prom that I hear the tyres screech, even from that far away, and two boys on the prom have to jump out of the way to avoid being run over.

Jean is back in her trolley and she's staring straight out at me.

My tummy grips me with a really hot pain.

A *really* hot pain.

This wasn't the time the old bags asked me about my mummy. This was much later than that.

The hot pain was there because it was the day my period started.

I was twelve when this happened.

My father came back for me when I was twelve.

It's not that I forgot it. I just didn't realise.

I didn't put two and two together.

And Aunty Jean saw him off . . .

Thirty-Seven

'EXCUSE ME,' RAYMOND SAID TO LOZ, STEPPING INTO HER PLACE by Peg, who was standing next to Jean at the exit to the chapel, shaking hands with the mourners as they filed out. 'This is where family stand.'

Without acknowledging him, Loz stepped back so that she was next to the two wheelchair-pushers. Peg noticed the set of her chin, though, and it didn't bode well.

Jean looked up at her brother. 'You came, then,' she said.

'Oh yes,' Raymond said, standing at the other side of Peg, looking away, rubbing his hands together against the biting December cold.

It was an odd greeting for a brother and sister who supposedly hadn't seen each other for fifteen years.

'I'm so sorry,' one of the distant cousins said, dabbing at her drooping eyes with a lace-edged handkerchief, and trying to avoid looking at either Peg's haircut or Jean's bulk.

'Thank you for coming all this way,' Raymond said, shaking her timidly surrendered hand.

'Your mother was a formidable lady,' one of the old Masons

said, patting Jean's hand. He looked at least a hundred years old, like he had stepped out of a cupboard full of cobwebs.

'She was that,' Raymond said, working his jaw and looking up at the sun, which pierced sharply through a cold blue sky, bringing a lot of light, but very little in the way of warmth.

The pub buffet was everything a funeral luncheon should be – fried chicken wings, wobbling bacon quiche, sausage rolls. Nothing too outlandish, and nothing on the savoury table that a vegetarian could touch.

'Get this down you.' Loz put a large gin and tonic into Peg's hand as she listened to two old dusty Masons talk about what a wonderful woman Doll was and how she had held the whole family together through an extended 'nervous illness' that Frank had suffered when Jean and Raymond were 'nippers'. This was yet another revelation. No one had ever said anything about Frank ever being ill.

'He wasn't the same after,' one of the old boys said. 'He lost his pep. Became a bit of a mouse, really, poor old Frank.'

Poor Frank.

Having learned that Raymond intended to go back to the bungalow after the funeral, Peg was in no hurry to speak to him at the wake. While the part of her that had urged him to come had many reasons to be glad that he had turned up – the closure he seemed to so despise, the fact that Doll would have wanted it, and so on – a newer part of her now realised that she wished he hadn't.

Speaking with him would be too much like hard work, which, against the emotionally strained backdrop of Doll's death, she didn't feel much like facing. It would involve too much verbal ducking and diving, too much dissemblance. Not only were there all the things she had learned about him that he had no idea she knew, but there was also the weight of Loz's suspicions. Although Peg wanted to write them off as the product of a feverishly inept amateur sleuthing, a tiny voice in her head kept persistently asking: *What if she's right? What if she's got a point?* To all this was added her own ambivalence about the flat and the money – she knew Raymond would at some point want an answer from her.

The result of all this was that his presence so complicated this already difficult day that she felt her stomach turning over whenever she caught sight of him.

She circulated among the guests, keeping an eye on Loz, who seemed to constantly have a drink in her hand. She ducked Mrs Cairns's inappropriate questions about her plans for the bungalow, instead listening to the stories about her grandmother's incredible nursing prowess, and how everyone in the street turned to her.

'She ran her front room like an operating theatre,' one woman said. 'It was like our own little hospital.'

'Of course, she were never the same after the accident with little Keith,' a woman who had introduced herself as 'Dolly's mum's sister's girl' said. She wore a silk scarf knotted round her stringy neck and had a voice that bore witness to half a century's addiction to tobacco. 'She doted on that little boy, and her world ended when he went. It's where it all started to go wrong for that one, too.' The woman waved a knotty hand at Jean, who had been parked at a table with a mounded-up plate of food, a pint of Guinness, and a selection of sympathetic old boys around her.

'What do you mean?' Peg said, as Loz weaved towards her to replace her empty glass with a full one.

'After the accident with poor little Keith, well, Dolly

wrapped the other two up in cotton wool and never let them out of her sight again. He –' she pointed her angular chin at Raymond, who was talking quietly with Archer at the bar – 'he escaped through his business and all that, that dodgy club racket, and all that other business with your poor mother.' The woman waved vaguely in the air, and Peg wondered if everyone in the world had known the truth but her. 'But poor old Jeanie,' Dolly's mum's sister's girl went on. 'Well, she never got away. And you see what happened to her.'

Peg took a slug of her drink. But surely Doll had *looked after* Jean, not kept her prisoner? She had single-handedly kept her daughter alive.

She made her excuses and left the woman, who she had decided was a spiteful old cow with nothing better to do than speak ill of the dead.

Irked, she looked around the overheated room. Despite the small number of funeral guests, it was full enough for all the windows to be fogged with condensation. Two double gins on an empty stomach had made her woozy. Had she not been, she might have noticed what was going on before it was too late.

Loz was standing right next to Raymond, yet again waiting to be served at the bar, her eyes glinting over at him, like emeralds sharpening themselves on his jaw.

The she moved in and said something to him – something Peg couldn't hear.

He froze for a second, like a cobra before a strike. Then, his eyes half closed, he leaned towards her and whispered something back at her.

It didn't look like a declaration of love.

'Don't think you can scare me like you do everyone else,' Loz said, loud enough for Peg, who was still hovering over at the other side of the room, to hear. At the sound of Loz's words, the buzz of elderly conversation faded for a second, then politely picked up again.

It was time for Peg to move over and intervene.

'Why don't you just leave?' Peg heard Raymond say, as, with the sense that she was heading towards two colliding tornadoes, she crossed the room. 'You don't know what you're talking about. You don't belong here, if that's what you think.' A vein throbbed in his temple, and he looked like he had when he choked on the piece of meat back in Spain.

He stood and squared up to Loz. He wasn't a tall man, but next to her he looked enormous. Archer, who was standing at his other side, put a restraining hand on his arm.

'Enough, Raymond,' he said. 'We don't want any trouble, remember?'

'You're not welcome here. And what the fuck you doing with my daughter, anyway?'

Peg moved in next to Loz, ready to step in and take the blow for her, should it come.

But like a tiny terrier, Loz faced Raymond up and, with a protective arm round Peg, she addressed him, her voice loud and clear. 'You don't even know her. I love her and she loves me, and if you want anything to do with her, you're going to have to deal with that. *Raymond.*'

The cousins, positioned by the buffet with their plates, gave a slight but perceptible gasp.

'Can we leave it, please?' Peg whispered, pleading, wincing, wishing they would both just melt into the floor. 'Can we deal with this later?'

'I don't think we can,' Loz said, balling her fists. Peg really thought she might try to land a punch on Raymond, which would be a very bad thing indeed. She could imagine that he might be good at fighting.

She could imagine that he might even carry a gun.

'Stop this right now!' Jean exclaimed, thumping her big fist down onto her table, making the old boys near her jump.

'*Shut up Jean*,' Loz said, her eyes still on Raymond.

The cousins gasped, far more audibly this time. Then the room fell silent. Everyone was poised, trained on Loz and Raymond.

'Go on. Tell me about Mary Perkins,' Loz said. 'What did you do to her? And what's in the garage at Heyworth Court, eh? Or don't you want to talk about that, either?'

'This is my mother's *funeral*,' Raymond said. 'Show some *respect*.' His chin twitched and his lower lip stuck out. He flexed his fingers and Peg couldn't tell if he were preparing to throttle Loz or trying to restrain himself from doing so.

'Like you showed respect to Mary?' Loz went on.

'Loz, please,' Peg said.

'You don't know what you're talking about,' Raymond said, his voice now dangerously low, his eyes narrowed.

'For God's sake, shut UP!' Jean thundered, her flesh wobbling.

The air in the room had grown as thick as fur. Peg realised that her heart was racing so violently, she was finding it hard to breathe.

'You've ruined Mummy's funeral,' Jean went on. 'Are you satisfied now? Haven't you punished her enough?'

With a shock, Peg realised that her aunt addressed this not at Loz – who she actually thought deserved it – but directly at her father.

The silence that followed this accusation was like a violin string in the moment before a snap.

'It's dreadful. Dreadful,' Jean said, at last, wheezing and purple. 'Dreadful.'

No one moved.

No one said a thing.

Then one of the cousins coughed.

The spell was broken.

Like so many Cinderellas, people started to put their plates and glasses down and make for their coats and bags.

'Thank you so much, Margaret. It was a lovely send-off, er . . .'

Pulling on her mothball-scented fur coat, the cousin who coughed came forward to shake Peg's hand, then moved on to say goodbye to Raymond and Jean. She was followed, one by one, by the rest of the gathering, until there were no guests left except Peg, Loz, Raymond, Archer, Jean, her bearers and Julie, who, after the upset, had helped Jean on with her oxygen mask. Two bemused waitresses in black skirts and white polyester shirts moved among the empty tables clearing up half-finished plates and half-empty glasses.

'I'll be up day after tomorrow.' Raymond turned to Archer and touched him on the shoulder, dismissing him. 'Thanks for your help, mate.'

'Are you all right to get my aunt back to her bungalow without me?' Peg said to the ambulance driver, who made to object but, given the situation, just nodded. Then, unable to stay in the room any longer, she left.

She just walked out.

She needed to find some air.

Thirty-Eight

'FOR FUCK'S SAKE,' LOZ SAID, RUNNING BEHIND PEG AS SHE streamed along the freezing low tide sand, heading eastwards, away from The Street. She wanted to walk out to the very corner of Kent and keep going, striding out into the North Sea until she reached mainland Europe and left all this mess of a life behind her. 'Stop, Peg, please.'

An easterly wind had got up, whipping sand in their faces. Seagulls circled like vultures above them, eyeing a strange crop of blighted dogfish corpses that littered the exposed seabed around them.

'Why?' Peg turned and shouted at Loz, nearly backing into a muddy pool as she did so. 'Why the hell should I? You come in here, into my family, which you know nothing about. You start getting all these stupid melodramatic ideas about my father – my FATHER – being some sort of serial killer; you wind up my aunt and make trouble, and now you fuck up my grandmother's funeral because what? – because you don't want to share me with anyone else?'

363

'It's not that. I—' Loz tried to grab Peg's hand. 'Can't you see he's no good? I'm just worried for you, that – that he's going to lead you into trouble.'

'I CAN LOOK AFTER MYSELF!' Peg yelled, pushing Loz so that she fell backwards onto the mud, ruining her smart interview suit. Undeterred, Loz scrabbled to her feet, not even pausing to knock the dirt from her trousers.

'He's no good,' she said, running after Peg, who was striding on over the sandbanks. 'Don't you see? This is your chance to break away from them. You don't need to have anything more to do with him or with Jean. They're . . . toxic! They're infecting you.'

'Infecting me because I'm standing up to you?' Peg said, stopping again and whirling round to face Loz. 'Don't you think I'm capable of having an opinion of my own? You just want a piece of me. You want me as some sort of leper project of yours, put me together like some recipe and cook me up. And you want all this drama because your own right-on, sad-fuck family is so fucking well adjusted and so fucking boring there's nothing you can do for them.'

'Is that what you think of me?' Loz screamed above the gulls and the wind that howled round them, scudding fresh grey clouds over the sun, tugging Peg's dress across her knees and blowing her own duvet coat about her like a black sail. 'Is that what you really think?'

A gull, fed up of waiting for them to move, dive-bombed to the ground, tearing up a ribbon of rotting dogfish flesh. Emboldened, others followed, then fought, their struggle mirroring that of the two women sharing their seabed.

Peg picked up a stick and swiped at the gulls with it, sending them scattering, wheeling and regrouping for another foray.

'I think you've built up some kind of sick fantasy in your

head about what this family is all about,' she said, turning back to Loz.

'Sick fantasy? We've got *facts*. Evidence. Enough to go to the police.'

'Police?'

'Now we don't have to worry about upsetting poor Doll, I'm going to prove to you that I'm right,' Loz said, folding her arms and sticking her chin out – the tiny embodiment of determination.

'Don't be ridiculous. You'll waste their time and you'll look like an idiot.'

'Watch this space, Peg. Did you know that Mary Perkins's mum tried to kill herself three years after her daughter disappeared? And then, what about poor Colin Cairns topping himself? And that schoolgirl's parents? What about them?' Loz looked at Peg sternly. 'They weren't lucky like you were today.'

'Call *me* lucky?'

'Unlike you, she didn't even have a body to bury. Can you imagine? It's not just about your own little family, Peg. Don't be so blind and selfish.'

'But—'

'And it's all down to him,' Loz yelled over the top of Peg, pointing towards the shore. 'He's not only ruined the lives of his victims. He's also fucked up everyone who loved them. And you, Peg. He's royally fucked you over *all your life*.'

'NO,' Peg said.

She felt like drawing her hand back and hitting Loz smack across the mouth, sending her flying across the rocks and mud. Instead, she flung the stick she was still holding far out to sea, flipping it like a helicopter blade, slicing it through the thick, cold air until it splatted muddily down in the distance. She hurled it with so much force she wrenched her arm.

'Just go,' she turned and said to Loz. 'Go!'

And, turning her back on the woman she loved, she set off again, trudging over the mud, heading for the sideways horizon, where the sands seemed to run out. When she finally stopped, the icy incoming tide now covering her boots, cold water soaking into her tights, she turned and looked over her shoulder.

There wasn't another soul on the wind-blasted beach.

As if Peg had imagined her entirely, Loz had disappeared.

Thirty-Nine

PEG DIDN'T GET AS FAR AS THE CORNER OF KENT. THE TIDE seethed in and, before she reached Reculver, she was forced up on to the shingle. She crunched on, increasingly half-heartedly, until the sky darkened and dusk arrived, heralded by sharp needles of ice-cold rain that picked at her red cheeks and stabbed into the churning surface of the sea.

The cold and the walking had dissipated the gin that had fired her blood. But it hadn't quite forced out her anger. Loz had ruined Doll's funeral. She had bulldozed through everything, only concerning herself with her own pet theories. It was idiocy, and Peg felt violated on behalf of her own flesh and blood.

She climbed the shingle bank to the concrete promenade and started to head back to Tankerton, the wind behind her now. She was beginning to wish she hadn't walked quite so far. By the time she turned inland to the grid of streets that led to the bungalow, it was gone five, and as dark as a moonless midnight. She couldn't feel her sodden, frozen feet and even thrusting her hands deep inside her parka pockets didn't stop them stinging as if the skin had been peeled from them.

As she approached the bungalow, she saw a big black Lexus parked in the driveway. Behind drawn curtains, a light glimmered in Doll's lounge.

Raymond was there.

She wondered if he was specifically waiting for her, or if he had some other business to attend to.

Quietly, she opened the front door. The full blast of central heating shocked her frozen blood back into circulation. A telling layer of cigar smoke hung in the hot, dry air. Shrugging off her parka and stripping off her salt-waterlogged boots and socks, she peered through the half-open lounge door.

Raymond sat on his mother's chair in front of the gas fire, which he had turned full on. In one hand he held the school photograph of Peg, in the other he had one of Loz's bottles of champagne.

As he lifted it shakily to his mouth to drink, Peg saw that he was crying.

She hesitated in the doorway, unsure whether she should show herself. He might not take kindly to being seen like this, defences down.

She wondered if she should be scared of him. Could this frail piece of flesh and blood weeping on the settee really be the monster of Loz's imaginings? The evidence against him was pretty compelling – even viewed through her own eyes. But seeing him there, his wet cheeks pink like a little boy's, his sorrow stripped bare . . . He didn't look capable of harming a dying dog, let alone a pretty young woman in her prime, or a schoolgirl the same age as his own daughter.

No, Loz could still be discredited in Peg's mind.

She coughed. An irrational fear stabbed at her as he jumped to his feet in a movement that suggested that, if he had a gun, he would have drawn it.

But when he saw it was her, his face softened.

'Hello, Dad,' she said.

He stood and, carefully putting the bottle and photograph down on the occasional table, crossed the room and put his arms round her.

Astounded, Peg could only respond in kind. Because she was that bit taller than him, it felt as if she were comforting him.

It went very one-way like that.

After a couple of minutes, he drew away from her, pulled a starched white handkerchief from his breast pocket, blew his nose and wiped his eyes like a woman tidying her mascara.

'Want a drink?' he said.

'Yes please.'

He went through to the kitchen and came back with another bottle of champagne and two glasses. Peg knew she should really eat something before she drank again, but didn't feel able to intrude on this moment with something so mundane as needing food.

He popped the top off the champagne, filled the glasses and handed one to Peg.

'There you go, girl. Get that down you.' He had regained his composure on the trip to the kitchen, although there was still a catch in his voice.

They sat, he on Doll's chair, she, nails scraping, on the edge of the settee.

'You were right, in a way, Margaret. I should have come back earlier,' Raymond said. 'I should have seen Mum before she went.'

Peg nodded.

'But it was too complicated. It was better for everyone if I stayed away.'

'What do you mean?'

But Raymond just shook his head and looked down into his glass, where the bubbles fizzed and popped like little bullets.

He looked utterly dejected.

Then Peg had a thought. 'Wait there a minute, Dad.'

She jumped up and went out into the freezing shed, where she found the Raymond box that Doll had kept on top of her wardrobe.

'She kept all this,' she said, bringing it back into the warm and placing it in front of him. Kneeling beside him, she pulled out the old school reports, the photographs of him as a boy and his caul, which she opened and put into his trembling hand. 'This was round you when you were born. She kept it to protect you. She loved you, you know.'

'I know she did,' Raymond said, fingering the papery husk. 'Too much.'

'What do you mean?'

'It was too much, that's all.' He put the caul back in its box and replaced the lid, then he closed the Raymond box and pushed it away, brushing the dust from his fingers.

'It's a pity Paulie never met her, though,' Peg said.

'It's better for him how it is,' Raymond said. 'Better that he never met her.'

Peg frowned. She couldn't work out what Raymond was saying to her.

He sat, lost in thought, offering no further explanation. Eventually he shifted in his seat and refilled his glass, holding the bottle out to Peg. Then he pulled a cigar out of his breast pocket and lit it.

'I've got to go back tomorrow,' he said. 'It's Paulie's birthday day after and I'm throwing this big party. Forty kids, their parents and a full sit-down meal and entertainment. I've got that boy band, what they called, the ones with the hair like that –' he held his hand about a foot above his head – 'coming as a surprise too. Not even Caroline knows about that.'

'Lucky boy.' Peg couldn't stop the wave of jealousy that passed over her, the now-familiar feeling of *what about me?*

'Well, I like to make it special for him with his birthday being on Christmas Eve and all that. Hey, you could come if you want.'

'I think I'd better stay here,' she said, gesturing at the dividing wall between Jean's and Doll's. 'How is she?'

'Who?'

'Aunty Jean.'

'Out blotto,' he said, nodding at the dividing wall. 'She was in bits after all that business at the funeral, so I gave her a couple of her pills. That girl Julie what looks after her come back because she was in such a state. She showed me which was the right ones.'

'Thank you for sorting her out.'

'Think nothing of it,' he said, misunderstanding her. 'I don't want her to be the burden on you or me that she was on my mother. She's got no one to blame but herself for how she is. It was possible for her to get away, but she chose not to. Look at me. I managed, didn't I?'

Peg frowned. This talk of escape echoed what the cousin had said at the wake, and it puzzled her. 'I don't know what you're saying.'

'That's just as well, Margaret, believe me.'

A night seagull wheeled past outside, unseen beyond the nylon net curtains, its staccato caw puncturing the silence in the room.

'Sorry about all that,' Peg said eventually. 'Back in the pub, I mean.'

371

'That friend of yours is dangerous,' Raymond said. 'Accusing me of God knows what.'

'She's got a bee in her bonnet about some photos we found,' Peg said.

'Mary Perkins.'

'Yes. And there's this.' Peg rummaged in her rucksack for her key ring, to which she had attached the garage key for safekeeping. She handed it to Raymond. 'Loz has some fanciful notions about what you got up to in there.'

'Heyworth Court,' Raymond said, rubbing the label. He leaned forward, carefully arranged Peg's keys on the coffee table, then sat back and sucked on his cigar. 'Where'd you find it?'

'On top of Nan's wardrobe. Under that box.'

'Ah.' Raymond nodded.

'We even went there to see if we could get in.'

'Could you?' He looked up sharply.

'No.'

He breathed out and Peg waited, like a diver on a high board, for what he was going to say next.

'All right then,' Raymond said, leaning his head back against Doll's old chair headrest and, for the first time since she had arrived, looking Peg straight in the eye. 'I've got a confession to make.'

Peg swallowed.

'I used to be a naughty boy,' he said.

'What do you mean?'

'I played around, Margaret. I'm not proud of it, and I certainly keep my nose clean now, but until your mum . . .' He checked himself and started again. 'You see. After you was born and until your mum got poorly, I wasn't a very good husband to her. Well, I was out every night at the club. They were all around me, pure gold. Temptation.'

Peg sat rigid on the settee. She needed to hear his explanation, but that didn't mean she was going to like it.

'Ah,' he said, flicking his cigar into the empty champagne bottle. 'All them pretty girls. Throwing themselves at me because I was the boss man with the slick car and the fancy suits. And the booze, and the party powders.'

Peg raised an eyebrow.

'Don't look at me like that, girl. You lot with your hair and ironmongery all over your faces didn't invent drugs, you know.'

Peg bridled at this. The closest she had ever been to an illicit substance was the Valium Doll had slipped her from time to time when she was younger, to calm her nerves.

'What was a man to do?' Raymond went on. 'After she had you, your mum, God rest her soul, well she got, how can I put it? Homely. She went straight from fox to mumsy, without passing go.'

'She had a baby to look after,' Peg said.

'That's right. She couldn't come out with me any more because of you. And I had to go out because that's how I make my money. So what was I to do? Besides, I'd got a taste for the girls in the club before I met her. Shit, it was *how* I met her, if you have to know.'

'I know.'

'Do you?'

Peg nodded.

'You've been busy, haven't you?'

'She was my mum. I wanted to know about her.'

'What else did you find out?'

He looked at her and, for a moment, she thought she saw fear in his eyes. Something in her wanted to keep it there, as security. She decided not to tell him quite yet exactly what she had found out about the life and death of her mother.

'Why are you telling me all this, Raymond?'

'Ah, can't you call me Dad, girl? It's what I am to you.'

She avoided his eye. 'Sex and drugs. You're telling me things a father shouldn't tell his daughter.'

'I'm telling you the *truth*,' he said. 'It's what you was banging on about when you came out to see us, wasn't it? The truth. That's what you said you wanted.'

Peg sighed and flopped back against the settee.

He emptied the bottle into his glass, which was standing on the coffee table. He filled it so much that he had to bend forward and slurp the top off before he could pick it up.

Then, wiping the fizz from his lip, he continued. 'Look. It just happened that one of the birds I had on the go, that Mary Perkins, met with a sticky end. A tragedy. But sadly that kind of thing happens from time to time with the sort of girl who goes out to work just as the normal ones are heading home.'

Peg didn't believe him. This 'confession' was nothing but a disappointment, a fudge. Nothing that she didn't know already.

'And what about the garage, then?' she said, shaking the key at him.

'*It's just a fucking lock-up*. Just a place we used for storing stuff for the club and that.'

'And Anna Thurlow? What about her?'

Raymond jerked his head round, as if wrong-footed. 'What do you mean? Who's Anna Thurlow?'

'You said you'd tell me the truth, Raymond.'

'IT IS THE FUCKING TRUTH. I don't know nothing about no Anna Thurlow.'

'I don't believe you.'

'Suit yourself.'

He got up. Peg noticed that he was swaying, quite drunk –

374

there were two other empty champagne bottles on the floor beside Doll's chair. The bottle they were sharing was the fourth, the last of Loz's hoard.

He crossed to the door.

'Where are you going, Raymond?'

'Can't I take a fucking piss if I want?'

He stumbled out of the room.

She waited.

'Now then, girl,' he said, coming back and adjusting his flies. Despite the stifling heat of the bungalow, he still had his very well-cut camel coat on, a coat that somehow made even this overweight little mousy man fiddling with his trouser zip seem elegant. 'I've given you my confession. Now what about yours? What you doing with that ugly little gobshite, then?'

'She's my girlfriend.'

'You don't say.'

'But you know that, don't you? Don't pretend you don't know everything about me. We live together. We've been together for a year.' Peg could feel the redness rushing to her cheeks.

'Tell me something.' He sat and shuffled his elbows forward on his knees, a one-sided smile smeared over his face. 'Have you ever *had* a boyfriend?'

'No.'

'Never even done it with a bloke, one-night stand or nothing?'

'No.'

'Fuck me.' He slapped his thigh. 'I send you to that school to keep you away from all that. Boys and stuff. All that can spell proper trouble for young girls. If anyone knows that, I should. And you end up with a dyke. Fucking rich, innit?'

Peg looked at him through narrowed eyes.

'Tell me something, girl. How do you know you don't like blokes if you never done it with one?'

'I just know, that's all,' Peg said. 'I love Loz.'

'Love Loz? And what kind of name is that? Loz the lez. Well, there's no way you're going to live in that flat I bought you with *that*. No way, doll.' He sat back and crossed one leg over the other. 'She's a liability.'

'Well then you can stuff it,' Peg said, the words finding their way out of her mouth before she could even start to engage her brain. 'You can stuff your flat and you can stuff your money. You liar.'

'Whoah, whoah,' Raymond said, holding his hands up flat. Then he got up and squatted down in front of her, pushing his face right into her personal space. 'Now, I'm a liberal-minded bloke. I've seen the world. But do you know what this would have done to your nan, eh? She would have thought you were a right disgusting pervert.'

'Nan wasn't like that.' At the mention of her grandmother, Peg's mouth turned down and her eyes prickled hotly. Her father knew which buttons to press, and he clearly wasn't going to be held back by the fact that Doll was still warm in her grave.

'Oh yes she was. She'd have seen that Lez off—'

'Loz.'

'Lez, Loz, what difference does it make?'

'You think you've got some sort of right to tell me what to do? Nan would have wanted anything for me that made me happy.'

'Oh my mother had *very clear* ideas about right and wrong. And you don't look or sound very happy to me, Margaret.' He moved in even closer to her, his nose almost touching hers, his face red, the sweat gleaming on his forehead. 'You don't look or sound happy at all.'

'Why do you think *that* is?' she said, holding his gaze. 'Do you think it could have something to do with the fact that my father couldn't bear to hang around while my mother died naturally, so he finished her off nice and neat and then fucked off out of my life completely when I was just six years old?'

'I didn't—' Raymond spluttered, showering saliva in Peg's face. His hand went to his chest.

'You did. You did, "Dad". You did. And you killed your baby brother, though you were only a boy then, so I suppose we have to excuse you of *that* murder, don't we?'

'Who told you that?'

'Who do you think?' Peg looked over at the door in the lounge wall that led to Jean's.

'Bitch!'

Gasping for air, Raymond staggered over to the bookcase and punched the wall.

'Fucking bitch! Sooner she's locked up in a home the better. Fuck her. Fuck.'

His hand to his chest, he fell to his knees and put his head on the swirling carpet.

Peg watched as he stayed like that.

Was he having another heart attack?

Did she care, she wondered?

Eventually, whatever it was passed enough for him to look up at her.

'You don't know the half of it,' he said.

Peg stood, drawing herself up to her full height.

'You don't know the first thing about me, or what I know. And you think you can buy me. It's pathetic, Raymond.'

'I'm just trying to pay you back,' he said, his voice tiny. 'I'm trying to make it up to you.'

Peg wobbled. Trying to ignore the pleading note in his voice, she steeled herself. 'Then you have to accept that I love Loz and she is as much my wife as Mum was yours,' she said. 'More, by the sound of it. At least neither of us fuck other women.'

Raymond thumped the floor.

Suddenly, shockingly, Peg felt a barely resistible urge to take his head and smash it down on the ground like he had just done with his fist. She wanted to hurt him badly for every wrong he had ever done her.

The air hung heavy in the room. The peppered sweetness of his cigar, mixed with his coal-tar soap smell and the sour stink of champagne, made Peg feel sick, like someone was pulling a knotted rag up through her entrails.

Then Raymond turned.

'Look. I'm sorry, Peg.'

Peg blinked, momentarily taken aback.

'I spoke out of turn. I'm a bit pissed. Pissed off, too. That little dyke is mental, Margaret. She's got these crazy ideas about me killing that girl—'

'Killing *those* girls.'

'And they're all wrong. Believe me. But you believe her above me, don't you? Why the fuck shouldn't you? So what do I do with that, tell me, Margaret? What do I do?'

'I don't know,' Peg said. 'That's up to you, isn't it? As Loz would say, it's your problem, not mine. But here's a thing.' She tried to control her breathing, but the urge to get at him had returned. Her knees were shaking; buckling with a fury she had never allowed herself to feel before, her throat contracting with it. 'If you're as innocent as you say you are – and yes, a growing part of me tends to believe her over you – you're going to get your chance to prove it pretty soon. She's going to the police. She's taking those "crazy ideas" of hers to the police. At first I didn't want her to, but now I'm not so sure. Perhaps they'll be interested, "Dad". After all, with what you did to Mum, you've got form, haven't you? Perhaps they'll make more sense of all this than I can.'

'The police,' he said, the words dark in his mouth. 'You silly little girls. You have no idea what you're getting yourselves into.'

They stood and stared at each other. Then Jean's intercom buzzed, cutting across the crackling silence of the room. Raymond jumped and almost stood to attention.

'You said she was out blotto,' Peg whispered furiously. *Had Jean been listening in to this entire conversation?*

'Raymond?' Jean croaked. 'I need you in here. Now.'

He crossed to the box and pressed the answer button. 'Yes, Jeanie,' he said, his voice artificially softened. 'I'll be with you in a second.'

Then he turned to Peg.

'Over my dead body she's going to the police. You get in touch with this Lez and tell her that from me. She'd just better bloody not. Or else.'

'Is that some sort of threat?'

He didn't reply.

'Get out,' Peg said. 'Go to someone who needs you. Go to Aunty Jean. My life was a lot simpler before you came back into it and I want that back again. Get out. Go back to your darling Paulie and your stupid Caroline and fuck you and fuck your flat and fuck your money.'

Raymond stood still for a moment processing this. Then his features narrowed and he levelled his eyes at her. 'Just tell her to keep her bloody trap shut,' he hissed. Then he turned and left.

Alone, Peg rushed through to the kitchen, shut the door, put the radio on and, with shaking hands, pulled out her mobile phone, desperate to talk to Loz. But there was no reply. The phone just rang and rang. It couldn't be because she was at work – the plan was that she should have been with Peg that night, after all. Peg imagined Loz looking at the caller ID and, in a huff, refusing to pick up. Eventually, the voicemail cut in and Peg left her message, which was just that she was sorry and that she loved her, and that she must do whatever she saw fit. She must go to the police if that was what she wanted.

Then Peg went back to the lounge, to Doll's cocktail cabinet, and poured a glass of the potato wine. It smelled truly disgusting, and fulfilled its promise with its flavour, but it was clearly potent and it complemented the evil taste that already tainted her mouth.

She knocked it back in one, then stumbled up the ladder to her bedroom, where, still in her smart funeral dress, she curled up on the bed and fell into a deep and dream-filled stupor.

Then

or ten.

It's a sizzling, muggy day and I've spent the whole afternoon in the sea, floating on my back and looking at the dirty haze in the sky above me, wondering how far it goes on upwards. Nan sits on the beach, leaning against a breakwater and reading her *Mail on Sunday*.

I have a last wee in the sea. I love the feeling of the warm me flooding the colder, muddy water. Then I get out and Nan wraps me in the towelling poncho and feeds me hot chocolate from a thermos, and chocolate digestives. The poncho smells lovely, all of fabric conditioner, and it's soft on my pruney, sea-soaked skin.

She puts more sunblock on me and we sit and chat a bit about the people around us. There are some very common people a bit further along the breakwater, and we have a bit of a laugh about them, with their stupid voices and ugly, tattooed bodies.

Then it's time to go, because Nan has to make tea. I carry

the picnic basket and Nan takes the blanket and the towel. The sky is still heavy and hot, pressing down on us. Some of the tarmac bits where they've mended the pavement have gone all sticky, so I'm careful not to step on them.

And now I remember that I was upset about something, or I wasn't feeling too well, or something – I'm not sure which – which is why Nan put on this treat for me, coming down to the beach for the whole afternoon with a picnic, even though I know she didn't really like to leave Aunty Jean on her own for more than an hour.

'Pooh,' I go, as we turn the corner into our street. Something's burning.

'Who'd be having a bonfire in this close weather?' Nan says, shaking her head. 'Some people haven't got the slightest bit of sense in their heads.'

'Look!' I point at the plume of smoke rising from behind our bungalow.

'Oh no,' Nan goes, pushing the blanket and towel into my arms and rushing off. 'Jean? Jean, dear? Are you all right?'

I follow her up the driveway and dump the stuff outside the front door, then I go after her, down to the side-entrance to the back garden.

'Frank! What on earth are you doing?' I hear her say, before I turn the corner, so I hang back and listen, just peeping out to see what's going on.

Gramps is there, in his gardening shorts and vest, a knotted hanky on his head to keep his bald scalp from burning. According to Nan, the sun can burn and tan even through thick cloud, which is why I always wear sunblock.

He's standing there, completely still, staring at a bonfire

burning in the middle of the lawn as if it had hypnotised him. He is as wet with sweat as if someone has thrown a bucket of water over him.

'I burned them, Dolly,' he says, turning to face her, and I see his eyes are flame-red where they should be white. This isn't my gentle Gramps. He looks like someone else entirely.

'NO!' Nan cries, and she pushes him to one side – right to one side, even though she's so much tinier than he is – and runs for the hosepipe, which she yanks out of its neat roll and turns full on to the fire, putting out the flames.

Then she flings the hosepipe aside, never mind it sprays all over the place, getting Gramps even wetter than he had been with the sweat, and she starts stamping on the fire in her sandals. It must really hurt her feet.

She falls to her knees and starts pulling things out and I gasp, because I see that it's some of her Commonplace Books Gramps has been burning. Nan is on her knees now and is making this strange little wailing sound. She flips open one of the books that hasn't completely burned up.

'Why?' Nan says to Gramps, who is still standing there, now completely drenched by the hosepipe as well, just watching her. 'Why have you done this?'

'It's not right, Dolly,' Gramps says. 'It's not good. It's got to stop.'

'I'll be the judge of that,' Nan says. She scrabbles together the other surviving books. 'I'll be the judge of what's right and good.'

Nan is really cross. Crosser than I've ever seen before.

Crosser than I ever saw again, in fact – except perhaps those two or three moments of dementia-fuelled confusion when she mistook concern for violation.

She stands up, holding to her chest what she has rescued from the bonfire.

'Have you took your pills?' she says to Gramps.

Gramps just stands there, still. Looking at her with his red old eyes.

'You haven't, have you? You know you have a turn when you don't take your pills. I don't know what you was thinking.'

'I don't like them, Dolly. They make me all woozy.'

'The doctor SAID you have to take them. Remember? You HAVE to take them. Otherwise you do bad, bad things, Frank. Remember?'

Gramps opens and closes his mouth. He looks like a poor fat goldfish out of its water.

'I'm going to take these in,' Nan goes. 'And I'm going to come back out here with your pills and a glass of water, and I'm going to stand here and watch you while you take them. I'm going to watch you every day now, to make sure you take them. You're not to be trusted, Frank Thwaites. I don't know what I'm to do with you and Jeanie and the girl to look after. Truly I don't.'

Does she mean me? Am I a trouble to her like Gramps? I shrink back a bit against the brick wall.

Nan goes into the bungalow, her head held high.

Gramps slumps against the wall and puts his head in his hands. His shoulders are shaking and, for a minute, I wonder why he's laughing. But then he looks over at the back door where Nan has disappeared and I gasp, because I see his eyes are wet and red and he's crying.

I stay where I am for a couple more seconds. Then I sneak into the bungalow through the front door and sit quietly in the lounge with my book, trying hard not to be a bother to anyone.

Forty

PEG WAS TIED TO A HOSPITAL BED AND THE MAN – WHO although she could only see his silhouette had to be Raymond – positioned a whining power drill over the centre of her forehead. As it bored through her skull, it stuttered on the bone, but he kept revving it, insistently starting up again and again, as if—

She forced herself awake and sat bolt upright in her little bedroom, narrowly avoiding banging her head on the low eaves ceiling.

'Meggy! Meggy!' Through the fathoms of her hung-over daze, she could hear Jean wailing. Downstairs, the intercom buzzer was repeatedly being fired off.

That had been the drill noise.

In the darkness, Peg stumbled down the ladder, flicked the light on in the lounge and found the white box. Her head pounded and her mouth tasted of stale Brussels sprouts.

'Meggy! Meggy!' the buzzing and calling continued.

'Yes, Aunty Jean?' Peg said, hitting the respond button.

'Oh, thank goodness you're there. I'm all alone in here. I thought you'd gone away without saying goodbye.'

'Isn't he in with you?'

'Raymond? He had to go off. It's dear little Paulie's birthday tomorrow,' Jean said. 'He's gone back to Spain.'

'But he said he was staying the night.'

'He did, darling.'

'He did? But—'

'He stayed and he waited and waited for you to wake up this morning, but you didn't, so he had to go. He went to Hamley's to get a present before his flight. I said to him, "Go to Hamley's," I said. "There's toys there you can't buy anywhere else in the world."'

'Are you saying I've slept right through the whole day?'

'That's what it looks like, Meggy, doesn't it? You youngsters. I wish I could still sleep like that. I can't sleep at all unless I take me pills. Anyway, I need you to come over and help sort me out.'

'OK, Aunty Jean. I'll be with you in a tick. I'll just get myself properly dressed.'

Back up in her room, Peg peeled off her funeral clothes. She was glad her father had gone without saying goodbye. It's how she wanted it to be. No more contact.

It was a liberating thought.

She looked at the dress as it lay in a heap at the floor and winced at how much she had spent on it. A sum she would never have paid had she been sure she was going to tell Raymond to stuff his money. She picked it up and sniffed at it, then held it out to examine it. There was mud on the hem, and it smelled as it should after thirty-odd hours of continuous wear. Even Loz would think twice about taking it back for a refund.

Loz.

She flipped the dress over the back of a mouldering Lloyd Loom chair that she had used to sit at her desk when she was a child, and grabbed her phone from the bedside table. There were no messages. Loz had not tried to return her call. She tried phoning her again, but, as before, it just rang and rang. Peg felt a flash of her new, all-too-accessible anger.

Loz was holding out for too bloody long. She had apologised, hadn't she?

Perhaps Loz had gone to the police and been detained for wasting their time. But that was a ridiculous thought. More likely she had lost her mobile phone, left it on the train or something, like she had twice before in the year they had been together.

Would they be together for another year? Could they survive all this? The thought of not being with Loz made Peg feel so empty she ached.

She took a quick shower, washing away the mud that had crusted through her tights onto her legs. Standing under the feeble jet of water, she let it slide over her face. It was hardly invigorating, but it was what she knew, and it went some way towards waking her up.

She dressed, towel-dried her hair then, just as Jean started buzzing again, she let herself out of the back door and through into the extension.

'I was wondering where you had got to,' Jean said. 'Thought perhaps you'd slipped in the shower like Mummy did one time.'

Sitting upright in her bed, propped up by purple floral pillows, Jean looked strangely well – at least, she appeared to have more vim than she had since Doll's death.

'Oh, Meggy, I'm so hungry. The girl left me blasted salad again, and it's only touched a tiny corner of my stomach. Is there any way we could get hold of a bit of fish and chips? My purse is on the side over there. Treat yourself, too.'

Peg realised that part of the feeling in her belly that she had put down to frayed nerves, tension and a hangover was mostly deep hunger. She had not eaten since breakfast the day before.

'All right, Aunty Jean. I'll just be a tick.'

She went to the end of the road where the chippy stood rather too conveniently. She remembered that on certain days, when the wind came more from the north, it would carry the intoxicating scent of hot fat and frying potatoes right into the bungalow, making it impossible for her young self to concentrate on anything until she had satiated the urge by going to buy a portion of chips.

She remembered all this now. She remembered everything – almost.

'Oh, hello, darlin',' Mei the chippy owner said, looking up from the fried fish portions she was arranging in the hot cabinet. 'Long time no see. I'm so sorry to hear about your nan, my darling.'

'It was a bit of a shock,' Peg said.

'We'll miss her in here,' Mei said, nodding her red face to her husband, a skinny, drooping man shifting the chips around in the fryer. 'Won't we, Jimmy?'

'Eh?' he said, looking up from his hot, greasy task.

'I said we'll miss old Dolly coming in here every night, won't we?' Mei shouted over the sizzle and pop of the fat and the racket of the extractor fan that piped the seductive smells out into the street.

'Oh, yes, we will.' Jimmy rested his hand on the edge of the stainless-steel fryer and wiped his flopping hair back from his eyes with the other, glad of the chance to pause his hot work. 'We'll miss the business too!'

'Jimmy!' Mei scolded. 'So rude. I'm so sorry about that, Meggy darlin'. The chip fat gets into his brain.'

'No, no, that's all right,' Peg said, keen to find out more. 'Nan came in every night, you say?'

'Oh yes,' Mei said. 'You could set your clock by her. Every night at eight, for your aunty's supper. Big fish and chips, chow mein and the surprise.'

'The surprise?'

'She'd always take her something else. "Jean's little treat", she called it. Sometimes a big bar of chocolate or bottle of pop from there.' Mei pointed to a refrigerator unit full of soft drinks and confectionery. 'Sometimes another portion of something. She liked the sweet and sour pork balls, I know that. Dolly really looked after your aunty, didn't she? Poor lady. If we were quiet, I'd send him –' she nodded at her husband – 'with her, to help her carry it all.'

'When did she last come?' Peg asked.

'The night the ambulance came.'

'When she went into hospital?'

Mei looked a little uncomfortable. 'No, the very last time. I said to him –' she pointed her spatula at her husband again – 'I said that she didn't look too clever, didn't I, Jimmy? And, for the first time, it was early, about half four. But she'd been in hospital for a few days, hadn't she? So we thought she just wanted to celebrate with your aunty or something. We thought nothing of it. I'm sorry, darling.'

Jimmy, who had returned to his chips and was now shaking the excess fat off them before putting them in the hopper to keep them warm, nodded. 'She was some lady,' he said.

Peg walked away from the chippy, balancing the heat-wilted thin plastic bag and its large portion of fish, two of chips and one chow mein against her chest to ward off the cold. Her parka pocket swung with the weight of the family-sized bar of Fruit and Nut that Mei had insisted was Jean's favourite. She didn't have to imagine what a nightly dose of this, on top of a full day's eating, could do to a person. The evidence lay piled on a bed not more than a couple of hundred feet away.

'That looks good,' Jean said, as Peg carried a tray mounded with steaming fried food into her bedroom.

'Mei at the chippy said Nan used to go and get you supper every night.'

'She looked after me,' Jean said, cramming a handful of chips into her mouth. 'Got any ketchup? And what about a drop of Guinness, then?'

'Hoo, your dad was in a right old state when he came through last night after your little set-to,' Jean said, as Peg returned from the kitchen with cans and ketchup. She tipped the chow mein so that it landed like a heap of worms on top of her fish and chips. 'I told him not to worry, that it's just a bit of a phase, that you'll come through it. All girls have crushes on other girls, and fights with their dads. It's quite normal, and it's just happening to you a bit later than usual, because you didn't see him for so long. But you need to have this little bit of arguing now.'

Peg popped a couple of chips into her mouth, enjoying the way the warmth instantly soothed the weak, low-blood-sugar hunger that had dogged her since she had woken up. As she worked to prevent Jean's words annoying her, the realisation hit her that she didn't have to put up with her aunt's rubbish any more. Now Doll was gone, she could just do what Loz had always told her to do. She could turn her back on the whole lot of them, step out of the mould they had made for her.

It had nothing to do with her!

She popped the top of her can of Guinness and took a deep swig, as if toasting that thought.

'So me and your daddy had a bit of a talk last night after your ding-dong,' Jean said between mouthfuls. 'And we realised that there's one way to help you and that's to bring you back into the family.'

Peg spluttered on her drink.

'What?'

'I think Mummy, God rest her poor soul, rather neglected you in the past couple of years. Letting you move away and all that.'

'I wanted to go, though. It's what I wanted.'

'That's what you think, but you're only a girl. What do you know, really?' Jean said, licking salt and grease and congealed chow mein sauce from her fingers. 'This is really and truly delicious, you know, Meggy. I don't know why you didn't get it too. You don't know how much I've missed me chow mein since Mummy passed away. That Mei said they were too busy to do home deliveries, so I just had to make do with curry from the Taj Mahal. Which, as you know, doesn't always agree.

'So anyway. Me and your daddy had this talk and it turns out he's going to be very generous. He's going to build us a lovely bungalow, right by his villa. In Spain, no less. Well, you'll know how lovely that is, because you went there behind our backs. And it'll be all mod cons and specially built for a person of my size. He's going to pay you to look after me. Very handsomely, he says. More than you earn in that library, anyway. And there'll be no rent or anything for you to pay. All bills taken care of. Just think!'

Jean looked at Peg, a wide smile almost cleaving her face in two.

'But I don't want that,' Peg said.

What was this new plan Raymond had cooked up, in complete contradiction to all the putting-Jean-in-a-home business? Was it some sort of revenge on her for telling him to stuff it? Or was it just another of Jean's fantasies?

'Oh, but you can't turn it down,' Jean said, still smiling. 'You'd be an idiot.'

'But I want to live with Loz and get on with my own life.'

'Meggy, see sense, dear,' Jean said. 'This isn't like you, looking a gift-horse in the mouth. And it won't last, believe me, this little thing you've got with that Loz. She looks like a flighty sort of person to me. Not your sort, not at all. And anyway, it's not a proper sort of thing, is it? Not really? Not proper family. No, girly, you belong with me. I wouldn't be surprised if that Loz just drops right out of the picture.'

'What do you mean?'

Jean avoided Peg's eyes. 'Like I said, she looks proper flighty. Pass us a serviette, dear, will you?'

Somehow, even though she had been talking all through the meal, Jean had managed to ingest every last scrap of the mound on her plate. She took the napkin Peg handed her from the dispenser on the bedside table and dabbed her mouth. 'Anyway, like I said, your daddy's going back to Spain and he'll get it all sorted for us. He says it'll only take a couple of months, he says six at the most, and I can get you trained up in what you need to do for me while we wait. Though of course, Mummy taught you most of what she knew, didn't she?'

Peg clasped her hands in front of her face and screwed up her eyes. She couldn't believe what she was hearing. How could her father have performed such a complete about-face in less than twelve hours? To say she had been stitched-up was something of an understatement. She had been double-hemmed, overlocked and smocked.

But she had the power to walk away from this grotesque future they had decided for her. A power that was beyond that of her aunt. Putting her half-finished meal to one side, she stood. She had to talk to Loz.

'Sorry, Aunty Jean. I need to take all this in.'

'You do what you like, dear. You'll see it's for the best.' Jean folded her hands comfortably on her belly, burying them underneath the flesh of her breasts.

Peg headed for the door.

'Oh, Meggy?' Jean called.

Peg, who had reached the kitchen, stopped. Her shoulders stiffened. She could smell the cigarette Jean had just lit. 'Yes?' she said.

'Could you just clear away the supper things, dear? They'll make the whole place stink like a chip shop if they stay in here overnight. The girl'll complain. And we need to keep her sweet just for a little bit longer.'

Peg sighed and turned, and then she went back into her aunt's bedroom to do as she had been told.

Forty-One

HAVING PACKED HER BELONGINGS, STRIPPED ALL THE BEDS AND put the rubbish out, Peg walked away from Tankerton early the following morning for what she thought was the last time.

In her haste to escape the suffocating way the bungalow seemed to have crept into her bones, trying to bind her to it like a tortoise to its shell, she forgot her London keys. She didn't realise until she was sitting on the train, halfway there.

When she arrived at the flat, Loz didn't answer the doorbell, so Peg had no choice but to rouse Sandy, the PARTYBOY downstairs. They had perhaps rather recklessly given him a spare in case of emergencies. Luckily, he was still up – his nocturnal lifestyle meant he had only just arrived home, conquest in tow.

'Peg love, how are you? Haven't seen you for ages. This is – um,' he vaguely gestured to the boy standing behind him in the doorway. Techno music throbbed from inside his flat.

'Simon,' the boy said, removing one hand from the sheet draped round him and holding it out for Peg to shake.

'Loz doesn't seem to be in and I've forgotten my keys. You haven't seen her, have you?'

'She was here yesterday during the day, darling,' Sandy said, licking his fingers and wiping the mascara smudges beneath his eyes. 'Woke me up making a hell of a racket. About lunchtime, I think it was.'

'Sorry about that,' Peg said.

'Don't think a thing about it,' Sandy said. 'I'm not exactly the dream downstairs neighbour anyway, am I?'

'Can't argue with that,' Peg said, taking the key from him. 'Thanks.'

'Happy Christmas, darling,' Sandy said, kissing her on the cheek.

'Happy Christmas.'

'You girls should come down for a drink tomorrow. If you haven't got any family commitments.'

'We haven't. That'll be lovely. I'll talk to Loz.'

When Peg opened the door to her flat, the first thing that struck her was the Christmas decorations. Loz had garlanded the living room with streamers and tinsel. A small tree stood on the dining-room table, hung with baubles and fairy lights. A bunch of mistletoe hung over the defunct fireplace. Loz's favourite song, Fleet Foxes' 'White Winter Hymnal' was playing from the kitchen, set on repeat on her iPod speakers, adding to the seasonal splendour.

But as Peg searched the flat, all this adornment only served to underline the absence of its creator. And it was so unlike Loz to go out and leave the flat in such a state. The bed was unmade, her drawers open, and a towel had been left flung on the bed, leaving the mattress damp underneath it – something that usually made her very cross indeed when Peg did it.

Even odder, in the kitchen, a glass had smashed on the floor, with the orange juice it had contained pooled around it, and a cup of coffee sat half-drunk and cold on the draining board. The weirdest thing was that Loz had been baking, but had not cleared up the ingredients. There was flour all over the work surface and the floor, and the bowl of her food processor – which she treated like a beloved child, washing and drying each part lovingly by hand – sat dumped in the sink, cake mix crusting its expensive innards. And the cake itself stood on the counter in the heart-shaped tin Peg had bought Loz for her birthday, its sunken surface leathery for having been left out unbaked and uncovered.

Peg switched off the music at last and tried to phone Loz once again, which, she noticed from her recent calls list, was the thirtieth unanswered time in a row.

Perhaps Jean was right. Perhaps Loz *was* flighty. Perhaps she didn't know her as well as she thought. But a tiny kernel of clarity inside Peg's head held fast. And that is what made her worry.

She called Loz's mother, but Naomi said she hadn't been back home.

'It may be nothing,' Peg said. 'We had a bit of an argument, though . . .'

'Oh, she can be like this sometimes,' Naomi said. 'She's an awful sulker. Why don't you check round your friends, see if she's gone to ground? I'm sorry, Peg, I must go. I've got a patient who's not very. Patient, that is.'

'Yes, of course,' Peg said. 'Sorry.'

'Don't apologise. You're always apologising.' Naomi spoke so like her daughter it made Peg's longing for Loz even more urgent. 'She'll turn up. She knows what she's doing.'

Praying Naomi was right, Peg pocketed her phone and sat

back on the armchair she and Loz had dragged home from a skip one night. Where could she be? She called round the few mutual friends she had phone numbers for, but no one had seen her. Then she called the restaurant.

'Nah,' Cara, the owner drawled. 'I've been trying to contact her all morning. She was due in at eight today because we've got like this mega lunch party booked?'

Peg glanced at the clock on the microwave. It was a quarter past nine. Loz was never late for work.

'If you hear from her,' Cara said, 'tell her she's in serious big trouble with me and she'd better get her sorry ass here as soon as.'

Peg could feel her heart pounding. If Loz was letting the restaurant down, something was very wrong. She might moan about Seed all the time, but she was truly professional in her attitude to her work. Peg hung up and went to the coat hooks by the front door to the flat. Loz's duvet coat wasn't there, nor was her bag. She searched the flat, but couldn't find her keys, phone or wallet.

Was that encouraging? She thought it might be, but even so a sense of panic was rising in her throat. She sat at the dining table, put her head in her hands and tried to breathe it away.

She thought about calling the police. But she had it in her mind they would only respond after an adult had been missing for twenty-four hours, and Sandy had heard her yesterday lunchtime. Or, Peg corrected herself, he had heard noise coming from the flat. There was no guarantee that it had been Loz. And anyway, if she told the police everything about the argument, they'd just put it down to a lovers' tiff and wouldn't take her seriously.

But then she remembered Ray's reaction the night before last when she told him what Loz was planning to do.

Over my dead body is she going to the police.

There was also his evasiveness over Mary, and the awful things he had said about Loz . . .

What if Loz – and Jean – had been right?

What if Raymond was a truly bad man, rather than just a useless father and a man who had loved his wife so much he couldn't bear to see her suffer any more and complied with her final request? What might he have done to or with Loz in that case?

Peg shook her head sharply. Raymond would be in Spain now, organising darling Paulie's precious party. She toyed with the idea of calling him, but, even if she could have borne to speak to him, she couldn't think of a way of asking him if he had any idea where Loz might be which wouldn't be met with ridicule or disgust. A sudden, crazy thought grabbed her and she rushed to the box-file where, librarian-style, she kept Loz's and her own papers. Loz's passport was there, so she was still in the country. Raymond couldn't have taken her to Spain with him – could he?

Or was that something Archer could arrange for him?

She was being absurd. She was allowing her imagination to run away with her.

She was being like Loz.

As she was pulling on her parka to go out and ask if Loz had dropped by to pick up her daily *Guardian* from the newsagent's, her phone rang. Grabbing it from the table, she saw it was a number that she didn't recognise.

'Hello?' she said.

'Is that Peg?' A crackled, South-East London voice said at the other end.

'Yes. Who is this?'

'It's Parker. From the garages.'

'Parker!'

'Do you know where your friend is?'

'No. I can't find her anywhere.'

'I think you'd better come here as soon as you can. Something fucking odd's going on.'

Then

'WHERE'S THE KEY?'

I'm ill, in bed.

Cuddling my sniffy blanket.

Everything's woozy.

I hear voices but I can't make out who they are, how many there are, or where they're coming from.

'Where's the bloody key?'

'You'll not find it.'

I can't even tell if it's a boy or a girl or a man or a woman or a horse or a tree.

Then it's all black again.

Forty-Two

'I WAS OUT DOWN THE SPAR YESTERDAY PICKING UP SUPPLIES FOR the holiday season,' Parker said to Peg as he hobbled alongside her, away from his garage. 'And, fuck me if I don't out of the blue bump into my old mate from the regiment. So I go off for a jar or two with him, and it turns into a bit of a session.

'Then, much later, as I get back, I'm nearly sent flying by this big black Lexus as it comes out of the alley. Whoosh!' He gestured wildly with his hands to demonstrate how he avoided being knocked over. 'Which is well odd because no one uses these places got a big car like that. Not any more, anyway. Not since your dad was down here. Anyway, I don't get a chance to see the driver's face but I reckon whoever it is is up to no good.'

Raymond, Peg thought, fear splintering her heart.

'It had pulled up outside your nan's garage,' he said. 'I know that because these was never here before.' He squatted by a tyre track in the frosted mud surrounding a puddle in front of the door they hadn't been able to open.

'Anyway, while I was looking at the tracks, I found something. Must've fallen out the car. Hang on a tick there.'

He led her back to his garage and disappeared inside, leaving Peg standing in the grey, cold air as snowflakes whirled down from the leaden sky. She didn't know what to think, or what to do.

A minute later, he shambled back out holding a very distinctive sequinned Union Jack purse.

Peg gasped and her knees nearly buckled.

Parker flipped the purse open and there was a photograph of Loz and Peg, giggling, taken when they were newly in love, in a photo booth at Victoria Station.

It was a picture of past history, of happier, more carefree times.

A sort of Eden.

'I tried calling her when I found it, of course, but there was no reply,' he went on. 'And look. There's all her cards and sixty quid, so she must be missing it.' Parker showed the wallet to Peg. 'I found this in it, though, which is how I managed to find you.'

He handed her a Starbucks receipt. Peg flipped it over and saw her name and phone number scrawled on the back, in her own hand. She had written that when they went to coffee after Loz turned up at the library, before they decided to go back to Peg's flat.

And Loz had kept it.

Peg was surprised – she didn't have Loz down as the sentimental type.

'We need to get in there,' she said, nodding over to the garage.

'You still got the key?'

Peg groaned. 'No, I—'

She had left it on the occasional table, along with her flat keys, in front of Raymond.

In front of Raymond.

'What?'

'I don't know where Loz is, Parker.' The panic rising in her throat made her speak so quickly her words almost ran into each other. 'I haven't seen her since Nan's funeral. We had an argument and she's disappeared. I thought she'd just left the flat in a mess, but now I think there might have been a struggle. And if so, my dad's involved somehow.'

They both looked over at the silent, locked garage. Then Parker turned to face Peg.

'Fuck it, girl. I'll get me angle grinder out.'

The security bolts on the garage were tougher than Parker had expected. He worked at top and bottom of the door, cutting through two locking posts which, he explained, ran right through on both sides.

'Whoever got these put in knew what they were doing,' he said, lifting his visor which, on top of his outfit of beaten leather jacket and grubby Belstaff trousers, made him look like an aged extra from *Mad Max*.

He set to work again. Peg had to stand back to avoid the flying sparks sizzling into the snow-dusted air.

'I hope you don't get into trouble for this,' she said, as he moved to the other side.

'Look, girly, I've got a feeling this is serious.' He raised his visor and looked at her, his face grim. He fired up his angle grinder again and, shortly after, he stepped back.

'We're in,' he said, bending to grasp the bottom edge of the up-and-over garage door. As he lifted it, the scene he revealed was so bizarre that it took a few minutes for Peg to register what she was looking at.

'Shitting Christ,' Parker said, his sparsely toothed mouth

hanging open. A wave of ancient rottenness hit Peg's nostrils, overlaid by a sweet, chemical smell, a smell she recognised from her childhood, a smell that spelled comfort and being tucked up in bed.

The smell of her sniffy blanket.

The garage was laid out like a cramped living room, with what might have been a dining table in the middle, a couple of armchairs facing the back wall at the far end, and a desk and chair up against the side.

What set it apart from a living room were the stained and rusty implements hanging neatly from hooks on the wall: saws, scalpels, axes and knives, all arranged according to size. A load of brown-stained sheets were mounded up in one of the far corners, and the walls and floor – which was covered in exactly the same lino used for the bungalow bedrooms – were decorated with sprays of reddish brown, as if . . .

Peg passed a hand over her forehead. Something was itching at the back of her memory, but before she could pull it into focus, someone unseen groaned from one of the armchairs.

As she rushed in, followed by Parker, she nearly tripped on a brown bottle, sending it flying.

'Chloroform,' Parker said, stooping to catch it and glancing at the label.

But Peg didn't stop, because she knew who it was in that chair.

'Loz!' she cried.

Pale as the snow just settling outside, Loz was slumped in the armchair. Her body was limp, her eyes rolled back under half-closed lids, showing only the whites, and her lips were dry and ringed with sores. Her arms and legs had been tied with circulation-stopping tightness to the armchair.

Peg shook her, but she flopped as if she were only held together by a fragile thread.

'Let me at her,' Parker said and Peg stood aside as he scooped his oily fingers inside her mouth.

'What are you doing?' Peg said.

'Checking her airways. See them sores? Chloroform. Bastard. But if it was that bloke in the car last night, he would've had to use something else too. Chloroform don't last that long unless it kills you.' As he took Loz's pulse, he scanned the garage. 'What's that?' He pointed to a packet on the desk.

Peg rushed over and grabbed it. 'It's Aunty Jean's sleeping pills,' she said, handing the package to Parker.

'Jesus, that's a hell of a dose,' he said, reading the package. 'If whoever did this gave this little girl more than two of these, she's lucky to still be breathing. Here, go and get some snow while I get her untied.'

'Snow?'

'It's our best shot at waking her up.' He worked at the knots that bound Loz to the armchair. 'That and getting her moving around.'

Peg rushed out into the freezing air, chucked her parka on the ground, scooped snow into it, then hurried back in to Parker.

'Rub it round her face,' he said, battling with the last rope.

As Peg did so, Loz began to move her head. Her eyelids fluttered and she licked her sore lips. Then her eyes shot open, distorted with terror, and she kicked and struggled to be free of Peg's arms.

'It's all right, Loz . . .'

'Steady on there, girly,' Parker said.

Startled by the strange male voice, Loz turned her head.

'It's me, love. Parker, from the end garage.'

Loz looked around her wildly.

'We're in the garage,' Peg said. 'You're all right now.'

Freed, Loz fought her way up out of the armchair. But her feet gave way underneath her and she crumpled, landing against Parker, who took her in his arms and settled her back down.

'Take it easy, girly,' he said. 'You'll be a bit woozy for a while.'

'War . . .' Loz said, her voice hoarse and indistinct.

'Give her some water,' Parker said.

Peg packed some snow into a ball and held it up for Loz to suck on. It wasn't very successful because, as well as trembling all over, she was trying to say something.

'Th-th-th . . .'

'What is it, Loz?'

But she couldn't string her words together. It was as if she were drunk.

'Let's get her out of here and into the warm and I'll try to get some coffee down her,' Parker said.

He went to pick Loz up, but first she yelped in pain, then she resisted, struggling out of his arms, trying to pull him back into the garage.

'The b-b-b . . .' Loz lifted a shaking hand up to point to the mound of sheets. 'L-l-look . . .'

'What's she saying?' Parker said.

'No, look . . .' Loz said. She wrenched herself away, then lost her footing again. As she fell to the floor, her head took a hit on the corner of the table.

'Jesus, Loz!' Peg threw herself to the ground and scooped Loz up. But she was still struggling, grasping her way towards the sheets.

Parker moved past the two women and pulled the sheets away.

Then he stumbled back, his hand to his mouth.

'Fuck.'

Loz strained against Peg's own unsteady arms and vomited onto the lino that Peg now knew – from the evidence in front of her – was splattered with blood.

The skull hung back from the rest of the small body at almost seventy degrees. Leathered skin gaped at the throat where once it had been cut, making a second, obscene mouth to match the one lined with braces in what remained of the face. Apart from the reddish curls which lay like floss around the little sundress – whose flowery pattern had been all but obliterated by a flood of blackish-brown bloodstains – it looked to Peg like an Egyptian mummy she had once seen on a school trip to . . .

She knew instantly who this papery corpse had once been.

The hair was too horribly familiar. And the dress, too.

The dress, too . . .

The truth burrowed through Peg's brain, like a worm making tunnels. But try as she could to drag it out, it was still stuck there, unable to gather its constituent parts to make something coherent, something that could give meaning to all of this.

All she had to go on was a dense sickness combined with a heavy feeling of guilt, of responsibility.

'Burned,' Loz said, struggling to get up. 'He – he said find the burned . . .'

'Burned what?' Peg said, holding onto her.

'Burned books . . .'

'Let's get her out of here,' Parker said, backing away from what he had uncovered. 'She's had enough horror. So have I, come to that.'

Between them they managed to pull the struggling Loz from

this place of nightmares: this last resting place – if rest were the right word – of ten-year-old Anna Thurlow, who, twelve years previously, had vanished without trace from her parents' three-million-pound Hampshire home.

Then

IT'S THE START OF THE SUMMER HOLS AND I'M NINE YEARS OLD.

Wayne has fetched me from school and, before he's even finished taking my bags up to my bedroom, I'm in tears in Nan's arms.

I'm so glad I'm back.

All term I've wanted to be back here.

'What is it? What is it, Meggy?' she asks me.

'I don't want to go back to school ever again,' I say, bawling through my words. 'I want to stay here and go to the normal school with the normal kids.'

'But Meggy, your school's ever such a good one. If you want to be a doctor, it's the best place to be.'

I've never actually said I want to be a doctor, but Nan has decided that's what I've got to do. It stands to reason in a way, because that's what she always wanted to be and now there are loads of women doctors, she says there's no reason why I shouldn't be one.

Except that I don't want to be one.

'It's hell at my school,' I cry.

'Come on now, Mrs Fubs. You come in and tell me all about it. See what we can do to make it all better.'

She leads me in, telling Wayne off for walking through the kitchen with his muddy shoes, although I can see that they're not muddy: they're as shiny as ever.

'Good afternoon to you too, Mrs T,' he says, tipping his hand to his forehead in a sort of salute. Then he bends and gently puts his knuckle up against my cheek.

'Cheer up, Meggy. Your nan'll look after you now. See you in September.'

And he's gone.

Nan leads me through to the lounge, where the table's set with the coming-home tea. But for once I'm not hungry. I just sit there with little sobs still coming out of me.

'Come on, Meggy, have a little bite,' she says, scooping up a big, creamy slice of chocolate cake on a fork and holding it out in front of me.

I shake my head.

'I'm fat, Nan.'

'What?' Nan says, astounded. 'Who on earth's been telling you that?'

'Everyone at school says I am,' I say, the tears once again breaking through. 'And ugly. And stupid.'

'What complete and utter nonsense!' Nan says. 'Who's this everyone? What are their names? I won't allow this sort of thing to happen, Meggy. Believe me. We're going to do something about this.'

I write Anna Thurlow's name on the piece of paper she puts in front of me.

* * *

Later, when we're unpacking my bag upstairs in my bedroom, Nan finds the school photograph I've brought back. It's a big print, about the size of a normal sheet of paper.

'That's a lovely picture, Meggy,' she says.

I shrug. I don't think it's lovely. It's just proof that Anna has a point: I *am* fat. I certainly *look* fat in the photo. And ugly.

Nan unwraps the photo and turns it over.

'I suppose this is the photographer what took the pictures,' she says, pointing to a gold label with Happy Days Photography and an address and phone number printed on it.

'I suppose it is,' I say.

A few days later, while Nan's in with Aunty Jean, the post arrives.

There are two envelopes: one has Private and Confidential printed on the front and the other has a gold sticker on the back with Happy Days Photography on it.

I think perhaps Nan likes my photo so much she's ordered another copy. But then I realise there must be some mistake, because it's addressed to Mrs Thurlow, and Nan's name is Mrs Thwaites.

Forty-Three

'SHUDOOR . . . SHUDOOR!' LOZ WHEEZED WHEN THEY WERE inside Parker's garage. She was still unable to stand, and her speech was hard to decipher. 'He – he –'

'He's not going to get you again,' Peg said, as Parker first ran back to close the garage they had just escaped, then returned and slammed his own door shut against the cold. Peg sat down next to Loz on a camp bed in the corner, and Parker tucked a rough woollen blanket over her.

'Rub her, get her warm,' he said to Peg. 'And here's one for yourself.' He tossed another blanket to Peg, who hadn't noticed how cold she was without her parka.

Either cold or in shock.

Anna Thurlow.

She would never get the image of that desiccated body out of her mind. She knew that already. But worse than that, she knew that somehow it was entirely her fault the poor girl had ended up there.

'You *were* right, Loz. He killed them all,' she said at last as she tried to warm Loz out of her tremors. 'All of them. And

Nan and Aunty Jean must've covered up for him.' She closed her eyes and shook her head. 'And if it hadn't been for Parker finding your wallet, you would've been his next victim.' She put her forehead against Loz's and closed her eyes. 'I'm so sorry I didn't believe you. So sorry.'

'N – n – n . . .' Loz said.

'Keep rubbing her, getting her warm, there.' Parker reached up and twisted a bare light bulb in the ceiling, turning it on and casting a thin yellow light over the garage. 'It don't stand to reason though,' he said as he poured water from a plastic container into a kettle.

Peg's eyes took a moment to accustom themselves to the gloom, but when she could focus, she saw that half of this odd, makeshift home was neatly arranged as living quarters, with a small portable stove, a bed, a pile of tidily folded clothes. The other was some sort of metal workshop – a blowtorch and various hammers, spanners and cutting tools lay on the floor by what looked like a collection of small horses made from scrap metal.

'My statues,' Parker said, seeing Peg's look at them. 'I make them and sell them to this shop down Bermondsey Street. They pay all right for them.'

'What do you mean, it doesn't stand to reason?'

'Well why didn't he finish Loz here off too? If that's what he done to that poor girl in there, then he's got all his tools to hand and no compunctions . . .'

'Perhaps he thought he'd done the job with Jean's horse pills. Thing is, the bastard doesn't know how tough my Loz is.'

Loz shivered and groaned.

'Oh Loz. What did he do to you?' Peg whispered. Her mind was red with hate for her father. She wanted revenge. Blood and revenge. 'What did he want?'

'He – he . . .' Loz's eyes rolled back into her head and she passed out.

'Oh God,' Peg said. 'Parker!'

He moved in and lifted Loz's eyelids. 'Hard to tell because she's still so out of it from the sleeping pills, but I reckon she's concussed too now from that hit she took when she fell down. Loz, love, wake up,' he said, gently shaking her. 'We've got to keep her awake. Sit her up and keep shaking her and I'll get on with the coffee.'

'Come on Loz, wake up,' Peg said, putting her arms round her, trying to get her to her feet. But because she was so floppy, her meagre seven or so stone seemed like a dead weight. As Peg grabbed her, she came to, jolting with agony. Again, she tried to speak.

'He – he . . .'

'Shhh!' Parker said sharply. He stopped what he was doing at the stove, stood, and held his hand out flat.

Peg froze, motionless, head craned, ears tuned to the alleyway outside.

Soon she heard it too: a vehicle roared up the lane into the garages, coming to a screeching halt somewhere up the far end.

Parker hobbled over to the wall where the door was and held his eye up to a tube protruding from the wall. 'Knobbing shite,' he whispered.

'What?' Peg asked, still supporting a wilted Loz, who, now she was coming round, seemed to be in a lot of pain. 'What's that?'

'My periscope. Take a look.' Parker took hold of Loz while Peg peered into the tube. 'I rigged it up for security, see. It pans round the whole alley in case of bastards or bailiffs, so I know when to stay schtum. What is it, girl?' he asked Loz. 'Does it hurt here?'

Loz nodded.

'You've probably got a broken or bruised rib or two. Did he rough you around?'

Loz nodded again.

'Cunt. I never liked the look of him. I'll strap you up once we're in the all-clear.'

With one eye up against the periscope, Peg made out a white van that had drawn up in front of what she now thought of as Raymond's garage.

A white van. Not exactly a surprise.

A fat bald white man got out of the passenger side, ran and opened the van's back doors then climbed inside.

As the driver walked into view to join him, Peg drew in her breath.

He was fat, black and bald, and not only the glimpsed driver of the white vans that had followed her, but—

'Wayne!' she gasped, under her breath. Tearing her eyes away from the periscope, she turned to Parker.

'They're my dad's men,' she said. 'His driver Wayne and some white guy.'

'Fuck me.'

Peg put her eye back to the periscope. 'The white guy's handed Wayne something. A sleeping bag, I think. Now he's climbing out of the back of the van with a canister of something. Pretty full and heavy from the look of it. They're going to the door now . . .'

She watched, holding her breath as Wayne jiggled something in the main lock. He stopped and looked puzzled, then called over the white guy, who moved the handle and opened the door with a jolt that suggested it gave way far more easily than he was expecting.

As the door swung fully open, the two men frowned at each other.

'They've gone inside,' Peg whispered to Parker, stepping away from the periscope.

'Shit.' Parker leaned in, breathing on his hands and rubbing them together to warm them. Peg took hold of Loz, whose eyes were wide open now, like a scared rabbit.

'Don't worry, Loz, it's going to be all right.' Peg winced at how unconvincing she sounded.

'The fat boys are out again,' Parker hissed from the periscope. 'And they're having a bit of a ding-dong,' he went on. 'Some sort of argy bargy. White guy's looking all around him. Looking this way. Shit. That Wayne's coming down the drive towards us. Hold your breath, girls. Kill the light Peg, love.'

Peg was sure that anyone out in the drive would be able hear her heart, so loudly was it pounding against her ribs. In the darkness, she could make out the white of Parker's eye as he held it to the patch of daylight let in by the periscope. Then it was gone, as he put his hand over the eyepiece.

They held their breath as Wayne's footsteps passed Parker's garage, on their way to the end of the block. Then, after a moment's silence, they heard him speak.

'No one down here, mate,' he said, the sound of his voice conjuring instantly for Peg the image of the back of his head, seen from her position on the rear seat of The Car. 'She's just disappeared.'

His footsteps passed back along the alley then retreated towards the van and the garage.

Parker cautiously uncovered the periscope and put his eye up to it again.

'That Wayne's on the blower,' he whispered. 'Now he's telling the white guy something. They look pretty fucked off. Someone's been giving them a bit of a shitting-off on that phone. They're moving pretty nippy now. Ah, Whitey's got that canister and he's spilling it all round the garage, going inside with it, splashing it all up the walls.

'Wayne's gone in the back of the van, rummage, rummage, rummage. And he's out again. And he's got some sort of box he's taking in there now.

'He's out now and he's got his phone in his hand again. Nope, it's some sort of remote control or something. Fucking shite. I should know what the fuck that is – hold on! Whitey's closing the garage door. Fuck!'

'What?' Peg said.

'He's only setting fire to the fucking building,' Parker went on. In the reflected daylight of the periscope, Peg could see the muscles twitching in his wasted cheek. 'He's running back to join the black guy in the van. Now they're reversing, right past us. Getting out of it pretty sharpish.' Parker turned, swivelling the tube one hundred and eighty degrees as he did so. 'No, they've stopped at the end of the lane. Oh fuck. I know what – GET DOWN GIRLS,' he yelled suddenly, turning to them. 'Under the table.' His drawn features, side-lit by the periscope, showed energy, authority and just a tiny trace of excitement. Twenty years dropped from his face as a forgotten part of him stepped back into focus.

Peg dragged Loz to the shelter of the table and threw herself on top of her.

'DOWN!' Parker shouted – to himself, essentially, because he was the last man standing. As he hit the garage floor, an almighty explosion shook the concrete beneath them, shuddering and clattering the many metal contents of Parker's garage like some sort of anarchic percussion section. Peg felt her eardrums strain with the wave of pressure that followed.

For a while, there was nothing but jangling and dust and whiteness. It was as if everything had gone into slow motion.

Peg was just thinking about tentatively creeping out from under the table when a series of smaller explosions further shook the ground and she redoubled her grasp on Loz, who was shivering like a chick fallen from its nest.

'Everyone all right?' Parker asked, once the last blast had faded. Or at least, that's what Peg thought he said, through the ringing in her ears.

She sounded her assent.

Parker moved back to the periscope. 'All clear.' He helped Peg get Loz out from under the table. 'They won't be back in a hurry, I reckon.'

He hauled open his garage door and, supporting Loz between them, they stumbled out into the smoke-filled air, blinking in the greyish light.

Except for a pile of blackened smouldering rubble, there was nothing left of the garage where Loz had been held prisoner. The wall to the side of it had also been completely demolished, as had five neighbouring units.

'If we hadn't got Loz out of there . . .' Peg said, a fist drawn tight inside her.

'Nah.' Parker shook his head. 'Like I said. If they wanted her dead, she would've been dead when we found her.'

Peg shuddered.

'They were here to bundle her out and destroy the evidence. And they're in trouble now they've lost our girly here. They're going to want to find her.'

He looked around and sniffed the air. Then something inside him turned over, switching him into another mode. 'Look. I don't want to seem like a selfish fucker or nothing, but I don't plan on being here when the filth turn up, which they will in about four minutes.'

He darted inside his garage and came out with a rucksack.

'I always keep this packed ready in case of emergencies and I reckon this situation qualifies. You coming, girls? You don't have to. You can stay if you want. Give statements and all that shit. I'm out of here, though.'

Peg looked at Loz, shaking her head.

'Bunga . . .' she mumbled.

'What?' Peg said.

'Doll's . . . book . . .' Loz had become agitated again, and was trying to pull Peg away. 'Quick.'

Of course. The bungalow. The last place Raymond would think of looking for Loz. The place where Peg would find the answers.

Jean knew exactly what Raymond had done and to whom, she was sure of it. And she was now prepared to use anything to get the truth out of her – truth she finally realised she badly needed.

'I need to talk to my aunt,' she said to Parker. 'Will you help me get Loz back to my nan's bungalow?'

Without a second's hesitation, Parker nodded.

To the din of fast-approaching sirens, he helped Peg support Loz away from the garages. At the side of the buildings, he lifted aside some brambles to reveal a hidden footpath that led them to the other side of the boarded-up demolition site.

As they worked their way up to London Bridge, the worm burrowed its way out of Peg's memory. But the piece of truth it held in its sharp little mouth was too horrific for her even to start to examine.

She did know, however, that it was her fault.

As much as it was her fault that Loz nearly died in that lock-up, it was also down to her that poor Anna Thurlow had ended up there too . . .

Forty-Four

THE LONG WALK TO THE STATION HELPED LOZ COME BACK INTO focus, although she still had difficulty forming words.

By getting her to nod or shake her head, Peg and Parker learned that it had indeed been Raymond who had abducted her. Using the keys Peg had left on the bungalow occasional table, he had let himself into the flat.

'And he knocked you down, drugged you and took you to the garage,' Peg said.

Loz shook her head. 'First . . . first, he . . .'

'What did he do? What did that bastard do to you?' Peg said.

'No – no. He – he was trying to show me . . .' Loz said, shaking her head as if trying to force her eyes to focus.

'What?'

'Wh-what she did . . .'

'Who?'

Loz just shook her head and looked away. 'We've got to find the books,' she said. Even though her eyes were loose in her head, for one split second she looked Peg in the eye with a lucidity that shot a cold, leaden feeling through her.

'What books?'

Peg looked at Loz, but her eyes had rolled away again, and she had lost track of what she was saying.

'What is it?' Parker asked, watching what was going on between them.

Peg shook her head. 'I can't say. I need to speak to my aunt.'

Parker shrugged and scratched his wispy stubble. 'Suit yourselves,' he said. 'But I'm sticking with you. For one thing, sleeping beauty here might need a bit of extra support.' He nodded at Loz. 'And what if your old man or his charming fucking mates turn up? What then? You might be grateful of an old squaddie. Besides, I've got nowhere else to go till all the hoo-ha dies down.'

So they made their way out to Tankerton like a band of grubby post-apocalyptic survivors, two Tank Girls – one who looked to any casual observer as if she had taken too much of something – and one raddled Mad Max. Despite the crowded, standing-room-only train out of Victoria, no one took the empty seat next to Parker.

'You two'd better go and wait in Nan's,' Peg said to Loz and Parker as they approached the bungalow. 'It's best Jean doesn't know you're with me. Silence when we go in. She's got the place bugged.'

'I'll stay outside a bit,' Parker said. 'Just keep my eye out while you're in with your aunt. Just in case. Make sure she's warm,' he added, as Peg took Loz from him and led her through the back door to Doll's lounge, where she quietly settled her on the settee, swaddling her in one of Doll's crocheted blankets.

'Time to turn Aunty Jean's weapons back on her,' she

whispered to Loz. She got hold of the intercom and fiddled with the buttons until she could hear the rise and fall of Jean's anti-bedsore air-bed.

'You've got to stay awake,' she whispered, settling the box down by Loz. 'Listen in. Be my witness. Whatever you hear me say, I love you. Remember that.' She kissed her, then grabbed the bottle of potato wine from the drinks cabinet and let herself out of the back door.

'Hello!' she called, as cheerfully as she could.

'Oh, Meggy. Where did you get to?' Jean said, as Peg walked into the bedroom. 'Pass me my ciggies, will you, darling? Ooh, you look a bit rough.'

'I've had a busy day. Didn't Julie pass the message on?' Peg said, lighting Jean's cigarette for her. 'I decided to go up to London to get some more books and that. As I'm going to be here pretty much permanently.' She was testing the water, to see what Jean knew about the day's events.

'Ah,' Jean said, relaxing back against her pillow and exhaling. 'I do like my ciggies. One of the small pleasures left to me. No, the girl didn't say a thing. I'll be glad when we can send her packing, won't you, Meggy?'

'If you don't like her, then she has to go, Aunty Jean.'

'Make us a cuppa, there's a dear. And some biscuits wouldn't go amiss.'

Peg rifled in the kitchen cupboards and assembled a large platter of almost all the cakes and biscuits she could find. Putting it on a tray, she added two glasses and the bottle of potato wine, then she steeled herself and took it into the bedroom.

'Goodness!' Jean said, rubbing her fat purple hands together. 'A feast!'

'I thought we deserved to treat ourselves,' Peg said. 'Given everything we've gone through over the last few weeks. And I thought it would be nice to drink some of Nan's wine in memory of her, God rest her soul.'

Jean nodded, her face passing from greedy glee to mournful sadness in a beat.

'And we also need to celebrate!' Peg said, unwrapping a Galaxy cake bar and handing it to Jean.

'Celebrate?' Jean hungrily pushed the whole thing in her mouth and swallowed it almost in one gulp.

'Oh yes. I've been thinking. About Dad's plans for your house in Spain,' she said. 'It's all good, Aunty Jean. Have a glass of wine.'

'Do you think so?' Jean said, looking delightedly at Peg as she handed her a large glass of the potato wine and a slab of Battenberg. 'Well, that's lovely. How exciting!'

'It is. And I'm very much looking forward to it. But,' she said, settling down on to the chair by Jean's bed. 'Before we do anything else, I need to know the truth, Aunty Jean.'

'The truth, dear?' Jean chewed on the cake, looking puzzled. Peg handed her a chocolate digestive.

'Yes. I want to know why Raymond changed his mind so quickly about you. When I last saw him he was all for putting you in a home.'

Jean narrowed her eyes.

'What are you playing at, Meggy?'

'What did you say to him?'

'I don't know what you're talking about.' Jean drained her glass, folded her arms and looked away. 'I don't know nothing about none of it.'

'But you do, Aunty Jean.' Peg broke a large Kit Kat into four and laid the fingers out in front of Jean like dog treats. She refilled her aunt's glass – her own was untouched. 'If you're not straight with me, then how can you expect me to look after you in that specially built place in Spain? If you can't treat me like the family I am, then where do we go? If I'm not on the inside, I'm on the outside.'

Peg leaned in very close, so close she could smell the fear on her aunt.

'I need to know what's going on between you and Raymond.'

Jean broke her gaze, and, with surprising agility, reached a cigarette from her pack and lit it. Then she alternately smoked, drank, and ate Kit Kat until cigarette, wine and biscuits were finished.

Then finally she looked at Peg.

'Are you threatening me?' she said, wiping a bit of chocolate from the corner of her mouth.

'Me? No. I'm just asking you to tell me the truth. I also want to know about what happened to Mary Perkins. And what about your fiancé, come to that. Did he really just disappear?'

'Tony? He deserved everything he got,' Jean spat.

'What did you do to him?'

'What did *I* do to him?' As slowly as a snail, a smile crept across Jean's face. She was just about to say something when a movement outside made her look sharply over at the window. 'What's going on out there?'

The thought that her father's men might have turned up made the adrenalin prickle across Peg's face. She jumped across the room and pulled the nets slightly apart so that only she could see out. But it was only Parker, standing in a studiedly casual way, smoking and watching the road. Sensing the twitch of the curtain, he looked round. With her back to Jean, Peg motioned to him to get out of the way of the window.

'It's only Mrs Cairns having a nose at the state of the garden.'

'I thought the girl said she'd gone away for Christmas.'

Shit, Peg thought. But, surprised at how easily she could brazen it out, she turned back to Jean with her face level. 'Oh no. She's definitely out there.'

'Interfering old cow,' Jean said, taking a moment to decide from the box of Fox's chocolate biscuits Peg offered her, then finally plumping for a chocolate-coated strawberry wafer. 'I'm worried about you, Meggy. What we need is a quiet life. If you start telling people all this—'

'All what, Aunty Jean?'

'If you start telling people any of this, then we'll all be dragged down. It'll be the end of the family, all that Mummy fought so hard to keep together.' As she spoke, she sprayed pink wafer on the bedspread.

Peg shook her head and took Jean's hand, even though it now made her flesh crawl to touch her. A change of tactic was needed if she was going to get any concrete answers.

'Oh, I was never going to tell anyone. I mean, there's no point in raking up the past. Not after so long. You see, Aunty Jean, I just need to know the truth. If you'll only tell me the truth, I'll not tell a soul.'

'You won't?' Jean said, that smile again working its way into the flesh of her mouth.

Peg took a deep breath and dived in. 'I promise. I've been thinking about what you said. You've been like a sister to me. You know me better than I know myself, and you were absolutely right about that Loz. She's no good. She was leading me astray, when of course, where I really belong is here. She wasn't at the flat when I went back, so I left her a note saying I never want to see her again. I'm staying here now and I'm coming with you to Spain to look after you in that lovely house that Dad's going to build for you.'

Peg didn't think she sounded all that convincing. But it looked like it was working on Jean, who, drunk both on sugar and Doll's wine, had taken on a misty look, all disbelief well and truly suspended.

'I'm so glad, Meggy. So glad,' she said at last, shaking her head to bring herself back to earth. 'People don't understand this family, you see. Mummy only did what was best for us. For your daddy, for me. For you.'

'I know that.'

'Mummy was a saint. I'd hate to think of what she'd feel if she looked down and saw you dragging our family name through the dirt.'

Unable to cross her fingers against her lie – she was still holding Jean's clammy hand – Peg folded her toes over each other inside her boots. 'Oh, no chance of that. I'd never tell on family. But I want to know about what you did, Aunty Jean.'

'Me? I didn't do nothing.'

'Nothing?'

'Nope.'

Jean was so slippery. Peg had to fight the urge to slap her. Instead, she pulled her hands away and faced her aunt.

'So why did Raymond kidnap Loz, then?'

'What?' Jean jolted and stared at Peg, a mess of chocolate and biscuit falling out of her open mouth.

'Why did he kidnap Loz and leave her in the garage for some thugs to come and finish her off?'

'He what?'

'He left her in the garage. At Heyworth Court. With the body of poor Anna Thurlow for company.'

'How do you know—?' Jean's face turned red, her eyes bulged, and her lips pursed like a pincushion.

'I was there. I saw. And yes, I would also like to know about what happened to Anna, but right now, I mostly want to know why he did what he did to Loz.'

'How? What? Oh, THE STUPID LITTLE BERK!' Jean exploded. Like a hurricane making landfall, Jean's anger forced her words from her mouth. 'He wasn't supposed to *leave her* anywhere.'

'What? Are you saying you told my father to kill Loz?'

'SHE WAS GETTING IN OUR WAY!' Jean lurched herself up and roared, spitting biscuit over her duvet. 'SHE HAD TO BE DEALT WITH.'

Then she collapsed back onto the pillows, her chest heaving. She scrabbled behind her for her oxygen mask, and Peg made no move to help her.

'Thanks, Aunty Jean,' she said, holding up her voice recorder, which she had turned on and hidden in her pocket the moment she stepped into the bedroom. 'You and Raymond: you're both as bad as each other, aren't you? That's what I need. I've got all of that on here. For the record.'

'Give that to me!' Wheezing, Jean tried to haul herself up to grab the recorder, but she missed.

'I've got Loz next door,' Peg said. 'She's been listening in too.'

Jean gasped and put her hand over her mouth.

'Yes. She's all right, no thanks to you. And in a short while, because of what I've got on here –' again she waved the voice recorder in front of Jean, who again tried to swipe at it – 'we'll be calling in expert help to uncover the rest of the truth about what you and Dad have got up to.'

'Expert help?' Jean said, her nostrils flaring. 'What does that mean?'

'Police, Aunty Jean. It really is time to go to the police.'

Turning her back on her bloated, outraged aunt, Peg left the bedroom and went out of the extension, shutting the back door behind her and firmly turning the key in the lock.

She had Jean. There was no going back from her admission, and, trapped by her own flesh, she couldn't go anywhere until the police came for her.

But Peg was all too aware that she didn't yet know the whole story.

Perhaps, though, she was going to have to leave that to the professionals.

Forty-Five

BUT BACK ON THE OTHER SIDE, DOLL'S SETTEE WAS BARE, THE crocheted blanket thrown to one side.

Loz had disappeared.

Panicked, Peg scrambled up the ladder to her bedroom, but she wasn't up there.

The front door was still bolted, so there was no way she could have gone out that way. Peg fell out of the back door.

'Parker!' she called, panic raising her voice a full octave.

'What?' Parker said, appearing at the gate to the back garden.

'They've got Loz again . . .'

'No love, look.' Parker pointed at the shed behind her. Peg turned. The door was open wide and Loz was staggering out with an armful of Doll's Commonplace Books. The burned ones with charred edges and blackened covers.

The burned books.

'Loz, what is it?' Peg said, seeing the tears that rolled down her cheeks. Loz never cried, not ever.

Then, at last, the words spilled hoarsely from her.

'He said it wasn't him. He explained and I didn't believe him. He begged with me. He said I needed to find the burned ones. That there was proof there. Frank had tried to burn them. He said they'd be here somewhere. I knew where they were. I had to see . . . Sorry, Peg,' Loz said, stumbling as she handed the books over to Peg. 'Sorry.'

'You need to get back inside, girl,' Parker said, and he scooped Loz up. Clutching Loz's find to her chest, Peg followed them back into the lounge, ripping the intercom out of the wall before she sat down in Doll's rocking chair.

She hesitated before opening the first book. She had only ever looked at Doll's Commonplace Books before with her permission. To do so unprompted seemed like a violation of some law of nature.

Even now, with Doll in her grave.

But, as she flicked through the pages, the assault was all on Peg.

The words were bad enough. Rendered in Doll's meticulous pre-senile handwriting and tucked in among recipes, patterns and shopping lists, the poisonous denouncements squatted like ugly beasts.

There was a litany of Tony's wrongdoings and lists outlining what kind of conniving, unfaithful, thieving, ungrateful BASTARD he was. Mary Perkins was a WHORE, a FLOOZY, a JEZEBEL who had set a trap to bring the family down. Anna Thurlow – and here Peg wavered, unable to breathe – was a VILE CUNT who had MADE POOR MEGGY'S LIFE A LIVING HELL.

But it was the images that accompanied each burst of text that really churned her nausea.

In everything but subject matter, they were like the diagrams

430

and drawings Doll had taught Peg to make whenever she learned a new skill.

But instead of crochet patterns, or the labelled parts of a flower, these were detailed drawings of human bodies. They reminded Peg of experiments she had done at school with frogs and ox's eyeballs; the kind of experiments where at least one girl – usually Philippa – would faint, or throw up. But these were dissections – no, dismemberments – of human bodies. No detail was spared, and the rendering of the facial features was uncannily accurate.

Doll had quite a skill, it had to be said.

Frank had been right: she could have been an artist.

But instead, she had been something quite different.

There was no mistaking Jean's fiancé or Mary Perkins, and the depiction, in the final book, of Anna Thurlow's cut throat was detailed and accurate. There were several blank pages after that drawing, as if put aside for future use.

And like a rude, slapped awakening, the unspeakable nugget of worm-truth revealed itself to Peg.

Then

HOW OLD AM I HERE?

I'm ten.

I'm waiting.

Waiting in a car. Not a posh car, but it's got leather seats. I know it because I know the smell of the pine air freshener. It's Nan's car. The special car big enough for the trolley.

It's parked right up against a fence in a place I don't recognise.

I've been sleeping all laid out on the back seat and I've just woken up, my sniffy blanket over my face.

I really need a wee.

But I'm all on my own.

I didn't used to be on my own in this car. There were other people here.

Where had we been? Some sort of park. It was a playground. Out in the countryside. They'd been mowing the grass and it had made me sneeze and I had got out to meet the girl, who was on a swing, in her flowery dress.

I was scared, but Nan said it was going to be all right.

She said the girl would be surprised to see me, because I wasn't at school and I was to bring her back to the car to say hello to Nan and Aunty Jean.

And then . . .

And then Nan looked at the photograph with a gold sticker with Happy Days Photography on the back of the cardboard frame, then at the girl. And then she said to Aunty Jean, 'That's the one,' and she turned to the girl and said, 'Hello, Anna Thurlow. Look. We've got your photograph here. Look.'

And Anna leaned into the car to take a look at her school photograph and then . . .

I don't know.

It's dark outside the car and I don't like it.

I'm shivering, even though I've got my pink and lime jumper on and it's summer.

I'm confused. Everything's woozy.

There's no one else around: no cars, no people, and the only light is coming from some sort of shed nearby.

It's at the end of a row of other sheds.

They're not sheds. They're garages.

The garages.

'Nan?' I go.

'Nan? I need a wee,' I say in the empty car. But no one comes.

I try to open the car door, but I can't. There's a child lock on to keep me safe. So I climb over to the front seat, sort of diving, sort of enjoying it, sliding over the leather seats, and I pull on the handle to open the front door.

I slide out on the fence side and catch my jumper on a sticking-out nail, snagging it and pulling a big hole in it.

I'm very upset, because Nan knitted this jumper for me, even with her sore knuckles.

But I'm desperate now, bursting for a wee.

I only just make it out onto the road when I wet myself, the wee running down warm inside my tights, steaming up the night air.

I start to cry. Ashamed, because I'm too old to wet myself.

'Nan!' I wail. 'I've had an accident!'

There's a clatter from inside the garage and the door opens. Aunty Jean's in her trolley and her big shape almost fills the doorway, but I can see light round her edges like a halo.

'Oh no,' she says.

She steers the trolley towards me.

'Meggy, you should've stayed in the car,' she goes, the bulk of her getting bigger, so that it's everything I can see.

'I needed a wee. I didn't know where you were. Where's Nan?' I say, in great gulps of air between sobs.

'Nan's busy in there. She'll be done in a bit. Now let's get you back in the car and I'll cuddle you to sleep.'

Aunty Jean lifts me up onto her trolley and I wipe my eyes on her big, cosy shoulder. As she drives the trolley back to the car, I look up and see behind her, inside the garage.

I see Nan, and she's got her nurse's uniform on.

And there's blood, and the girl.

I see . . .

I see . . .

And Aunty Jean puts something over my face that smells like my sniffy blanket but it isn't my sniffy blanket.

And then it's all a blank and I don't know what I see.

Forty-Six

PEG SAT IN DOLL'S ROCKER AND PUT HER HEAD IN HER HANDS, trying to hold her reeling thoughts in place, trying to reconcile her little, sparky nan with the monster who had created these books.

As far as Peg was concerned, Doll had given her nothing but love. But perhaps that's what it was all about, because she was family. She remembered Jean's words:

Mummy would have done anything to protect this family.

Peg sighed, trawling up nothing but blackness. Then she turned to face Parker and Loz, who had been watching her all the while.

'It was Nan,' she said.

Loz closed her eyes and nodded.

'Nan killed them all, didn't she?'

Parker looked at the two of them, his mouth hanging open.

'He tried to tell me,' Loz said, her voice so hoarse and low that both Peg and Parker had to strain to hear what she was saying. 'I didn't believe him.'

'Raymond?'

Loz nodded again. 'He said Jean had told him to kill me. He was going to deal with her, he said. I just had to wait till then. Not go to the police. I didn't believe him. He said . . . it was in the books somewhere. Burned books. I knew – I put them in the shed when we were clearing up. Piles of books.

'But I didn't believe him . . . I still thought it was him. How could he blame it on his own mother? I said I was going to the police. So he had to shut me up. He was crying, and still I didn't believe him. I'm sorry, Peg. Sorry, sorry, sorry.' Loz fell back onto the settee cushions, tears streaming down her face.

Peg went to her and held her close, the last parts of her world collapsing about her, like great Stonehenge-sized rocks crashing to the ground.

'What you going to do now?' Parker whispered.

Peg looked up at him with empty eyes. 'I'm going to call the police.'

'Good call.' Parker nodded. 'I'll go and keep lookout till they come, then. Then I'd better clear off. Take care, little Loz. Mind them ribs of yours. Take it easy.'

Loz nodded and tried to smile, her eyes closed against her tears.

Peg showed him to the back door.

'Thanks for everything Parker. What are you going to do now?'

'Don't worry about me, girl. Something'll come up. Can't see it'll be any good back at the garages now. Not for a good while, anyhow.'

'I'll call you once we've got everything sorted,' Peg said. 'If there's anything we can do to help . . .'

'Thanks.'

'See you, then.' As he went to shake her hand, she gave him an enormous hug. 'Thank God for the good people,' she said.

Blushing bright red beneath his oil-smudged skin, Parker mumbled his farewell.

'What number do I call?' Peg said, heading back towards the lounge and getting her phone out. 'Nine-nine-nine? It's not an emergency any more, is it?'

'You don't call no number.'

Peg froze with shock in the lounge doorway.

In a scene she never could have imagined, Jean was standing in Doll's lounge, leaning against the partition wall. With one massive hand, she had Loz clamped to her, pinioned to her chest. The other held a carving knife at her throat.

Behind her, the one-way door stood wide open in a wall that was bulging under her weight. Barely conscious, Loz whimpered, the pressure on her sore body almost too much to bear.

'Put that phone down now, Meggy,' Jean rasped. 'I'm not letting you do this.'

Stunned, Peg stood her ground.

'Put it down!' Jean said. She drew the knife a fraction of a millimetre across Loz's throat. Just enough to draw a tiny bead of blood.

'Please . . .' Loz gasped, her eyes wide with terror.

'Shut it,' Jean rasped in Loz's ear. 'Put that phone down now, Meggy.'

She redoubled her grip on Loz, squeezing her sore ribs tightly, making her yelp in agony.

As if it were a gun, Peg put the phone down on Doll's chair and stepped backwards, hands up in the air.

For a moment, no one moved or said a word. The only sound was Jean's menacing wheeze and a small, frightened noise, something like a strangled hum, coming from the back of Loz's throat.

'So what are you going to do, Jean?' Peg said. 'Are you going to kill Loz? And then what? Are you going to finish me off too?'

'You silly little girls.' Jean was panting heavily under the strain of carrying her massive bulk. 'Along with that stupid brother of mine, you've gone and spoiled it all.'

'You knew what Nan was up to, didn't you?' Peg said. 'You even helped her, didn't you? I remember now, I saw you with her, doing that.' She gestured at the singed Commonplace Book, which she had left open at the diagram of Anna Thurlow.

'You shouldn't remember, Meggy. You shouldn't remember ANYTHING.'

'And what about Raymond? Did he have anything to do with any of this?'

'Your father?' Jean spat. Actually spat on the carpet in Doll's lounge. 'What a waste of space. What a useless wimp. A lily-liver. He was no use to us at all. He never helped out, you know? Not with the cleaning up. Not even with the driving.'

'Driving?'

'We'd come out here with it and throw it all off the edge. Good currents here. It's how we found this place. Thought it'd be a nice spot for us to end up. Why we moved. Oh, Mummy . . .'

A wave of grief momentarily engulfed Jean. For a moment it looked like she was going to melt into the wall, possibly release her grip on Loz. But then she gritted her teeth and wrenched Loz's arm further up her back.

Loz screamed.

'Stop your racket, you stupid little bitch,' Jean hissed. 'And that milksop brother of mine cried when we helped your poor sick mummy out.'

'What do you mean?'

'She couldn't go on being sick like that. It was breaking his heart. But when Mummy helped him out, he cried like a baby.'

'Nan killed Mum, too?'

Jean chose not to hear Peg. 'And then when they found out it wasn't natural causes and I said he had to own up to it to save Mummy, that he had to say he done it for a mercy killing and there was no way out of it for him because it was two against one and who'd believe him anyway against the voices of an old lady and her handicapped daughter, he almost jumped at it. Like he was trying to get away from us. Like being in prison was better than being in the family. He'd always been an ungrateful little shit.

'And all Mummy wanted.' Jean's voice was quivering on the edge of hysteria, her breath coming in short, rasping gasps. 'Was to look after us. Is that so much to ask? After he pushed Keithy off that dock . . .'

'He pushed him?'

'I TOLD YOU HE PUSHED HIM,' Jean roared, 'WHY DON'T YOU EVER BELIEVE ME?'

'It's OK, Aunty Jean . . . Calm down, please,' Peg said, holding her hands out.

'All Mummy was doing was looking after us.' Her voice was coming in gulps now – the effort both of standing and of restraining Loz was putting her body under unaccustomed stress, and, to make matters worse, the partition behind her looked as if it might any minute give way under her weight.

'She looked after me with Tony. She looked after Raymond with that little floozy and your mother, and she looked after you with that nasty piece of work bully-girl. Don't you see? Don't you see, Meggy? SHE DID IT FOR US. And now I'm going to do the best thing for all of us and see to this girl the way that weak squit of a brother of mine should've done WHEN I TOLD HIM TO. I've called him and told him now.

439

I've told him there's nothing doing any more. It's all off between me and him.

'If you want a job doing properly, you've got to do it yourself. It's always the men let it down, isn't it, eh, Meggy? Believe me, you're better off without.

'If it hadn't been for Daddy hiding the key to Heyworth and burning Mummy's books then we wouldn't have to face any of this. We could've finished with that bullying little nasty piece of work and everything would've been tidied away nice and proper.

'So now it's just up to me, isn't it? I'm the last one with any sense left around here. Leave it to poor old Jeanie.'

With her eyes reddening at the rims and sweat pouring from her brow, she tightened her grip on Loz, wrenching her and making her squirm in agony. 'Yeah, poor old Jeanie. She'll have to deal with *this* first. Then she'll shop that brother of hers. Who'll believe his word over hers? He's a convicted murderer and she's just an invalid lady in a bed. She's just Mummy's handicapped daughter.'

Alarmed, Peg saw that Jean was shaking all over – even her knife hand, whose knuckles were white with the strain of gripping, juddered against Loz's frail white neck.

Peg had no idea what her next step should be.

If she did nothing, Jean could strike at any moment and carry out her threat. But jumping her would be worse: Peg would never reach her in time to stop her drawing the knife across Loz's throat.

She could see it now: quick, brutal, deep.

The only chance she had was to reason with her. She tried to muster her own quaking voice that had somehow stuck in her throat like a stone. Nothing came out but a dead little squeak.

She felt, as always, helpless.

Then suddenly, something inside her gave way.

'PARKER!' she yelled, the word jerking out from somewhere under her ribs.

'What?' Jean said, wheeling round towards Peg.

The lounge door flew open and Parker stormed in.

Taking advantage of Jean's stumbling shock at his sudden presence, he launched himself at her and wrested the knife from her hand.

'Oh!' Jean yelled, her body shuddering as Parker pushed her away from Loz. 'Oh!'

Somehow, perhaps because he had underestimated her weight, he lost his balance and ended up pulling her down towards him. Coughing with the shock, Jean toppled forwards, landing on top of him and bringing the TV and bookshelf, which she had grabbed hold of in an attempt to steady herself, shattering down on top of her.

Loz only just managed to escape being at the very bottom of the pile by rolling away and curling up to shield her head from the falling bodies. As she did so, she screamed at the agony of her cracked ribs as they ground against one another.

'Parker,' Peg cried. Pulling the bookshelf away, she launched herself onto her aunt, trying to pull her off him.

'I'm OK, Peg,' Parker said, his voice muffled underneath Jean's immobile bulk. 'Just pull her up as much as you can.'

Peg hauled with all her might, cantilevering herself against the weight of her aunt, but she was barely able to raise her, because she was as still and as heavy as a quarter-ton sack of potatoes. She carried on trying. Unable to seize a whole limb, she could only grab handfuls of fat, which she worried would rip off under the pressure.

At one point Jean's head flopped backwards and Peg saw

that her eyes were open in her bloated, purple face. But even with all the pulling and tugging, she didn't make a sound.

Finally she managed to get a purchase and lifted her enough so that, with some pushing and squirming against the floor, Parker managed to wriggle his way free of his fleshly prison.

'Fuck,' he said, wincing and hugging his torso. 'I think I've joined the cracked rib club, Loz love.'

Unable to hold her up any longer, Peg let Jean's body flop down face first on to the ground.

'What's happened to her?' Peg said, watching her stillness.

Carefully, nursing his sore chest, Parker knelt at Jean's side and worked his hand underneath her to extract her arm. He pinched her pulse point on her wrist, then shook his head.

'No dice, I'm afraid, girly. Her heart must've given out. Hardly surprising. Jesus.'

A sudden commotion in the hallway made him jump to his feet. Before he, Peg or Loz knew what was happening, two bald fat men – one black, one white – were standing in the doorway, looking at them. The white one had a gun, and it was pointed at Loz, who was curled up on the floor, barely conscious.

'Stand back or I'll shoot,' he yelled. He was wired up – his face was red and his nostrils flared. He clearly meant what he was saying.

'Wayne!' Peg said.

The black man looked at her and nodded. 'Do as he says, Margaret,' he said.

Parker and Peg put their hands up.

'Sit,' the white guy barked, and they both sat on the settee.

Wayne stepped gingerly towards Jean and took her wrist where Parker had let it go.

'She's gone,' Parker said. 'Heart.'

Wayne nodded and let go of her arm. He stood, got his

phone out and punched a number into the beeping keypad.

'It's done,' he said into the receiver, his eyes on Peg and Parker. 'The witch is dead.'

Everyone waited for a moment as he listened to the person on the other end, nodding at what was being said.

'Yeah. She's just fallen,' he said, walking round Jean's carcass. 'Looks like natural causes.'

The white guy adjusted his grip on his gun. It was still trained on Loz, who was whimpering softly, her eyes closed. Still on the phone, Wayne moved towards Peg.

'Please,' Peg whimpered. 'Please, Wayne.' She too closed her eyes, certain that something bad was about to happen.

'Yep. Yep,' Wayne was saying.

Presumably he was talking to Raymond. She thought perhaps that might possibly be a good thing, but she had no idea. Never a great believer in certainty, after the day's events she had completely abandoned any hope of second-guessing what anyone around her was thinking or doing. She hoped she had plumbed the depths of depravity of which her family was capable, but she wasn't sure. What else was going to turn up?

She was weary beyond belief, wrung out.

For a passing second she thought perhaps being killed might come as some sort of relief.

Then she felt a nudge. She opened her eyes, expecting to see the gun levelled at her. Instead, Wayne was holding out the phone.

'He wants to talk to you,' he said.

Carefully, Peg held the phone to her ear.

'Margaret?' Behind the newly familiar voice on the other end, a boy band sang a chart hit from a couple of years back.

'What's going on, Raymond?' she said. 'Who are these men, and why are they following us?'

443

'OK, love. Just calm down. These are my boys and they're here to help. They're on your side.'

'Doesn't look like it. They tried to kill Loz, you know.'

'Nah, love. They were just going to pick her up and get her out of the way, keep her quiet for a bit. Look. What happened was—'

'I know. She didn't believe you.'

'Didn't believe me? I'd say she tried to beat the living daylights out of me. I needed to keep her quiet until I could have a word with you, tell you what—'

'I know the truth, Raymond. I know.'

'You know?'

'Loz found Nan's book.'

'She did?'

'She believes you now. I do too.'

She heard him sigh heavily on the other end, as the carefree whooping of Paulie and his friends at the end of the song filled the background.

'I didn't mean to hurt her,' he said, his voice cracking with relief. 'I panicked. Jean knew you had the second key to Heyworth – she always had the first. She wanted me to burn the place. Then after the fight I had with your mate, I knocked her out with some of Mummy's old chloroform, then I called Archer and he told me to take your friend over to Heyworth and he'd deal with it, get this bird from Flamingos, Carleen – I think you know her – to look after her, keep her out of the way—'

'Carleen?'

'Carleen. See, she's another one keeps an eye on things for me on the UK side. Keeps in touch. You know.'

Peg blinked. 'Were you expecting me when I got to Spain?'

Raymond sighed.

'Jesus.' Peg breathed in and out. 'You were, weren't you? So how long were you going to "look after" Loz for, then?'

'Till I could get back after the party and tell you the truth—'

Everything stops for Paulie.

'And deal with that sister of mine.'

'Deal with Aunty Jean?'

'Oh yes. She was the last bad apple, darling. She's the end of all that.'

'How do I trust you?'

'You just have to really, don't you? And I never knew about that poor little girl, nor was I expecting to find her in Heyworth.' Peg heard him shudder. 'Your mate woke up just after I saw the body. Saw me freaking out. Then I gave her a couple of that fat bitch's horse pills.'

'And nearly killed her.'

'She's alive now, isn't she?'

'No thanks to you.'

'All thanks to me. No thanks to that cow of a sister of mine.'

'Why did you hate Aunty Jean so much?'

'She's had me just like that all my life, darling. That's why.'

'What do you mean?'

'Keith.'

'Keith?'

'Ever since our brother died she told me I done it. You have to think what that done to me. I was just a kid. And she held it over me all my life. "It'd kill Mummy if she found out it was you, Raymond, doing it on purpose," she'd say to me.

'She was right, and all. It would've.' His voice was wavering again. 'And if she was right about it being me – and I have no way of knowing for sure, Margaret: I was only a nipper so how am I supposed to know what was true and what that sister of mine chose to lie about?

445

'If she *was* right about it being me, then it was *my* fault my mother went off the rails like that. Keith dying sent her mental, Margaret. She was like a tiger after that, blamed herself for not watching her family all the time, and watched us like a bloody hawk after. There was nothing she wouldn't do.'

Peg realised that it was now or never. It was time to ask the big question that she had never really understood, which now seemed impossible to fathom, given the facts.

'Raymond?' she asked.

'Can't you call me Dad?'

'So why did you leave me with them, if you knew she was doing those terrible things, Raymond?'

'I didn't have a choice, did I? I was in the nick for six years. Then I tried to get you back, but Jean still had that bloody hold over me. Said you was making Mummy so happy that it would break her heart if I took you away. And of course, she'd have to tell her about Keith and all if I tried. My hands were tied. And I knew, at least, you'd be looked after. You were family. You'd certainly come to no harm. But I had to get out. I couldn't be near my sister any more. And there were business concerns keeping me out of the country and all. I made my choice. I made a clean break. I'm not proud of it. Look, Margaret,' he went on. 'Or Peg, is it, you want me to call you? All right then, Peg it is.'

Peg sighed and closed her eyes.

'It's all over,' he went on. 'We can all live our lives how we want to now.'

'But what do we do about Aunty Jean? She's just lying here in the lounge.'

'I want you two to leave the bungalow quiet as you can. Just get out of there. Go back to your little flat and have a nice Christmas. Archer's on his way down now. Him and the boys

446

will take care of everything else, make sure it looks kosher, like there's been some sort of break-in and your aunt met her end that way.'

'What about the girls they killed? And Tony's family? Don't they deserve some explanation?'

'It's a tough world, Peg. Look at what you got handed in life. Look at what I got handed, come to that. Nah. Sometimes you just got to look after number one, darling.'

Peg paused. She needed to think this through; work out what Raymond was asking her.

'Look, girl,' he went on. 'My big concern now is keeping you safe and protecting our name. My old offer still stands. I can set you up. You can go in that estate agent's day after Boxing Day and pick up them keys. You'll have somewhere to live, you'll be able to go to uni or whatever you want to do. Like all this never happened. Don't you see? We're free now, Peg.'

Peg looked at Loz and at Parker, both still held at gunpoint, their hands on their heads, both looking at her expectantly.

Eventually she spoke.

'OK, Raymond. I'll do it. But I've got two conditions.'

'And what might they be?' She could sense a smile in his voice. But it was more admiring than mocking.

'The first is that you accept Loz as my partner and the fact that we will be sharing our lives, living together in the flat you bought for me.'

Loz looked sharply up at Peg, a frown on her face. Raymond paused on the other end of the line. Peg could hear applause, and the overexcited shouting of children in the background. The concert must have finished.

'All right. All right. I suppose I owe her one. So long as you keep her quiet,' he said at last. 'And the second?'

'I want you to help a friend of mine with a job,' she said,

looking at Parker. 'Ex-military, good with surveillance.'

'Sounds interesting. I'll see what I can do. Now pass me back to Tweedledum.'

But Wayne had to take the phone from her because she had her hand over her mouth.

The last piece of horror had slid into place.

Then

TWEEDLEDUM AND TWEEDLEDEE
Agreed to have a battle.

It's late at night and they think I'm asleep, but I've got earache and I'm wide awake. I'm trying to read *Alice in Wonderland*, but something is keeping me from concentrating. My eyes just skitter over the lines and I'm not taking anything in.

I've not said anything to anyone about what I saw. I've not said anything at all in fact. I'm having difficulty believing that I actually saw it.

I have bad dreams, Nan says. It's difficult, she says, to tell the difference between dreams and real life. I have to forget my dreams.

She gives me medicine to help me with my bad dreams.

In the end I give up on my book. The dark up in my room is too scary to be in, so I get out of bed and crawl across the lino to the trapdoor where the ladder goes down, where the light is coming through from the hall downstairs.

They're in the lounge, but for once I can't hear the telly. They usually have it on pretty loud at night because, as Nan says, Gramps is deaf as a doorpost. If I put my eye in the far corner of the trapdoor hole, I can see right into the lounge. I can see Gramps in his chair, fast asleep, and Nan's little legs sticking forward from her rocker. She's got some knitting and the needles are going clickety-clack. She's also talking to Aunty Jean over the intercom.

Because the telly's off, I can hear every word.

I decide not to shout down to Nan about my earache. It's more fun spying on them from up here. I'm like George in the Famous Five.

'You're sure no one'll be able to tell?' I hear Aunty Jean say. Her voice sounds croaky and crackly.

'Nothing caused it,' Nan says. 'Just air.'

'You're ever so clever, Mummy.'

'Poor old Frank. But he didn't give us any choice, did he, Jeanie?'

'No, Mummy. I'd like to know what he did with that key, though.'

'Search me. I've looked everywhere.' Nan puts her knitting down and crosses the room. 'He could've thrown it in the sea, for all we know.'

'What a bother.'

'It's a real bother. We've left all that mess in the garage, Jeanie. I don't like messes.'

'We had to leave after Meggy saw, Mummy though. And you weren't to know Daddy'd hide the key. You were going to go back and clear up later, remember.'

'I know. It's a worry though.'

'But if we can't get in, then no one can get in, can they?'

'I suppose not.' Nan sighs heavily. 'Poor Frank. It's a real pity. A crying shame. He was a good man. A good husband. But he was going to tell, wasn't he?'

'Oh, he was, Mummy.'

'I did the right thing, didn't I?'

'You had to, Mummy.'

'Because what would you do without me?'

'I wouldn't be able to cope. Or Meggy.'

'Or Meggy, you're right, Jeanie.'

'I am, Mummy.'

'I'd better get rid of this then,' Nan says, picking up a syringe from the table beside Gramps's chair. 'It's dreadfully sad,' she says, stopping to stroke his face. 'But it's better than him going to the police. If he – a *member of this family* – didn't understand what I was doing, the police wouldn't have the foggiest, would they?'

'No, Mummy. They wouldn't.'

'And then where would you be, Jeanie? Without me to look after you?'

'I'd be lost, Mummy.'

'You'd be lost.'

'And Meggy'd be lost, too.'

Nan sighs and shakes her head.

I duck back behind the trapdoor so that she doesn't see me as she goes through to the kitchen. I hear the clanking of the bin as she drops the syringe in it.

'You ready then, Jeanie?' Nan says.

'Nighty-night then, Mummy.'

'Love you, my darling.'

There is a buzz and a crackle as Nan turns the intercom off.

The next thing I hear is Nan pressing the beeping buttons on the phone. Just three beeps.

'Hello?' I hear her say, her voice completely different now, all panicked and fluttery and helpless.

'Hello?' she goes. 'Ambulance please. It's, oh it's so dreadful. I think my husband's just had a heart attack. I don't think he's breathing.'

As quietly as I can, I crawl back into my bed and grab my sniffy blanket.

I pull it right over my head and put my fingers in my ears and I try to wipe it all out.

I make myself . . .

Forget.

Forty-Seven

DOING AS RAYMOND HAD ORDERED, THE BAND OF THREE – bruised, limping, shell-shocked – hobbled surreptitiously out of the bungalow under the cover of a dark Christmas Eve, leaving the two men behind to cover their tracks.

'Can we go down to the sea before we get the train?' Loz asked. 'I just need to sit for a bit.'

'Are you sure?' Peg said. 'It's freezing.'

'Nah, let's do it,' Parker said. 'I could do with a breath of fresh air myself after all that.'

They made their way down Tankerton Slopes to the promenade. It was a still, clear, piercingly cold night. The tide was high, right up and in, and a heavy moon lit the oily sea as it heaved and sighed. Had you not known that The Street was there, you wouldn't have believed it existed.

'Can we take a breather?' Loz said, when they came to a wooden bench in front of one of the luxuriously beautiful converted wooden houses on the front. 'My ribs are killing me.'

The three of them sat down and Peg put her arm round her Loz.

'I do worry about the families of those girls, though,' Loz said.

'But would knowing what happened be better for them?' Peg said. 'Whatever they imagined might have happened, surely the truth is even worse.'

'It's best to let sleeping dogs lie,' Parker chipped in. He had been very quiet since Peg had told him about the deal she had struck with her father, but he had clearly now thought it through. 'Sometimes, girls, it's best to just aim for an easy life. I'm looking forward to getting to know your dad a bit better out there in the sun. Look after number one, that's what I say.'

Peg nodded. She had a lot of processing to do. Her brain felt like Doll's bungalow at its worst, when the dirt and disorder had made it difficult even to enter. She had to recast her entire life, and she wondered whether the thought that Doll had done what she did with the best of intentions was going to be of any help to her.

'Happy Christmas, girls,' Parker said. He rolled two skinny cigarettes and offered one to Loz.

'Happy Christmas,' Loz said hoarsely, taking the roll-up from him.

Peg kissed Loz on her head, then she stood and jumped down onto the shingle.

Crunching down to where the cold sea heaved at the shore, she pulled the burned Commonplace Books out of her bag. They felt filthy and poisonous, untouchable, like raw shit.

In a sudden, jerking frenzy, she ripped the books into shreds, into paper dots that joined the real snowflakes, the purer snow, whirling in the wind, out over the shifting, icy waves.

Then she reached into her parka pocket and pulled out the voice recorder.

It felt heavier than it had before.

She glanced at it once, then, using a movement she remembered learning in school cricket, she lobbed it far out into the water, flinging it with such might that she thought perhaps she had ripped a muscle in her arm.

She watched as it arced through the air, splashing down to the surface. It paused there for a couple of seconds, as if to take a breath, before it was gulped down by the murky estuarine cocktail of North Sea and Thames River.

She stood, rubbing her arm, staring out into the devouring, moonlit waters.

Then, when the last piece of paper had whirled out of sight and the final bubble dispersed on the surface, she climbed back on to the promenade to join the others.

'Everything's going to be great now,' she said. 'And I'll look after you, Loz. For ever.'

And somewhere, deep beneath the surface of the sea, the mud shifted.

Every Vow You Break

Julia Crouch

The Wayland family – Lara, Marcus and their three children – are leaving England to spend a long, blisteringly hot summer in Trout Island, upstate New York. Marcus has been offered the lead in a play and Lara, still reeling from the abortion Marcus insisted on, hopes the time away from home will help her learn to love her husband again.

A chance meeting at the play's opening-night party reacquaints the family with an old actor friend of Marcus's. Stephen is everything Marcus is not: attractive, successful – and interested in Lara. As Lara feels herself increasingly drawn to him she knows it's a dangerous game she's playing. What she doesn't know is that it's also a deadly one.

Praise for Julia Crouch:

'Brilliant, truly chilling' Sophie Hannah

'Crouch excels at creating an atmosphere of low level menace, slowly ratcheting up the tension to full-on horror' *Guardian*

'A tale of slow-burning suspense . . . Crouch deftly avoids the obvious and builds up a very convincing air of menace' *Daily Express*

'Totally compelling . . . leaves you feeling shaken and out of sorts' *Heat*

978 0 7553 7802 9

headline